"I LOVE YOU."

"That doesn't matter."

"It does matter. It makes all the difference in the world."

Brett began sobbing into her hands. After a minute she wiped her eyes. "How will I face him?"

"Don't think about that, Brett."

"What am I supposed to think about?"

"Us. Think about us."

"I can't."

He turned her to face him. "Listen to me. What we did, didn't happen by accident. It was what we both wanted. And there was a reason for it. It wasn't just sex. You wanted to be with me as much as I wanted to be with you. And we've got to find out what it means."

"What could it mean?"

He stared at her, his face hidden in the darkness. She could barely see his features. "That we belong together."

Janice Kaiser

Private SINS

MIRA BOOKS

Authors' Note:
This book was written by Ronn and Janice Kaiser.

ISBN 1-55166-024-5

PRIVATE SINS

Printed in U.S.A.

For our mothers:

Edris Smith Bender

and

Ruth Small Kaiser

PART I

New Delhi, India

August 23, 1985

Elliot Brewster lay in bed, listening to the birds in the garden and the traffic on the boulevard, a hundred yards away. When the wind was right, he could smell the dung smoke from the cooking fires over in the old town. But most mornings he awoke to the nearer, more exotic smells of sandalwood and saffron. He stared at the ceiling, wishing he were still asleep. He'd been having a pleasant dream of Paris. The reality was that he was in his bed in Delhi, and Monica was beside him.

The heat was rising rapidly and already there was a fine patina of perspiration on his brow. He would have to get up soon, close the windows and turn on the air-conditioning so that she could sleep on, even as the air grew more sultry.

Elliot turned to look at his wife, but her face was hidden, her features obscured by her dark hair. The sheet was halfway off her, exposing one breast. He couldn't look at her without feeling aroused, yet at the same time saddened.

Monica didn't like India; she didn't like their bungalow; nor, he knew in his heart, did she particularly like him. Hating him was easier and less destructive than hating herself. Dr. Farelli, the psychiatrist at the embassy compound, had told him that. The information was superfluous since Elliot already realized that.

He watched the ceiling fan turn, its motor groaning softly. For a fleeting moment he wished that he could slip back into

the sanctuary of sleep. Now that he thought about it, he
must have been dreaming about sex.

Again he looked at Monica's naked body, wanting it sexually while despising the woman herself. How could their
marriage have come to such an end? It *was* at its end. He
knew it—and felt helpless to do anything about it.

Sex was one of the few things left between them. Not
physical love, just sex; the mutual surrender to a coincident
need—his to screw, hers to be screwed. They accommo-
dated each other, but only with resentment, with anger and
in self-pity.

Elliot heard a scratching sound outside in the garden. He
sat up on the edge of the bed, his head a bit dull from the
vodka tonics he'd consumed the night before—something
he'd been doing more and more, lately. It was not a good
trend. Booze was Monica's indulgence and soon, if he
wasn't careful, he'd no longer have grounds for complaint
about her excesses.

The scratching continued and he peered toward the open
louvered windows and into the walled garden filled with
mango trees. He saw nothing. He got up and padded across
the tile floor to the louvered door, which accessed the veranda and garden.

Jamna, their houseboy, was sweeping the dirt at the foot
of the stairs. He was wearing his usual attire: a dhoti, white
cotton shirt and sandals. Seeing Elliot, he bowed respectfully. Elliot nodded in return and leaned on the doorframe,
watching the man work in the slanting rays of the morning
sun.

Jamna was a young man, quite thin, but healthy and energetic. Though he did his work with near-religious zeal,
Elliot found himself distrustful of him, for no particular
reason except, perhaps, the extent of the man's devotion to
Monica.

Jamna worshiped her. Early on, she had complained that
he always lingered about, hoping to catch glimpses of her
dressing or entering her bath. Elliot spoke to him about it,
and the practice had abated for a time, but then it resumed.

He'd made up his mind to fire the houseboy, but Monica decided she didn't mind after all, perhaps because Jamna had proved to be so amusing in his devotion.

Still, she often mistreated the servant, particularly when she was drunk. In recent months she'd taken to calling him Spot because, she said, he seemed more like a guard dog than a man. In her better moments, though, she showed him small kindnesses, giving him trinkets as compensation for her harshness.

On a couple of occasions she had even favored Jamna with a naked walk through the house, figuring, probably correctly, that a glimpse of the goddess in the altogether was the rarest and most treasured favor of all. Elliot suspected that she had deliberately left the shutters open so that the servant would be driven to a frenzy. To everyone but Jamna, Monica's teasing was cruel, but he was clearly in ecstasy, and she had her petty amusement.

At the moment the houseboy was bent over, sweeping the ground with a short-handled rake made of closely bound sticks. His efforts sent a small cloud of dust onto the veranda. Elliot never understood why Jamna employed the crude rake when there were perfectly good long-handled ones in the garden shed. But he did, and Elliot knew no amount of lecturing would change things.

Indians were, in many ways, a stubborn people. Not so insouciantly as the Chinese, or as deceitfully as the Arabs, but they knew their minds. In the long run, it was easier to let them make their way, trusting that failure alone was a worthy teacher.

On balance Elliot was content with their living conditions. By almost any standard save Monica's, their life was pleasant. Still, he was well aware of India's limitations. There were things he could never get used to, but he understood the place better than most foreigners.

Over time, India had given him much, including insight into his marriage. As Dr. Farelli had said, "This place will strengthen the good marriage, and destroy the weak one."

Aware that he had to get cleaned up, he went to the bathroom to shave and shower. After a breakfast that Jamna had set out, he would go to the embassy.

It was scheduled to be a busy day. He had asked for a few minutes with the ambassador first thing. After that there would be an important staff meeting and then a dusty ride out to the airport to greet Amory and his new bride.

Elliot hadn't been looking forward to his stepfather's visit. Monica was rarely well-behaved around his family. She had hated Amory from the start, making relations among them tense, to say the least. Still, the invitation was hardly one to be withheld, even though Monica had complained bitterly when he'd told her what he planned.

Elliot hadn't attended the wedding because Monica had wanted to go home in December for the holidays, which allowed no time for even a quick trip to Washington. He probably couldn't have gotten leave anyway, because the ambassador had been out of the country and had only just returned to Delhi earlier in the week. So, when Amory had written to say he and Brett would be in East Africa for their honeymoon and were thinking of continuing on around the world, Elliot had felt obliged to invite them to visit.

Shaving, he nicked himself on the chin and slammed down the razor in disgust. It took several applications of septic stick and a compress before he managed to stem the bleeding. It wasn't going to be his day.

After he'd finished his shower, Elliot went back into the bedroom. Monica had kicked off the sheets and was lying naked on the bed, still asleep. Jamna was sweeping the veranda now, his bobbing head visible through the louvers. Elliot's first impulse was to close the shutters so that the houseboy couldn't see in. But since Monica would do as she wished in the end, he saw no point in denying her.

He was finishing his tie, looking at himself in the mirror over the chest of drawers, when Monica rolled over and groaned—the usual indication that she was waking up. He glanced over at her.

"How do you feel?"

She cleared her throat. "Like shit. How else?"

"I was hoping this might be one of your bright, cheerful days, darling. We're having company today. Remember?"

"Who?"

"Amory and Brett are flying in from Nairobi."

"Oh, crap. Is that today?"

"And dinner tonight at the ambassador's residence. I left a note for you yesterday, as a reminder. I guess you didn't see it."

She rubbed her head. "No, I was out all day."

"And all night, too, it seems."

"Jesus, Elliot, are you going to start on me first thing?" She sat up. "Amory's not your father, for Chrissake. You aren't even close to him, so why do you give a shit?"

"Amory's the only family I've got. And anyway, I don't have to justify myself. I've invited them. They're on their way and that's that."

"You just want to meet the little bimbo Stepdaddy married, that's all. You're curious. You want to see what sort of girl would marry an old fart like Amory who's twice her age." Monica laughed. "Your new stepmama would even be young for you, Elliot. And it galls you, doesn't it? Amory's got a sweet little virgin and look at what you're stuck with—a witch who hates your guts."

"You managed to zing everybody in that speech, didn't you, Monica? Me, Amory, Brett, even yourself."

"Fuck you."

He gave her a sardonic smile. "I know mornings aren't a pleasant time for you, dear, but I would be ever so grateful if you would make an effort. Just for a couple of days while they're here. Then you can go back to your familiar ways. I don't ask much of you, but I am asking this."

"You know what your problem is, Elliot? Your ego can't handle the truth. You just can't accept the fact that this marriage is fucked up."

"My failing aside, will you make an effort while they're here? Will you be decent?"

"I'll have the house ready for your goddamn relatives. All right? So don't get on my case. Just having to look at you first thing in the morning is bad enough." She got up and went to her dresser for underwear.

Elliot noticed Jamna peering through the louvers as he pretended to sweep. Monica acted as though he didn't exist. Elliot abhorred that about her, but as she padded off to the bathroom he couldn't help looking her over, right along with Jamna.

Monica had a wonderful body. She was as curvaceous as the day he'd married her, though of late she seemed to have put on a little weight. Her breasts were full, her hips nicely rounded, her derriere ripe. He'd always liked her ass. Monica had a wonderful ass.

Elliot looked at himself in the mirror over his chest of drawers. Behind him he could see Jamna maneuvering for a better angle to see into the bath. The servant's clumsy desperation struck him as nearly as pathetic as his own. Their obsession with Monica was quite different, of course. Jamna's was a desperation of want. Elliot's was a desperation of pain. She was right. It was his ego she wounded more than anything.

"What the fuck did you do in here?" she called from the bathroom. "Slit your wrists?"

"No, I missed my wrist and got my chin by mistake," he replied.

"Tough luck."

Elliot smiled, despite himself. There was a time when they might have laughed together, but no more. The joy in their marriage hadn't lasted long—no longer than their love.

He truly thought that he had loved her once, though in retrospect it seemed more like a period of delusion. The only passion between them now was sexual. It was customary to want and detest her at the same time—sustaining himself on a diet of joyless sex.

Elliot moved to the bed where he could see her standing at the basin. For the first time he noticed a large bruise on the back of her leg. She certainly hadn't gotten it playing tennis.

Monica had always liked her sex rough. More than once she had laid open his shoulders with her nails, inviting him to hurt her in response, always playing to the darker side of his sexuality. But he knew he hadn't caused this bruise. A flash of jealousy went through him, which was ironic, considering. Maybe she *was* having an affair.

That had occurred to him more than once, over the past few months, though he'd never questioned her about it—perhaps because he didn't really want to know. The time would come when she would throw it in his face. He wondered if that was where they were now.

With Monica it was difficult to tell. She was a bundle of contradictions—beautiful, well-bred, intelligent, educated and sophisticated on the one hand; foulmouthed, common, acerbic and cruel on the other. With her clothes off, she was an animal with only one thing in mind—to conquer or be conquered.

Early in the marriage their game had been played with manners and a certain flair. They could ravish one another, laugh about it, then go to the theater or to a sit-down dinner for twelve in Georgetown or East Hampton, Grosvenor Square or the Île St-Louis. He had never been sure whether he pleased her, because she refused to give him the satisfaction. So the first years had been a challenge match, a libidinous contest of one-upmanship and defiance.

Sexually it had been stimulating, but it had taken its psychic toll. The contest had become bitter. The more pleasure he gave her, it seemed, the deeper her loathing for him became.

Monica had been brushing her teeth, glancing at him in the bathroom mirror from time to time. Then she bent over to spit into the basin, pointing her ass at him defiantly.

"What happened to your leg?" he asked.

She wiped her mouth with a hand towel, ignoring him. He knew she'd heard him. "Monica?"

Still no response.

Behind him Jamna was sweeping like crazy. Elliot flushed with anger. He got up and went to the door of the bathroom.

"Jamna and I both would like to know where you got the bruise, Monica."

She leaned close to the mirror to examine her skin. "Tell Jamna it's none of his fucking business."

"Shall I invite him in so you can tell him?"

"Do whatever you fucking want, Elliot."

He stood in the doorway. "Maybe you'd like to tell *me* where you got it."

Monica turned around, folding her arms just below her full breasts as she rested against the basin. "Maybe it's none of your goddamned business, either."

"I think it is."

"Well, fuck you."

She started to turn around and Elliot stepped forward and grabbed her arm. Monica jerked free and, when he reached for her again, her eyes flashed. She slapped him hard. Elliot slapped her back, just as hard.

She put her hand to her jaw. "You sonovabitch."

"Who are you having an affair with?" he demanded. "Somebody I know or somebody you picked up in the street?"

Her eyes narrowed. "Oh, somebody I picked up in the street, of course." She pushed past him and returned to the bedroom.

Monica saw Jamna peering in the louvers, hardly making any effort to pretend that he was working. She did a pirouette in the middle of the room and faced Elliot.

"This seems to be my day. Everybody's interested in looking at me in the altogether."

He glared.

"What do you think of that, Elliot? How does it feel, knowing your wife can keep the servants happy just by walking across the room? Does it make you feel like a stud? Lord and master of the household?"

"You're a whore, Monica."

She grinned. "And part of you loves it." She walked back over to him, looking up through her lashes. She swayed her hips for the houseboy's benefit, her smile mocking.

Elliot loathed her as much as a man could loathe a woman, and yet she was right—she incited him as much as any woman he'd ever known.

"I was beginning to worry about you," she said, fingering his tie. "I was wondering if maybe you'd lost it." She reached up and put her cool hand on his neck, then dragged her finger across the cut in his jaw.

He didn't move, though a shudder went through him.

Monica inched closer. Over her shoulder he could see Jamna staring in the window. Monica rubbed his chest with both hands. "So what's the verdict? Do I do it for you anymore?"

"You're a slut," he mumbled.

"Oh, I think we've established that."

Elliot knew her performance was for Jamna's sake as much as his. Maybe more. But mainly it was a way to show her contempt.

She ran her hand to his crotch. "Do whores turn you on, Elliot? It seems they do. How else can you explain this bulge in your pants?"

She began stroking him, delighting in the fact that she'd aroused him. Jamna was a statue at the window. Elliot hated her. He hated himself for wanting to fuck her.

"We used to get it on pretty good in the old days, didn't we?" she purred. "Is that what you're thinking about? You thinking about bending me over a chair and ramming your cock up my cunt?"

He swallowed hard, wanting to stop this, but at the same time not wanting to stop. This, he realized, was her revenge. He fought the urge to crush her, telling himself she was despicable, unworthy. Finally he took her wrist and pulled her hand away from his crotch.

"Oh," she said. "Elliot is trying not to want me. Would you rather see Jamna do me? Is that what you're thinking?

That it would be more fun to watch? Want me to spread my legs for him?''

A violent tremor went through him, and she smiled. He stared at the red splotch on her jaw, wanting to hit her again, but knowing his desire to hurt her made him no better than she.

"Not everybody can fuck a whore," she said, taunting him. "I wonder if you're still man enough."

"You're sick," he said.

"If I am, then so are you. How many times have you turned it down? Huh?" Her mouth twisted. "Never thought of it that way, have you?"

Elliot told himself to walk away, but his contempt was matched, even exceeded, by his desire. He *did* want to fuck her. It was the only way they communicated anymore.

Monica looked into his eyes. She sensed she had him. And he was as aware of it as she.

Reaching out, she began to unbuckle his belt. Then she unzipped his fly and let his trousers drop to the floor. He stared at her, his loathing now full-blown lust. There was no sweeping sound coming from outside. The room was quiet except for the groan of the fan.

Monica reached into his shorts and grabbed his cock. She stroked it, squeezing it every once in a while to the point of pain. She liked it when he winced.

When she had his penis rigid and pulsing, she let go of him and slunk over to the bed, glancing at Jamna to make sure he was still watching. She lay on her back, opened her legs and began massaging her breasts.

"Are you man enough to fuck me with Spot watching?"

Elliot stepped out of his trousers and walked to the bed. Monica glanced at his penis. "Hope you don't mind if I close my eyes and think about somebody else," she said. "No offense, but I like it better that way."

He glared at her, knowing the thing to do was walk away without a word.

Monica feigned remorse. "Did I hurt your feelings, Elliot? Is that why the sad face?"

He said nothing. She touched the end of his penis with her toe before rubbing his thigh. She twisted her nipples between her fingers and closed her eyes, focusing on her own pleasure.

"I'm getting wet," she purred, "but I won't say who he is."

A cold anger went through him. Monica, watching, laughed. Unexpectedly she jumped up and threw herself against him, grabbing his head and kissing him violently. She bit his lip so hard she drew blood. Then she pulled him down onto the bed on top of her. "Fuck me, you sonovabitch," she said through her teeth.

She wrapped her legs around him and scraped his shirtfront with her nails, keeping her head turned to the side, her eyes closed. She was wet and he slipped into her easily, driving himself deep into her, making her gasp.

Holding her down, he rammed into her so hard that she cried out, her face contorted with pain. A drop of blood fell from his lip onto her chest. She took his punishment, her arms limp at her sides, her face still turned away, her eyes closed, only her lips moving with each gasp. He wondered if she really was thinking of someone else.

Glancing up, Elliot saw Jamna staring at them, mouth agape, eyes wide. It was just what she wanted. Well, he'd given it to her, but that was enough. His anger flared.

"Get the hell out of here!" he shouted.

Jamna scampered away. Monica began to laugh.

"You just don't want to share me, do you, darling?"

There was only one answer for that. Elliot started driving himself into her as hard as he could, making her gasp with each thrust. Her nails sank into his flesh. Monica moaned and whimpered, then wedged her hand between them and began caressing herself.

Within a minute, they both came. Elliot collapsed on her. She tolerated his weight for a few moments. Then she said, "Get off me."

Elliot got up. He looked at the window to make sure Jamna was gone, then glanced down at his wife. Monica's skin was damp, her cheeks still flushed.

She stared at him with contempt. "Like I said before, fuck you," she said. Then she got up and staggered off to the bath.

Elliot's shirt was wet and there were a few drops of blood spattered on it. He wiped his lip with the back of his hand and loosened his tie. Then he began unbuttoning his shirt. He took a fresh one from the closet.

The shower started and he heard Monica groan as she stepped under the spray. He couldn't say whether she was feeling triumph or defeat. He suspected she felt neither. Or perhaps both. That was the way he felt at the moment—victorious and defeated, good and bad. Empty. Alone.

Elliot went into the bath and washed himself at the basin. He wiped the steam off the mirror so he could see his face. Between the razor and Monica's teeth, he looked like he'd been in a fight.

He stopped the bleeding with a septic stick, and went into the bedroom to dress again. He'd just finished putting on his tie when the shower stopped and Monica appeared at the door, drying herself.

"You still here?"

"Don't worry," he said. "I was about to leave." With Monica watching, he fetched his suit coat from the closet, then went to the kitchen to have his breakfast. She wouldn't be joining him. She never did.

The Indian Ocean

Brett Maitland pressed her face close to the aircraft window and peered down at the broken patches of cloud drifting slowly by. She could see the sun reflecting off the water, so she knew they hadn't made landfall yet. They were between two continents—Africa and India—places she'd never dreamed she'd see. It wasn't all that long ago that the drive from Mount Ivy to Atlanta had seemed like such a wonderful adventure. And now this.

They had left Kenya in the night. India, only minutes away, was yet to be discovered. The subcontinent was little more to her than a collage of images from *National Geographic,* but that would soon change.

The last months had been a voyage of discovery. She had been a neophyte in so many ways, and still was, though for the sake of her self-respect she'd tried to take each new step with an air of assurance. But she hadn't pretended to be something she wasn't. Especially with Amory. She'd been brutally honest with him. That made their relationship so very special. Brett knew he loved her for who she was. There was nothing more important than that.

She glanced at her husband, asleep in the seat beside her, his silver head cocked at such an uncomfortable-looking angle. At least he was getting some rest, the poor darling. That bug he'd picked up in Tanzania had torn up his insides.

She studied his face. He'd been pale and drawn the last few days, looking older than his fifty-five years. She felt so sorry for him. Despite her assurances that it didn't matter, he was upset that he'd become ill on their honeymoon. Yet what were a few days out of a lifetime together?

This train of thought made her smile. Being patient had never been her long suit growing up, but in the past year or so she had learned so much from Amory. He was a special man, the kind whose wisdom and goodness tended to rub off on others.

Because she was twenty-two, Washington had regarded their marriage as practically scandalous. She hadn't quite been able to pretend that she didn't care what people thought, but she was mature enough to know that if Amory didn't mind, then it really wasn't important.

Her relative inexperience was something she had to live with. Thank God she hadn't been a virgin. That would have been too much, even though Amory probably would have preferred it. But he wouldn't have said so. He'd never do anything intentionally to make her feel inadequate. He was too kind. Besides, he was determined to be modern. That was to be his challenge in this marriage. Hers was to learn wisdom from him.

Brett sighed and told herself for the thousandth time that their different life experiences didn't matter. Relationships did not have to be symmetrical to work. Amory had had a long-term marriage and a career that had taken him to the pinnacle of the American legal profession. He had a step-son who was twelve years older than she.

If she was insecure, it was because of her background. She might have graduated from Georgetown University with honors, but the fact remained that she'd been a poor girl from the hills of north Georgia. Her family were simple country folk, none of whom had been either educated or wealthy.

Washington knew—and was not shy about pointing out—that were it not for her marriage to an associate justice of the United States Supreme Court, she would have been hard-pressed to get a job as a staffer on Capitol Hill. Washingtonians reserved their respect for those who attained power and position by winning it on the battlefield. Brett could accept that, because it was true. What hurt her most were the jabs that Amory had to endure because of her.

An article Sylvia Quinn wrote in the *Washington Post* the week of the wedding had been especially unkind. She'd implied that Amory was having a midlife crisis and hinted that Brett might be a social-climbing opportunist. The worst was the implication that Amory had been taken in by a chance at some firm flesh.

To his credit Amory had laughed it off, but Brett knew it must have been hard for him. He'd been one of the few leading figures in Washington who was rarely criticized, even by the standards of the justices of the Supreme Court. It was a source of great pride to her that he was universally admired for his integrity and fair-mindedness. That made the ribbing he was getting especially unfair.

She'd tried to keep her chin up and not let it bother her. Amory had been wonderful about it, very supportive. But the simple fact was, he was used to living in a fishbowl, and she was not. Adjusting wouldn't be easy. Nonetheless, she was determined to succeed.

Africa had been a perfect and much-needed respite. It had been more than merely an escape from Washington. It had been a journey to another world.

Their first few days at the Mount Kenya Safari Club were relaxing. They'd spent their time playing tennis, walking across the grounds under the acacia trees, and observing the wildlife. Nobody knew them and nobody cared who they were. They'd focused on each other. It had been ideal.

They had seen so much beauty, but their first morning in Nanyuki stood out most in her mind. She'd awakened well before dawn and had gone out on their balcony to stare in awe at the jagged snow-capped peak of Mount Kenya, illuminated by the moon and rising conelike from the earth. The fresh morning air smelled so foreign and exotic.

Despite the coolness, she'd stayed on the balcony for an hour, waiting for the first light. Below, on the shadowy lawn, she'd seen a peacock and also some sarus cranes and ibis. It had been a magical time. The dawn of a new life.

Their photo safari to the Masai Mara and the jaunt to the Ngorongoro Crater in Tanzania during their second week was more spectacular, though somehow not as moving. Camping in the bush, they'd seen what the real Africa was like—unspoiled, unforgiving and harsh.

Brett had been enthralled, lying awake on her cot, listening to the rumble of the lions and the cries of the hyenas. It made her appreciate how little she knew about life beyond civilization. Africa had touched her deeply, made her question things she hadn't given a lot of thought to, even as she was embarking on a new life.

But if Africa had given Amory an opportunity to look into his soul, he hadn't let on. That made her wonder if maybe he was beyond that point in life when important questions remained to be explored. Perhaps he'd faced all his demons and made his peace with them. She'd already learned that a big part of maturity was coming to terms with the way things were, not just the way she wanted them to be. Amory, she realized, was now finding his excitement in her quest, rather than in his own. The love implicit in that was very reassuring.

Brett settled back against the seat and put her hand on his as she listened to the steady purr of the jet engines. Amory was sleeping soundly and didn't move. The poor darling was completely exhausted.

She ran her fingers over the veins on the back of his hand, liking the weathered maturity of his skin. He was a handsome man, in excellent shape for his age. Still, her physical attraction to him had always been secondary. Amory Maitland was above all a cerebral being, an intellectual presence, a moral force. And she was in love with his spirit—she had even told him so.

He'd laughed. "Spirit? My God, you make me feel like a priest. I'm far from a saint and certainly don't want to be thought of as one."

His humility was his most endearing quality. It was never more evident than when he was compared with his brother. Harrison Maitland was the junior senator from Maryland, and a powerful man in his own right. But the brothers couldn't have been more different—in appearance as well as personality and character.

The senator was shorter and stockier. His coarse hair was salt-and-pepper rather than silver. And while Amory was cool and patrician, Harrison was florid and, in her opinion, more than a little dissolute-looking.

Amory was even-tempered and contemplative, whereas Harrison had the jocular, extroverted demeanor of a politician. She had discovered early on that her brother-in-law could be charming and witty without necessarily inspiring trust. He would frequently goad her into political debates—especially after he'd had a couple of Scotches. He wasn't mean-spirited, exactly, but neither did he have Amory's inherent goodness.

If Harrison had a redeeming feature, it was his wife. Brett had grown very close to Evelyn, who had become both a mentor and a friend to her. Of course, due to the differences in their ages they were more like mother and daughter than sisters. If it weren't for Evelyn, she would have had a lot more trouble with the social quagmire that came with marrying into the Washington political elite.

Harrison and Evelyn were the only family members she'd met. That was one of the reasons she had mixed feelings about India. The real world was waiting for her there—not only embassy social events, but Elliot and Monica, as well.

Maybe she was more afraid of that than she'd been willing to admit. Though she'd tried not to dwell on it, she knew she would always be compared to Catherine. That was the lot of a second wife.

She had no illusions about Amory's first marriage. Only death had separated him from Catherine—he'd told her that—but that in no way diminished his love for her. Amory had told her that, too, and she believed him.

And yet, she had to deal with the ghosts of the past, even if at the moment they remained largely unknown. All she knew for certain was that Amory and Elliot had not been extremely close, and that made it even harder to understand why her husband was so adamant about going to India, whether he was ill or not.

"In a couple of days I'll be as good as new," he'd said when they'd talked their last evening at the Mount Kenya Safari Club. "I hate to be this close to Elliot and not take advantage of the opportunity."

"Surely he'll be coming to Washington sometime soon? Don't foreign-service officers have to visit the home office now and then?"

"I've never visited Elliot and Monica at their home, darling. There may not be many more chances."

"Do you think they'll divorce?" she asked.

"I'm afraid they may."

"It might be for the best, Amory. I mean, if the marriage isn't working..."

Amory had given her a dark look. He took his Catholicism very seriously. To his credit, he didn't impose his faith on her, but he was traditional and had orthodox beliefs. He was sometimes considered to be a little out of step, even with modern Catholics, but his views were his own and he was fiercely protective of them.

"I suppose that's a matter for them to decide," he'd said. "But I personally wouldn't counsel it."

Brett had known it wasn't a time to engage him in debate, though she didn't shrink from disagreeing with him when she felt it was appropriate. They often had intense discussions, even arguments. But his fairness kept their "departures," as he called them, from becoming acrimonious.

"You want to be the healing father, don't you?" she'd said as he looked up at her with weary blue-gray eyes.

"The last few years, Elliot and I have gotten along all right," Amory had said. "Once he went away to college, I was forgiven for having married his mother. But we've never had the necessary conversation to make our peace. We weren't able to do it when Catherine died, nor when he married Monica. I was hoping this might be the opportunity."

She had discovered early on that Amory's weakness was that he cared too much about other people's feelings. It was, of course, a virtue, as well. It was his conscience more than anything that made him such a fine jurist and decent human being.

"Elliot's complex," Amory had continued. "A very private man. I'm not sure whether he'll be receptive to my efforts, but I feel the need to reach out to him, especially now that my life has changed."

It pleased her to think that she might have made the difference. She'd squeezed his hand. "If it's important, then we'll do it," she'd said. "All I want is for you to be happy."

Amory had reached up and caressed her cheek. "I love you, Brett," he'd said.

His words had brought tears of happiness to her eyes, but they hadn't eliminated her doubts.

The pitch of the engines changed slightly and Brett looked out the window. Then she heard Amory moan. He blinked awake and gave her a faint smile.

"Well, good morning, darlin'! Did you have a good sleep?" she asked cheerfully.

He reached over and took her hand. "You are my sunshine, Catherine. What would I do without you?"

He didn't see her face fall, nor did he notice his slip. Brett passed it off, knowing that it didn't mean anything, that he was groggy from sleep.

"Are we still over the ocean?" he asked.

She peered out the window again. Sure enough, the shiny blue-gray sea had been replaced by the muted brown of the land. "No, we're over land!" she announced happily.

"Good," he said. "I'm looking forward to that hotel bed."

"Tummy bothering you again?"

He nodded. "I believe it's time for another visit to the john." He roused himself partway up, pausing to lean over and kiss her temple. "I'll be back in just a minute."

He moved tentatively up the aisle. Brett drew a long breath and sighed. She knew his slip was meaningless, that Catherine no longer occupied a central place in his heart. She was Mrs. Amory Maitland now. Nothing mattered but that.

New Delhi

Elliot Brewster arrived at the sprawling embassy compound and was waved through the gate. To him, Americaland was like a little chunk of the States. There was a commissary, a movie theater, tennis courts, a school, a hospital, a swimming pool and even a Little League baseball field.

He parked close to the embassy building, and went directly to the ambassador's office. Eugene Welty, the incumbent, had attended Ivy League schools and considered himself a spokesman for both the mind and soul of America. Elliot didn't mind the presumption. Gene was twenty-five years his senior, and was a short-timer to boot. He had earned the right.

India was Welty's last posting before retirement. One of Cy Vance's boys, he had been dispatched back to Delhi when Reagan's man left abruptly after only two years on the job. Now they were six months into the president's second term and the new appointee was still languishing in committee on the Hill.

Elliot liked Welty, at first because they both were alums of Fletcher, and later because they could talk about the real India. Welty had the well-deserved reputation of an American who could listen—an admirable trait.

When Elliot got to the ambassador's office, Dorothy, Welty's longtime secretary, told him the boss had gotten an eyes-only dispatch from Washington and was now on the phone with the undersecretary. She pointed to the Naugahyde couch under a lithograph of the Jefferson Memorial.

"Latest *Time* is there on the table, Elliot."

He sat down, but didn't pick up the magazine. He was glad for a chance to reflect. He'd decided on investigating the possibility of a transfer and wanted Gene's advice. After all, his problems with Monica were no secret; nowadays they couldn't go to a social function without him getting lots of sympathetic glances, whether because of her drinking or her flirting, he couldn't be sure.

Monica had always been a tease, taking up with somebody at a party and carrying things to a ridiculous extreme before dropping the poor bastard and moving on to somebody else. He'd once overheard some matron marvel that it was amazing Monica had kept the same husband so long, since she was the type who seemed to change her men as often as her nail polish.

It had gotten worse of late. But he was beginning to realize that Monica's drinking had become his excuse as much as hers. He winced, knowing the time had come to take action.

Elliot felt his lip crack open, and he took out his handkerchief to dab at the cut. He knew he looked like hell. The wounds he'd received that morning—self-inflicted and otherwise—were bound to provoke questions. He hadn't decided what story he'd give yet, assuming something would come to mind when the time came.

He picked up the magazine and flipped through it for a couple of minutes, but his mind soon wandered, and he began thinking about Amory. His former stepfather couldn't be paying a visit at a worse time. Things had been coming to a head with Monica for weeks now. And she was sure to raise hell. Somehow, in some way, she would cause trouble.

"Jesus Christ, Elliot, what happened to you?"

Startled, he looked up to see Gene Welty standing at the door to his inner office. Elliot frowned, not understanding.

"Your face. You look like you've been in a brawl."

"I stood a little too close to my razor this morning," Elliot said, touching his jaw. "And this happened when Monica and I collided." He got up, taking his jacket from the arm of the chair.

"Adrianne and I bent over to pick something up once, clunked heads and damn near knocked each other out," the ambassador said affably. "As I recall, I had a mild concussion."

"Marriage can be dangerous."

Welty smiled and signaled to him. "Come on in."

Elliot went into the spacious corner office, furnished in an understated yet tasteful way. Adrianne Welty's hand was in abundant evidence, particularly in the selection of antique prints.

Gene Welty, medium height and paunchy but with a certain air of crispness, headed for his large teak desk. "We're looking forward to meeting Justice and Mrs. Maitland this evening," he said, smoothing his slicked-back hair. It was an affectation he repeated unconsciously. "Adrianne's been in a dither for a couple of days. This is her first Supreme Court justice ever."

Elliot chuckled. "She'll find Amory a welcome change from the usual congressman on a junket, I think."

"This trip isn't at taxpayer expense," Welty said, gesturing for Elliot to sit down. "That alone will make it different."

Elliot tossed his jacket on one of the visitor chairs and dropped heavily into the other. "You'll like Amory. He's very intellectual, well-informed. I don't know about his knowledge of India, but it wouldn't surprise me if he'd done some reading in preparation for the trip."

"I like that in a man. I'm sure we'll get along quite well." Welty folded his hands and looked at Elliot pleasantly. "This is the first time you'll be meeting Mrs. Maitland, if I recall correctly."

"Yes," Elliot said. "They weren't yet engaged the last time I saw Amory."

"She was his law clerk. Wasn't that it?"

"Not even that. Amory had sponsored her on a financial-aid program for undergraduates at Georgetown. They became friends and in her last year of college the friendship turned to romance. Sort of a case of the professor marrying his student, with a twist."

"She's quite young, then."

"Graduated in June."

"My, I had no idea. We knew there was a difference in their ages, but..." Welty smiled. "It's nice to see a man of my generation recovering his youth. They say a young wife will do that for you. But then you're young yourself, Elliot."

"I manage to feel old at times."

"Could that be the purpose of this chat?"

"In a manner of speaking." He took a deep breath. "I think I've got to get Monica out of India, Gene. She's not doing well. And I'm sure I don't have to tell you my career is going to suffer for it, if it hasn't already."

Welty looked down at his hands. "No, I understand and I sympathize."

Elliot could tell by Gene's reaction that the perception of others might even be worse than he'd thought. "Naturally, you'd be key to any decision, that's why I'm talking to you first," he said.

"Does Monica want to leave? Is that the principal impetus?"

Elliot hesitated. "Can I be frank, Gene?"

"Certainly."

"I don't mean to burden you with my personal problems, but there's some doubt whether Monica and I will even stay together."

Welty didn't look surprised. "I thought it might be serious, but I didn't know how serious." He leaned back, smoothing his hair. "Do you think a change of environment will make a difference? There's no guarantee where they'll send you."

"I appreciate that, but I've recently come to the conclusion things can't continue on as they are."

"Have you considered sending Monica home for a while first? Sometimes a girl just needs a little time back in the States to get grounded. I've seen it make the difference in the gravest of situations."

"I don't think that would do it in this case," Elliot told him. "But I'll talk to her about it."

"Perhaps having this family visit will raise her spirits," Welty said hopefully. "I take it Monica will be at the party this evening."

"That's the intent, but she's unpredictable, as you know. As for the family angle, I'm not optimistic. In fact, I'm concerned."

Welty looked like he wanted to ask why, but let the remark pass. "Well, do as you see fit," he said. "I'll do my best to keep any dirty linen that turns up here in Delhi. I can promise you that much."

"I appreciate it, Gene. I'm more aware than anyone that my career is hanging in the balance, right along with my marriage."

Welty nodded. "We'll see you through this."

Elliot got to this feet. "I've got to prepare for the staff meeting, and I know you do, too." He grabbed his jacket. "I'll get out of your hair."

Welty came around the desk, putting a hand on Elliot's shoulder as he walked him to the door. "My sympathies are with you, Elliot."

In the middle of the staff meeting it was apparent to Elliot that he wasn't going to be able to get away to greet Amory at the airport. So he slipped out of the meeting long enough to make arrangements for an embassy car to pick them up. He had his secretary send along a message that he'd drop by their hotel before the end of the day.

Elliot couldn't decide whether to try to take Monica along with him that afternoon, or if their first encounter should be at the party. A public setting could be better or worse, depending on her mood. In the end, he decided to let her make her own decision, without pressuring her either way.

As for Amory and Brett, he had no idea of their attitude toward either Monica or the party. Were he in their shoes, an embassy dinner would be about the last thing he would choose. Of course, he attended diplomatic functions for a living, so maybe they would be more receptive. There'd be plenty of time later for a visit to Agra and Jaipur.

Just before noon the staff meeting broke up and Elliot went to his office. His secretary, Joni Hammond, had a message from Monica. "She said to tell you she'd meet you at the ambassador's residence at eight. She has an appointment this afternoon and can't go with you wherever you wanted her to go."

The words were innocent enough, but Elliot felt the same old suspicion. "Did she say what kind of an appointment?"

"Something like an art show, or an exhibit. I forget which."

"At the Ministry of Culture, maybe?"

"Yeah, now that you mention it. I think that's what she said."

During the staff meeting Robert Farrens, the cultural attaché, had said something about attending an exhibition at the Ministry of Culture that afternoon. Elliot thought about the man, trying to picture him with Monica. He couldn't believe either of them would be that stupid, but he knew his wife was capable of anything. He didn't know Farrens, who was fairly new at the mission, well enough to judge.

"When did she call?" he asked.

"Not long ago. Maybe fifteen minutes." Joni made no secret of her dislike of Monica, and Elliot could hardly blame her. Monica had the annoying habit of treating her like hired help. At times she was downright rude. There'd been no serious blowup, so Elliot hadn't said anything to either of them, but the situation was an embarrassment.

Taking the classified-documents file Joni handed him, Elliot went into his office and sat at his desk. Robert Farrens kept going through his mind. With only the slimmest shred of evidence—an offhand remark made in the staff meeting and Monica's message—he sensed that he may have solved the riddle of who she was having the affair with.

His pulse quickened. Even in the beginning, he couldn't say he'd trusted Monica. That was too much to expect. Still, this was the first time she'd gotten involved with somebody he worked with. In the past, her flirtations had been with men who had been remote, anonymous, harmless—men Elliot could safely ignore.

In his heart he'd known this current interest was different. Yet he'd never acted on his suspicions, never pressed her or accused her until that morning. As he thought about it, he realized she hadn't bothered to deny the accusation.

Elliot realized it wasn't jealousy that made his heart race; it was wounded pride. Jesus Christ. Robert Farrens. Why had she picked him?

The new cultural attaché was not a particularly imposing figure, and certainly not attractive. Farrens was in his mid-forties, but looked ten years older. He was a widower on his first field assignment after his wife's death and years behind a desk in Washington. Like a lot of people in the culture game, he was a frustrated artist—one who lacked the guts to live without a salary. But he had friends in high places at State, and was thus not without resources.

Elliot didn't dislike the man; he'd considered him marginal, unimportant in the greater scheme of things. Obviously, if his suspicions were true, Farrens wasn't equally indifferent toward him. Elliot shook his head at the irony. Christ, the son of a bitch was saying hello in the hallway while secretly fucking his wife. That made his blood boil. For the first time, he knew what it was to be a cuckold.

Elliot immediately started speculating how many people knew. Was it one of those situations where he was the only one in the dark? Did Gene know? How about the rest of the senior staff?

Elliot was sweating, though his office was cool. He took out his handkerchief and wiped his brow. Could he be wrong? Could he have jumped to conclusions? Maybe the exhibit was a coincidence. No. Somehow he knew it was true. It all kind of fell into place.

He realized now that he had intentionally turned a blind eye to the evidence that was probably there all along. He swallowed hard, trying to think. His relationship with Monica had gotten much worse in recent months. But when did it start? When Farrens arrived?

The timing made sense. He'd noticed a change in her within a month or so of Farrens's coming to Delhi. For a while they must have been careful. Elliot tried to recall the way the attaché had behaved toward him. Had he avoided eye contact? Conversations?

He shook his head, realizing how naive he'd been. When he thought about it, Farrens was a logical choice. The bastard was one of those long-suffering, world-weary types who agonized with charm. He was a lush, too. There had been talk about that almost from the time he'd arrived in Delhi. Actually, he and Monica made a great pair. The angst, the booze, the dissipation. It wouldn't be like Monica to choose some appealing, really together guy. That wouldn't be as much of an affront to him. A sleazeball was so much better. Yes, it all made sense.

The question now was how to deal with them. Self-righteous indignation hardly seemed the appropriate response. Nor could he claim she'd betrayed his love. He didn't love her; he'd only possessed her. They shared a house, a bed, and his name. There was little more to their marriage than that.

The hell of it was he'd slipped himself, once, and that limited his options. His dalliance had almost been accidental. To Monica's ears that would sound hypocritical, but it was true.

There'd never been a shortage of opportunities. Women were attracted to him, and a disproportionate number of them were married. However, unlike Monica, his sex drive wasn't so overwhelming that he couldn't be prudent, especially when it could prove detrimental to his career. There'd been a time, though, about three months earlier, when he had slipped.

He had been in Jakarta for a meeting with the trade-committee staff of ASEAN. Elise Morgan, the wife of the Australian ambassador to Indonesia, had buttonholed him at a cocktail party. She was a tall blonde in her late thirties who had all but propositioned him. Only the ambassador's personal intervention had saved him that evening.

The next night, however, after the final session of the working group, Elliot was in his hotel room, already half drunk from the wine he'd had with dinner, when Elise came to his door. She wasn't in the room more than five minutes before she had her clothes off and was astride him on the bed.

He hadn't resisted, rationalizing that Jakarta wasn't Delhi. Even when her screams of pleasure carried out the open window, bringing amused laughter from the people in the garden below, neither of them was deterred. Elise didn't care about anything. And that night, anyway, neither did he.

She made him make love to her a second time and tried for a third. When he couldn't get it up again, she dressed, kissing him goodbye without so much as a plea for discretion. Elliot assumed that she had a reputation, but he never found out. His work complete, he left town in the morning without learning the story behind Elise Morgan.

So he'd made his mistakes, too. But if Monica was fucking Farrens, he had to intervene. Two careers were on the line. Shit, if she was unwilling to think of her husband, she might at least consider her lover.

Elliot picked up the telephone and dialed home. Monica didn't answer until the seventh ring.

"I'm about to go out the door, Elliot."

He fought hard to keep his calm. "Joni said you were going to an exhibit."

"Yes, but I'll be at the dinner tonight, don't worry."

"I wasn't able to pick up Amory and Brett because of scheduling problems, so I thought I'd leave here early and drop by their hotel."

"You do that."

"I thought it might be nice if you went with me."

"Elliot, you know I've made plans. That's why I called you, for Chrissake."

"Is the exhibit that important that you couldn't miss it, or go another day?"

"This is the opening, and everybody who's anybody will be there. Besides, I want to go."

"Since when has Indian society gotten so interesting? Until a few months ago they were all ragheads and the women's perfume made you gag."

"Some things you adjust to, I guess. Anyway, it beats sitting around here watching the ceiling fans."

"Yes, I suppose it does."

"Can I go now, or do you want to grill me some more?"

He considered coming right out with it, but that wasn't something he could do on the phone. To accuse her of infidelity, of playing with his life and his career, he had to look her in the eye.

"No, Monica, go ahead," he said. "Enjoy your exhibit."

The phone went dead. Goodbye, it seemed, had gotten to be too much to expect.

Brett leaned against the counter, peering at the man anxiously.

"I am sorry, *madame,* but there is nothing more I can do," he said, pushing his thick horn-rimmed glasses up off his nose. "I have looked twice and it is not here."

"I don't understand how y'all could lose our luggage. The flight was nonstop from Nairobi."

"All I can tell you, *madame,* is that your luggage is not where it is supposed to be."

"I know that," she said with exasperation, "otherwise I wouldn't be standin' here!" She sighed. Brett heard her Georgia accent grow stronger as she became annoyed. Since she'd moved up north, it had softened considerably, but when she got angry it tended to roll off her tongue as if she'd never left Habersham County. "Look, my husband is ill and we simply have to have our suitcases. Please do something."

The man, who was slight and very dark-skinned, allowed that perhaps he could contact Nairobi and ask if the luggage had been left in Kenya. He invited her to have a seat while he checked.

There were half-a-dozen chairs against the wall of the small baggage office. She sat down next to a toothless little man who was wearing a turban. Brett was frustrated, on the verge of tears. Amory was miserable, too, but at least she'd gotten him settled in the VIP lounge where a lovely young woman in a sari had taken him in hand and served him some tea.

Their flight got in early and Elliot wasn't there. She wondered whether she'd get the baggage mess straightened out before he arrived. As if traveling with a sick husband wasn't enough, now she had to contend with lost luggage. At least she'd had the sense to put her jewelry in her purse, and they did have a change of underwear in their carry-on bags. Other than that, they only had the clothes on their backs.

The little man next to her smacked his lips as he chewed something. Brett glanced at him and smiled. He nodded. She had no idea what had brought him to the baggage office, but whatever it was, he seemed resigned to the wait. Patience came with old age, apparently. Or maybe it was an example of the weighty inevitability of life in India.

She'd only had the barest glimpse of the country so far, but the swarming crowds were something to behold. She'd seen quite a few Indians in Washington—both at Georgetown and in the city generally—but it was different seeing them in their own environment. It reminded her of the story one of her professors related about what a student of his said after returning from a trip to China: "My God, I've never seen so many Chinese!" Brett understood that statement now better than ever.

During the flight Amory had given her a travel book. Leafing through it, she'd found a letter Elliot had written to Evelyn, whom he was obviously very fond of, when he'd first been posted to India. Evelyn had passed it on to Amory, who'd stuck it in the book before their trip. Brett had been impressed with what she read. It had given her an insight into Elliot—one that she'd felt might be useful if she were to help Amory mend fences. She took the letter out of her purse and read it again.

India can take its toll on Westerners. I can't pass someone lying in the street without thinking of the young daughter of a colleague who arrived in Delhi after finishing school in the States. Her father was driving her from the airport when she saw a man lying in the road. She screamed for him to stop, but he continued on, telling her it was too late, that the man was dead.

The dark side of the subcontinent is undeniable, but there is the other side, as well—the gentleness of the people, their stoic outlook on life. And there are the cultured elite, the rich and powerful who look down on Americans as coarse middle-class Philistines cloistered in Americaland, the U.S. Embassy compound, cut off from the host country as though it were a hostile sea.

I have already made close friends in Indian society and in the halls of power in Delhi. It is my job to do so, but I also do it for myself. I try not to be a Babbitt in their eyes, the stereotypical American, preaching grace by virtue of economic worth.

Ironically, though, I do not love this country greatly. Its weight is too much for me. India's problems, I fear, are too overwhelming. In that sense I am truly American. I need challenges that include an attainable goal— that have a beginning and an end. That, it seems to me, is both the strength and the weakness of the American mind. Conversely, India's intractability is both her dynamic and her damnation.

Brett closed the letter, feeling a profound respect for Elliot's mind, though she only knew him through the words he'd written. He was obviously intelligent, but there was more—a sensitivity that was rare. She liked the letter as much for what it said about him as for what it said about India. Something told her that despite her misgivings, she would like Amory's stepson.

In a way, she'd gotten to learn more about Amory through his writing, too. Early in their relationship she'd asked for a sampling of his legal opinions. Reading them, she'd discovered how measured, honest and fair he was as a jurist.

The clerk returned. "Please, Mrs. Maitland," he said.

Brett got up and went to the counter. "Did you find our luggage?"

He shook his head. "No. I am sorry to say it is not in Nairobi. The information that I have is that it was put on the plane."

"But it isn't here. Obviously somethin' has gone wrong somewhere, wouldn't you say?" The accent again.

"That certainly appears to be the case," the man said. "I have ordered another search. We must consider that perhaps the cases were accidentally sent on to another destination. I will check with the cities where there were flights departing about the time of your arrival."

Brett had a sinking feeling. Elliot Brewster's insights were growing in wisdom by the moment. "How long will that take?"

"Some time, I'm afraid. May I suggest that you go to your hotel. We will notify you as soon as your baggage is found."

She saw that there was no point in staying. She told him they would be at the Taj Mahal Hotel, thanked him and turned to go. As she left, she glanced at the old man, who was still waiting patiently. She couldn't help wondering if he was prepared to die before his problem was solved.

When she got to the VIP lounge the hostess told her Amory was in the "water closet." The poor man had virtually been living in the bathroom when he wasn't in bed.

"May I bring you a cup of tea?" the girl asked.

"I'd love one, thank you."

The hostess gracefully draped the trailing end of her sari over her shoulder and went off. Brett sighed. The lounge was tranquil compared to the clamor outside, and she was grateful for the respite. When she looked around the room, she noticed two rather distinguished Indian businessmen sitting at a table in the corner, drinking tea and talking. They had interrupted their conversation to admire her when she'd come in, and only reluctantly resumed talking when she sat down.

Nearby, a heavyset woman in an elegant sari, her arms draped with gold, slept in a chair. Soft sitar music played in the background. The hostess returned with the tea, smiling sweetly as she placed it on the table. Brett immediately took a sip. The milk and sugar were clearly intended to be added, but she passed up both. With the air-conditioning the room was quite cool and the brace of tea felt good. She took a few more sips and looked toward the rest room, hoping Amory was all right.

The India segment of the trip had certainly begun on a down note. Brett thought of her lovely black cocktail dress, the one she'd brought for the embassy party, adrift somewhere in a sea of baggage—assuming it wasn't already in some thief's hands. She shuddered to think of going to the party dressed as she was. The notion of borrowing something from Monica went through her mind, but she quickly dismissed it. The prospects of that working out weren't good. Perhaps she could buy something in a hotel shop.

Having grown up with so little, Brett found the prospect of losing her things especially painful. She'd really enjoyed putting together her trousseau. At first, though, she had worried that it would be an insurmountable problem, given her meager finances. But Evelyn had stepped into the breach. In June she had invited Brett over to offer her help in planning the wedding.

It had been a pleasantly warm day. The air in George-town had been soft and fragrant with blossoms. They'd sat in the small garden in back at a glass patio table. It had been set with the quiet elegance so typical of Evelyn Maitland— a Waterford bowl filled with yellow roses, Georgian silver and antique Spode china.

"Let me get right to the point, dear," Evelyn had said in her soft patrician voice. She'd smiled, her blue eyes gentle and full of warmth. "As the wife of a Supreme Court justice, you're going to need a trousseau. And I don't mean a couple of dresses and a suit. We're talking about a serious wardrobe."

The mere mention of clothes had made Brett uneasy. She'd been all too aware how limited her wardrobe was from

the moment she'd first set foot in Washington. Living on a
student's stipend hadn't allowed her to acquire much, and
although Aunt Leona tried to slip her a little money from
time to time, the Wallaces had problems of their own,
making ends meet. "I realize I'll need some things," she'd
said, trying to maintain her dignity.

Evelyn had patted her hand endearingly. "I'm sure
Amory intends to give you some money, but I want you to
let me buy your trousseau so that he doesn't have to."

Brett was as touched as she was surprised. "Evelyn, I
couldn't let you do that."

"Why not? Give me one good reason."

Brett sighed.

"It would make me happy," Evelyn went on. "Isn't that
reason enough?"

"I do have my pride, Evelyn."

"You and I are family, dear. Pride is for outsiders." Evelyn had taken her hand. "Please, Brett, let me do this."

Brett had been overwhelmed with gratitude, but she'd
been embarrassed, too. Catherine had undoubtedly gone to
Amory with a complete wardrobe, a houseful of furniture
and silver and china, and maybe even a trust fund. Brett
didn't have any of that. She only had her love. Evelyn knew
that and didn't want her to suffer for it.

"You've been so good to me," she'd told her, "but I
don't want to be in your debt."

"It wouldn't be a sacrifice. Besides, I'm really being selfish. My mother and I spent weeks selecting my trousseau. I
believe it was one of her greatest joys, and perhaps our
happiest time together. I haven't a daughter, Brett, but I
would like the experience. So give me this little pleasure."

Brett shook her head, feeling both gratitude and admiration.

"You'll have to let me help you choose things, though,"
Evelyn said warmly. "That's a condition."

"You're much too generous."

"I have a selfish motive. You're my only chance, dear. I'll
never have another."

There had been no way Brett could refuse. Evelyn was utterly sincere. That was the kind of person she was. And Brett had been deeply grateful that Evelyn had framed her offer in a way that had made it so easy for her to accept.

Once Brett's exams were behind her, the two of them had spent a lot of time together shopping. It had been wonderful fun. And they'd both done a lot of secret pretending. They were the mother and daughter the other had never had. Dear, sweet Evelyn.

Brett was drawn from her happy recollections when the two Indian businessmen got up to leave, both of them glancing her way. One reminded her of Omar Sharif. His hair was tinged with gray and he looked very elegant in a double-breasted suit that might well have come from Savile Row.

"Good afternoon," he said pleasantly, smiling and checking out her legs as he walked past.

Brett nodded in response, aware that he'd been eyeing her. She was used to the attention of men, though she'd never particularly relished it. Younger men in particular were too single-minded in their intentions. She wanted to be admired for the person she was, and not just her beauty.

Watching the men go out the door, she suspected that in this case her honey-colored hair and fair skin—rare commodities in this part of the world—added to the interest. Regardless, flirtation was not a game she enjoyed.

She was still learning to adjust to being married. Men, she'd already discovered, treated a woman differently when they knew she was taken. In Kenya she'd experienced it firsthand.

The pilot who'd flown them from Nairobi to Nanyuki was a rakish Brit who'd initially mistaken them for father and daughter. He'd flirted outrageously until Brett had made things clear by putting her hand on Amory's knee and addressing him as "Darling." Afterward, Amory had said he was rather proud to have a wife who could turn so many eyes.

The door to the lounge swung open and an Indian, appearing more harried than most, barged in, looking about the room. Seeing her, he made his way over. "Mrs. Maitland?"

"Yes?"

"A thousand pardons. I am Bhagwant Kumar from the American Embassy. I learned only now that you arrived early. We checked on the arrival time, of course, but these people never get things straight. This is not Dulles International, as you can see. I hope you have not been greatly inconvenienced by the delay." He only then stopped to take a breath and bow.

Brett did her best to hide her amusement. "Are you with Mr. Brewster?"

"No. Forgive me. Mr. Brewster was unable to come due to pressing matters at the embassy. He asked me to carry you to your hotel."

"I see. Well, I'm about to add to your burdens, Mr. Kumar. My husband is indisposed at the moment, and it seems the airline has lost our luggage. They're looking for it and promise to deliver it to the hotel if and when they find it."

Kumar nodded. "Then you understand what I mean that this is not Dulles." He smiled. "I have been to America myself, so I know."

Just then Amory came out of the rest room. Brett introduced Bhagwant Kumar, and explanations were made concerning the luggage and Elliot's absence. They decided the best thing to do was to get to the hotel as fast as they could.

Amory was so weak that Brett asked if he wanted a wheelchair, but he declined. "I refuse to be wheelchair-bound on my honeymoon," he said with a wan smile.

"Better than ending up in a hospital."

"A few hours' sleep," he promised, "and I'll be a new man."

Kumar gathered their carry-on bags. As they left the VIP lounge, Brett held Amory's arm. They walked slowly through the terminal building with their driver talking nonstop. He and Amory had instant rapport, laughing at the small world it was when they discovered that Kumar's brother lived in Easton, not far from the Maitland family home on Maryland's East Shore.

"I know Oxford, yes!" Kumar said excitedly. "And the Tred Avon River. Yes. My brother took me on a sailboat there when I visited three years ago. Yes, yes. I know it well."

Amory seemed to like the coincidence.

"You must live in one of those elegant houses on the river, Excellency," Kumar enthused. "There are some very beautiful palaces. I saw them. From the boat, of course."

"Palaces might be a bit strong," Amory said, as they moved along through the crowds.

Brett was able to share the irony. Rosemont had seemed like a palace to her, too, the first time she'd seen it. The big old brick two-story mansion overlooked the river, sitting on a vast grassy slope that swept down to the water. It had been in the Maitland family for four generations and Amory and Harrison owned it jointly now.

Brett had certainly never dreamed of owning such a fabulous estate—not for years, anyway. But Amory had the place in Chevy Chase in addition to the East Shore house, and over the months she had gotten used to the idea of owning two such lovely homes. Since their wedding reception had been held on the terrace of Rosemont, it had a special place in her heart. She was part of the Maitland family history now. The thought of that made her proud.

They found the embassy limousine just outside the terminal building. Kumar and Brett helped Amory into the back. The way he dropped into the seat told her the respite had come none too soon. She climbed in beside him, giving him a comforting kiss on the cheek.

Bhagwant Kumar climbed into the driver's seat, placing their carry-on bags on the seat beside him. Brett had made sure of that.

"Don't worry, Excellency," Kumar said over his shoulder. "I will have you at the Taj Mahal Hotel in very good time."

They sped off a bit faster than Brett would have liked. The guidebook had said that the traffic in India could be a nightmare, and the indifference, even the hostility of some of the drivers, was to be feared.

Brett was nervous, seeing how close they skimmed to pedestrians, animals, bicyclists and other slow-moving vehicles. It didn't help that Bhagwant Kumar was as interested in talking to Amory as in paying attention to where he was going.

They made it to the city without incident. The streets of Delhi teemed with people, bicycles, motorized rickshaws, bullock carts, vehicles and animals. Indian film music blared over radios made in Taiwan. The air smelled of smoke and cooking food and excrement.

Amory lay back, but Brett was on the edge of her seat. She wanted to be out among the people, though after she'd caught a glimpse of a body cart and realized what it was, she had second thoughts.

Kumar impatiently blasted his horn. To Brett's relief, he was paying more attention to the road than before, though he still kept turning to look at them. Suddenly, a scrawny cow lurched in front of the limousine. Brett cried out, but they struck the animal before Kumar could stop.

All eyes turned on them. Over the hood of the car, Brett could see the cow thrashing about. The struggle continued for a while, then stopped. Bhagwant Kumar sat stunned, motionless. He didn't say a word. Before she knew it, people appeared from out of nowhere, closing in on the car, pressing their faces and hands against the windows.

"Good Lord," Amory said. They were the first words that had been spoken.

Brett's heart was racing. She heard thumps on the sides and roof of the vehicle. A couple of people jumped up on the bumper, rocking the car. She searched the faces, looking for signs of anger. The children were smiling, but that didn't reassure her. She could hear Kumar mumbling in dialect. He finally uttered his first intelligible words. "This is not good," he said. "No, no. Not good at all."

"Should we do something?" Amory asked, leaning forward.

"I must talk to them," Kumar said, more to himself than to them. "It was not my fault. It is the fault of the stupid cow. Can't they see that?"

Brett grew even more anxious when she saw Kumar begin to shake. She looked at Amory, already pale from his illness. He appeared more concerned than afraid. She slipped her hand in his.

"I must talk to them," Kumar said again, as though trying to find his courage. He opened the door and a small roar went up from the crowd.

Brett didn't exhale until the door closed again. She considered locking the door after him, but was afraid to look panicky. She watched Kumar move to the front of the vehicle. People crowded around him, but other than some pushing from the rear and inadvertent bumps, there was no serious jostling, no violence.

Through the windshield she and Amory watched Kumar stare down at the cow. He spoke to those closest to him, gesticulating with his hands, obviously blaming the cow for the calamity.

Brett heard Amory groan. "Damn," he said, "what a time for an attack. What do you suppose the chances are of finding some facilities around here?"

"If there isn't anything nearby, maybe we can go on to the hotel in a taxi," she said.

"I'm not so sure you should be out in this mob," Amory said. "But I'm going to try to find a toilet. If I end up squatting in the gutter like everybody else, so be it." He scooted to the edge of the seat.

Brett glanced at Kumar. He was making his case and two or three people seemed to have taken the side of the cow.

"Listen, Brett," Amory said. "As soon as I get out, I want you to lock the door behind me. Don't let anybody in. I'll try to be back in a few minutes."

Amory climbed out of the car. She was relieved to see the crowd open to let him pass. It could be a sign they weren't too hostile, though she couldn't help but be afraid, especially when the curious faces pressing against the window began to multiply. She closed her eyes and tried to calm herself.

A terrible fear began welling up inside her. Accidents did that to Brett. Ever since that big semi had snuffed out

Kady's life over on the road to Cornelia. Her sister's death had been a terrible blow. Things had never been the same after that.

And here she was in India, grown, married and twelve thousand miles from home, yet unable to get that wreck out of her mind. She could almost smell the pine trees on that sweltering August day, the hot asphalt and spilled oil. She shivered, blinking back her tears as she watched the mob.

Over the hubbub, she could hear a siren. A minute later a police jeep pulled up, scattering the crowd. The officers quickly took charge. Brett was relieved, but her recollections of Kady's accident had left her anxious.

The police were examining Bhagwant Kumar's papers when Amory returned, rapping on the window to get her attention. She immediately let him in.

"Well, I can now say I've experienced India," he said. "Guess we might as well go home." He laughed.

She didn't respond. When he saw the distressed look on her face, he asked what was wrong.

"Oh, I don't know. It's hitting the cow, I guess. I'm upset and . . . thinking about Kady again." She bit her lip, trying not to cry.

Amory put his arm around her.

"Look at me, getting all worked up," she said. "And you're the one who's suffering. Are you all right, darlin'?"

"I'm fine, considering."

"India is starting out badly, isn't it?"

"I'm sorry you're upset. We definitely did not need an automobile accident."

Brett shook her head. Despite herself, she was back in Georgia again. She could picture her Uncle Earl looking at his pickup, wringing his hands as the firemen struggled to get Kady out of the mangled wreckage. Why she was feeling so emotional about something that had happened so long ago, she wasn't sure, but she began to cry.

Amory stroked her head. "My poor Brett."

"I'm sorry," she sobbed. "I don't know what's gotten into me." She wiped her nose. "I'll be all right."

Amory gave her his handkerchief. She blew her nose. She tried to smile.

"Ghosts from the past."

"Ghosts?"

Brett drew a ragged breath. "I didn't mean my sister. I suppose I was thinking about Earl."

"Your uncle? Why?"

She shivered, closing her eyes.

"Brett, what's wrong? It isn't just the accident. Something else is bothering you."

"The accident made me think of him, that's all. It's nothing, Amory. Don't worry about it."

"You've always acted so strange when the subject of your sister and uncle comes up. I thought maybe there was something you needed to talk about."

She could see how genuine his concern was. It gave her a warm feeling. "Dear Amory. I can't hide a lot from you, can I?"

"Are you hiding something?"

Brett sighed again. "The situation with Kady is a little more complicated than I've let on. But I'm not so sure this is the time to burden you with it." She wiped her runny nose.

"Why not? We're prisoners in a car in the streets of New Delhi. What else is there to do?"

She took his hand and pressed it to her cheek. "I'm not very rational when it comes to my baby sister. The truth is, I blame Earl for what happened to her."

"I thought she was hit by a truck while she was out driving."

"Kady didn't even have a license. She took Earl's truck to get away. To escape."

"Why?"

"Because he'd beaten her."

"He beat her?" Amory sounded duly horrified.

"I know I'm making my family sound like a bunch of redneck crackers," she said. "But then, maybe that's exactly what we are."

"Why did Earl beat her, Brett?"

She drew a long breath, trying to settle the turmoil still roiling inside her. "Kady had been caught with a boy, doing something she shouldn't. In rural Georgia, that's not well regarded, unless a wedding is planned."

"So he beat her?"

"And me, too, because I knew what Kady was doing and I didn't do anything to stop it."

"My God."

"But it was Kady who really suffered. He beat her up pretty bad. Not all the marks on her body came from the semi running into her."

Amory shook his head. "I understand your bitterness."

"It's a different way of life, Amory—one I understand, if not fully accept."

"I was not terribly fond of your uncle," Amory said, "but I have no respect for him whatsoever now."

"That's all right. I've hated him for years and even though I've tried to put it behind me, what he did to Kady still haunts me." She wiped her eyes. "I'm sorry to be such a baby. This isn't like me. I don't want to burden you with troubles from the past."

"I'm here for you, Brett, just like you're here for me. Husbands and wives don't really know one another until they've seen each other's wounds and scars. This is the way it's supposed to be. I want you always to feel you can talk to me. About anything that bothers you."

Brett put her hand around his neck and kissed him. "You're so good, darlin'. You really are."

Amory held her close. The people outside had been staring in at them, watching everything, but she didn't care. She felt relieved. It was amazing how that awful secret had festered.

"Looks like things are being resolved," Amory said.

Brett looked out and saw one of the policemen directing some men to drag the carcass to the side of the street. The officer in charge, the one who'd been inspecting Kumar's papers, sent the chauffeur back to the car.

He climbed in, seeming greatly relieved. "I told them it was the fault of the cow," he said. "Very simple. I was not to blame." He turned and looked back at them. "Very sorry for the delay, Excellency. Now we shall go to your hotel."

"We'd like that," Amory said, squeezing Brett's hand. "We really would."

Elliot spent the afternoon at his desk, reading and re-reading memos, opening and closing files, without comprehending a thing he saw. In his mind he'd had half-a-dozen confrontations with Monica—some coolheaded, in which he'd laid her open with biting sarcasm, others more hostile, ending in a shouting rage of indignation. All of them were right. All of them were wrong.

He'd fantasized about having it out with Robert Farrens, as well, in words dripping with contempt and disdain. Scorn was his only weapon. Somehow it didn't seem enough.

He'd seriously considered surprising the two of them at the exhibit, publicly embarrassing them. But he knew he'd embarrass himself even more, and perhaps look like a fool in the process. There was so little a cuckold could do.

Under the circumstances, he had no particular desire to see Amory and Brett. But Joni had come in with news of a traffic mishap on their drive in from the airport, so a courtesy call seemed not only politic, but the decent thing to do.

He looked at his watch and decided he ought to get over to their hotel. He wasn't accomplishing anything anyway.

Elliot returned the classified files to the proper folder, stacked the others on the corner of his desk, put on his suit coat and went to the outer office. He handed Joni the classified folder, saying he was on his way to the Taj Mahal Hotel.

"What about the political summary?" she asked. "Didn't you want me to type up a final draft before going home?"

"We'll do it in the morning."

She gave him a look. "Give me time to type it, Elliot. The ambassador wanted it by ten."

"I'll come in early," he said. The truth was, he'd forgotten all about it. "For the moment it's diplomacy over paperwork."

He bade her goodbye and left. As he walked down the hallway, he imagined that every friendly look or word from his co-workers masked awareness of his domestic troubles. Making him the object of ridicule—whether real or imagined—was the worst part of Monica's sin. And he suspected she was perfectly well aware of it.

The Taj Mahal Hotel, like other places of opulence, was another island of refuge. The uniformed guards who kept things quiet and peaceful motioned him through the gate. A bearded doorman of great stature, wearing a smart uniform and a turban, greeted Elliot, taking the keys handed him.

"I won't be long," Elliot said to the man, who bowed respectfully.

"Yes, sir."

Some people considered the Taj Mahal Hotel the finest on the subcontinent. The architecture was modern; the decor—with its tapestries, lanterns, latticework and stylized peacocks—was traditional. Elliot liked the place for its impeccable service, though in his present mood nothing pleased him. It would probably appeal more to Robert Farrens, he thought—matters of aesthetics were more in the attaché's purview than his own. He wondered if the bastard had brought Monica by to contemplate the art.

Inside he approached the desk, asking the clerk for the Maitlands.

"I'll ring for you, sir."

A brief conversation followed, then the man sent Elliot to the elevators. Upon reaching the appropriate floor, a bellman escorted him to the door of the suite, rapping on it crisply with a gloved hand. Elliot handed him several rupees and gestured for him to go. The man withdrew, and a moment later the door swung open.

She was not what he expected. Brett regarded him with equal surprise. Then she beamed, saying, "Elliot, we meet at last!"

He knew she was just a kid fresh out of college, but there was something in the soft drawl and faux—or not so faux, he couldn't be sure—Southern charm that was suggestive of a more mature woman. She extended her hand, shaking his with a crisp sincerity.

"I understand you had a little trouble on your way in from the airport."

Brett rolled her eyes. "Don't even mention it. We ran over a cow! I was sure the mob that gathered was going to stone us or something."

He smiled. "In this country, people get their entertainment where they can. As a novelty, your value is quite high."

"That's a different way of looking at it, I suppose." She gestured for him to enter, closing the door behind him.

"Well," he said, "on behalf of the ambassador, the prime minister and forty million cows less one, welcome to India."

She laughed. "It's not really a joking matter, I guess. I felt just terrible. And so did Amory."

Elliot looked into her eyes. There was a genuineness about her that he detected immediately, though by nature and training he tended to be cautious in his appraisals of people. But then he reminded himself that she was a bride, and probably deserving of the benefit of any doubt.

"Speaking of Amory," he said, glancing around the sitting room.

"I'm afraid there's bad news," she said.

"You didn't lose him on the way from the airport?"

"No, but he picked up a nasty bug."

"Already?" he said. "Delhi belly usually takes a day or two, at least."

"This is Kenya cramps, or whatever. He's been under the weather for the better part of a week. Even flying out here was an adventure, Elliot, believe me."

"Is he in bed?"

"He's taking a nap at the moment."

"I'm sorry to hear he's not feeling well. Traveling's not a very pleasant time to be sick, especially on one's honeymoon."

"I think Amory'd agree with you on that," she said. "He actually feels guilty about it, if you can imagine. I told him he's the one suffering, not me." Brett guided him toward the sitting area. "Poor thing's only just gotten to sleep, so if you don't mind, I'll let him rest awhile."

He noticed the scent of lilacs about her. It was stronger than the general smell of sandalwood in the air. As she turned to take a seat on the sofa, he let his eyes drift down her to satisfy his curiosity. Brett had on a tan safari dress. Her skirt was slim, and short enough to show off what may have been the longest, most shapely pair of legs he'd ever seen.

Elliot sat in the chair opposite her. She gave him a warm smile.

"The cow wasn't our only catastrophe of the day," she said. "On top of everything else, the damn airline lost our luggage. I had visions of our things ending up in a street market in Bangkok or someplace, but it turned out to be a false alarm. They called half an hour after we got to the hotel. Some ninny had left our bags sitting on a baggage cart in a corner somewhere."

"It's always darkest before the dawn," Elliot said, touching his throbbing lip.

Brett noticed the wound. "Did you have an accident, too?"

"A love bite."

She grinned. "Lucky you."

He shook his head. "Things are not always as they appear. I use the term *love* loosely."

"That sounds like a subject not to be pursued," she said.

"You're probably right."

He watched her cross her legs, thinking how ironic it was that he found her attractive. He'd known she was pretty, of course. There'd been a photo in the clipping Evelyn had sent, but newspaper pictures never told the whole tale. In this instance, they hadn't done her justice. What he was seeing struck him at a visceral level.

There was an aura about her, a presence, an intelligence that went beyond the physical, though all the elements of beauty were there. She had flawless vanilla skin and bones that were delicate without being fragile. Her golden hair was straight, falling to her shoulders, though she had the habit of tucking it behind her ear, a gesture she'd made a couple of times already.

As he looked at her, she did it again, exposing her neck. His gaze shifted from the gold earring that looked like a cluster of berries to her sherry-colored eyes. Brett seemed embarrassed by a scrutiny that had gone on a bit too long.

"So," he said, assuming the burden of the conversation, "I guess you didn't expect the 'in sickness and in health' business to come quite this soon."

She laughed gratefully. "Amory and I have been joking about that. He thinks I ought to be entitled to a money-back guarantee, but I pointed out that all the money's been his to this point, so I may just be stuck with a lemon."

"Nice to see you taking it in such good spirits."

"A nurse, I'm not. But I do the best I can. Amory would do the same for me."

Elliot wondered why such charity only came at the beginning of a marriage. What was it that inevitably turned the milk of human kindness sour? It wasn't inevitable, of course. There were couples he'd known that escaped unhappiness altogether, but it was rare.

"When will I get to meet Monica?" Brett asked. "I was hoping she might come with you."

"I was, too, but unfortunately she had another commitment. She'll be at the ambassador's party this evening, though."

The last thing he wanted was to create expectations about Monica. The chances were good there'd be a knock-down-drag-out fight of some sort—most likely before Amory and Brett left India. But not knowing himself how and when it would transpire, he didn't feel it wise to say anything.

"We've been looking forward to seeing y'all and going to the party this evening," she said. "At least, we were until Amory got this bug. It was very thoughtful of Ambassador and Mrs. Welty to include us, though."

Elliot's mind started wandering and it took an effort to concentrate on the social niceties. One moment he'd think of the dull throb in his lip and Monica, the next he'd be aware of the beautiful young woman in front of him—Amory's wife.

His instinct was to be critical of her, to reject her because she seemed so flawless, a little too good to be true. But that was probably only because of his own pain. Brett, he decided, covered her youth and inexperience well, despite the tiny signs of nervousness. On the surface she'd seemed so confident, but when he looked closely, he noticed how her hands trembled slightly, and he heard the occasional quaver in her voice.

"Elliot, you have such a funny look on your face," she said. "What are you thinking?"

He smiled at having been caught. "I guess I'm just curious about you."

"In what way?"

He wasn't about to tell her. That was the danger with honesty. It was why diplomats rehearsed their lies carefully. "Curious who's under all the Southern charm," he said glibly. "I'm sure Amory didn't marry you for that."

The comment seemed to fluster her. "I don't know whether to consider that a compliment, or to be offended."

"Oh, don't be offended," he said quickly. "That would ruin our fledgling relationship and upset the family equilibrium."

She studied him sternly. "I can't decide if you're teasing me, or if you're just cynical."

"Oh, cynical, Brett. By all means."

"And is that because you're a diplomat? Or is it your nature?" She arched her brow in question.

"Let's say it's because of my job. Diplomats can be jaded . . . and, yes, cynical."

She contemplated him, trying to look serious despite the hints of amusement on her face. "They say it's a diplomat's job to lie. Are you a liar, too, Elliot? Or can I take what you say at face value?"

The irony of the question, coming on the heel of his own thought about the diplomatic lie, amused him. He also liked her gumption. He wondered if that quality had attracted Amory.

"Trust is a very delicate thing. I don't think it's wise to trust anyone too easily," he said.

"How depressing."

"The gloomier one's outlook, the nicer the surprise when things work out."

"That sounds suspiciously like self-deception to me."

She had him pegged. Brett wasn't just beautiful, she had brains. Maybe that's what had attracted Amory, considering he was so cerebral. Elliot liked her intelligence himself. He liked their jousting. But maybe, in the process of being so clever, he'd exposed himself.

"I think you may have put your finger on an undeniable truth," he said.

His admission seemed to please her. "I hope you won't hold that against me."

"Never."

They sat regarding one another for several moments when there was a knock at the door. Brett got up.

"That'll be room service. I ordered tea as soon as the desk called to say you were here."

He watched her walk to the door, admiring the enticing curve of her hips. She was more of a woman than he had expected. Amory's taste had always struck him as somewhat pedestrian. Elliot had to hand it to him. He'd done well.

The room-service waiter wheeled in the cart. At Brett's direction he began laying out the meal. There were finger sandwiches, pappadams, chutneys and fruit pastries. After the man left, she scooted forward on the sofa, her knees canted demurely to the side, and asked how he took his tea.

"Black's fine."

Brett poured, then handed him the cup and saucer.

"You've really taken to this wife business, haven't you?" he said.

"What do you mean?"

"You seem rather comfortable. 'Amory and I' rolls off your tongue as though you'd been saying it for years. And you appear to have done this before," he said, gesturing toward the table.

"Well, I don't mean to disillusion you, Elliot," she said, pouring herself some tea, "but I'm as nervous as a June bug on the fast lane of the interstate. You're my first official relative since the wedding, you see."

He found her candor endearing. "How undiplomatic of you to admit it."

"I'm not yet to the point of cynicism...still naively honest." She took a sip of tea. "As for being able to pour tea, you can learn with a cracked pot from Wal-Mart just as easily as with fine china. The aunt who raised me was a humble woman, but not without her graces. Anyway, for a couple of years I've been watching Evelyn very closely."

"I have colleagues with daughters your age," he said. "They're not as grown-up."

"Is that a compliment, Mr. Brewster, or a break in your diplomatic veneer?"

"A compliment."

"Thank you. The way I see it, my husband is a mature man. I consider it my duty to behave accordingly."

Elliot drank some more tea, watching her. She was disarmingly shrewd. But something about what he saw bothered him. It wasn't so much Brett, he finally concluded, as the fact that she was married to Amory.

His stepfather did not seem the sort of man who would appreciate her nimbleness and subtlety. There was almost too much there for Amory—layers that would escape his notice. That wasn't being critical or unfair. Amory, to him, had always been a creature of intellect—a man of principle, a repository of values, a person who lived foremost in his mind. If he lacked anything, it was a sense of humor—an appreciation for how fatal being deadly serious could be.

Brett seemed to span a broader range of frequencies. Or was he simply projecting? Did they have a special rapport, or was he engaging in wishful thinking?

What bothered him, he realized, was why Brett had been so taken by Amory that she'd married him. How could that moral purity and stodginess appeal to her?

"Can I fix a plate for you?" she asked when no conversational gambits had been forthcoming.

"Please."

She selected a sampling of what was on the tray. Elliot watched her hands, her long, tapered fingers. She handed him the plate and a napkin.

"So tell me," he said, "how did Amory convince you to marry him?"

She chuckled. "Aren't you really asking how I convinced him to marry me?"

"No, Brett. Even if I were that rude, I wouldn't let it show. We diplomats are cynical. We're liars and we're jaded, but we're unfailingly polite."

"Point taken. The simple and honest answer to your question is that Amory and I love each other," she said.

Elliot chewed on his finger sandwich. "I don't doubt it for a minute."

She looked skeptical. "I know you're thinking I married him because he's a catch, but it's not true. Being married to a veritable institution is not something I'm looking forward to. Amory's a remarkable man. That's what I married. An exceptional human being who happens to love me. Sometimes it's hard for me to believe I'm a part of his life."

"If I may remove myself from my shroud of cynicism to utter a simple truth, Amory's fortunate to have you, Brett."

"Coming from you, that's especially flattering. Thank you." She drank some tea, eyeing him over the rim of her cup. "Does this mean that we're friends now?"

"I think that's a safe assumption," he said.

"Good."

"Is that important to you?" he asked.

"I've been told you're the black sheep of the family. I didn't want you to be my only failure."

His mouth twisted with amusement. "I'd say you're doing just fine."

The bedroom door opened. "Do I smell tea out here?" It was Amory, in pajamas and a silk robe.

"Well," Elliot said, rising, "the rumor of your demise was a gross exaggeration, I see."

"Hello, Elliot."

They walked to each other and shook hands. Elliot was aware of the customary awkwardness that seemed to underscore their meetings.

"Good to see you," Amory said.

"And you. How you feeling?"

The justice put his hand on his stomach. "I wasn't sure I was going to make it across the Indian Ocean in one piece, if you want to know the truth."

"Revenge of the Third World."

"Come have some tea with us, Amory," Brett called to him.

Amory walked over to her. Brett put her arms around his neck, giving him a kiss. He turned to Elliot. "I'm glad you two have met. Brett has been the joy of my life, Elliot."

"I can see that," he said. "And I think it's fair to say you're the joy of hers."

"Let's sit down," Brett said. "Can I pour you some tea, darlin'?"

"That sounds wonderful." Amory looked decidedly content, despite his illness. "Monica wasn't able to come?" he asked Elliot.

"No, she had another commitment."

"I'm sure we'll see her."

"It remains to be seen, but I hope so."

Amory took the cup and saucer Brett handed him. "How is Monica?"

"You really mean how are we, don't you?" he said.

The justice grudgingly nodded.

"I suppose it's the relevant question," Elliot said, glancing at Brett, who seemed duly sympathetic. He had known this moment would come, and he didn't want to lie—not about this. "To tell you the truth, we aren't doing well."

"I'm sorry," Amory said.

"But it's not a topic for the occasion. The beginning of a marriage is much happier than the end of one, and Brett has told me what a good start you've gotten off to."

Amory smiled and put his arm around her. She blushed, looking her age for the first time. Elliot could see there was no duplicity on either of their parts. The happy couple.

He did not need their bliss any more than they needed his gloom. Feeling entirely superfluous, he consulted his watch. "Will you be up to the dinner party tonight at the Weltys'?" he asked Amory.

"I'd like to attend. I just don't know. This thing goes and comes. The flight was miserable, but I've had a good nap. I feel a little weak right now, but I may well feel up to it later. It's hard to say." Amory sipped his tea. "I want Brett to go in any case. No sense spoiling her evening, too."

"Of course I won't go," she said. "Not unless you do."

He brushed her cheek with his fingers. "Darling, that sort of devotion belongs in some earlier generation, even before mine. I'm not on my deathbed."

"I'd prefer to stay with you," she said.

"We'll see how I feel. But if I'm not up to it, I want you to go." He looked at Elliot. "I want you to insist."

Elliot had been trying to remove himself from the conversation. What he wanted to do was leave. Now Amory was putting the burden on him. "You're the boss here, not I."

"Right now, the boss seems to be this microorganism that's taken over my life." He put his cup down. "Speaking of which, I'm going to have to pay a visit to the bathroom." He got up. "Elliot," he said, shaking a fatherly finger, "convince her to go to the dinner party. I'm counting on you."

Elliot and Brett exchanged looks.

"For being such a nice man, you can certainly be severe," Brett said.

Amory laughed and started for the bedroom. "As long as I get my way," he said over his shoulder, "I'm as pleasant as can be."

They watched him disappear through the doorway.

"There isn't a word of truth in that," she said. "He's the gentlest person I've ever known."

"Yes," he said. "He is." Elliot got to his feet. "I should be going, Brett. You've got your hands full."

"Don't be silly. I'm enjoying our conversation."

"I've enjoyed it, too. But we can talk later. If not tonight, then another time."

She rose as well. "I know you want to go," she said, "and I won't keep you. But I would just like to ask if there's anything we can do to help."

"With what?"

"Monica. One of the reasons Amory wanted to make this trip was because he hoped to smooth things over. We'd hate to think us being here is making things worse."

"I appreciate the thoughtfulness, Brett. I really do. But Monica's and my problems have nothing to do with Amory, or the fact that you're here."

"Maybe she'd rather not see us."

"This sounds harsh, I know, but the sad truth is she doesn't give a damn about you one way or the other. Don't even think about her."

Brett seemed at a loss.

"As far as tonight is concerned, do whatever you wish. Don't feel any obligation to put in an appearance. If you'd really prefer to stay with Amory, I'll tell them not to send a car."

"I'd rather stay with him, but he'd have a conniption if I did. We've only been married a couple of weeks, but I can tell when he's dug in his heels."

"I defer to your wifely judgment."

He went to the door. Brett followed him over. She gave a hint of a smile and extended her hand. "I'm glad we've finally met, even if it's not under the best of circumstances."

Elliot took her hand, aware of how slender and cool it felt. He looked into her warm eyes, feeling an unexpected stirring. "It's always nice to welcome someone new into the family," he said.

"Is it?"

He ignored her gentle challenge. "Amory did well," he said, continuing to hold her fingers. "Welcome to the family, Brett."

She seemed to appreciate the kindness. "I'll be ready when the car arrives," she said, "and looking forward to the evening."

Elliot nodded and finally let go of her hand. "Yes, I will, too."

He left the suite, thinking that what he'd just said was ironic, considering the day he'd had. But it wasn't diplomatic prattle. It was quite true. For the first time in a long time, he did feel as if he had something to look forward to.

Amory sat propped up in bed, watching Brett in the bathroom, applying her makeup. She had on a black bra and panties and, judging by the way she was posed, he decided she was aware of his observation.

"You know, Brett," he said after several minutes, "there must be a law in India that says that when husbands are incapacitated, wives have to cloak themselves from head to foot, so the poor chap can maintain his sanity."

She turned and smiled. "Am I being too immodest for you, darlin'? I can close the door, if you'd prefer."

"Heavens, no. The deprivation I already feel is bad enough. I was teasing, of course."

Brett put down her mascara and came into the bedroom. She got on the bed and crawled over to him, giving him a kiss on the lips. "Maybe you aren't feeling so bad, after all," she chided. "Maybe you ought to come to this dinner party with me." She kissed him again. "Or maybe, if you're feeling a whole lot better, neither of us should go to the party." She gave him a devilish grin.

Amory caressed her face adoringly. "How did I ever deserve you, Brett?"

"The same way I deserved you, I suppose."

"This honeymoon was perfect until I picked up that damned bacteria."

"It's still perfect. Don't you know deprivation makes the heart grow fonder?"

"Is that how the saying goes?"

She tapped the end of his nose. "Sounds pretty good to me." She laughed and kissed him again. Then she glanced at the clock. "Yikes, I've got to get going or I won't be ready when the car comes."

Amory sighed as she returned to the bath. She was far more exquisite than he deserved. With her on his arm he felt awfully proud, but at the same time a little guilty. He was well aware most people assumed her beauty had attracted him, but it wasn't true. Oh, he found her irresistible, all right, but she was alluring in so many other ways. She was an absolute delight to be around, but even that wouldn't have mattered if he hadn't fallen in love with her mind. Brett had a mature intellect and a depth of character that he found terribly stimulating.

Catherine had been intelligent, well-educated and cultured. They'd shared important things, even aspects of his work, but not with the kind of mutual understanding he had with Brett. Her intense interest in the law partly explained it, but it was broader than that. She cared about ideas the same way he did. It was remarkable, actually, that he could be mentor and lover and partner, all to the same woman.

Still, the decision to propose hadn't come easily. There were so many arguments militating against it, not the least of which was the way other people would regard them. Harrison's reaction had been typical of what people were most likely thinking.

Even before Amory had spoken to Brett, he'd gone over to Harrison and Evelyn's to tell them about his plan and—truth be known—to ask for their blessing. They'd been aware of the relationship, of course, but not of how serious things had become.

It had been a Sunday in January, Super Bowl Sunday, though he hadn't realized that until he'd gotten to his brother's place in Georgetown and had found him sitting in front of the TV set in his den. Amory had felt he couldn't interrupt the game, so he watched for a while.

Both of them had had a passion for sport. At Yale, Amory had played tennis and fenced. Harrison had preferred contact sports. He would have been a football player if he'd been able, but lacking the size, he'd played rugby, having given up wrestling after high school to spare disfiguring his ears—Harrison's athleticism was tempered only by his vanity.

As the 49ers and the Dolphins and Harrison continued battling it out, Amory had slipped off for a chat with Evelyn. He was glad, in a way, to be able to tell her first. He'd found her in the salon, doing needlepoint. . . .

"Amory, I'm so happy for you!" she enthused when he told her. "That's the best news I've heard in ages! I think it's wonderful."

"Do you really?"

"Of course. And Brett must be overjoyed."

"I haven't officially proposed yet, but we've had conversations—let me put it that way."

"I think it's perfect," Evelyn said. "Perfect for you both."

He shouldn't have been surprised by her generosity. Evelyn was the most giving, warmhearted human being he'd ever known. She'd gone through Catherine's death with him and, as a result, they'd grown very close. Over the years he'd confided in her more than he had in Harrison.

"I have to be frank, Evelyn. I'm a bit worried that Brett and I have both been caught up in the moment, that we aren't looking at this thing clearly."

"What are you talking about?"

"I *am* thirty-three years older than she."

"I assume Brett is as aware of that as you, Amory. If it was a problem for her, I'm sure you'd have heard about it. Besides, you never know about the future. Harrison and I were both kids when we met and we're growing old together, but that certainly hasn't guaranteed us a unity of spirit. Sometimes I wonder if sharing all that isn't as likely to spawn bitterness as joy."

Amory fell silent.

"But listen to me," she said. "You didn't come to hear about the woes of marriage. I'm supposed to be cheerful."

"Our friendship should be a two-way street, Ev."

"Yes, and you've always been very understanding. The best brother-in-law a woman could hope for. But it's my turn today to be cheerleader." She smiled. "Your happiness is written all over your face, Amory."

"I love Brett, and I do want to marry her," he said.

"Then what's the problem? She's mature enough to know her own mind."

"I don't want to take advantage of her."

"Discuss that with her frankly."

"I have. At length. I don't doubt Brett's sincerity. And you're right, she's very mature and serious-minded." Amory smiled self-deprecatingly. "But I wake up some mornings, asking myself how I can possibly be so happy. I guess I'm afraid I've turned a blind eye to reality."

"What reality?" She reached out and patted his hand. "If you don't mind me saying so, dear, I think you're doing the same soul-searching every man does when he wants to ask a woman to marry him. The issues vary from relationship to relationship, but we all have our questions. And our insecurities."

"You're right, of course."

Evelyn gave him an appraising look. "I think you'll make a wonderful couple."

Amory leaned back in his chair, looking out the window at the icy branches of the trees. He stroked his chin thoughtfully. "I appreciate you saying that because I have to tell you, Ev, I've never felt like this about anyone before. Not even with Catherine, bless her soul. I loved her, but this is different. Brett has me head over heels, to use the vernacular."

"I can see that." She'd hesitated then, before going on. "I'd like to share a conversation I had with Catherine a month or so before she died. I haven't told you this before because it was never particularly relevant, but it is now. Catherine's biggest worry was that you would settle into the widower mode and lock out any chance for happiness with someone else. She asked me to encourage you to keep an open heart."

"Catherine said that?"

"Yes. And I was rather moved by her generosity. But she was right, Amory. I've shared her concerns about you. I also knew there was nothing I could do except encourage you, if and when that special someone came along."

"So here we are," he said, his eyes shimmering.

"Yes," she said. "Here we are."

"You're a gem, Evelyn. You truly are."

"I've got one important piece of advice," she said. "Trust Brett. Trust what she feels and what she thinks. And trust yourself, as well."

"That's very good advice, I know." He reached over and took her hand. "Dear Evelyn."

"Well," Harrison said, appearing in the doorway. "I've got 49ers murdering Dolphins in my den and a love-in going on in my parlor."

"You don't know what a jewel you've got for a wife," Amory said.

"Please, I've spent years instilling due modesty in her, brother, dear, so don't stir up trouble by telling Evelyn how wonderful she is. Uppity women quickly become a pain in the ass."

Amory and Evelyn both laughed.

"Is your game over?" she asked.

"It's in its dying moments. Why?"

"Amory's got wonderful news."

"News?" Harrison looked back and forth between them. "Is it something I sit for, or can I remain standing?"

"Oh, come sit down, Harrison, and talk to Amory," she said, getting up. "I'm going down to the cellar and get us a bottle of champagne."

"Oh, God," Harrison said. "It's one of *those* occasions?"

Evelyn left and Harrison dropped onto the sofa. Amory came right to the point, describing his plans. Harrison froze for a second, then an appraising, vaguely annoyed look crossed his face.

"For Chrissake," he'd said, "what do you want to marry her for? Why don't you just fuck her like any other normal middle-aged man would? By this stage in life, you ought to understand the difference between lust and love."

Amory didn't appreciate Harrison's cynicism, but he knew his brother was given to brash overstatement. "This is not a sexual thing. It's not like that at all."

Harrison acted genuinely surprised. "You really mean to say that firm, nubile flesh isn't what's caused you to take leave of your senses?"

Amory flushed. "I love her, Harrison."

The senator leaned back, screwing up his face in consternation. "For God's sake, Amory, you're a justice on the Supreme Court. Maybe you don't fuck college girls, but you don't marry them, either. Do you have any idea what sort of ridicule you're in for? Do I have to tell you what people will think?"

"I don't care what they think."

Harrison shook his head. "You're in love so you're going to throw everything out the window. The world be damned."

"Harrison, what are you afraid of? That you might somehow be embarrassed by this? Is that your concern?"

"I realize family is of secondary consideration in these matters. And I admit your approval wouldn't be essential to any decision I had to make, but I can't help wondering if you haven't failed to think this through, ignored the broader implications."

"Just say what you mean."

"For Chrissake, Amory, she's young enough to be your daughter. I understand the attraction. Believe me, I've felt it myself. I've been there. Jesus Christ, just the other day a dolly in a miniskirt put her hand on my crotch in the elevator. And she wasn't some slut. She was deputy counsel of one of my committees. We'd been working together for weeks!"

Amory turned red. "It's *not* that kind of thing."

Harrison got up and went to the window. "It doesn't seem like it because this is your first time. Christ, by the time the third or fourth sweet little thing comes along, you begin to understand what those rumblings inside you really mean. I've been there, Amory. I know."

"You don't know about this. I'm not interested in the sex."

Harrison turned around. "Then maybe you need a shrink, not a wife."

"You know what I mean."

Harrison returned to the sofa. "Live with the girl for a while. See how it holds up. See how the sex is. Shit, screw a couple of others before you decide it has to be this one."

Amory had tried to control his emotions, but he couldn't help snapping. "I can't live that way and you very well know it."

Harrison groaned.

Their attitudes about so many things were completely at odds. Harrison didn't believe in the sanctity of the marital vows, nor had he taken their Catholicism nearly as seriously as Amory had.

Growing up, they'd been as different as a choirboy and a streetwise ruffian. Harrison had jokingly referred to Amory as the Pope of Talbot County, saying he should have gone to the seminary rather than law school. As they grew older they came to realize it didn't benefit either of them to argue. So, for the most part, they'd adopted a live-and-let-live attitude.

"I don't think either of us is benefiting from this," he told Harrison. "I know you mean well. I know you've said what you've said out of love. But I'm going to ask Brett to marry me. And if she accepts, I'm going to marry her for what I consider to be the right reasons."

"It's your life."

"I'd like to think you approve of what I'm doing," Amory said. "But if you can't, I at least hope you won't resent me."

Harrison looked at him. "What do you mean by that? Are you suggesting that I'm jealous?"

"If there's been jealousy, Harrison, it's been on my part. You have a wonderful wife, and I've always felt you haven't sufficiently appreciated that fact."

"Shit, you aren't going to lecture me on my marriage, are you?"

"No. I just want you to know that if Brett ends up being half the wife to me that Ev is to you, I'll consider myself fortunate. And I want you to know I love Brett for the person she is, not because she's a sweet young thing who makes me feel like a boy again."

Harrison smiled sardonically. "Maybe *you're* the one who doesn't appreciate what he has."

"Right now I'm concerned about you and me, Harrison."

Harrison sat back on the sofa. "I've been spending the afternoon watching a couple of football teams kick the shit out of each other. After it's over they'll shake hands and put their arms around each other. That's the way it should be with us, brother dear. You apparently want my blessing, so consider that you've got it. Now, unless there's something else that needs to be said, I think it's time to get drunk."

"I suppose it is."

Harrison turned toward the back of the house. "Evelyn, what the hell's keeping you?"

"Coming!" she called. A moment later she came into the front room carrying a tray with a bottle of champagne in an ice bucket and three flutes. "As I was going past the den I heard the final score," she said. "It was thirty-eight to sixteen, San Francisco."

"Great," Harrison said. "I lost a hundred bucks." He winked at Amory. "Win a few, lose a few, eh, big brother?"

Evelyn put down the tray. "Well, if not the outcome of the game, we definitely have something to celebrate. Amory is taking a bride at last."

"Ah, yes," Harrison said. "It's not even spring, but love is in the air...."

They'd toasted then, and Harrison had never brought up the subject again. Yet, in spite of the silence, Amory suspected that his relationship with Brett had caused Harrison more consternation than he was willing to admit. His brother had a reputation as a player. Everyone in Washington was aware of it. Brett's beauty—her "firm, nubile flesh," as Harrison called it—was what he would have cared about, were he in Amory's shoes. Perhaps Harrison was incapable of thinking of a woman in any other terms.

Amory was grateful for his sense of proportion, and deeply regretted that Harrison was so lacking in that quality. He felt sorry for his brother, and even sorrier for Evelyn. If there was a family tragedy, it was the lot his sister-in-law had drawn.

"Amory, you have the most wistful look on your face," Brett said, bringing him back. "What can you be thinking about?" She was standing at the chest of drawers, removing the wrapping from a new pair of panty hose.

"I was thinking how happy I am that you're my wife, darling."

"Is that true?"

"You know that's the way I feel."

"But is it true that that's what you were thinking?"

"I was thinking about the months that brought us to this point."

"Really?"

"Yes, indeed."

She grinned. "Aren't you the romantic, though?"

"I'm just a happy man."

Brett came back over to the bed and snuggled up beside him, nuzzling him and running her hand inside his pajama top. "And I'm a happy woman."

"So happy you're willing to be late?"

"Amory Maitland, don't you go making any promises you can't keep."

He smiled and pressed his head against hers, feeling warm and happy inside. Brett stayed a moment longer, then hopped up to finish dressing. She slipped on her panty hose. Amory watched her gyrations as she pulled them up.

Catherine had been extremely modest, even after years of marriage, and seldom dressed in front of him. Brett was not only a different person, but of a different generation. Her frankness appealed to him, even if it took some adjustment on his part.

The big difference between his first and second marriages was the part religion had played. Catherine had converted, but Brett refused to. Again, the explanation might be generational, but that wasn't the whole story. By nature Catherine had shared his modesty and traditional values. In a first wife, that had been very important. With Brett he'd been more tolerant, more open-minded. His work as a judge had given him that.

Brett was standing at the closet now. His eyes skimmed down her. The lower half of her body was several shades darker because of the black panty hose. She was a sexual creature, and yet that was all right with him because of her fundamental virtue. He watched her looking over the raw silk black cocktail dress she planned to wear that evening. She seemed thoroughly delighted by what she was doing, and that amused him.

"Are you going to wear the pearls?" he asked.

"If you think I should. They'd be pretty with the dress."

"Then do."

She looked at him as she stepped into her dress. "You don't think it might upset Elliot, seeing me in pearls his mama wore?"

"To the extent that he would remember them at all, he'd be aware they're the Maitland pearls, darling. Besides, I don't think jealousies toward the second wife extend to stepchildren."

"I'm sure you're right. I just don't want to step on any steptoes." She gave him a wide smile, then sat down on the bed with her back to him so he could help her with the zipper.

When he'd finished, she went and got the pearls. She stood at the mirror, struggling with the magnificent diamond clasp. Finally, in exasperation, she returned to the bed so he could help her again.

"You know these far better than I do," she said.

"I guess I've fastened them a few times."

Brett looked at him over her shoulder, the stricken look of a child on her face. He'd seen it before, but not often.

"Please tell me, Amory. You don't think of her when you see these, do you?"

He shook his head. "Now I think of you."

She searched his eyes until she'd found the reassurance she needed. Then she returned to the mirror. Her hair was done up in a French twist, the way he liked it. She looked lovely, but the pearls did bring back memories. The spirit of what he'd told her was accurate, though. Now the pearls belonged to her.

She turned to face him. "Well, what do you think? Will I do as your personal ambassador to the ambassador?"

Amory smiled. "You look gorgeous, darling. The most beautiful wife in the world."

"Maybe I'd better go before your compliments get way too outlandish for belief. It's enough if I please you."

"You do, Brett. You do."

She got her purse, checked the contents, then came to the bed again to kiss him goodbye. Caressing his cheek with her cool fingers, she said, "You get better, darlin'. Soon."

"I'll do my best," he said.

Brett went to the door. "I wish you were coming with me."

"Do what you can for Elliot. He's really suffering."

She nodded. "He's not a happy man."

"I hope Monica's decent to you," he said.

"I guess I'll soon find out." She blew him a kiss and glided out the door.

The evening was not as hot as usual, so Elliot elected to wait outside the ambassador's residence for the arrival of the embassy car, or Monica, whichever showed up first. All afternoon his mind had moved back and forth between Brett and his wife, from curiosity to misery to fascination and back to misery again.

He was aware that Monica was a problem he had to deal with; that the time had finally come; that he couldn't put it off any longer. But Brett wouldn't go away. She was there at the edge of his awareness—her perfume, her long legs, the wry connection of their intellects. He couldn't shake her, and it surprised him.

Maybe it was his way of compensating for his unhappiness—to seek out beauty when the world around him was filled with ugliness. He knew, though, that it wasn't just a physical thing. It wasn't lust. It wasn't hormonal. It was Brett's purity and perfection, her happiness, that contrasted so markedly with his own abysmal life.

Elliot had to smile at his self-pity. He wasn't like this normally. His nerves were a little frayed. He was tired. His pride was wounded. He had to pull himself together. *Never allow your personal life to impinge upon your career.* All his mentors had told him that, perhaps knowing the burden he was carrying in Monica.

Elliot began pacing in the dappled shadows. The air was particularly fragrant. He inhaled deeply, wanting to sense something, to get his mind on something—anything—more positive. He thought about his work, his conversation with Gene Welty, the new posting he wanted. Yes, a change of scene was key. He knew he had to get out of India.

Dorothy Hughes, Gene's secretary, came up the drive, having walked from her apartment in the compound. When she attended these functions she was always alone. A spinster in her fifties, dedicated, efficient, looking ahead to retirement, Dorothy was a fixture at the embassy. There was something vaguely sad about her. It could be a sad business.

"Hello, Elliot," she said softly as she passed him.

He got a whiff of her heavy perfume. "Hi, Dorothy."

She went to the front door of the residence.

Elliot was in his dinner jacket, as per the hostess's request for semiformal attire. Adrianne Welty, like her husband, had a bit of the Raj in her blood, preferring her parties on the formal side. She had hired her favorite Delhi group for the evening, a trio that played both traditional Indian music and a kind of modern jazz. When the door opened to admit Dorothy, the soft sitar music coming from inside the house grew louder momentarily, then died back down. Elliot continued to pace back and forth in the shadows.

This sort of function had long since lost its charm. When they'd first gotten to India he had enjoyed the parties—first because they were different and secondly because Monica liked them. She was not one to endure isolation and needed to be around people. Now, apparently, she'd taken that requirement to the extreme.

Monica hadn't made it back to their house to change before he'd left. Her infidelity had become blatant and she'd made no effort to cover up. She was forcing him to picture her fucking his rival. It was as though she were saying, "Hey, Elliot, here it is. What do you think?"

Their confrontation would have to wait until later. He couldn't imagine things ending quietly, without a final blowup. No, that wasn't Monica's style. These were the moments of her life. He'd come to understand they were all she really had.

Not surprisingly, Robert Farrens hadn't put in an appearance, either, even though it was eight-fifteen and most of the guests had already arrived. He wasn't sure if something should be read into that, but it made Monica's tardiness all the more apparent.

Needing a respite from his wife, Elliot let his mind drift back to Brett. The image of her was so pleasing, especially in contrast to Monica. Yet, when he let himself think about her situation, he felt a rush of anxiety.

Brett Maitland was not just a woman, she was his stepfather's wife, his mother's successor. On the face of it it seemed absurd, but it was the fact. Brett was a new bride and wife to the man who'd once been pseudofather to him.

Elliot hadn't focused on it particularly, but the fact was he was jealous. He was envious of his stepfather, envious of Amory's picture-perfect wife and her picture-perfect devotion.

When he'd thought about them that afternoon he'd decided they were deluding themselves, and was convinced that their bliss would one day give way to the harsher reality. Elliot knew well that his cynicism was a product of his envy and that his distrust of their happiness was a direct result of the impossibility of his believing in his own. Predictably he'd put down what they had, finding Brett's love for Amory a bit too saccharine, and therefore suspect.

Brett was young, which meant she was in love with being in love. His smug appraisal didn't really make him feel better, but it was necessary as an ego defense. The thought brought a smile to his face. Elliot knew he was on the verge of becoming pathetic. Why couldn't he suffer through his unhappiness without bringing Brett into it? Why did he have to complicate things by allowing himself to get obsessed?

Several more guests arrived, their voices carrying up the dark drive as they approached the residence. Elliot exchanged greetings with them. Salome Nugent, the Lebanese wife of his closest friend in the mission, patted Elliot's cheek, telling him he looked devastatingly handsome. Salome was a buxom olive-skinned woman and the mother of four who loved her husband but refused to deny her romantic soul. Fortunately Fred understood, and Salome had the wisdom to confine her acting-out to public displays.

"You the official greeter?" Fred Nugent asked, as the others went inside.

"Thought I'd wait for the guests of honor out here," he replied. "It's a lovely evening."

Fred, a man of fifty-five with thinning hair and a laconic manner of speech, called to his wife that he'd be in shortly. He lit a cigarette, looking up at the moon as he exhaled. "It is a nice night."

"Yes." Elliot thrust his hands in his pockets. "Heard anything juicy on the new skipper?"

"Not a word, except that he was an extremely generous contributor to the president's campaign and is aware that New Delhi is the capital of India."

"I was hoping we might get another professional instead of a hack."

Nugent sighed. "No such luck. It's not all bad, though. The rest of us get to work more and party less."

They stood listening to the symphony of frogs and insects.

"Is Monica inside?" Nugent asked.

"No, she hasn't arrived yet."

"Have you talked to her since this afternoon?"

Elliot searched Nugent's face. "No. Why?"

"I hesitate to bring up a sore subject, but I had a call from Ranjit Banerjee, my pal over in the ministry. It was one of those I-thought-you'd-like-to-know conversations."

Elliot felt something ominous coming, and his gut tightened. "What's she done?"

Nugent took a deep drag on his cigarette before he spoke. "Apparently she called some deputy minister's wife a slut in front of a dozen people at a reception this afternoon."

"Shit."

"From what I understand, she was with Robert Farrens. He hustled her out of wherever they were. It was an art exhibit, I think."

Elliot's heart lurched. She *was* with Farrens. So much for any benefit of the doubt. He'd known, but hearing about it in such matter-of-fact terms made the sting all the worse. So they were at the point of running around together in public. And he had to hear about it from a colleague. At least Fred wasn't making anything of it—or he was kind enough not to appear to be doing so.

"It looks like I have to have a talk with her," Elliot said, barely able to disguise his shame.

"It might not be a bad idea to say something to the lady and the deputy minister. I expect they'd appreciate hearing from you."

"Undoubtedly."

"The names weren't familiar, but I've got them at the office. I'll give them to you on Monday."

"Thanks, Fred."

Nugent dropped his half-smoked cigarette on the pavement, crushed it and kicked the butt into the bushes. He put a hand on Elliot's shoulder then went inside.

For several moments Elliot stood in the balmy air, fuming. He probably would have killed Monica if she'd been there. Damn her. It wasn't enough to kick him in the balls; she had to knife him in the back, too. Shit.

An embassy car came along the drive. Elliot figured it was the one that had been sent to pick up Brett. He peered into the dark interior, wondering if Amory had come along. In a way he hoped he had, but as the car stopped Elliot was able to see there was only one passenger. Through the side window he saw Brett Maitland's face in the light coming from the house. His heart gave a little lurch.

Elliot went over to the car. He opened the door for her and offered his hand. "Good evening, Mrs. Maitland."

"My," she said, smiling up at him, "your duties for Uncle Sam extend all the way down to opening car doors?"

"All the way *up* to opening car doors," he replied. "Diplomacy in the electronic age is not what it once was."

She stepped onto the pavement, taking in the air as he had, glancing about, some thought of "exotic" India undoubtedly going through her head. Elliot discreetly looked her over.

She had on a sexy black dress with a sassy short jacket. Her hair was swept up. She wore large pearl-and-diamond earrings and the Maitland pearl necklace. He recognized it immediately. "The justice wasn't up to an evening of diplomacy, I see."

"No," she said, engaging Elliot's eyes. "I left him with a cup of broth and a pot of tea."

Now she smelled of roses—each time a different blossom. He momentarily considered her mouth. "The only thing worse than the bugs in the Third World is the inflation."

Brett laughed and looked into his eyes. She seemed so happy. There was still adrenaline surging through his veins because of what Fred Nugent had told him about Monica and yet, here he was, looking wistfully at his stepfather's wife. He offered Brett his arm and she took it. They headed toward the front door.

"Is Monica inside?" she asked.

"No, I'm afraid she's late, as is her custom. She may even have defected, in which case we won't see her at all."

"Defected?"

He rapped on the door. "It's a long story."

An Indian servant admitted them to the party—a cacophony of cocktail chatter, sitar music, the smell of food and incense. Brett glanced up at him, her face bright and happy.

"This is my first diplomatic affair," she confided. "I'm pretty nervous."

He liked it that it didn't bother her to be seen as an neophyte. He patted her hand. "Two deep breaths, relax and don't let the smile go brittle. You manage that, and you'll be a success."

She squeezed his arm like she would a favorite cousin's, and they stepped inside. "You make it sound easy."

"Like falling off a bicycle," he replied.

"Tell me if I make some horrible mistake," she said. "I consider this a learning opportunity. Better I cut my teeth here than in Washington."

He could see he was to be her handler for the evening— the friendly face, the family member she could confide in. Somehow, he didn't mind. Watching her having her big adventure almost appealed to him. Plus it might help keep his mind off Monica.

Elliot introduced her to Adrianne Welty and the ambassador. Adrianne, a kind of Julia Child figure with the same kind of overpowering voice, took over. She led Brett off and Elliot dropped back. He ordered a double vodka tonic and watched the spectacle from a distance.

His stepmom-once-removed did well, her smile never becoming plastic, each gracious comment sounding sincere. He realized he shouldn't have doubted it; their little diplomatic outpost was small potatoes beside the Washington power centers.

Of course, Brett was still on her honeymoon, so she hadn't yet had a chance to do her wifely thing with *tout*

Washington. Still, Elliot suspected Evelyn had been giving her a few tips beyond what Brett had indicated.

Inside of ten minutes she appeared to have charmed everybody in the room, and what's more, seemed to enjoy it. He wondered how long before this sort of thing would start to bore her.

With a mind like hers, playing helpmate to Amory wouldn't satisfy her for more than six months. Monica hadn't lasted that long, the tragedy being she'd never found a constructive alternative to simply being his wife. That is, until now. And Farrens was certainly not the most constructive choice she could have made. Elliot could picture Monica, her voice rising so that everybody could hear, calling that poor Indian woman a slut. His jaw tensed. *Damn her!*

Now he was sorry he hadn't had an excuse to skip the party. Word about Monica's indiscretion had probably started getting around. Fred wouldn't have said anything, though Salome might have. Others in the mission had their contacts in the government, as well, and there was little doubt every official in New Delhi would be aware of the incident by noon tomorrow.

Adrianne Welty hadn't given any indication she was aware, but then Adrianne could play the perfect hostess even if Gene had just told her that a nuclear war was imminent. As he moved toward the table with the hors d'oeuvres, Salome Nugent intercepted him, pressing her copious breast against his arm—the usual prelude to intimate conversation. "What a delightful girl Mrs. Maitland is."

"Yes, she is charming," he said, relieved it wasn't going to be a comment about Monica. He took a long sip of his drink.

"And so bright. I suspect she'll end up on the Supreme Court with her husband."

"Why's that?"

"She's going to be an attorney. Didn't you know? She told me she's starting law school next month."

Elliot glanced over at Brett, who was holding forth with half a dozen of the key embassy staff, including Gene Welty. "As a matter of fact, I didn't know, Salome. I guess I shouldn't be surprised."

The woman turned to watch Brett. "Delightful girl. It's a shame the justice was too ill to come. I would have liked to meet him."

"Amory's a solid human being."

"He must be quite a man to turn the eye of a girl like her." Salome smiled, grabbed a canapé from a tray, and drifted off.

Elliot continued to observe Brett. Her sexuality jumped out at him. The thought of her making love to Amory had gone through his mind, but he hadn't dwelled on it. Now he found the notion upsetting, though he wasn't quite sure if it was because of the associations concerning his mother, or pure and simple jealousy.

Elliot had always felt some guilt with respect to Amory, perhaps because he knew his feelings toward him were basically unfair. He'd never come to terms with Amory's righteousness or his Catholicism. The man was almost priestlike. Maybe that was what made it seem so wrong that he had Brett. Ah, that envy again.

Elliot sensed someone beside him and turned to see the Weltys' majordomo, a Sikh of imposing height by the name of Ram. Though with his uniform, turban and beard he presented a most fearsome presence, he was in fact an engaging man whose dark eyes always seemed to sparkle with laughter.

"Good evening, Mr. Brewster."

"Ram, how are you?"

"Excellent, sir. Thank you."

"A festive evening."

"Quite, sir. Yes, indeed."

Brett said something that made her entourage laugh uproariously, turning heads throughout the room.

"There's a new jewel in the crown this evening," Ram said.

"Yes, the wife of one of the judges on our highest court."

"His Excellency isn't here?"

"No, Ram. The duty of escorting the lady has fallen on me this evening."

There was little meaningful that a man in Ram's position could say in response, but Elliot read his thoughts easily. They both continued admiring her.

"There hasn't been a call from Mrs. Brewster by any chance, has there?" Elliot asked.

"No, sir."

"Robert Farrens hasn't put in an appearance yet?"

"No, sir."

Monica and Farrens weren't a subject he and Ram could discuss, either, even if Elliot was so inclined, but that didn't mean the majordomo wasn't aware. Ram knew more than anyone in Delhi; Elliot and many others were convinced of that.

When Elliot put down his empty glass, Ram signaled a servant, who promptly brought another vodka tonic. It was an indication of the way the household was run.

"Ram, what tidbits of interest do you have this evening for a lowly diplomat?"

"Tidbits of what nature, sir?"

"I've heard enough social gossip today to last awhile. Tell me something important about India. What do your soothsayers have to say these days?"

"As has too often been the case in our country, Mr. Brewster, forces on the extreme threaten to undo us."

"You're speaking of the assassination of Harchand Singh Longowal?"

"Yes. He could not get a concession for the Sikhs from the mother. He succeeds with the son and he is rewarded with death." Ram shook his head.

"What's your prognosis?" Elliot asked.

"In India the future rises from the earth like the crops, Mr. Brewster. Some have an eye for what the harvest will be like. There are false prophets, and others not so false."

"What do you see in the future for Mr. Gandhi?"

"Trouble, Mr. Brewster. The son is not the politician his mother was." Ram leaned closer, lowering his voice. "Nor is he blessed with the manly endowment she was. He may be able to hang on to power for some years, but eventually he will fall from his own weakness. Not unlike your Mr. Carter, if I may be so bold."

"You should have been a diplomat, Ram."

"Thank you, sir."

Elliot admired the man's subtlety. For a time they surveyed the party in silence.

"Mr. Brewster," Ram said, nodding toward the door, "you inquired about the cultural attaché. I see he's arrived."

Elliot looked up to see Robert Farrens standing at the entry, surveying the party. Their eyes met briefly and Farrens quickly looked away. Obviously aware that word of the afternoon's events had reached Elliot, Farrens seemed to be in no mood to deal with the matter unless forced to.

Elliot watched him closely, feeling more contempt than jealousy. Despite a gaunt, dissipated look that came with years of drinking, Robert Farrens managed to appear effete and cultured. He was a man who had lived a great deal and wore his suffering like a bud in his lapel. Some women—Monica being a notable example—found the quality appealing. Elliot didn't understand it, but then he wasn't a woman.

Farrens was of medium height, with brown hair and dark penetrating eyes. His grooming sometimes bordered on careless, as one might expect of the idle rich, though not of a diplomat. Tonight he was a bit more disheveled than usual.

Farrens's manner was smooth. He spoke three or four languages fluently. No one disliked him, nor did he particularly evoke affection. He was a hard man to categorize.

Elliot glanced at the door and wondered if Monica was standing out front, waiting a few discreet moments before putting in her appearance. He was not eager to find out, considering he couldn't say much to her at the party.

The attaché, for his part, quickly mixed with the crowd in order to make an encounter more difficult. It was rapidly becoming apparent that he and Farrens would have to come to terms.

Ram excused himself to tend to his duties, leaving him alone. Since Farrens had arrived, people had been glancing Elliot's way from time to time, but it was difficult to tell if it was to see the cuckold's reaction, or simply because of the little drama that had played out at the art exhibit that afternoon.

Elliot had had a reputation as one of the bright young stars of the foreign service—a sure bet to make ambassador at an early age. At the moment, though, he was on the verge of becoming an object of ridicule. Monica certainly had found a way to exact her revenge.

Guts, someone once said, was grace under pressure. This, he realized, was his chance to show he had guts.

To help keep his cool, he watched Brett instead of Farrens. The more he observed her, the more he decided she seemed like a rose in a field of thistles. She was almost too pure, too perfect. That made him worry. Fate had a way of humbling perfect lives. His own had been far from perfect, but it had certainly given him a lesson in humility.

It was hard not to be aware of Farrens, though. Elliot watched him over the rim of his glass, fighting his feelings of contempt. People continued to glance his way, but he tried not to notice. He almost would have preferred ridicule or scorn.

Adrianne Welty saw Elliot standing alone and signaled for him to join her. He complied, knowing he couldn't hang back all evening. He conjured up his most provocative smile as he approached Adrianne and several other woman. They all responded positively. Any pity this particular group felt was well hidden.

Listening to the mindless banter, Elliot wondered how the situation with Monica was going to turn out. Divorce seemed inevitable. It was the last resort for the cuckold—besides violence.

After several minutes of conversation, he decided it was time to show his balls. He made a diplomatic tour of the crowd, chatting with as many guests as he could, while sparing Farrens. A public confrontation would only make Elliot look weak. Better to rise above his humiliation.

Before long it was time for dinner. Adrianne seated Brett between Elliot and the ambassador, whose place was at one end of the long teakwood table. The group was large enough that some of the younger people were shunted off to the patio, where several more tables had been set up.

The dinner began with no sign of Monica. To make things worse, Robert Farrens had left minutes before they moved to the dining room. Elliot wasn't close enough to hear his excuse, but Adrianne did look his way as she was bidding Farrens goodbye.

Elliot tried not to let Monica's treachery get to him, though his anger wouldn't go away. He wondered if she'd been so embarrassed by the incident at the exhibition that she couldn't face him. Somehow he doubted that was the problem. It wouldn't have been unlike Monica to tell the story to the whole dinner party, turning, in her view, a point of embarrassment to one of triumph.

Gene Welty, who had imbibed a bit more than usual, was in rare form, regaling Brett with the best stories of his diplomatic career. One would have thought that it was Rajiv Gandhi himself at his elbow.

Brett was a delight, to be sure, and so very self-assured for someone her age. Still, he wondered if being someone's wife wasn't a misuse of her talents. The news that she was going to law school, though, had changed his perspective somewhat. Could she be more Machiavellian than he'd thought? A lawyer married to a Supreme Court justice would hardly be at a disadvantage.

When Gene finally gave her the chance, Brett turned to him. "Elliot, am I doing all right?" she whispered. "Should I be pulling back a little?"

He was flattered by her request for approval. "You're doing great, kid. Keep it up."

"I was afraid I might be going overboard."

"No, they love you."

"I don't want to let Amory down."

"I'm sure he would be proud."

Brett looked deep into his eyes, perhaps in search of sincerity. She had allowed him to see her vulnerabilities, though he wasn't sure why. In a funny way, it endeared her to him. Maybe her motives weren't any more complicated than simple honesty.

"Was Monica detained?" she asked. "I was hoping she'd be here."

Elliot gave a half shrug. "She's AWOL, Brett."

"I hope nothing's wrong."

"I've had to deal with it before," he said. "Don't worry."

Gene turned his attention back to Brett, forcing Elliot to chat with the woman on his other side. As he did, he glanced down the table at the spot where Monica likely would have been placed. With the extra people, Adrianne had shuffled the guests so there were no empty chairs, but Elliot saw the hole anyway. It was like a bleeding wound in his side.

Mercifully, the party came to an end. Elliot's sole remaining duty was to see Brett on her way. They said their goodbyes to their hosts and went out to where the embassy car was waiting. The driver held the door, but Elliot motioned for the man to take his place in the driver's seat.

Brett paused, gazing up at the night sky. "Aren't the evenings wonderful here?" she said. "Reminds me of home in the summertime. The air's so rich and heavy and nice."

She was incredibly beautiful by moonlight. It was difficult not to notice—not to stare at her mouth, her cheekbones, her eyes that were full of innocence and happiness and another mysterious quality he hadn't yet put his finger on. There was a joy in her soul. That was something he didn't see much anymore. As they stared at each other, her expression slowly turned to concern.

"I'm worried about you," she said.

"How so?"

"I can see you're suffering. Is it Monica? Are you concerned about her not coming?"

"Monica does what she wants."

Brett seemed uncertain how to proceed. "I wish I could help," she finally said.

He was amused, yet at the same time touched. "There's nothing to be done."

"I can listen, if you want to talk," she said earnestly.

Elliot thought for a moment. Then he glanced around. "If you want to, we can take a stroll. There isn't a safer place in Delhi than here in the compound."

"I'd love to."

Elliot told the driver they'd be a few minutes, then closed the door. They started down the drive. Nearly all the Weltys' guests had gone. Only a couple of cars remained, including his.

Brett inhaled. "What an exotic, wonderful country this is." She glanced at him shyly. "Of course, I said that about Africa, too. Maybe I just like to travel." She laughed.

"India's infinitely fascinating," he said. "It's one of the cradles of civilization. A source of what we have become—the mother's milk of modern insanity."

She seemed surprised. "Why such a harsh appraisal?"

"I don't know. It's my mood. Forgive me. Don't listen to what I say."

"But you do keep saying these things," she said. "That tells me you're suffering."

"Suffering?"

"It's in your eyes, Elliot."

"Hmm. Maybe this walk wasn't such a good idea, after all."

"I didn't mean to pry or make you uncomfortable," she said.

"Don't worry. You're not."

He'd been resisting telling her the truth. It was mostly pride, but already the evening had become an exercise in learning to live with humiliation. Maybe he ought to tell her. There was no need to go into detail, but almost certainly part of Brett and Amory's concern was due to the fact that they didn't know what was going on.

"I've been reticent, Brett, because I didn't want to burden either you or Amory with my problems. I see now that all I've done was add to your concern. You might as well know, Monica and I are likely to split up."

"Oh, Elliot, I'm sorry."

"It's been a long time in coming. If I seem distracted, it's because things seemed to have come to a head today. It's at a point where our problems are impacting my job, and that's a concern. I won't get into specifics. Suffice it to say it's a rather unpleasant situation."

"Out-of-town guests are the very last thing you need."

"The timing is not good, true, but to be perfectly honest, I'm glad for the distraction. It always helps to get your mind off your own problems."

"You're certainly being brave about it," she said.

"Not brave. Resigned. But enough about me. I'd much rather talk about you than myself."

"Me? That's hardly an interesting subject."

"I don't know a thing about you, Brett. If we're going to be in the same family, I probably should learn something."

She laughed. "There's not much interesting to say. Not yet, anyway. But feel free to check back with me in a few years."

He liked her cheerfulness. It made him feel good. That was the point. Maybe that was the reason he'd wanted another conversation with her. "I understand you plan to go to law school," he said, trying to get her talking.

"Yes."

"What are you going to do with it?"

She had her hands clasped behind her and she looked up at the moon. She stared off dreamily, as though she was visualizing the future. "Do you really want to know?"

"I asked, didn't I?"

"Promise you won't laugh?"

"Brett, I'm a diplomat. The most inane things are said within my hearing and I'm trained not to so much as blink."

"It's okay to have a reaction," she said. "Just don't laugh."

"All right. I promise."

"I think I want to be president."

He took in the comment, nodding slowly, as if considering it. She was watching him, waiting.

"Well?"

"It's good not to aim too low," he said evenly.

She punched his arm playfully. "You're teasing me, Elliot. That's not nice."

"But I'm not laughing," he said, raising an admonishing finger. "That was our bargain."

"You broke the spirit of our agreement," she said.

"No, actually I'm impressed by your ambition. Tell me, what makes you want to be president?"

"I just said that. What I mean is I want to do something important. Hell, I'd be a justice on the Supreme Court with Amory—assuming I get through law school—or a senator like Harrison, or a member of the House of Representatives, or a dogcatcher, if that's only as far as my talents take me. The point is, I want to do something meaningful."

"That's admirable. I commend you."

She smiled. "Thank you for not laughing. I know I sound like a thirteen-year-old at junior-high graduation, but you asked a serious question, and I tried to give you a serious answer."

"Well, you've married into the right family, if power is your thing. Harrison can hand carry your résumé right into the Oval Office. And Amory... Well, I don't have to tell you what he can do. Lawyers can't go any further in the profession than he has."

"You're the family diplomat," she said. "We've got all the branches of government covered, if you think about it."

"I'm afraid I'm pretty small potatoes," he said.

"But you're young. Thirty-what?"

"Thirty-four."

"So you're only ten years or so ahead of me." She laughed.

Elliot couldn't help admiring her. He liked Brett for her willingness to be herself, to talk from the heart. Actually, he just liked her.

She took his arm. "So, I told you my secret ambition. What's yours? Are you going to be secretary of state? An ambassador? What?"

"Right now I'm trying to figure out how to finish my present assignment in one piece," he said.

"That's diplomatic obfuscation. You have to tell me honestly what you aspire to do. Like I did."

"You know, Monica's never asked me that—what deep in my heart I wanted to do."

"Well, I'm not Monica."

He chuckled. She delighted him. "All right. I'd settle for secretary of state. There. Now I've said it."

She beamed. "Good for you! See, saying it wasn't so hard, was it?"

"No, saying it wasn't so hard."

"When do you think you'll make it?"

He laughed. "Secretary of state? Well, I don't expect it to be my next post. There'll have to be a change in the White House before any political job is feasible. And that's the first step."

"You mean to say you're a Democrat, Elliot?"

"Shh," he said. "Not so loud. The Foreign Service is a nonpartisan outfit." He winked. "Not that anybody really gives a shit. Pardon my French."

"That's all right. I use the word myself. Though not around Amory."

Elliot opened his mouth to say something, then thought better of it. It wouldn't be fair to comment, though he understood what she was saying. He'd watched his tongue around his stepfather when he was a kid. Not that Amory would be unpleasant about it. Some people were just that way.

But Brett's comment made him think about their marriage again. What a shame she didn't feel free to be herself around her husband, to use the language she wished. On reflection he decided it might not be so bad, though. God knows, with him and Monica things had become *too* loose. Restraint was something his wife knew little about.

"Well, I'm glad to hear you're a Democrat," she said. "I was afraid I was the only one in this clan."

"My, not a Republican and they let you in anyway?" he teased.

"Amory's not like Harrison," she said.

"No, that's certainly true."

"How did *you* get to be a Democrat?" she asked.

"I'm not really part of the family, if you want to get technical about it. I sort of came in on my mother's coat-tails. She became a Maitland. I didn't."

"Funny, but now that I know you I don't think of you as Catherine's son. I was very aware of it before we met."

"Yeah, I suppose that could make for some awkwardness, if we allowed it."

"I hope it doesn't," she said.

"You're the second wife, Brett. If it bothered anybody, it would be you."

"Then it's not a problem."

Her adamancy pleased him.

They strolled. Brett was beautiful in the silvery light of the moon. It was hard not to stare at her. He wondered if Amory had seen her often by moonlight, if he fully appreciated what he had.

Brett glanced about her, seemingly content. Except for the fact that she held his arm, she could have been oblivious to his presence. But he was very much aware of her. He felt a strong attraction. He drew in her perfume, wanting to take in more of her. And then he realized how terribly stupid that was. He was torturing himself, and for no good reason.

"Maybe we should head back," he said.

"Okay. If you want. I've enjoyed our walk, though." She turned, letting go of his arm, and they started back the way they'd come.

Neither of them spoke for a while. Elliot felt obliged to put things on the right track, even though anything that might have been improper had occurred exclusively in his head. "Have any plans for sight-seeing?" he asked.

"If Amory's up to it we wanted to see the Taj Mahal and that other city with the sandstone buildings, and the Maharajah. What's his name?"

"Bubbles, the Maharajah of Jaipur."

"Yes, that's right. I've read all about him."

Brett's buoyant enthusiasm came to the surface again. Elliot was glad. Earlier he'd considered offering to accompany them on a tour of the nearby attractions, but now he decided it wouldn't be a very good idea. It was becoming obvious that the less he saw of Brett, the better.

"Hopefully Amory will feel up to a long car ride," he said.

"I imagine he will. If not tomorrow, then the day after. Ambassador Welty said he wanted to take Amory to his club, so I'm sure he'll want to be doing that, as well," she said.

"The Gymkhana?"

"Yes, I believe that was it."

"Gene's a secret imperialist under his Midwestern populism. He likes to go to his club and pretend he's an old Brit swigging pink gin."

"That's the sort of place it is?"

"They're mostly old Indian duffers now, but the theory's the same—out-British the British."

"It sounds colorful."

"It's worth the trip. Amory should go."

They were within sight of the car. They slowed their gait. Elliot's thoughts had left him feeling vaguely uncomfortable, if not actually guilty.

"Monica and I won't be having you over like we would if things were different," he said. "I hope you and Amory will understand."

"Of course. Don't worry about us. You've got enough on your mind."

"I really regret the way things worked out," he said. "I'd like to take you and Amory to dinner before you go."

"That would be nice, but don't feel an obligation. We understand. Honestly."

They came to the car. He opened the door. Brett turned to him. "Thank you for the evening. For looking after me, Elliot. I know Amory is appreciative, too."

He smiled. "I'm glad you had a good time." He held out his hand and Brett took it. They didn't shake, they just made a connection. "Tell Amory I'll figure out something the three of us can do."

"The poor darling had better get over the Kenya cramps soon," she quipped. "I told him if he doesn't, he might have to take me on another honeymoon."

They smiled at each other. Her hair appeared midway between gold and silver in the moonlight. She searched his eyes.

"Uh...rattling on the way I did, I've said some pretty silly things tonight," she said. "Could I ask a little favor of you?"

"Certainly."

"Could that speech I gave about being president be our secret? Some things said in friendship sound funny out of context."

"Your secret's entirely safe with me, Brett. I won't even tell Amory."

She beamed and slipped into the back seat of the car. "Thanks." She peered up at him, the light falling full on her face. "Good night."

"Good night, Brett." He closed the door and rapped the top of the car with his knuckles. The engine came to life and they drove off, leaving him alone in the Indian night.

As the taillights disappeared into the obscurity, Elliot realized what his infatuation with her was really all about. He'd made a terrible mess of his life. If he'd been smart, instead of marrying Monica, he'd have waited to find a girl like Brett.

The effect of the vodka had practically worn off, which Elliot figured was well and good because driving at night was twice as challenging and dangerous as in the day, since Indians considered it a luxury to use lights of any kind. Crossing a dark boulevard in Delhi was like being a soldier in World War I, trying to dodge the artillery shells screaming over the trenches—about the time you were aware a vehicle was coming, you were dead.

Elliot managed to get home without death or mutilation. Jamna opened the gate, bowing and grinning into the glare of the headlights. Elliot parked in the carport and got out. The servant was waiting at the foot of the steps, ready to accompany him to the door.

Elliot noticed the house was dark. "Isn't Mrs. Brewster home?"

"No, sahib," he said, shaking his head with worry. "Not all day."

"She hasn't called?" Elliot asked.

"No, sir. Nothing."

Elliot cursed silently as he mounted the steps. Jamna rushed to open the door. Elliot went inside and the servant followed.

When Jamna was alone he kept the house dark, using only a solitary candle to light his small cubicle. Elliot had offered to have a light bulb installed, but Jamna refused, preferring his way. The small space just inside the front door was indisputably his—it was where he slept and rested during the heat of the day, and where he stayed except when he was cleaning, cooking or working outside.

Elliot turned on a light in the sitting room as though something meaningful might be revealed. But the room was as it had been when he'd left to go to the dinner. He turned the light off, said good-night to Jamna, and made his way through the dark house to their bedroom.

It, too, was as he'd left it. For a while Elliot sat on the bed, trying to unravel the senseless puzzle his life had become. Fatigue overwhelmed him after a while and he got undressed and lay down on the bed. He listened numbly to the night sounds—insects competing with the distant hum of city traffic.

Monica had pushed things over the edge, giving him no choice. He would have to have it out with her. The final break.

The sheets felt hot and soon he was perspiring. Despite his anger, Monica drifted out of his mind and Brett insinuated herself into his thoughts. He recalled how beautiful her face had been in the moonlight. He remembered how she'd looked, surrounded by admirers at the party. He could almost hear the lilt in her voice as she'd spoken about Amory and their happiness.

Shit. Which was worse—feeling contempt for the woman one had, or being attracted to one who was forbidden? That was his dilemma. He simply hadn't faced it until now.

For two hours he lay restlessly, growing more and more uneasy. Finally he got up and went, barefoot and in his shorts, to the front room. Jamna had closed the shutters, but Elliot tilted them open so he could peer into the garden.

The grounds lay in the warm, moonlit shadows of mango trees. Beyond the bougainvillea, the lush tropical vegetation and the iron gate, he could see the street, dappled with light. Barely visible across the quiet avenue was a much larger house, a white-columned mansion built by the British and presently occupied by the ambassador from Malaysia.

Elliot was beginning to think Monica wasn't coming home. She always had in the past, regardless of the high jinks she'd been up to. He began pacing, wondering at what point he should notify the police. Not until he'd rung Farrens, certainly. That was probably the place to start.

Jamna heard the footsteps and watched through a gap in the curtain with dark, curious eyes. Elliot paid little attention, resenting the fact that the houseboy was yet another witness to his humiliation.

Jamna didn't seem any less upset than he did, however. By the look of things the servant hadn't slept, either. They both waited for Monica's return, Elliot with his eyes, Jamna with his ears.

As he continued staring out the window he heard the sound of Hindi love songs in the street. Moments later, a young man walked by the gate with a portable radio on his shoulder. He was stopped by a policeman whose job it was to ensure the tranquillity of the neighborhood. The music died instantly and the young man moved on. Jamna's curtain dropped again.

Elliot had about decided it was fruitless to wait when he heard a vehicle approach. Moments later a taxi appeared at the gate. The houseboy drew his curtain back.

Outside, Monica's laughter drifted to the house. The door of the cab opened and her creamy legs appeared. Her white gauze skirt was hiked up halfway to her crotch. A man's voice came from the darkness of the taxi. She leaned back inside. A hand slid over her bare back. Elliot could only see a silhouette, but the voice was American. It was Robert Farrens's. Monica left the taxi and staggered toward the gate.

Jamna had already unbolted the door. He glanced at Elliot before trotting down the steps to greet his mistress.

"Sure you're all right?" the voice called from the cab.

"Yes, Robert. Spot's coming. He'll see I get inside without falling on my ass."

When Jamna opened the gate, the taxi pulled away. Elliot watched them making their way to the porch, the servant offering his body like a walking stick. Monica was still giggling as they mounted the steps.

"Shh!" she whispered at the door. "Mustn't wake sahib."

"Sahib's still awake," Elliot replied, his voice giving Monica a start.

She peered in the direction of the sound, locating his silhouette in the darkness. "Well, the whole damned family's up to greet me. First Spot, now you."

"And the whole damned family's disgusted."

"What for? Because I don't need you to enjoy myself?" Monica removed her hand from Jamna's shoulder and took a couple of defiant wobbly strides toward Elliot. The servant retreated.

Elliot grabbed her arm roughly, knocking her off balance. "Time for a talk."

Monica started screaming as he dragged her through the house to their bedroom. Breathless, she cursed him as he gave her a shove toward the center of the room. She spun around as he closed the door. A lamp cast a mellow glow on her once-lovely face.

"What do you want from me, you sonovabitch?" she seethed.

"To quit your whoring around!"

"Oh, go to hell!"

"Farrens summoned the decency to at least put in an appearance at the Weltys' tonight. Where the hell were you?"

"None of your goddamn business." She had trouble standing.

"The hell it isn't." He pointed his finger at her. "I'm only going to tell you this once, Monica. Your days of screwing my co-workers are over. You're going to sober up, and you're going to go someplace to get help. As soon as I can arrange it, you're out of here."

"The hell I am!"

"The hell you aren't. You're going to do exactly as you're told."

"What do you think I am, Elliot? Your fucking harem girl? Your servant? You can't tell me what to do!"

"Monica, you're too drunk to understand what I'm saying."

"Bullshit! I know what you expect. You want me to wait on you hand and foot like I was goddamned Spot! You think whenever there's an ass to kiss, I'm supposed to run and kiss it just because it pleases you. All you've ever wanted was a dutiful wife who'd spread her legs for you when you felt the urge. Or have I left out something?"

"It would have been nice if you'd learned to keep your mouth shut in public. You know how long it took for that remark you made to the deputy minister's wife to get back to me?''

"Fuck you and fuck her." Monica swayed. "She was a whore and she deserved it. The cunt did everything but grab Robert's crotch."

Elliot shook his head. "You are disgusting."

"Not so disgusting as you. I hate you! I hate the day I married you!''

He took a threatening step toward her, but she didn't cower. He stopped, the adrenaline flooding his veins. He could have struck her so easily if he'd let himself.

Monica stood her ground, though, her dark hair a mess, her chin red from whisker burn, her skimpy white dress barely holding together, barely containing her defiant sexuality. There was a beast under her beautiful facade—a beast as flagrant and unsubtle as a bitch in heat. Sadness and a curious sort of desire overcame him.

"Why do you insist on drinking?" he demanded, forcing a calmness into his voice.

"Because I like it."

"It's bad enough to destroy yourself. Why take me down with you? Does it give you some kind of sadistic pleasure?''

She wavered. "I don't know what you're talking about."

"Everything you do, Monica, is designed to destroy me."

She gave an incredulous, drunken laugh. "Destroy you? You think that's all I care about? Do you really think I lie around plotting ways to do you in?''

"It seems that way."

"Ha! What a fool you are, Elliot! You can't see beyond your own ego. Didn't it ever occur to you I'm trying to find my own happiness? Didn't it ever occur to you that I'm miserable being married to you? That every day I live as your wife, I die a little?''

"Then why the hell did you marry me? Why the hell don't you leave?''

"Don't think I'm not considering it. Don't think I'm not trying to find a way."

"You seem to have found a way already—right into the gutter!"

"If that's a swipe at Robert, you're wrong! You don't know him. He's kept me from losing my mind. Robert is twice the man you are! Robert loves me. He adores me! I love Robert as much as I hate you! If I could, I'd kill you, Elliot. I swear I would!"

He knew she was drunk, but more than the booze was talking. It was becoming patently clear how hopeless their marriage had become. The plans he'd once had to save it seemed pathetically futile. Even when Monica was sober, not much was different—the alcohol only smothered her inhibitions. "I feel sorry for you," he muttered.

"Oh, save your sympathy. Better yet, shove it up your ass!" When she saw the utter disgust on his face her anger turned to rage. "I hate you!" she screamed, lifting her fists to strike him.

He grabbed her wrists.

She jerked free. "Keep your hands off me!"

Elliot was close enough to see the love bites on her neck and shoulder. Her dress was scooped low in front, revealing more marks on her breasts.

He was disgusted, but at the same time he was in pain. He'd once loved this woman, or thought he had. How could things have gone so terribly wrong?

Monica saw the sorrow, the ambivalence in his expression. She smiled, and walked away from him to the mirror, where she stood drunkenly studying herself.

"Do you like this dress?" she asked. When he didn't answer, she said, "I do. Every man who sees me in it gets a hard-on."

Elliot refused to rise to the bait. He looked at her face in the mirror. Monica began posing, using her body to taunt him. Her attitude had changed. She ran her finger over her cleavage. He watched impassively.

"I like this dress a lot," she said, her eyes meeting his. "And if you don't appreciate it, maybe I'll wear it around the house to amuse Spot."

He watched her studying herself, examining the silhouette of her body through the light fabric. There was a time when he might have been overcome with desire for her, even when she was behaving this way. Intellectually he understood how he'd wanted her. Even now, amid his profound contempt, he could remember, could almost feel what he'd once felt.

There was a trace of a smile on her lips when she turned to face him. "What do you think of that, Elliot? How does it feel knowing your wife can keep the servants happy just by walking across the room?"

"I don't feel anything anymore."

She grinned. "Oh, I think you do. You don't want to admit it, but it's true." She walked over to him, looking up through her lashes. "Don't you still feel something deep down? Doesn't a part of you love the fact that I'm a whore?" She stood there, swaying, her smile mocking him.

He felt sick inside. He loathed her as much as a man could loathe a woman, and yet she was partly right. He didn't want her now, but neither could he forget how much he'd wanted her in the past.

"You know, I was beginning to worry about you," she said. "I was wondering if maybe you'd lost it." She reached up and put her cool hand on his chest.

He didn't move.

She ran her fingertips over his shoulder. "We used to get it on pretty good in the old days, didn't we?"

He fought the urge to slap her.

"I don't know if you're man enough anymore." She ran her fingers along the band of his shorts. Her mouth twisted into an ironic smile. "Not everybody can fuck a whore. Especially if he knows she's fresh from somebody else."

Elliot snapped. He grabbed the bodice of her dress, jerking it so hard it ripped open. Monica was nearly knocked to the floor. She staggered, but managed to keep her footing.

The dress hung from her shoulders like a rag. For an instant she was livid, but then she smiled. She let the tatters slip to the floor and stood there completely naked.

He looked at her body. "Were you too drunk to remember to put your underwear back on?"

Her eyes flashed with rage. She slapped him as hard as she could. He slapped her back.

Monica shrieked hysterically, lashing at his eyes with her nails. Elliot swung again, catching her on the jaw and knocking her onto the bed.

"You sonovabitch!"

He moved forward, wanting to hit her again and again. But before he could do anything, Monica brought her foot up sharply, catching him in the scrotum and doubling him over. She scrambled to her feet, but he managed to throw her back onto the bed, falling on top of her.

She tried to claw his face, but he grasped her wrists, pinning her under him. They lay panting, their faces inches apart.

"Let go of me, you bastard!"

He didn't reply. Monica squirmed, but she was helpless. She tried to bite him, but he pulled away.

"Let go!"

She spat at him.

"You're a whore, all right, Monica," he said in a low voice. "That much you got right."

She struggled for all she was worth, but he wouldn't release her. After a minute or two she collapsed with exhaustion, her face and neck scarlet, her hair soaked with perspiration. "I hate you," she muttered in a half whisper. "I hate you."

Elliot knew the combat had run its course. He eased the pressure on her wrists and lifted himself off her. She didn't move. She just looked at him.

He drew his gaze down her voluptuous body, wiping the spittle from his cheek with the back of his hand. Monica was soaked, her skin gleaming. His chest was wet, partly from his own exertion, partly from her perspiration.

He glanced at her pubis, which was moist and glistening like the rest of her. Her raw sexuality, the combat, stirred him, and he almost wanted her, almost pictured himself taking her.

Monica rubbed her jaw, continuing to stare with glazed eyes. It was as though they were poised at a summit and didn't know which slope to slide down. Then her hand moved between her legs and she began to caress herself.

"Fuck me, Elliot," she finally said. But she could have been addressing anyone. He could tell. "Fuck the hell out of me," she said. "Please."

He watched her pleasuring herself, and in spite of everything, he felt himself harden. His muscles grew taut as he fought his desire.

"Elliot, I want you," she whispered.

He shook his head. "I wish you did, Monica. I really wish you did." He turned then and went to the window, opening the shutters so he could look out into the garden.

The moon was very low, its silvery beams reflecting off the foliage. When he inhaled he could taste the heavy richness of the air. Behind him he heard Monica sob. He heard her get up from the bed and pad across the floor to the bathroom. He heard the door close and the key turn in the lock.

A minute passed before the first scream. Glass began shattering and her screams turned to horrible shrieks. She was tearing the place apart—maybe herself, as well. There was rage and terror in her voice, and something he'd never heard before—madness.

When Brett entered their room she found it dappled in shadow, Amory asleep in bed. The only sound was the vague hum of the air-conditioning and her husband's breathing—a heavy, somnolent whisper. It disappointed her that he wasn't awake. She'd looked forward to telling him about her evening.

She sat on the bed beside him, causing him to stir. He lifted his head from the pillow and gave her a half-conscious greeting before immediately falling back to sleep. The poor thing was bushed. He'd had a rough time.

Brett stroked his silver mane, feeling a curious, almost-maternal love. Her Aunt Leona had told her before the wedding that marrying a man was the way to find the little boy in him. It wouldn't make a bit of difference that Amory was a Supreme Court justice or that he was more than twice her age. Men were men and a part of them would always remain little boys.

Brett hadn't found much evidence of that until Amory had taken sick. He wasn't a complainer, though he seemed fond of her nursing. She had no doubt he would have done the same for her, though—cherished the little girl hidden in a corner of her being.

Returning to her husband's side felt good. Already there was a familiarity about being with him that she treasured; a belonging, a partnership. He would have been interested in hearing about the party.

She had established a real rapport with Elliot and she knew that would please Amory. But recounting it would have to wait till morning.

Brett leaned over and kissed him on the temple. Amory didn't stir. That was too bad, because she would have liked for him to hold her just then. This was the first time she'd had feelings of deprivation because of his illness. She had a very strong desire for him.

It would be selfish to waken him, so she got up and began to undress in the darkness. She stared at her husband's motionless figure as she removed her bra and panties. There were times when she reveled in nakedness and this seemed to be one.

Brett didn't think of herself as a sensual person, but occasionally she had a desire to burst loose from the constraints of everyday life, to let go. She'd felt that way one night while they were on safari in Kenya. After a long day of photo-taking they'd been sitting around the fire in camp, drinking gin and tonics with their tottering old guide, Lionel Ellis, when she'd had an overwhelming desire to make love with Amory.

She'd taken him by the hand and they'd gone off to their tent at the edge of the camp and she'd made him watch as she undressed. After kissing him, she'd unbuttoned his shirt and pants and they'd made love. Lying in his arms afterward, she'd asked if she'd embarrassed him, and he'd told her she hadn't, but it was clear to her it had been a new experience for him.

Brett considered climbing into bed naked and snuggling up to him now, but Amory probably wouldn't appreciate it in his present condition. That was all right. It wasn't important. There would be other nights when she felt this way.

She went into the bath to wash her face and brush her teeth. After examining her body in the mirror she put on the white lacy nightgown that Amory had given her a week prior to the wedding. She brushed out her hair, then quietly crawled into bed. Amory groaned slightly, though he put his arm over her, an unconscious act of affection. Brett kissed his hand and sighed.

She was very happy being Mrs. Amory Maitland. Even happier than she'd imagined. She'd felt the usual trepidation before their wedding, but everything was working out wonderfully, though during their engagement she'd been a little concerned about the physical part of their relationship.

They'd slept together only three times before their wedding night, primarily because Amory hadn't been comfortable with the notion of premarital sex. Brett had been adamant, though, insisting that sex was an important part of a marriage and that she had no intention of playing Russian roulette. She knew she'd taken a calculated risk, considering how Amory felt about religion and morality, but it had paid off.

Shortly after their engagement he'd taken her to Rosemont on the East Shore. It was there, on a snowy evening, that they had first made love. Everything had been fine. He'd been a gentle and considerate lover, making the experience joyful and warmly fulfilling. He'd held her afterward, stroking her head, making everything right.

Although his conscience tugged at him, they'd made love at her apartment in April after she'd softened him up with a home-cooked meal and a bottle of wine. If she'd intended to seduce him, it had been unconscious. With a little prodding, Amory had admitted that their weakness might actually be a good sign.

They'd never made love in his home in Chevy Chase until the Fourth of July, a month before their wedding. The two of them had barbecued hamburgers in the backyard, and they'd each had a few beers. Brett had become aroused, lying in the sun in her shorts and bikini top. When Amory sat beside her on the lounge chair, she had begged him to make love with her.

"How can I say no?" he'd whispered. Then he'd taken her upstairs and they were intimate for the first time in the bed he'd once shared with Catherine. Brett had been aware of it as much as Amory. If that time had been less than perfect, it was only because of the guilt she felt. It had been an irrational reaction, but certainly understandable. Amory had said as much.

Their wedding night, spent at the Waldorf in New York, was like the other times—wonderfully loving and intimate. More than ever she'd felt a unity of spirit, a bond that was so very profound. Brett couldn't have asked for more.

Lying beside him now, she found his newly familiar scent comforting. In the course of only two weeks, they'd developed a physical familiarity she'd never felt with anyone else—even Drew Croft, the naval cadet whom she'd thought she'd been madly in love with, the man who'd taken her virginity.

Brett had originally come north to be close to Drew. For a while she'd been sure they would marry. Whenever he'd gotten leave she'd taken the bus up to Annapolis, or he'd come to Washington and they'd gotten a room in some hotel. Their sex life had always been full of enthusiasm, but little subtlety.

She clearly remembered the first time she'd ever had an orgasm. It was in early spring, and she'd only been in Washington a few months. She and Drew had spent the day in a cheap motel on the edge of Annapolis. There had been heavy thundershowers all afternoon. Drew had gone out in the rain to get a pizza, which they'd eaten in bed. They'd made love three or four times with the television blaring. But she hadn't had her orgasm until the middle of the night.

When she awoke he'd been caressing her. She was already moist and soon began throbbing. It had been the best sex she'd had, perhaps because it had come straight out of her unconsciousness.

She felt herself moisten at the recollection. It was no time for sex, though, with Amory sick. She scooted away from him, before she got too excited. Soon he would be better and wanting to make love with her.

Brett stared up at the dark ceiling, too aroused and keyed up to sleep. She was physically exhausted after a day that had begun in Africa, but her mind as well as her body was alive, full of thoughts and images. The events of the past few weeks rolled through her brain, but her mind kept coming back to the party that evening, and to her conversation with Elliot as they'd strolled about the compound. She kept seeing his face as he'd said goodbye, under the boughs of the mango trees.

She'd felt such compassion for him. She understood his pain and she'd told him so. But now, in retrospect, she knew she had seen something else in his eyes, something other than his unhappiness. She remembered the way he'd held her hand. They'd talked about family and friendship and innocent secrets, but she realized now that they had really been talking about *them*. Brett shuddered to think what might have been in his mind.

There was no disputing that Elliot Brewster was an attractive man. In his dinner jacket he'd been an arresting figure, a man who drew women's eyes even while their hands were on their husbands' arms. Of course, she hadn't thought of him that way herself. True, she'd been aware of his green eyes watching her as they'd walked in the moonlight, his face dramatized by shadow. But it was his sorrow and Amory's concern for him that had preoccupied her.

Brett hoped Elliot hadn't misread her friendliness. Surely he'd understood that all she intended to offer was simple compassion. Of course he had. He was no fool. He was perfectly aware that she was his stepfather's wife.

And if there had been a wistfulness in his eyes, if in some quiet, understated way he'd reached out, it was only because he was so desperate and unhappy. His pathos touched her, affecting her not unlike the ragged children she'd seen in the streets. But in the excitement of the evening, she'd been blind to what was going on in his mind. It was evident to her now that he was attracted to her, that his wistful glances had said more than she'd realized.

Brett flushed at the thought. Twinges went through her, but she knew what had happened wasn't serious. Elliot's feelings were a product of the moment, having more to do with Monica than with her. Now it would be up to her to keep friendship the focus of their relationship. Elliot's feelings would fall into perspective soon enough. All she had to do was send him the proper signals and avoid the wrong ones.

Having worked it out in her mind, Brett felt better. The heat in her cheeks subsided and she began to relax. Even so, she kept picturing Elliot's face and hearing his voice, but now she told herself that she was thinking of him with the compassion of a friend. That was what Amory wanted, it was what she wanted. Given that, everything would work out fine.

Brett looked at the illuminated face of the clock. A couple of hours had passed since she'd returned. In his sleep, Amory reached out and put his hand on her arm. The quiet nature of his love was so heartwarming. It gave her strength. She slipped her hand into his, and he held it tightly, holding it as a father would hold the hand of his child.

Content now, she began drifting off. It seemed she wasn't in her dreams long before a telephone rang, jarring her back to consciousness. She lifted her head, noticing the early-morning light filtering through cracks in the curtains. Evidently more time had passed than she had thought. The telephone rang again, awakening Amory too. He mumbled something, obviously working his way out of a drugged sleep.

The phone was on his side of the bed. He half raised himself.

"The telephone, Amory," she said. "I think you'd better get it."

He looked at the offending instrument, shaking his head before crawling over to take the receiver from the cradle.

"Yes?"

Brett could hear the faint sound of conversation on the line. "Do you know how serious it is?" he asked, his voice taking on a grave tone.

"I see." He listened for a moment. "Where is she again?" Another pause. "I imagine we can take a taxi. That would be quickest, wouldn't it? All right. We'll be there as soon as we can." He put the receiver back.

"What's happened?" Brett asked.

"That was the ambassador's wife, Mrs. Welty," he said. "She wanted to let me know there's been an emergency. It's Monica. She's at the embassy hospital."

"What happened to her?"

"A breakdown of some sort. Apparently she tried to slit her wrists. They're very concerned. Elliot's with her. I think we should go."

"Of course." Brett pulled back the covers. Amory was already out of bed and heading for the bathroom.

Brett sat up, trying to collect herself. Just when things finally seemed to have fallen into perspective, the world was on its head. Poor Monica. Then she remembered the man who'd strolled with her after the party—his sadness, the way they had shared their dreams, teasing and joking and even laughing. She recalled the solemn tone of his voice when he'd promised to keep her secrets, even from Amory. Poor Elliot.

PART II

Washington, D.C.

Georgetown was just waking up as Harrison Maitland descended the steps of his house on P Street. He tossed the *Post* up onto the porch, then went through the wrought-iron gate, closing it carefully behind him.

Another jogger, a young man in an American University T-shirt, came padding up the leaf-strewn sidewalk. They exchanged silent nods, the senator wishing he could hire a young fellow like that to do his jogging for him, though he knew the task was simply another of life's burdens.

But this particular morning, exercise was the least of his problems. He would have to look as if he'd really been out for a run when he got back. Evelyn was no fool. At some level she knew he had a preoccupation apart from politics. But she couldn't possibly know he was leaving the house at this ungodly hour to see another woman.

After several halfhearted stretches and an attempt to touch his toes, he started toward the corner at a slow jog, turning on Thirty-first and heading up the hill toward R. If he was going to exhaust himself it would have to be now, because Dumbarton Oaks was only a few short blocks away. He began pushing himself until he could feel his heart thumping.

Although the air was still comparatively cool, he was perspiring and breathing hard by the time he reached Avon Place. His doctor, Mark Feldman, had wanted him to lose weight when he'd experienced heart irregularities the previous spring. All those years of smoking had taken their toll, Mark had told him. "You don't represent a major tobacco state, so you've got no excuse." And, except for occasional lapses, that had been the end of the smoking.

Recently, though, Harrison had found himself dipping into an empty pocket for a packet of cigarettes, only to remember. It was the pressure of an election year. He knew that. And so he forgave himself when he'd sneaked onto the patio the night before for a solitary cigarette—his first in a month. Everything seemed to go to hell when he was up before the voters—his work in the Senate, his personal life, and maybe, this time, even his health. It was all part of the game. Nobody knew that better than he.

With George Bush moving ahead of that Greek liberal from Massachusetts, it was starting to look like a good time for a Republican to be on the ballot. Thank God the Bush campaign had gone on the attack when it did. Harrison had been saying for weeks that they couldn't win sounding presidential. They had to attack, they had to make Dukakis look bad. Whether it was true or not, they had to make the case that the son of a bitch was soft on crime, a card-carrying member of the ACLU.

Come November, Harrison wouldn't be the only Republican who owed Willy Horton a debt of gratitude. God knows, he hadn't been shy about pointing out to the people of Maryland that the bastard had been furloughed from a Massachusetts prison. He suspected Willy and the Pledge of Allegiance flap would put the Old Line State in the Republican column, come election day. And coincidentally, it made his seat look a lot safer.

But he was damned sorry to see "Dutch" Reagan heading back to California. He'd been one of the president's staunchest supporters in the Senate, maintaining a tough posture on defense and, at opportune moments, speaking out on issues dear to the heart of the Moral Majority. Harrison was careful not to alienate the moderates unduly, though. They'd largely been responsible for his election. It was no small accomplishment. Harrison suspected his relations with a Bush administration would be just as good, though he recognized the necessity of going it alone, especially when the administration was doing something unpopular with the home-state voters.

His strategy in the Senate had been to line up alongside Republican liberals like Lowell Weicker and Mark Hatfield on social measures without selling out the administration when it really counted. Once, at a subcommittee meeting, Teddy Kennedy had admonished him for being cynical, but old Ted had winked when he said it. After all, the senator from Massachusetts had been known to crawl into bed with the conservative wing of his party when favors could be won cheaply enough.

The one social issue on which Harrison had gone whole-hog into the conservative camp was abortion. Jerry Falwell had managed to turn a politically sensitive issue into a popular cause and Harrison was convinced that it was a tide that could be ridden a long, long way. He'd been strongly in favor of a Constitutional amendment and felt betrayed when the White House did little more than pay lip service to the cause. Worse, his own dear brother sat on the court destined to eventually take up the issue, with nobody, including him, having the slightest idea how Amory would vote.

But taking his cue from Reagan's 1984 campaign, Harrison had decided to keep reproductive politics out of his speeches except for the routine pro-life endorsement. Fortunately his Democratic opponent, though Catholic, was even less enthusiastic about campaigning on the issue than he was.

To date, the campaign had centered on Chip Donlevy's close ties to contractors and union officials during his tenure on the state senate public-works committee. Harrison had the bastard in a corner. But he was not one to be complacent. Harrison had seen too many candidates let up when they should have been bearing down. His reputation for ruthlessness was a source of great pride. Being right, he was convinced, was never as important as being victorious.

By the time he reached the path leading to the informal gardens at Dumbarton Oaks, he had to stop to catch his breath. He slowly walked the last few dozen yards so as not to encounter Megan in a state of total exhaustion, though his heart was still pounding at top speed. To his mortification, he saw the auburn-haired young woman waiting outside the entrance.

He let his annoyance show as he walked up to her. "What are you doing out here? Anyone can see us."

"I'm sorry," she said contritely, "but the gardens aren't open yet. I didn't know the hours when I called."

Harrison read the sign on the gate. Opening time was an hour away. "I hope to hell this is important," he said between breaths. He glanced around, his chest heaving. "We can't stand out here. Let's go to the park." He took her arm and they started along the path.

Megan Tiernan had large dark eyes. They were as pretty as ever, but Harrison felt little charity for her just then. They walked in silence, an occasional leaf drifting down through the still air. He was anxious to get out of public view and find a place where they could sit.

"I told you never to call me at home," he said after a while, his breathing slowly returning to normal.

"I'm sorry, but I had to. Besides, your wife doesn't know me. I said I was a staffer."

"Evelyn knows my staff, Megan, or at least anyone who would call me at six forty-five in the morning."

"I was afraid you would be leaving to campaign. I wanted to speak with you before you left."

"I don't have any appearances until tonight. Except for a meeting with Tommy Bishop in an hour, it's family business today. I'm having lunch with my brother."

"I didn't know."

They found a bench well off the street at a fairly secluded spot overlooking the entrance to Rock Creek Park. Megan sat with her head bowed, not wanting to look at him. He studied her profile, his eyes drifting to her breasts under the blue velour jogging suit. Megan Tiernan was one of those pretty, full-bosomed females whose essence was sexual, whatever the context. He liked her intelligence and kindhearted nature, but every quality she possessed paled beside the physical effect she had on him.

Aware of his growing desire, Harrison managed to suppress his anger. That's the way it had always been with him and Megan. In the abstract, she could be dealt with. But when he was with her, something seemed to pop and his gonads took control of his brain.

He reached over and took her hand. "What is it, Meggie? Why did you have to see me?"

For the first time she looked at him, her face filled with anguish. It surprised him. Other people's distress often did. Even Evelyn would sometimes express unhappiness over some slight that to him had no basis whatsoever. Women were the worst offenders in that regard; frequently their grievances came totally out of left field.

"What's the matter?" he asked again.

"Oh, God..." Her eyes flooded. What remained of her composure started to give way.

"Megan?"

She looked as though she were about to cry out. Then she took his hand, crushing his fingers. "Harrison..." She fought for control. "I'm pregnant."

The junior senator from Maryland sat stunned. He blinked. "Pregnant?"

Megan lowered her eyes, letting large tears roll down her cheeks and drop onto her thighs.

"Jesus," he moaned, as the words finally sank in. He turned away, his head sinking into his meaty hands. He sat hunched, his elbows resting on his knees, his face buried. He was trying to get a grip on what she'd said. Then he looked up at her.

"Are you sure?"

Megan managed a nod.

"Have you seen a doctor?"

"Yes. I've had the tests. Several. They were all positive."

"Jesus Christ."

She let out a mournful cry. "Harrison..."

"You didn't say anything about us...to the doctor, I mean."

She shook her head. "No. They don't ask questions like that."

"No," he mumbled, "I suppose not." He was thinking. It was the sort of disaster he'd always dreaded, but never dwelled on—not so long as fortune had smiled down on him. "How in God's name could you get pregnant?" Anger was beginning to displace the mortification.

"I don't know. I always used something—a diaphragm, usually, but..."

"Shit!" he said, pounding his fist against the seat of the bench. "Goddamn it, Megan."

She looked up at him, terrified.

He took her chin, making her look at him. His grip was firm and she winced, but he didn't let go. "Is it mine?" he asked, his voice shaking.

Her eyes widened with horror. "Of course! Who else's could it be?"

He turned away, running his fingers through his salt-and-pepper hair. "I'm sorry, but I had to ask. It's doubtful I can have children and I thought—"

"Well, you *can* have children, Harrison...and you *are!* In about six and a half months!"

Megan Tiernan was not just another one of his playmates, though their relationship had begun that way. It had been nine months since he'd first bedded her. Their liaison had continued since that time.

He had never known anyone who'd captured his imagination so completely. Before her, sex had always been a game—like tag. Senator presses penis into willing female, gets rocks off, then moves on to next partner. The rules permitted a little giggling, occasional female assertiveness, but no long-term expectations.

For some reason, though, he could never get enough of Megan. Even when he'd screwed her until he couldn't get it up anymore, there remained a hunger for her, a desire to couple interminably. Now that the unconscious object of the game had been realized, he was shocked.

"You're going to have it, Megan? You're really going to have the baby?" he asked.

A splash of incredulity washed over her. "What do you expect? That I'd get an abortion?"

He didn't answer.

After a moment her eyes narrowed. "I can't believe you'd ask that. I do take my religion seriously—at least when it comes to an issue like this."

There was reproach in her voice—something he didn't easily countenance in a woman. "So do I," he snapped. "But...my God..."

For an instant she was stunned. "Harrison! What are you saying? *You*, of all people..."

"Yes, I know, but this could ruin me," he said.

"This is our baby we're talking about! A human being!"

He ran his fingers through his hair again, muttering, cursing under his breath. Megan began to weep. He had a sick, empty feeling in his gut. For the first time he could recall, his feelings toward Megan were akin to his feelings for Evelyn. The only thing he and Megan had ever fought over was how much time he could afford to spend with her. This was tragically different.

"Come on, Meggie, stop crying."

She looked at him with a scorn he'd never seen in her before. He hated this kind of emotion.

"You're worried about the voters, aren't you?" she said. "You're concerned about what people will think."

"Jesus, Megan."

"Am I wrong?"

"Of course I'm thinking about that. Aren't you?"

"Dear God," she said, her lip trembling. "Why did I have to fall in love with you?"

For an instant he wasn't sure whether he should be flattered or offended. He was still vacillating between anger and remorse. Harrison shook his head and stared off at the empty sky.

After a moment, Megan said, "What about Evelyn?"

"Please, let's not talk about that, too. Don't we have enough to worry about?"

"Well, what about us? Does this change things?"

During the past few months he had let their relationship drift into a state of ambiguity. He'd had conflicting feelings—convinced one minute he was ready to divorce Evelyn and marry Megan, certain the next that he wanted things to go on forever as they were. Once, in a moment of passion, he'd spoken of the possibility of marriage. Megan had fastened on it as only a woman could.

"What's changed," he said darkly, "is that you're pregnant. Evelyn has nothing to do with it."

She glared, not liking the implication. "She does so! It's a question of whether our child will be legitimate."

He returned her hard look. "It's too late. It's already a bastard."

"You mean as far as the voters are concerned, don't you?" Her voice was high and brittle.

"Oh, let's not do this. It won't help to get shrill. I know you're upset. So am I. I've got to think... I've got to get some perspective on this." He took her hand again. "Don't worry about us, Meggie. Please. I promise you, everything will be all right. We'll work it out so no one will get hurt." He kissed her cheek.

Megan felt the air going out of her. She heard something different in his voice, something she'd never encountered before. Harrison had always come first in their relationship. He'd never even tried to disguise the fact that his wishes mattered most. But now his tone smacked of deceit, manipulation. And even though he'd kissed her, she felt him pulling away.

Somehow she'd feared this, feared losing his love. Until this moment she'd never doubted it. Harrison was always very much his own person. He was obsessed with his career and his work. She'd known that. But he loved her. Now, that was in jeopardy. She sniffed and wiped her nose.

"If anyone's to blame," she said, "I guess it's me. I should have taken the damn Pill."

"Come on," he said, putting his arm around her shoulder, "let's not get into fault and blame. We've got to discuss this logically." He looked at his Rolex watch. "But this is not the time. I've got to get back. I've got to meet with Tommy."

His voice had grown reasonable, emotionless. Megan didn't like that. She preferred his anger. Tears filled her eyes as he touched her cheek.

Harrison looked at her still-fit body. Megan was thirty-four, in the autumn of her childbearing years. She was ripe, fecund, womanly. More than once he'd fucked her, imagining he was impregnating her. More than once he'd lain on her breast, craving her motherly essence. With Megan he could yearn to suckle and copulate at the same time. She appealed to every sexual instinct he had, base and exalted, innocent and profane.

He touched her hair. "When did it happen, Meggie?"

"I think when we went over to your place on the East Shore at the beginning of July."

He remembered the weekend well. It was just before his twenty-fifth wedding anniversary, when he and Evelyn had gone to Bermuda. It had been high adventure—taking his mistress to his family home. Megan hadn't understood the pleasure he found in the illicitness. She'd taken it as an acknowledgment of his feelings for her, which it was in a way—though not in the way she had imagined.

It was the weekend he'd admitted he didn't love Evelyn as he once had. He'd said it impulsively, yet he'd meant it. He'd wanted Megan to know her magic was special. With her, he could forget other things.

The rational side of him knew the whole business had been a mistake—one that could ruin his career, if he wasn't careful. And what would he have then? A woman who could arouse him with the slightest effort? A woman who could give him children? And an ex-wife whom he still loved in some distorted, unfathomable way?

"Look, I've got to go, darling," the senator said, rising. He knew he had to get away, to think. "I've never jogged this long in my life. Evelyn will have the paramedics out looking for me."

She stood, too. Harrison looked her up and down. She was beautiful, vulnerable and exciting. Just looking at her brought back the stolen afternoons at her apartment. He was a different man with her. In the past, when he was in bed with someone else, the mere thought of Evelyn or his mother could wilt him. But Megan was different.

He took her hands. She looked sad. He didn't like her this way. Megan was always so happy, so full of life. That's what he loved about her. Now she seemed even more vulnerable. There was something sexy about that, too. An unexpected desire came over him and he contemplated her body, picturing it naked. His loins started to tingle.

What irony, he thought. The woman had just told him she was pregnant, his whole career was hanging in the balance, and his cock gets hard. It was the sort of problem teenage boys had, not United States senators. God!

"I'm sorry to have to leave you like this," he said, "but I really must go."

"What are we going to do, Harrison? What's going to happen? Will it really be all right?"

He sighed. "Trust me. Right now I don't know how we'll work it out. I'll have to think about it. I need time, but I'll come up with something."

She gazed into his eyes, wanting to believe him, but feeling doubt. His anger had passed, but his face was solemn, ashen. He was already putting her news into the larger perspective of politics. He was weighing their child against all those other things he cared so much about—the damned election, the Senate, his wife.

Megan feared that somehow she and the baby would come up short. She had come to the park harboring some hope that he would find joy in her news, that their love would rise above everything else. It had been a silly dream; she saw that now. Politicians were too pragmatic. It didn't mean he didn't care. She knew he loved her. She always had that to cling to.

As she stared, Harrison seemed to come back from wherever he was. He looked into her eyes and took her hands in his.

Megan felt emotion building. "I'm sorry," she said. "I'm really sorry to have done this to you."

He nodded briefly, then leaned forward to kiss her. His lips pressed against hers. It was a perfunctory, distracted kiss, more spousal than loverlike.

As he pulled back, she examined his expression for some positive sign, some reason to hope. Suddenly his eyes widened. His mouth dropped open and he groaned. Then his face twisted with pain.

"Harrison, what is it? What's the matter?"

His lips opened wider, and he gurgled. He seemed almost frozen, as though he were unable to breathe.

"Harrison?"

He clutched his hand to his chest. "My heart..." he stammered, and his face contorted.

Megan felt her stomach drop. "Harrison! Oh, my God." She grasped his arm. "What shall I do?"

"Get help..." he wheezed. Then he dropped to the bench, his hand still clamped against his chest. He groaned horribly.

She stared at him, horrified, her hands covering her mouth. "Oh, Lord..." She looked around frantically. There was no one in sight. She had an impulse to scream, but she knew that wasn't right. She had to get help!

Megan dropped down beside him, taking his hand. "Will you be all right if I leave you?"

He nodded, waving at her to go.

She jumped to her feet and Harrison watched her run up the path toward R Street. Pain radiated throughout his chest and arms. It was a heart attack. This was it! He'd die. He had no doubt. His body had failed him. He was going to die.

He fell against the bench and tried to relax. The sharp pain had begun to abate some and felt dull now. Harrison closed his eyes and focused all awareness in his chest, every beat of his heart, each contraction and release, hoping he'd survive.

Maybe he wouldn't die. The pain was milder now, and the rhythm in his chest slowed. Maybe he'd live.

He looked up the path. Megan must have gone to a house on R to phone for an ambulance. What would she do then? Probably return. God, he hoped she'd have the sense to be discreet.

He could envision what the papers would do with this. A heart attack was bad enough for his career, but a phrase like "found in the arms of a young female companion" could be disastrous. Poor Nelson Rockefeller hadn't lived to bear those consequences, but Harrison was beginning to feel he might. And Evelyn! He had to get word to Evelyn!

He heard someone on the path and turned to see Megan running toward him, a terrified expression on her face. "Oh!" she exclaimed breathlessly. "Thank God you're...all right." She dropped down beside him. "An ambulance should be here soon."

He smiled weakly.

"Are you in terrible pain?" she asked, her chest heaving.

"It hurt at first, but now it's not as bad. I think I'm all right."

"Thank God, thank God." Megan put her arms around him.

There was the faint sound of a siren in the distance. "They'll be here in a minute," she said.

He nodded. "Maybe you'd better go...."

"No, I won't leave you."

"It's best that they don't find me with you. There's no point in taking chances."

She shook her head. "Nobody knows who I am. I could have been a jogger who found you. Besides, there won't be reporters here."

"They'll be at the hospital, though. Don't go with me to the hospital. Please."

"Okay, I won't." She looked up toward the street. The siren was getting closer. "Maybe I'd better meet them."

"After you show them where I am, go on home. Don't tell them who you are. Just show them and leave."

His words stung. But before she could say anything, he closed his eyes. Harrison was thinking about himself—just himself—which would have been natural enough, except it wasn't his heart that was preoccupying him, it was politics. He could be half dead and still worry about losing votes.

"I'd better go meet the ambulance," she mumbled, and got up and walked toward the street.

Minutes later, as the paramedics strapped Harrison onto the stretcher, Megan watched with a jogger who had been attracted by the commotion. Then she followed behind as they rolled Harrison toward the waiting ambulance.

She discreetly stood aside as they lifted him in. Then, while the attendant was preparing to give him oxygen, she heard him say, "Could somebody please get word to my wife? She'll be worried. I want her with me."

The words cut through Megan's heart. She felt weak, sick. It was as though he'd shut her out of his life.

The attendant slammed the doors closed and ran around to the driver's seat. Then the ambulance lurched into motion, the siren beginning to wail as it moved toward Wisconsin Avenue. When it disappeared around the corner, Megan looked down at her stomach, laying her hand against it. All she could think of were his last words to her: "Go on home."

Brett stepped into the elevator, her alligator briefcase in hand. She pushed the button for the sixteenth floor and watched the light on the indicator skip across the panel until it finally stopped and the door opened.

The floor lobby was richly carpeted in maroon, the wall opposite paneled in walnut and decorated with sconces bracketing a large oil—a hunting scene. Brett glanced at the painting, then turned toward the reception area. Over the entrance, in gold relief letters, were the names Horgan, Gotlief & Browning. A receptionist was seated at the far end of the spacious room.

"Hello, Mrs. Maitland," she said. "Please have a seat. I'll tell Mr. Horgan's secretary you're here."

John Horgan was Amory's personal attorney. Now in his mid-seventies, he'd represented Amory's mother for many years before the justice had put his affairs in the esteemed old barrister's hands. John was a friend, as well—practically a member of the Maitland family.

Several times during her years in law school, Brett had gone to him for advice. He'd become her father confessor regarding questions of career, which took a burden off her relationship with Amory.

After a wait of three or four minutes, a secretary escorted Brett to a large corner office at the back of the suite. Horgan, a heavyset, bald man with only thin wisps of white hair over his scalp, rose as she was shown in. He shuffled around his desk to greet her, fumbling to button the coat of his dark gray suit.

"Brett, my dear." He gave her a peck on the cheek. "Ravishing as always."

"Thanks for squeezing me in, John. I woke up this morning and decided I had to see you."

He beamed with pride. "I've only got one other appointment and I'm looking forward to two hours of crossword puzzles." He winked playfully. "I think the boys are beginning to suspect the only reason I come in is so they can't take my name off the door."

She laughed and he seated her in the comfortable leather chair across from his desk. John Horgan had a common touch while managing to be businesslike. His appearance and manner suggested a small-town banker from the South or Midwest, though he was from a prominent upstate New York family. He was a good listener and was utterly without prejudice, which made him such a respected counselor.

He installed himself behind his desk, unbuttoning his coat. He beamed a ruddy smile. "So tell me, how is it to have the bar exam behind you? I don't think we've talked since you took it."

"No, we haven't. Frankly, I'm relieved."

"I know how proud Amory is."

"I hope I don't embarrass him by failing."

"Posh. Top twenty in your class. I know you studied hard. You'll do fine."

"I hope so."

Horgan wiped his mouth with his handkerchief. "How is that husband of yours doing, by the way?"

"Amory's fine. A rock. You know that. But he's struggling with the problem of what I'm going to do right along with me, John. We're both aware that if I practice law there will be repercussions."

"You mean the possibility of conflicts of interest."

"Yes."

He considered the situation. "Amory aside, what sort of work would *you* like to do, Brett? Assuming you were single or married to someone else where there wasn't a conflict-of-interest problem."

"To be honest, what I care most about is women's issues. I'd like to be an advocate, if I were free to do what I want."

"You obviously feel you aren't free."

"John, my brother-in-law is a pro-life stalwart in the Senate and my husband will probably be deciding whether or not to overturn *Roe v. Wade* this term. How would it look if I'm carrying a pro-choice banner through the streets of Washington, or lobbying for the Equal Rights Amendment or campaigning against sexual harassment or for equal pay?"

"Do you feel resentful, Brett?"

She sighed. "I do and I don't. I knew who Amory was when I married him, but I also know that was before I got to really know myself. I wasn't radicalized by law school, John, but it focused my capacity for critical thought and made me more aware. Amory has been very fair with me. He's encouraged me to be myself and develop my own views. Under the circumstances, that's real enlightenment. We don't have problems at the personal level."

"But that doesn't resolve your professional dilemma."

"No, if anything I feel even more guilty because of Amory's decency. I know that sounds crazy, but it's true. He deserves a wife who believes what he believes, who supports him to the hilt and encourages him. Instead, he's married to a problem."

"Don't be unduly harsh with yourself, Brett," John Horgan said. "Amory might be from a different generation, but he knows the world has changed, that wives these days have careers. And he is enough of a realist to have known that the day would come when you would want to put your education to use."

"That may be true. But even if I practice tax law I have to be careful," she said. "Something that I was involved in could get to the Supreme Court."

"There are problems to be faced. But Sandra Day O'Conner's husband practices law. And there are many ways to contribute to causes you believe in, Brett. Some of the big firms have gotten into pro bono work. They've hired associates to take on charity cases and work on worthy causes in the community. These young lawyers become advocates within their firms."

Brett sighed. "I suppose I've made more of the problem than is justified. It's just that I've got fire in my belly, John, and I hate holding back."

Horgan folded his hands over his ample stomach. "What would Amory like you to do? Has he expressed a preference?"

She chuckled. "Amory would like for me to have a baby."

"And you don't like the idea, I take it."

"I'd like children eventually, but right now I'm itching for a career. Amory understands. But you asked what his preference is and that's it."

"I'm afraid family planning falls outside my area of expertise, Brett."

She laughed. But then, after a moment, she sighed. "Marriage is not an easy thing. Amory and I do love each other. That's what matters most. The rest will work out, I'm sure."

Horgan steepled his fingers, watching her. "Will you be job hunting?"

"Probably. I like your idea of a pro bono practice. Maybe I'll look into that. Regardless, I have a few months to kill until the bar-exam results come out. Amory and Harrison have decided to refurbish Rosemont, so I may spend some time over on the East Shore supervising the work."

"I imagine Amory's busy getting ready for the next term."

"Yes, he's been reading briefs the past week. They'll be deciding whether to grant cert on an abortion case that could negate *Roe v. Wade* sometime in the next week or so."

"That's what I heard." He contemplated her without saying anything.

"I don't know how he's going to vote, if that's what you're wondering, John. He hasn't raised the issue except in passing and I decided it's not right to press him. It's best for our marriage if he leaves his work at the office, though God knows if I'll be able to keep my mouth shut if the Court decides to hear the case."

"You're not the only woman in Washington who's faced the issue, Brett."

"No, and there've probably been a few men in my situation, as well."

"I stand corrected," he said with a wink.

"Abortion's not an easy subject. I wish no one ever had to face the issue—personally or professionally."

"Amory must feel the same way."

"He's been dreading it, I know. But for the good of the country, he's going to have to 'face the music,' as he puts it."

"I don't envy him. That's why we have judges, I guess."

There was a rap on the door. It was Horgan's secretary.

"Excuse me, Mr. Horgan," the woman said, "but there's an urgent call for Mrs. Maitland."

John and Brett exchanged glances. Brett's stomach dropped. She was certain that something had happened to Amory. She'd thought about that often lately—her husband's mortality—though he was in excellent health. He was nearing sixty and the passing years seemed to count more for him than for her.

"Who is it?" she asked warily.

"It's Justice Maitland. He's on line two."

Brett felt a tremendous sense of relief. Horgan handed her the receiver.

"Darling?"

"Amory, what's happened?"

"I'm so sorry to disturb you, Brett, but I'm afraid there's been an emergency. Harrison's had a heart attack."

"Oh, my God!"

"We don't know how serious it is, but he's still alive. Evelyn called fifteen minutes ago from George Washington. Apparently he was jogging when it struck him."

"Oh, no..."

"Now we mustn't panic," he said, his voice calm, his words deliberate.

"What do you want me to do?"

"I'm leaving for the hospital now. The chief's offered me his limo so I won't have to fool with parking. I can swing by and pick you up, if you wish."

"Don't bother. I'll leave my car here and take a cab. That way I won't have to park, either. I should be there before you."

"Okay, darling. Do give my apologies to John for taking you away."

"Don't worry, Amory. I love you."

"You're a dear heart."

She handed the receiver back to John.

"Problems?" the lawyer questioned, an air of tragedy registering on his face.

"Yes. Harrison's had a heart attack. They don't know how serious."

"Thank God it wasn't Amory."

It was a surprisingly candid admission coming from a shrewd old legal hand like John Horgan, and it said a lot about the people involved.

Yes," she said. "Thank God."

Evelyn Maitland sat in the hospital chapel, her blue-gray eyes brimming with tears. It was not a time to falter, she told herself. Harrison needed her now more than ever. She sighed. From the day she'd said, "I do," she had prided herself on being a good wife, though at times the task had seemed overwhelming. She knew she'd been as selfless as any woman could be.

Still, there was more weighing on her than Harrison's health. For months now she'd worried about their marriage. He had denied anything was wrong, but she'd felt him slipping away. Whenever they were together, he seemed to be somewhere else.

She had managed to remain outwardly calm, though a quiet terror had been building inside. A thousand times she'd told herself that if it were another woman, it would pass. Yet she sensed this one was special, different from the others.

A few months earlier, she'd convinced Harrison to take her to Bermuda for their anniversary, hoping the trip would change things between them. But his heart clearly hadn't been in it.

They'd taken an apartment at the Mid Ocean Club, with a balcony opening directly onto the sea. The first night they went to bed early and lay side by side, the ocean air gently wafting over them. Harrison was in his shorts, and she had worn a filmy gown, hoping to arouse him. He'd said nothing, though, acting as though it were any other night.

When she'd realized he wasn't going to touch her, she'd scooted closer, laying the flat of her hand on his furry chest. Harrison had a stocky, manly build that she'd always found attractive. He'd been an enthusiastic, if conventional, lover once. But the physical passions they'd shared were long spent. Sex had become tied to occasions, dispensed like a Hallmark card.

That night in Bermuda had been a turning point. Evelyn knew she had to reach out to her husband or lose him. And so she had resolved to do whatever it took....

Harrison lay motionless as she ran her hand over his chest, caressing him, coaxing a response. But he was off in some other place, his body languid, his indifference palpable. When she kissed his chest and he didn't respond, she became more determined than ever. She moved her hand to his shorts, letting it rest on the bulge at his crotch. He rolled his head toward her, his flat eyes studying her in the muted light.

"I know I haven't been very desirable recently," she whispered, "but I do love you, Harrison."

He sighed in a way that said a response would be too painful, too trying. She wasn't deterred. She began rubbing him. When he didn't harden, desperation rose in her like a frightened beast. She slipped her hand through the opening of his shorts and grasped his penis.

He stiffened slightly, and his member began coming to life in her hand. She'd never initiated sex so boldly before, and she suspected it had caught him off guard.

Still, he said nothing. He didn't kiss her as she'd hoped he would. He just stared at the ceiling—off wherever it was he preferred to be. His disinterest made her want to weep, but his penis was slowly growing firmer. That gave her hope.

She wondered if he was equally indifferent to the little tarts on Capitol Hill with their willing bodies. She doubted it. Harrison had left her with only two options—to surrender or compete—inviting her, in effect, to become another of his whores.

In desperation, she pulled his penis out of his shorts. The soft head protruded from her clenched fist. In her fifty years, Evelyn Maitland had never had a man's sex organ in her mouth. She'd never kissed her husband there. He'd never asked it of her. And yet how many young nubile women had sucked him off?

Her heart pounded. She kissed the tip of his penis. Harrison moaned, and grew harder. More desperate than revulsed, she closed her eyes and took the end of his member between her lips.

Soon Harrison was thrusting into her mouth. He pressed her face down hard, making her gag. She wanted to stop, but Harrison was into her game now. After a moment or two she jerked her head back, taking a few anxious breaths. "What do I do now?" she murmured, hoping she had satisfied him.

His eyes were closed, he seemed in the throes of some distant, impersonal pleasure. "Open your mouth wide," he answered in a hoarse whisper. "Don't stop."

She parted her lips and tried to do as he asked, but it wasn't easy. When he plunged deep into her throat, she prayed God to make him stop. But he didn't. His intrusion became more forceful. When his pelvis convulsed against her face, she choked, wrenching her mouth free.

"Oh!" she cried out, feeling the full flush of panic. She looked up at his stormy face, the grimace, the labored breathing. "I'm sorry, darling," she gasped. "I just can't anymore."

He held his posture a moment, then rolled onto his side, turning away from her.

"Harrison?"

"I didn't ask you to do that," he said coldly. "I don't know why you did."

Tears welled in her eyes. "I wanted to please you."

"Starting something you can't finish doesn't please me."

"I'm sorry." She fought her mounting agony. "Can't we make love the usual way?"

"I'm not in the mood."

"Don't do this to me," she cried. "Please don't do this."

He turned and looked at her in the darkness. "For Chrissake, Evelyn, what the hell's wrong with you?"

She had begun to cry. "I don't want you to hate me."

He moved to the far side of the bed and sat up, his back to her.

"Harrison..."

He got up, went to the open slider, and gazed out into the black, tropical night.

"Harrison, please..."

He didn't respond. Evelyn stared at him through a blur of tears, having now a full sense of the disaster. Then, when he stepped out onto the deck, ignoring her pleas, she fell sobbing on the pillow....

The hospital chapel at George Washington seemed so far removed in time and place from Bermuda. And yet the crucifix on the wall was as appropriate a symbol as there could be for the state of her marriage, her failure.

To her surprise, that night hadn't been the end. The next morning there were no solemn speeches on divorce, no funeral orations. Harrison ignored the incident, leaving her to wonder what it was in her he still wanted. Eventually she decided it was her loyalty and support. That was all the marriage had been for a long time, and perhaps all it could be.

Yet she craved more. She wanted his respect as a full partner. She'd wanted that for years now, though she'd never once gotten it.

Harrison had steadfastly refused to deviate from his limited expectations for her. Her function was mandated by his needs. He had all the advisers he required. He wanted her safely in the background. It was a role she'd willingly accepted, and yet a part of her chafed.

If to the world Evelyn's persona had a political tinge, it was because of her father as much as her husband. She was often teased about having walked both sides of the political street. The attention secretly pleased her. She laughingly called her conversion the political imperative of the wedding vow.

A woman could do that in Washington more easily than a man. Pamela Harriman had not only moved from one end of the political spectrum to the other, she'd done it while crossing the Atlantic.

If Washington saw Evelyn as the quintessential good soldier, they only saw the uniform. She'd played her role well, it was true. She'd made a pact to do so. But Harrison had never given her a chance to do more, and Evelyn—to her shame—had never insisted on it. If frustration burned under her happy facade, she was coming to realize she was partly to blame.

She looked up at the crucifix again, realizing that if in the last fifteen minutes she'd prayed at all, it was to the political gods, rather than the Almighty. But it didn't matter. She'd come to the chapel not so much to plead for divine intervention, as for refuge. Mark Feldman had assured her that Harrison was in no immediate danger. Barring the unexpected, he would be all right.

Earlier, when she'd been allowed into his room, she'd kissed him and held his face against hers, trying to ignore the tangle of tubes and array of machinery.

"Thank you," he'd whispered when he saw her, his eyes moist with emotion. But his second or third sentence had shown what was already on his mind. "Get Tommy Bishop over here as soon as you can," he'd said. "We've got to manage this thing carefully. He'll know what to say to the media, but he's got to be here. And for God's sake, ask Mark not to say a word to anybody. No statements. No medical jargon. Nothing. And ask him if we can downgrade this thing to an episode, something that makes it sound like I've been working my ass off, and that I'm not particularly ill."

"But Harrison, you *are* ill," she'd said.

"No, a senator is not ill unless he's dead, or he has to be carried onto the floor for a roll call. Remember that, Evelyn."

"My father was in poor health his last four terms."

"Your father could have been reelected from the mortuary. I don't have to tell you that. I'm up against a tough reelection fight. Even with Bush coming on strong in the polls, I can't take anything for granted, Ev.''

"You're way ahead of Chip Donlevy."

"Which is exactly where he wants me at this stage. If he gains momentum and times his surge right, I could lose this. Anything's possible."

"This is no time to worry about that," she'd said.

"All right. I know I've got to rest. But please, get Tommy and Arthur Cadness over here on the double. And you might want to call Amory. He should know. But for Chrissake, tell him to be discreet."

She had left him then, knowing it was the only way she'd get him calmed down.

Evelyn got up from the pew where'd she'd been reflecting and went out into the corridor. Amory would be arriving at any time. Tommy Bishop was probably already there. Mark wouldn't let Tommy in to see Harrison—not for more than a minute or two—so she'd be her husband's contact with the outside world, she and Mark. It was the only way to keep Harrison from overdoing things. Wives, it seemed, did play critical roles at times. Occasionally they were even indispensable.

Harrison Maitland looked at the band of plastic on his wrist where he normally wore his gold Rolex. The sight made him keenly aware of his mortality—the fact that in the end all his senatorial splendor counted for nothing. He was just a piece of meat like any other, a specimen for medical science to play with.

When he'd arrived at the hospital, they had stripped him naked like they would the next man, given him a hospital gown, a bed, wired him to a machine, watched the little line blipping on the screen, listened to his heart, gone away, come back, given him a shot, then gone away again and left him with nothing to do but contemplate the piece of muscle in his chest that threatened to undo him.

It was dark outside now. He'd survived the day, but he still wondered if he had come to the end of the line. There was no pain. There hadn't been for a long time. But every once in a while he could feel an irregular beat, sending a surge of apprehension through him. Mark had said the first day or two would be the most critical. God, how he hated hanging from such a fragile thread.

He wished now he hadn't sent Evelyn home. Her comfort and support were constant. Never did she question or demand. She represented succor, fidelity, companionship—all admirable qualities in a wife, and all calculated to induce guilt. But he had sent her away after dinner, despite the fact that he felt better with her at his side. He was reasonably sure he wouldn't die that night, so he thought it best to be alone to think.

Tommy Bishop had been upbeat. "Shit, think of all the sympathy votes," he had said. "Don't worry. We'll find a way to make it a plus, Harrison. You'll see." Then, while Tommy, Arthur Cadness and Norm Samuelson—his brain trust—plotted strategy down the hall, Harrison lay in his bed, listening to the low hum of the machines, and waiting for God or man to make a decision.

Evelyn came in several times with questions and progress reports, and he had sent out his answers and comments. Since the major medical tests would be conducted the next day, they decided to delay the technical stuff until then. With reluctance, he had finally agreed they could talk to the media in terms of a heart attack.

"Better to start out gloomier and be in a position to downgrade it," Tommy had argued. "If Watergate proved anything, it was that you can bleed your credibility dry by first denying, then admitting everything."

Harrison had asked for a television set so that he could see the news, but Mark had forbidden it. "Have it taped and watch it tomorrow," he had said. "You can't do anything between now and then, anyway."

So he had given in to them, as he had on just about everything after his talk with Amory. Harrison loved his brother, but he'd never overcome resenting him. Amory had a way of making him feel guilty, regardless of what he did.

He gazed at the glow of the dials on the machine beside his bed. The lights had been dimmed. Outside it was dark. The injection they had given him twenty minutes earlier had made him drowsy. For some reason, though, he was resisting sleep.

His fingers lay absently on his chest, confirming the rhythmic beat of his heart. His head was rolled toward the blackened window glass. He didn't enjoy being restrained this way. It made him want to get up and do something—anything—if only to prove that he could.

Every time he managed to get his heart or the campaign out of his mind, Megan would come creeping in to fill the vacuum. He would picture her anguish when she'd told him she was pregnant. It was more than he could cope with just then, yet it gnawed at the edge of his brain like a persistent rat. Someone else would have to deal with it—one of his people.

Arthur Cadness was the logical choice. He was both levelheaded and loyal. And Arthur was discreet. Harrison's fondness for women was no secret among his advisers. In a perverse sort of way, he always thought they regarded it as a mark of distinction, unless it was simply indulgence on their part and he was too fatuous to recognize the fact.

But Harrison didn't care. He was in a position to do what he wished, so he did. That was something his sainted brother wouldn't understand in a million years. Amory couldn't comprehend what it meant to live in the gut—why Megan Tiernan, for instance, was so important to him. It was a pity, really. Amory had cheated himself out of some of the better gifts life had to offer.

Still, there was a price to pay for living that way. Harrison had come to understand that. He'd paid for it with his body, and he was on the verge of paying for it with his career. But why the hell did it have to catch up with him now, with everything on the line?

The door opened then, permitting the bright light from the hallway to spill into the room. He turned to see one of the nurses quietly approaching.

"Are you awake, Senator?"

"Yes."

"I'm sorry to disturb you, but there's a telephone call. Doctor said you're to rest, but it's from the Capitol . . . one of your staffers. Megan Tiernan, I believe she said her name was."

Harrison felt his heart tremble. He thought. "Did you tell her you'd ask if I wanted to take the call?"

"Yes, Senator."

"Well, I'd better take it then."

"I'll have it transferred," she said, and left the room.

Harrison knew he wouldn't be able to put her off for long. It annoyed him that she insisted on taking chances. Thank God she hadn't come to the hospital. He closed his eyes and tried to relax while he waited for the phone to ring. Megan. What should he do about Megan?

Brett lay in bed, listening to Amory on the phone, trying to reach Elliot in Geneva. It seemed he'd gotten hold of a maid who spoke little English. He was having a terrible time. The frustration in his voice was evident.

Harrison's heart attack had shaken Amory more than she would have expected. She'd seen something in his eyes she hadn't noticed before—fear. Even after he'd seen for himself that Harrison was all right, the yawning chink in Amory's armor hadn't fully fused.

The only other times she'd seen him falter were when he'd spoken of Catherine's death, or of his relationship with his mother, Anne Maitland. Amory hadn't dwelled on either subject, so his vulnerabilities were largely hidden. But Harrison's illness had brought them out afresh.

By the sound of the conversation in the other room, Amory had finally gotten Monica on the line. She heard him explaining. There was no way to know what Monica's response was, but Brett imagined it would be callous, indifferent.

Poor Elliot. Brett still felt sorry for him. She'd been doubtful when they'd heard that Monica's breakdown had been a turning point. She didn't see how moving to Switzerland could have made much difference in a marriage that seemed beyond repair. Then, when they heard that Monica was pregnant, Brett began to understand.

Jennifer was born at the end of May in 1986, which meant Monica had gotten pregnant about the time she and Amory were in India. Knowing what she did about Monica, she couldn't help wondering if the child was even Elliot's.

She'd discussed the matter with Amory. He'd said that since Elliot seemed to have accepted Jennifer as his, so should they. All the same, Brett had been skeptical.

She hadn't seen either Elliot or Monica since India. The sanitarium Monica had been sent to for a few months was on Long Island, near her parents' home—too far away for a courtesy visit. Amory had seen Elliot once when he had come to Washington for a meeting. They'd had lunch, but Brett had been in the middle of exams and couldn't get away. She'd extended a dinner invitation, but Elliot had had another commitment.

Other than an occasional picture of the baby, Christmas cards and so forth, Brett and Amory had had little news of Elliot and Monica during their stay in Switzerland. Elliot was assigned to the U.S. mission to the United Nations, where he'd distinguished himself, but the state of his marriage was a mystery.

The previous August, while Brett was studying for the bar exam, Amory had attended an international conference of jurists in Geneva. Elliot and Monica had had him to dinner in their apartment on the rue de l'Athénée. Amory later reported that they were living in an uneasy truce. Monica was clearly unhappy and resentful of both her husband and the baby.

It was a tragedy, considering the child. Even Amory admitted that it would have been better if Monica hadn't gotten pregnant. He did come home with a briefcase full of photos, which Brett studied with great interest. Jennifer was only a toddler, but she had every appearance of being her father's child. Still, Brett wondered.

"I know it doesn't seem important to you, Monica," Amory said from the other room, "but have Elliot call me anyway. He might like to know."

Brett heard an uncharacteristic touch of irritation in her husband's voice. She could tell he was losing patience. It hardly seemed possible Monica was drunk. It was very early in the morning in Europe.

"How's that little granddaughter of mine?" she heard him say, probably hoping for a more conducive line of conversation. And then, "Monica, I realize I'm not her grandfather, technically speaking, but I like to think of her as mine. Is it too much to give me that?"

There was a silence from the other room.

"No, no," Amory said. "That's all right. I didn't mean to be sharp. I apologize. . . . Yes, and I'm sorry to have gotten you from bed. I hope you feel better. . . . Yes, if you'll have him call me. . . . Thank you."

Brett heard him replacing the receiver. Then he appeared in the doorway in his pajamas, looking thoroughly beaten. There was a grayness about his countenance that wasn't like Amory.

"Poor darlin'," she said. "Monica was dreadful, by the sound of it."

Amory shook his head. "I don't know how Elliot can tolerate that woman. It's rare when I can't find charity in my heart for someone, but Monica pushes me to the limit." He sat down on the bed, his shoulders slumping. "I'm exhausted."

"Would you like a massage? Would that help you relax?"

"No, thank you," he replied, lying beside her on top of the sheets. "You're an angel, but all I need is rest. You've had a rough day, too."

Brett took his hand. Amory squeezed her fingers weakly. The lamp on his side was on, but he seemed content to leave it for the moment. He stared up at the ceiling.

"I sense things may be coming to a head with Elliot and Monica," he said vacantly.

"Why is that?"

"In August Elliot told me Monica was drinking heavily again. He didn't elaborate on what it was doing to their relationship, but it's not hard to guess. And just now, I thought I heard something in her voice."

"What did she say?"

"I'd mentioned being a grandfather and she got defensive, tossing off a comment to the effect that since Elliot was trying to co-opt Jennifer, she ought to expect it from me, as well."

"That's ridiculous. Maybe she *was* drunk."

"If so, it was from the night before. She didn't seem to know where Elliot was until the maid reminded her he was out of town."

"Well, you can't worry about Elliot, too. You've got enough on your plate right now with Harrison."

Amory gave a weighty sigh. Then he pulled her hand to his lips and kissed it. "Thank God for you, Brett. The staff of my old age."

"Amory! Don't talk that way!"

He chuckled. "A little self-pity, darling. That's all."

"I don't like that kind of talk, and you know it." She jabbed his side with her elbow. "Old age, my foot."

"You're much more sensitive about my years than I, my dear. Denying them is even less healthy than bemoaning them."

"Says who?"

He rolled his tongue into his cheek. "There must be an authority of some sort who preaches that."

"Yeah? If so, he was old and impotent."

Amory laughed and grabbed her waist, tickling her through her gown.

Brett shrieked with laughter and whacked his hand. "Stop that!"

"See what happens when you put wheat germ in my prunes!"

"Mr. Justice Maitland, one more crack about age and I'm going to give you a thrashin'."

Amory took her hand again and returned to his contemplative repose. They both lay thinking, the playful flurry over.

Then Amory said, "How did your meeting go with John this morning? I didn't get a chance to ask you about it."

"He's a dear. He listened like he always does. Let me ramble on."

"I once told John he should put a couch in his office and take patients," Amory said.

"He should. He'd do well. I'm truly fond of that man."

"Should I be jealous?"

Brett chuckled. "Why darlin', it's innocent. Same as when you and I first met and I was your little ingenue."

"That's what I mean."

She patted his hand. "We talked about my career mostly, about my indecision."

"What was John's advice?"

"In a nutshell, he said to take my time."

"That's probably wise," Amory agreed.

Again they fell into silence. Then Amory gave another heavy sigh.

"Would you like for me to call the hospital and check on Harrison?" Brett asked. "Would you sleep better, knowing he's okay?"

"No, that's all right. I'm fine."

Brett rolled onto her side so she could see Amory's face. She watched him, knowing his mind was working, that he was off in profound reflection. He was aware of her observing him, but didn't seem to mind; he would tell her what he was thinking if she asked. She liked that about Amory—the fact that he would allow her into his innermost sanctum.

"Is it worth a penny?" she whispered.

He turned to her. "Oh, a dime at least." He paused. "I was thinking about us, as a matter of fact. In a roundabout sort of way."

Brett propped herself up on her elbow. "Now that sounds interesting. What about us?"

He grinned, touching her lip. "I don't think you'll be pleased, Brett."

She gave him an inquiring look. "Maybe, but after that remark you have no choice but to tell me."

Amory continued to stare up at the ceiling, rubbing his chin as he did. "Harrison's heart attack got me thinking about my own mortality," he said.

"That's not surprising," she replied. "I'm kind of depressed myself."

"It's not that. I'm fifty-eight years old. According to the actuarial tables I've got another twenty or thirty years."

"You're going to live to be a hundred, Amory."

"Even if you're right, my children will be young when I go. I had this horrible vision today of trying to propel a baby buggy and a wheelchair at the same time."

"This is a conversation about career and family, not mortality."

"In my case they're not unrelated, Brett."

She, too, rolled onto her back and stared up at the ceiling. She put her arm across her forehead. She had a sick feeling in the pit of her stomach. It was the one issue in their marriage where she really felt at odds. And it was the only one in which the difference in their ages was a major factor.

"I don't mean to upset you," Amory said, "but I realize I've been repressing my feelings, knowing you've had the pressure of the bar exam. But seeing Harrison in that hospital bed with all that machinery holding him together really hit me in the solar plexus."

Brett didn't comment. She really wanted to establish her career before having children, but she knew that was a selfish desire. As it was, Amory would be in his sixties and seventies while their children were growing up. To push it back even further was probably unfair to both him and their children—Strom Thurman, the man of steel, as Amory called him, notwithstanding. Brett was beginning to see that starting a family might be one of those pivotal points of compromise most people faced at one time or another in a

marriage. It could be the major sacrifice she would be called on to make.

"Can I have a few months to think about it?"

"Certainly, darling. I'm not pushing for a decision."

"Even if I took a job, I could change my mind," she said. "And getting a year or two of work under my belt would probably be better than getting no time in at all."

"Yes," he said, "you may be right."

Brett put her hand on his arm. "It's been a bad day," she said. "Don't let what happened to Harrison get you down."

"I didn't say anything, but Harrison's fifty-five. He and Evelyn won't be having children. If I should go before we do, the Maitland line will come to an end."

"I really wish you wouldn't talk that way," she said, feeling anxious again. "I'll give you your heir, Amory. I promise."

"Have I upset you?" Amory asked, rolling his head her way.

She touched his cheek. "Of course not. I've been less than gracious."

"I truly don't mean to pressure you, Brett, though I know it sounds as though I am. The decision is yours."

Brett leaned over and kissed him softly. "It's our decision, yours and mine both."

That pleased him. He stroked her hair. Brett felt a well of emotion as she settled back on her pillow.

"Shall we turn off the light?" she murmured.

He looked at the clock. "All right. But if you don't mind, maybe I will call the hospital first."

Brett watched him sit up on the edge of the bed. He looked on the bedstand for the telephone number he'd jotted on a scrap of paper. His back was to her and she was glad. She didn't want him to see that her eyes were filled with tears.

Megan Tiernan sat in her car, double-parked on the Twenty-first Street side of the hospital. It was after one in the morning. She stared at the entrance. All she could think about was the telephone call she'd made a few hours earlier.

She'd waited for Harrison to come on the line, the phone clutched to her ear, her pulse racing. No one at the hospital would tell her anything; his office had no news. She'd been cut off, kept from the circle of insiders, even though it was *she* who'd saved his life, *she* who was carrying his child....

When she first heard his voice she felt euphoric. It didn't matter that his tone was cold, impersonal, indifferent. She only cared that he was alive, that her name was on his lips.

She couldn't help herself. All she could do was weep. "Harrison..." she sobbed. "Are you... all right?"

"Yes. Yes. Of course."

"I had to call." Her voice quavered. She tried hard to be brave. "I... I had to know."

"Well, I'm not dead. Yet."

Her tears flowed freely. She was glad he wasn't there to see. She wanted to be supportive, as Evelyn surely was. All day long the words he'd uttered as they put him in the ambulance had rung in her ears. "Get word to my wife. I want her with me." That, as much as anything, had devastated her. Why hadn't he wanted *her* at his side?

She sniffed. "I've prayed for you all day. For both of us." There was a long silence, and Megan closed her eyes, hearing the beat of her heart.

"I haven't had a lot of time to think about what you told me," he finally said.

"I know. That's all right." But it wasn't. Her soul was screaming for him to say something reassuring, if only that he loved her.

"Listen, Megan, we can't talk about it now. No telling who might listen in." He hesitated. "Why don't we get together when I'm out of here? Maybe by the end of the week. I'll call you."

"All right," she said. "I'll wait. Please call." Then she murmured, "I love you," but it was more to herself than to him. Harrison had already hung up....

For a long time afterward she'd lain on her bed, terrified that their love affair might be over. Oh, he would take care of her financially; she was confident of that. But could he handle the idea of a child? Maybe her pregnancy had destroyed his love. She wouldn't let herself believe that of him. Not Harrison.

Still, in her heart, there was doubt. She couldn't live with the uncertainty. How did he feel? Did he still love her? She desperately had to know.

Megan continued to stare at the entrance to the hospital, trying to summon her courage, trying to balance her need to see him against the consequences of getting caught. On the phone Harrison had seemed insensitive, but it wasn't really him when he was that way—it was the shadow of the man who loved her. She had learned to deal with that darker side of him, to buffer it.

He was often that way when he would come to see her—florid from whatever it was that had upset him, deep lines in his face, angry words on his tongue. She would put her arms around him and give him a kiss. He would fight her for a time, but eventually he'd settle into his favorite chair, the vexation draining. She would bring him a Scotch and sit on the arm of the chair. He would rub her thighs or her breasts, and before long they'd end up in the bedroom, his problem forgotten.

She watched a pair of nurses in white uniforms enter the hospital. They could be assigned to the cardiac unit, possibly one of them would be looking after Harrison. It killed her to think some anonymous female could be with him, but not her. They belonged together.

Until the campaign had gotten in full swing, Harrison had managed to see her nearly every day, saying he couldn't survive if they weren't together. He referred to her apartment as their home. He loved sharing it with her. They were his happiest hours, he told her.

Over the months he had helped her furnish the place, telling her it was his, too. She didn't feel like his mistress. Being with him was always comfortable and companionable. And as her love grew, she wanted to be with him all the time.

When she got lonely, she would go to the liquor cabinet and take out Harrison's bottle of Glenfiddich Scotch. She would caress it, remove the cap and sniff its distinctive aroma. It would remind her of the taste of his mouth when they made love, the flavor of his tongue brushing against hers.

At other times she would take his robe from the closet and press it against her face. It smelled of him—so intensely that his presence would almost seem real. And then she would wait until he came to her.

Oh, how she wanted him. Knowing a child was growing inside her—his child—her yearning became unbearable. There was a terrible danger, but she couldn't help herself. She had to see him. Now!

Megan pulled the car ahead and parked in front of a fire hydrant, the only space she could find. She got out and walked to the hospital entrance. Inside, the receptionist insisted that the senator couldn't be seen without his doctor's permission.

Megan noted Harrison's room number from the printed list in front of the woman. "Is there someplace I can get a cup of coffee?" she asked.

The woman glanced at the wall clock. "The cafeteria is only open to staff now." She paused. "I don't imagine anyone will get too upset if you want a cup of coffee. Take the elevator down," she said, pointing.

Megan went to the bank of elevators and brooded as she waited for a car. When one finally came she stepped in and pushed the button for the fifth floor. She wasn't going to be thwarted by some damned receptionist.

Moments later the doors opened to the sounds of anxious voices. Someone in a white uniform ran by as she stepped out. There was an urgent shout down the hallway, "Room 514! Five-fourteen!" Everyone was too busy to pay any attention to her.

The nurse at the station opposite the elevator was watching a panel of monitors as Megan slipped along the hallway and into Harrison's room.

The indirect lighting was bright enough that she could see his face. His eyes were closed, he looked serene. Beside him was a machine with glowing green dials, casting an eerie hue over his skin. Wires ran from the machinery to his body. He looked so terribly fragile.

She moved to his side and watched the slow rise and fall of his chest. It seemed strange to see him that way. She always thought of Harrison as robust—even knowing the doctor had been concerned about his heart for some time.

It was so good to be with him. She kissed his forehead. He didn't stir. Pulling over a nearby chair, she sat down and took his hand. His flesh felt warm. It cheered her to be touching him, even though he wasn't aware of it. What would she have done if he had died?

Megan remembered when Senator Henry Jackson had died of a heart attack back in 1983. She'd worked in his office as a clerk. It had been her first job in Washington and she'd only been there a few weeks when the tragedy struck, so she didn't really know him. But when word reached his Capitol Hill office, she remembered how staffers had broken down, crying and hugging one another. Because she'd been junior in the office, within two weeks she'd been unemployed again.

For a month after that, Megan had kicked around the Hill, trying to find a job. There weren't any openings anywhere, and she was having a terrible time. Then, one afternoon while she was in the staff office of the Senate Agriculture, Nutrition and Forestry Committee, waiting for an interview, Harrison came in with Senator Helms, the committee chairman. She and Harrison talked while Senator Helms was dealing with the staff, and before she knew it he was handing her his card, suggesting she make an appointment to see him.

Megan had considered taking Harrison up on his offer, but before she'd gotten up her nerve, a job opportunity had come up in the office of her own congressman, from Washington State's fourth district. She'd worked there until just before the election of 1986 when the seat was to change hands due to a retirement and she would be out on the street again. Megan had remembered Harrison's invitation and, being more mature and aware of the ways of Capitol Hill, she'd decided to go see him in his office in the Dirksen building, even though three years had elapsed since she'd spoken with him.

Megan sighed wistfully as she gazed at the face of the man she loved. Harrison stirred slightly, his mouth twitching. How very different he'd looked that time she had finally gone to talk to him about a job. He'd been so confident and self-assured. Senator Harrison Maitland had the world by the tail and he let everyone know it. . . .

Her appointment was on Halloween, a Friday, toward the end of the day. His staff had decorated the office a little, and a couple of the secretaries, while not exactly in costume, had dressed a bit outrageously.

One of them showed her into Harrison's private office, which had a great tall window looking out the back of the building, toward Union Station. He was in his high-back chair, facing the window, away from her, when she entered.

"Miss Tiernan to see you, Senator," the secretary announced.

"Have a chair, Miss Tiernan," he said, without turning around.

She sat down uncertainly, then the chair spun around very suddenly. Harrison was wearing a devil's mask! She let out an involuntary shriek, and he laughed. "You're supposed to say, 'Trick or treat.'"

Megan stared in total shock. "Jesus, Mary and Joseph . . . You scared me to death."

Harrison was still laughing as he tossed the mask aside and leaned back. "I hate job interviews," he said devilishly. "How about you?"

"Yes, I guess I do."

"So tell me, why has it taken you so long to come see me? Did I scare you that day?"

"You remember, Senator?"

"Honey, remembering names and faces is half my job. I *never* forget a face as pretty as yours."

Megan knew it wasn't true, that her call for the appointment had refreshed his memory, but she was flattered just the same. Still, that was so like Harrison, knowing just what to say, how to charm.

They chatted then, and Harrison asked her lots of questions about her background. She told him about having grown up in Ellensburg, Washington, the illegitimate child of a college librarian. She'd gone to Catholic schools until her mother had been stricken with Parkinson's disease.

Megan's major had been political science, and her dream was to go into politics. But she couldn't leave her mother, so she'd stayed in Ellensburg, teaching school and later on serving as director of the chamber of commerce. She kept her dreams alive by working in political campaigns. When her mother finally died, she packed up and came to Washington.

"And now you're all alone and unemployed," he said. "Hardly a condition for such a lovely young lady."

Megan liked Harrison's honesty. He wasn't at all stuffy, like so many of the legislators. And he seemed genuinely to care about her. She also found him appealing, though she didn't let herself think about that at first.

Harrison admitted that he didn't have any openings in his office, but he promised to talk to a friend on her behalf. Within a week she had a job with Lloyd Crenshaw, a Washington-based lobbyist whose firm represented a number of political-action committees.

The morning she was hired she dropped by Harrison's office to thank him. He was genuinely delighted for her.

"Congratulations!" he said. "Now you owe me lunch."

As it turned out, he took her to eat in the Senate dining room. Megan wasn't so naive as to think that a senator normally dined with a woman out of the kindness of his heart, so she was leery. But it didn't turn out as she had feared. Harrison was every bit the gentleman.

"If Mr. Crenshaw wasn't your friend, I'd never have gotten the job," she told him.

"Nonsense. It's your charm, Megan. The same charm that impressed me. It always helps to get a door opened for you, but the days of secretaries who can't type are over."

And so Harrison said goodbye, making Megan promise not to twist his arm too hard if she ever came up to the Hill looking for votes. "Drop in and say hello," he said. "I'd be happy to see you anytime."

By then she liked Harrison very much, and not just because he'd helped her. She liked his sense of humor, his kindness, and she found him attractive. When they parted after lunch she felt a keen sense of disappointment, thinking she might not see him again. Then two weeks later he invited her out to dinner, saying he was interested in how the new job was going.

He picked her up at her apartment, she offered him a drink, and they never made it to the restaurant. Before the night was over, she was in love with Harrison A. Maitland, United States senator....

Megan leaned forward, looking at his dear face. She was sure, now, that he would survive. That was the most important thing. All that remained was to come to terms with her pregnancy. And she knew deep down that their love was big enough for that. No matter what or who got in their way, she would see that they made it together, with their child.

Megan kissed his lips. She didn't want to disturb him, but she couldn't help herself. Harrison stirred. His eyes fluttered open.

"Megan?" he said, his voice a hoarse whisper.

"Harrison, darling, I love you so."

"What are you doing here?" There was a dreamy quality to his voice, as though he'd awakened in a place he hadn't expected.

"I sneaked in. Nothing can keep you from me."

He lifted his head slightly to look at the door. "What if they find you?"

"They'll make me leave, I suppose. But I had to come. I had to know you still loved me."

"Of course I do." His voice was dry, breathy.

He closed his eyes, and she realized he was only half awake. She didn't want to upset him, but she had to know the answer to the question that had been tormenting her. She leaned close to his ear. "You don't hate me because of the baby, do you?"

He rolled his head back and forth, as if to say no.

"We can still marry, and the three of us can be together. After the election. You'll win, darling, I know you will."

Harrison was only half aware of what was happening, but he felt a wonderful sense of contentment. Through the bedding he felt her breast against him. He knew Megan shouldn't be there, but he was too heavily sedated to care. The comfort she afforded was so pleasant. And so he let himself drift off, the wonderful scent of her hair filling his lungs. He did love Megan. He really did.

The morning sun came as a surprise. Despite Mark Feldman's assurances, Harrison had had doubts that he would see it again. The sunshine streaming in cheered him. It was great to be alive. Any other morning, a bromide like that would have made him laugh, but not this morning.

As he contemplated calling the nurse, he noticed a chair beside the bed. Then he remembered. His recollections were fuzzy, but he was quite sure it had really happened—that it wasn't a dream. Megan had been in his room. Had she slipped away as mysteriously as she'd arrived? He suspected he'd hear soon enough if she'd been caught.

Harrison reached for the cord to summon a nurse, then stopped himself, struck by a sudden realization. He was going to be a father! Him—Harrison A. Maitland. A father!

But in the middle of his euphoria, a sobering insight came to him. The issue was not fatherhood, it was responsibility and respectability. How did he square Megan and the baby with all that?

He sank back onto his pillow and closed his eyes. "Meggie," he muttered. "Oh, Meggie, what have we done?"

The day he'd gotten her pregnant was indelibly burned into his brain. In retrospect he wondered if he should have known—if God or Providence or the cynical hand of fate had tried to warn him. He often thought of the day, his cock getting hard on him every time he did.

For a long time he'd known Megan affected him differently. That day her full power, her magic over him, became undeniable.

He had decided to take her to the East Shore—something he'd never done with a woman before. In his mind it was an adventure, but also a test—a way of finding out how she felt to him in the sacred precincts of his family home. She'd had no idea what was going on in his mind, how his feelings for her had evolved. And so he'd kept his purposes between himself and the ghosts of his youth....

Having told Evelyn he was going fishing on the Chesapeake, he picked Megan up and they drove first to Baltimore, then over the Chesapeake Bay Bridge to Talbot County and the Tred Avon. As they cruised through the countryside in the warm July sunshine, Megan rested her hand on his thigh.

"I'm so happy, Harrison," she told him.

He ran his hand up under her skirt. "Does that mean what I think it means?"

She leaned over to kiss his neck, nibbling at his flesh. "Is that all you think about, Mr. United States Senator?"

"When I'm with you."

She laughed and crossed her legs on his hand, trapping his fingers between her thighs. It sent his desire soaring, and Megan knew it. When she slid her tongue across her upper lip, he said, "Damn you," and pressed down on the accelerator.

They flew through the village of Kirkham, then down the road leading to the river and the house. At the sight of the familiar countryside a bit of nostalgia crept in along with his excitement. All the land as far as one could see had been owned by his family at one time or another, and Harrison felt a tie to it. Whenever he passed through the level fields, marshes and woods, he had a sense of home.

He had known Talbot County from childhood, having been born in Baltimore only because his mother's pregnancy had been complicated and old Doc Knauf in Easton knew enough to send her across the bay to Johns Hopkins. As it turned out, Anne Maitland had nearly died anyway.

While still a boy, Harrison intuited that his birth had changed his parents' lives. He gathered that they never had sexual relations after that, which led his father, eventually, to find his pleasures elsewhere.

Charles Maitland was a landowner and businessman. And as his relationship with his wife became more distant, his business affairs took him from home with greater and greater frequency. When the war came he took a high-ranking job first in the War Department, and later in the War Food Administration, which he virtually ran. The family hardly saw him during those years, and Harrison later learned that his father had spent his time with a young woman in Washington.

Immediately after the war, Charles had a stroke. Amory and Harrison were teenagers when their father passed away; Amory was just a year from going off to college.

So it had been Anne Maitland who ruled the family domain. The daughter of the United States senator from Maryland during the Teddy Roosevelt and Taft administrations, she instilled discipline, moral and religious virtue, and a sense of political destiny in her sons. Amory, who favored her side of the family with his quiet intellectualism and tall athletic build, had always been her favorite. The fact that Harrison had his father's shorter, sturdier build and fiery temperament did not endear him to his mother.

Early on, Harrison learned to shift for himself, turning to outsiders for the attention he needed. He was popular in school, and soon learned he didn't need parental love to make his way in the world. He attended Georgetown University, graduating in 1951. He was commissioned as a second lieutenant in the army, spent two years on active duty, which included a tour in Korea during the last four months of hostilities. Three years after his discharge, when Amory was already on the faculty at Harvard, Harrison finished his studies at Notre Dame Law School. He entered the Maryland bar in 1958.

It was during a holiday visit to the family home on the East Shore, during his third year of law school, that he got to know Evelyn Daughton. Amory had brought a friend from Harvard to visit, and Harrison, bored by Anne Maitland's excessive attentions to Amory and his friend, had taken a rowboat out on the Tred Avon to amuse himself. It was an unusually warm day and, for the hell of it, he had strayed toward the far side of the river, near the "Daughton Shore," as they called it.

The Daughtons, Protestants and Democrats, had been rivals of the Maitlands for generations, though in the past few decades the competition had subsided considerably. Hanley Daughton, an eccentric bachelor, was residing on the family estate. All the other family members had passed away, save a brother, Ellis, from Connecticut, who happened to be a congressman. Ellis Daughton had been an antagonist of their father during Charles's Washington years.

That day, on the bank of the river, near the house, Harrison saw a slender young woman strolling under the trees. That surprised him. Old Hanley was somewhat of a recluse, and not known to entertain. Then it occurred to him that the girl might be the old boy's niece, the daughter of the congressman. The possibility was an interesting one, indeed.

From earliest childhood Harrison had been indoctrinated by their mother not only about the spiritual war between God and Satan, but also about the political war, championed on one side by Republican saints—like his father and maternal grandfather—and on the other by heathen Democrats—like the Daughtons. From his youth, Harrison had come to regard the Tred Avon as a line of demarcation, a bit like the River Styx—on one side the forces of good, on the other the forces of evil.

The Daughton girl—if that's who she was—posed a unique challenge. He'd felt reckless on that beautiful spring day. So, heaving to his oar, he steamed into enemy waters, approaching near enough to see the creature he'd spotted from afar.

It turned out she was a good deal more attractive than his most perverse imaginings would have allowed.

"Ahoy there," he called out. "Could I borrow a cup of sugar?"

"Are you friend or foe?" she called back.

"I'm a Republican law student, surname Maitland."

"Then I'd better warn you, the waters are mined!"

"Damn the torpedoes!" he shouted back. "Full speed ahead!"

After he had beached the rowboat, he and Evelyn sat on the lawn and talked for an hour. Then, feeling audacious, Harrison invited her to cross the river with him to meet his mother. She was spirited enough to accept. So they rowed back, taking Anne Maitland totally by surprise and earning her eternal enmity. After that, he had no choice but to marry the girl.

And Evelyn, knowing her uncle wouldn't recognize Harrison on sight, had introduced him as David Farragut—the historical character who had actually damned the torpedoes—much to Harrison's delight. She had come to the East Shore for the summer, enabling the liaison to continue. They courted surreptitiously, considering themselves much too modern to be deterred by ancient animosities.

Their marriage reduced what was left of the cross-river hostility to a low simmer, the feud ending officially with Anne's death in the fall of 1968, the day after Richard Nixon beat Hubert Humphrey for the presidency. "God always looked out for Mother," Harrison told Evelyn years later. "He let her see Dick win, but spared her Watergate."

Harrison, approaching Rosemont, the home his great-grandfather had built, slowed the car and rolled down his window, half sticking his nose out to smell the air. "Ah," he said to Megan. "Smell that, baby? That's home!"

She was duly impressed with the house, and Harrison knew immediately that his sweet-breasted beauty from out west was picturing herself living in it—a notion that amused him.

"The house," he explained, as they got out of the car, "belongs to both Amory and me, so really it doesn't belong to either of us. If anyone owns it, it's Mother. Her ghost still haunts the place."

"How do you decide who gets to use it?" she asked.

"Amory and I check with each other, and then come over whenever we wish."

"You didn't tell him we'd be here this weekend, did you?" she said with horror.

"No, I thought we'd live dangerously." Then he added with a laugh, "If you're going to be caught in the arms of a married man, it might as well be by a justice of the U.S. Supreme Court."

Megan rolled her eyes. "You are an evil man."

"Don't worry. For the weekend the place is mine. When it comes to the house, at least, Amory and I are equals."

"Better for you than if it went to the oldest son, the way they used to do it," Megan said.

"Oh, Mother had her eccentric ideas. We only have a life estate in the property. The house and land go to the eldest of our surviving children."

"But neither of you have children."

"No, and that didn't please my mother at all." Harrison smiled ruefully. "Wily old witch, wasn't she?"

He took Megan's arm and they walked around to the veranda. It overlooked a sloping lawn that went down to the water's edge. They stood there for a while, his arm around her waist as they surveyed the scene.

"That's a big house over there," she said, pointing across the wide expanse of water.

Harrison looked at the large white mansion more than a quarter of a mile away. "That's the Daughton place. An old duffer in his nineties occupies it. He also happens to be Evelyn's uncle."

"Her uncle's right there, within sight of us?"

Harrison grinned. "I'm not afraid of geriatric old Democrats any more than I'm afraid of ghosts." He lifted her face, then kissed her deeply. "Come on, Meggie, I'll show you my bedroom and my model planes."

He took their bags from the car, along with two bottles of champagne, which he immediately put in the refrigerator. Then he gave her a tour of the house.

"It's so clean," Megan said, looking around.

"We have a housekeeper come in once a week." Harrison pointed out the old porcelain rose vase on the mantel that had belonged first to his father's mother, and then to Anne. It had become the family chalice, he told Megan, the enduring symbol of the Maitlands' indomitable spirit.

"And who's that?" she asked, looking up at the great portrait above the mantel.

"That, my dear, is Mummy," he replied.

"She was a very serious woman, wasn't she?"

Harrison laughed. "She had a harder time making peace with F.D.R. after Pearl Harbor than the Germans and the Japanese."

"You don't look like her at all."

"No."

"Did she like Evelyn?"

He shook his head.

She turned to him. "Would she have liked me, Harrison?"

He contemplated the question as he took in her body with a sweep of the eye. "You know, I've never considered that before. Your politics are wrong, but your religion is right. She would have had trouble with the generation gap and couldn't have accepted our relationship in a million years. But to be honest, I think deep down she would have liked you—your essence, anyway."

"That's good, isn't it?"

"As far as it goes. But I like all the things about you she never would have approved of." He kissed her then, reaching down and running his fingers under the hem of her skirt.

Harrison showed Megan around the rest of house, then they took their things upstairs to the room where he and Evelyn always slept. Megan didn't ask him about that, though he suspected it was going through her mind. He sat on the bed and watched her hang some things in the closet, admiring the rounded curves of her ass and thighs. He felt desire, and it pleased him.

When she finished, Megan walked over to him and stood with her knees between his. She ran her fingers through his gray-flecked hair as he kissed a hardened nipple through her tank top.

"What about the champagne?" she teased.

"You're right. We must start with champagne."

They went back downstairs, and Harrison got the wine and two glasses. After he opened the doors to the veranda, they sat on the couch, facing the fireplace. He popped the cork and poured them each a glass.

"This seems like a special occasion," Megan said.

"It is, Meggie. It is."

In half an hour they'd both become drunk. Megan lay her head against his chest, telling him how much she loved him. She ran her hand over his polo shirt, slipping her fingers through the gap. She felt his heart pounding under her palm.

"I want you, Megan," he murmured into her hair. "I want you very much."

She ran her hand down to his crotch then, feeling the warmth of him through the fabric. "What do you want me to do?" she whispered.

"Take off your clothes," he said, sitting upright. "I want you to strip."

"Here?"

"No. In front of the fireplace."

She looked up at him. "Really?"

"You asked...."

She staggered a little as she made her way to the hearth. There she turned around with adolescent shyness, despite her intoxication. "Just take off my clothes?"

"Yes."

Megan kicked off her sandals and lifted her tank top over her head, exposing her pendulous breasts. She tossed the shirt aside, then stood motionless, watching him.

"Go on," he said.

She unfastened her skirt and let it drop to the floor, kicking it away. Giving him an inebriated smile, she slipped her panties off and stood totally naked under the portrait of his mother. She stared at him with a crooked grin. "Now what?"

Harrison got to his feet heavily. He grabbed an overstuffed armchair and pulled it between them, so that it was sideways. "Now come here," he said. And when she was before him, he bent her over the rounded arm of the chair, her head facing the fireplace, her buttocks pointed toward him.

Then he lowered his pants and moved forward, so that his already erect penis was poised at her haunches. Pressing against her then, he entered her forcefully, making her cry out. Megan grabbed the other arm of the chair as he clutched her hair with his fist and began to thrust.

After a while she started moaning, but he couldn't tell if it was in pleasure or pain. He didn't care. All he wanted was to fuck her. The slap of his flesh against hers became so loud he hardly heard her cries. She screamed louder then, and he pulled her auburn hair as he rammed into her.

She shuddered, and started screaming, "Yes, yes! Fuck me!"

He felt his orgasm coming then. He sank his fingers deep into the flesh of Megan's thighs, and looked down at her gyrating ass.

When he felt his scrotum clench, he looked up defiantly into his mother's eyes. A bestial grunt came from deep within his throat, his pelvis heaved against Megan's rump, and he filled it with his seed. When it ended, he collapsed over her and lay there panting.

Megan tightened her haunches on him and he whispered to her, "I love you. I love you."

Then, after several long moments, he braced himself and raised his face to Anne Maitland. His eyes filled with tears, and, inexplicably, he began to cry.

Harrison's body shuddered under the covers and he felt as though he were about to weep. With his eyes closed, he hadn't seen her enter or heard the door open. But when her cool hand touched his, he came to full consciousness from his dreamlike state.

"Evelyn!" He felt his heart trip.

"I hope I didn't startle you, darling. You looked so distressed."

"Oh . . . I was dozing. It was a sort of dream."

"You sure you're all right?"

"Yes, yes." He managed a smile.

"It's a beautiful morning. I expect we'll have good news from the doctors."

"I hope so."

Evelyn had some newspapers with her and she put them on his lap. "It's not as bad as I expected," she said.

Harrison opened the *Post*. The story was on the lower left corner of the front page. He read the headline and the first three paragraphs, then put the paper down. "It doesn't look like anyone expects the wheels of government to stop."

"No offense, Harrison, but I believe you are a lot more important to me than you are to the rest of the world. And I expect Nancy would say the same thing about the president."

"You think so?"

"A wife must."

He weakly took her hand. "Evelyn . . . Evelyn."

"What, darling?"

He shook off the question.

"What are you thinking?" she asked.

He hesitated a long time, then said, "Do you suppose I was any happier when I was David Farragut?"

She laughed. "You remember that?"

"How could I forget?"

She kissed the top of his head and stroked his cheek. Harrison glanced over at the sunshine coming through the windows.

"Do you think they'll make me rest before I get back to the campaign?" he asked.

"I would think so."

"Then maybe we should go to the East Shore."

"You want to?" There was delight in her voice.

His feelings about Rosemont were complex. He might have gotten his mistress pregnant there, but it was also the place where he'd sat on his mother's knee as a child and where he'd courted Evelyn.

"You really want me to go with you?" she asked when he didn't respond.

"I don't just want you to, Ev," he replied. "It's a matter of life and death."

PART III

Mount Ivy, Georgia

October 15, 1988

Two days after George Bush and Michael Dukakis debated on national television, Brett made the drive from Atlanta to the hills of north Georgia. It was a Saturday; she was going home to attend Earl Hatcher's funeral.

Leona had called the previous evening to tell her that Earl had died of a massive stroke while listening to a high school football game on the radio. She'd found him dead in his chair as the announcer was recounting the climactic moments of the game.

Amory had offered to fly down with her, but the new court term had just begun, and Brett didn't want him to miss the critical Monday meeting when they voted on certiorari petitions. She decided to attend the funeral without him, almost preferring to face her past alone.

As Brett drove she looked out at the countryside. Haze and woodsmoke masked the distant Blue Ridge, and the air, which she let circulate in the open window of the rental car, had a distinctive autumn smell that brought back sweet memories of her childhood. The memories evoked were not all happy, though she did embrace the warm familiarity of the place that had once been home.

The modest, cluttered, ramshackle homes that lined the country road housed families totally different from her neighbors in Chevy Chase. Country folk in dilapidated pickups and fifteen-year-old American-made cars were her people, and their way of life had once been hers, too.

Folks in rural Georgia had different priorities. They cared about Fred and Mae Ebersol's seventy-fifth wedding anniversary that was written up in the *Carlisle Independent*. They cared about the highway project east of Hope Junction that was delayed by the politicians down in Atlanta. They cared a lot about the Hempstead Central victory over Andrews High on Friday night— The Tigers hadn't beaten the Indians since Lester Maddox had last wielded a baseball bat in the capital.

The people of northern Georgia probably didn't give much thought to Mike Deaver's conviction for lying under oath to a grand jury, and they probably didn't much like either George Bush or Michael Dukakis a whole lot. Their lives, Brett knew, were defined by geography, relatives and friends. To them the outside world could be as incidental as paprika on potato salad.

The night before Earl died, she and Amory had attended a political dinner in Baltimore where Harrison and Chip Donlevy were making a joint appearance. Amory had taped the presidential debate between Bush and Dukakis that was taking place at the same time in Los Angeles so that he and Brett could watch it later.

So Friday after dinner, she had mixed Amory a Scotch and soda and fixed herself a vodka tonic to sip while they watched the governor of Massachusetts take on the wily utility man of the Republican Party. Amory liked George Bush because he considered him competent and reasonable. Brett liked the governor because he was liberal and seemed sensitive to human misery. She also felt sorry for him, having seen more than one liberal felled by the politics of racism and flag-waving when she was growing up in the South.

During the debate they good-naturedly chided each other's candidate. The vice-president was in the middle of his closing remarks when Leona called with the news about Earl.

The news didn't devastate Brett, but she grieved for Leona. And being her only relative closer than a distant cousin, she knew it was important that she be at her aunt's side when they put Earl in the ground.

When she arrived home, her aunt's friend and neighbor, Jeanette Johnson, twenty pounds heavier than when Brett had last seen her, was sitting with Leona in the parlor. Leona herself was a tall, rawboned woman like all the Wallaces. Kady and Brett both had taken their fine-boned beauty from their mother's side. But Leona was fair like the girls' father, and Brett had her sherry-colored eyes. The likeness was enough to give them a sense of kinship.

Seeing her aunt's tear-streaked face, Brett's eyes filled. They embraced. The familiar smell of Leona's skin, the perfumed soap of Brett's youth, made her feel like a child again. They wept freely together. Each of them, in an odd way, was relieved that Earl was gone.

Two days later, Monday morning, rain blew down out of the northwest, bringing with it dismal memories. Brett sat in the room she'd had as a girl, watching the boughs of the tree out front pitching in the wind. The day before, while Leona was in church, Brett had driven over to Ashton where Kady was buried beside their mother.

She had been so young when her mother died that Laura Brett Wallace was more an idea than a person. But Kady affected her differently. Brett's memories of her sister were crystal clear, and they came to her willy-nilly, like finding old photos in a drawer. All that was missing from the puzzle of the past was her father, Jack Wallace—the missing piece that she never expected to find.

Although he was Leona's brother, she had never talked about him much. And whenever Brett screwed up her courage enough to mention him, her aunt would change the subject. Even as a child Brett had suspected that the missing pictures from the photo album were of Jack Wallace.

Brett had no clear memory of her father. All that remained was the recollection of a dark figure in a brown felt hat. The December night when he'd brought her and Kady to Mount Ivy, he'd worn it pulled down, leaving his face in shadow.

Brett remembered the night of their arrival very clearly. During the drive she'd sat quietly in the back seat, watching the shadows dancing on the ceiling of the Rambler sedan every time they passed a car. Because the heater wasn't working, she and Kady were both under a blanket. Kady had fallen asleep, cuddled against her.

When they got to Mount Ivy, their daddy carried them to the porch where Leona was standing under the yellow light, her big bulky sweater pulled tight around her neck, her face wan. As Brett recalled, not much was said. Her father gave her a kiss goodbye—a last, faceless kiss from the man under the brown felt hat.

Brett shivered as the blustery wind gusted outside. It didn't blow through the walls the way it did when she was a girl. A couple of years earlier she and Amory had paid to have the house insulated and new siding put on. Still, just being there brought back memories of her impoverished childhood.

In the middle of her rainswept recollections, Brett caught the smell of bacon frying. Having indulged in enough sentimentality for one trip, she went downstairs to join her aunt for breakfast.

"Fittin' day for a funeral," Leona said.

"Yes," Brett agreed. "It is."

While they ate they talked of inconsequential things. During lapses in the conversation Brett listened to the patter of the rain, remembering, despite herself, her melancholy childhood. It was a necessary indulgence, as important as burying Earl.

Ever since the night of Harrison's heart attack and her conversation with Amory about starting a family, Brett had been thinking a lot about her childhood. Her father, especially, had been on her mind. It wasn't the most fitting occasion on which to raise the subject, but she decided to press her aunt about the man in the brown felt hat.

"Aunt Leona, have you ever heard from my daddy?"

"Jack? No, not since he left you and Kady on my doorstep."

"Do you have any idea where he might be?"

Leona sipped her coffee, before putting the cup down. "Your pa wasn't much for family, Brett. Guess that's obvious enough. If he's still livin', I expect he's got some old widow lady somewhere, lookin' after him."

The unapologetic candor in Leona's voice hit hard. It didn't square with the romanticized picture of her father Brett carried in her head. She blanched.

"Honey," Leona said kindly, "Jack was the sort of man who needed to be cared for. He wasn't up to lookin' after two little girls. Once your mama was gone, he was lost. That's just the way he was."

After sipping her coffee, Brett said, "Amory wants a baby. I haven't decided how I feel."

Leona studied her. "I expect if the judge wants a child, you should give him one, honey." Leona never referred to Amory by name, whether to his face or in reference. The few times she had seen him, she'd been so in awe she'd hardly spoken a word.

"The decision is mine as much as his," Brett replied. "The days of women existing simply for the purpose of breeding and cleaning are over."

"Perhaps that's so in the case of you educated gentleladies, Brett, but in these parts folks do what they have to do to get along, whether they're men or women. There's more than enough drudgery for most everybody. Menfolk could clean a house if they put their mind to it, but they ain't goin' to have babies."

Brett couldn't argue with that. But at the same time she knew there was no point in trying to explain her feelings further. She let Leona have the last word.

After cleaning up the breakfast dishes, they drove in the rental car to the clapboard church in Hope Junction. Brett put her father and Amory from her mind and began to think about Earl. She'd always blamed him for what had happened to Kady, and Leona knew it, even though they'd never discussed it openly.

Brett went forward with Leona to view the body. The only way she could look at Earl was to disconnect her feelings about the man.

The rain had stopped by the time they left for the cemetery. The boggy smell of wet leaves and earth filled the air. The service at the grave site was brief. Earl's deeds followed him into the ground, but Brett found neither relief nor satisfaction in that. After Leona received the condolences of her friends, they headed for home.

Neither of them spoke. Brett felt the weight of the past hanging heavily. There was a quiet desperation in her heart that she didn't quite understand. It couldn't be attributed to Earl, Leona, her father or any other ghost from the past. Maybe it was as simple as being home on a rainy afternoon.

The past few years when a little mood came over her like this, she'd cheer herself by thinking of Amory. For some reason he didn't provide the same solace as in the past. Brett didn't know why, unless it was the anxiety she felt about him wanting a child.

They hadn't discussed the matter again. Amory's spirits had improved right along with Harrison's recovery. Her husband was deeply involved with his work at the Supreme Court. They'd voted to hear the abortion case and Amory's energies were focused there. But in her heart she knew he was awaiting her decision.

The rain began falling again and Brett turned on the windshield wipers. They moved slowly behind a flatbed truck piled high with chickens in wire cages.

The rain stopped by the time they left the highway. Neither of them had said anything since leaving the cemetery. Then Leona said, "I had a surprise Saturday mornin' before you come up from Atlanta, Brett. Mrs. Croft called me with condolences."

"Madeline Croft?"

"Yes, the mother of that boy you was so fond of. I never spoke a word to the woman before then. Lord knows, it 'bout knocked me over."

"Is that all she said?"

"No, she went on a bit. Asked after you. Told me about her boy, seein' as you and him was friends, I guess."

"What about Drew?"

"She told me how he was married and all. His wife's havin' a baby come spring, she said. I don't know why she thought I'd care one way or t'other, unless it was just to gossip some. She knew about you marryin' the judge, of course."

"I didn't know Drew had gotten married."

"It was in the paper a year ago last summer. He married the daughter of an admiral or somethin'. Had their picture. I was goin' to clip it for you, but then I didn't."

"So Drew married an admiral's daughter. Seems fitting, somehow."

They arrived at Aunt Leona's place and, as they were climbing the steps, they heard the phone ringing. They hurried in, but got to it too late.

"Probably wasn't important," Leona said.

They both took off their muddy shoes and, while Leona put away her purse, Brett cleaned the shoes, standing at the kitchen sink in her stockinged feet. As she worked, it occurred to her the call they missed might have been from Amory. So, after finishing the shoes, she asked Leona if she could use the phone. Amory answered on the third ring.

"Darling, I just tried to reach you."

"The phone was ringing as we came in the door. I thought it might be you," she said, taking cheer from the accuracy of her intuition.

"Is everything okay there?" he asked. "Leona bearing up?"

"Yes, she's doing well."

"And you?"

"I'm fine, Amory," she said. "But I miss you."

"I miss you, too, darling."

"Otherwise things are all right?" she asked.

"Well, I have news. We certainly get our share of family misery," he said a bit solemnly.

"Not Harrison . . ." she said, afraid he'd had another episode.

"No. Elliot."

"What's happened?"

"He and Monica have split up. He's arriving tonight from Geneva with Jennifer. He asked to be reassigned to Washington so that he could see the divorce through. If you don't mind, I'll invite him to spend a few days with us until he can make arrangements."

"Of course."

Elliot. Brett felt sorry for him, just as she had from the time they'd first met. But she also was relieved in a way that he and Monica had finally called it quits. They were only making each other miserable. The tragedy was that they'd had Jennifer. What would he do, though, if he ended up with custody, as it sounded he might?

"What happened, Amory? Do you know?"

"He wasn't specific, but I took it to be more of the same."

"Monica's drinking?"

"I'm sure that's part of it."

"How sad."

"He'll be needing us, I'm sure. Not that we're all that special, but when you think about it, he doesn't really have anyone else."

"No, you're right."

"Elliot is fond of you, Brett, so I'm sure he'll be grateful for your moral support."

"I'll do what I can, darlin'. You know that."

"Perhaps it's for the best," Amory said. He paused a moment. "How long do you think you'll be staying with Leona?"

She glanced over at her aunt. "Not long. I may even leave as early as tomorrow. It depends."

"Well, she needs you, too, Brett, so do what you must."

"No, that's all right," she said. "I want to come home."

Washington, D.C.

Elliot ambled along behind Jennifer as she scampered about the waiting area, alternately giggling with glee or pulling up short when she found too many eyes focused on her. Finally he swept her into his arms and carried her to an empty seat where they settled down with her on his lap.

"Hey, angel face," he said, snuggling his face into her neck, "you've got to calm down. Brett will think I brought a little monkey to the airport to meet her."

"*You're* a monkey, Daddy!" She giggled. She squeezed his neck. "Down, Daddy. I want down."

"No, Jennifer. We've played enough. The airplane's arriving. Let's go to the window and see the airplane."

"Is Mommy coming?"

"No, angel. It's Brett."

She seemed to accept his statement at face value, though he knew she didn't have the vaguest idea who Brett was. But hell, how did you describe family relationships to a two-year-old? He couldn't very well say that Brett was her grandmother. The fact was, he wasn't too sure himself how to categorize her.

Three years ago, in India, Brett had been an innocent, a beautiful young woman with whom he'd had a connection of spirit. But who was she now? What would three years of marriage have done to her? Under normal circumstances a woman he'd encountered so casually would have faded from his mind by now. Yet his memories of Brett had stayed with him.

The explanation was simple enough. He'd been emotionally vulnerable at the time, and Brett's goodness—her virtue—stood out in marked contrast to Monica. He knew he'd idealized Brett, blinding himself to her flaws and imperfections. He didn't really know her, as either a woman or a person. She was, above all, a reminder of what was lacking in his life—of what, in wistful moments of reflection, he craved.

So naturally, the prospect of seeing her again intrigued him. Who could dismiss an image like the one he'd been carrying around in his head? He wanted to know what time, and Amory, had done to her.

As the plane approached the gate, Elliot held Jennifer up to the window so she could see it. She grew excited and he lifted her onto his shoulder.

"Look, Daddy! A *big* airplane!"

"Yes, angel, a big airplane."

The jet came to a stop at the gate. They watched a few moments longer, then, over Jennifer's objection, he carried her to the ramp where the disembarking passengers would be entering the terminal building.

He wasn't sure if Brett would be expecting him to meet her or not. Amory had intended to pick her up if he could get away, but when he'd offered, his stepfather was grateful to be spared the trouble. That morning, when Amory had left for the Court, he said he'd try to let Brett know about the change of plan. Elliot had no idea if he'd contacted her or not.

The first passengers began streaming through the doorway and he felt a twinge of nervousness. It was an odd feeling, almost like waiting to see an old love. Brett's impact on his psyche, he decided, may have been greater than he'd allowed.

"Mommy, Mommy!" Jennifer said, clapping her hands excitedly.

He found his daughter's confusion both amusing and ironic. Three years earlier, he'd wondered what it would have been like if he were married to Brett instead of Monica. And now Jennifer was expecting to see her mother, not the woman he'd once imagined in her place. The irony.

A third of the passengers had disembarked before Brett finally appeared. When he saw her, Elliot felt a little start, just as he had three years earlier in Delhi, when she'd first opened the door at the Taj Mahal Hotel.

She was wearing a navy blazer, a gray wool skirt and plain white silk blouse. A carry-on bag was in her hand. She appeared serene, elegant, perhaps a touch aloof. Gone was the twenty-two-year-old ingenue he'd escorted to the embassy party. Brett was a self-assured woman now, a beautiful woman with a presence and a sense of self. He could tell, just by watching her move through the crowd.

She scarcely glanced around as she made her way past the other passengers. He reached out to touch her arm as she went by. "Brett."

She stopped, taking a moment before she realized who he was. "Elliot!" She smiled warmly and looked at his daughter. "And this is the baby. Hello, sweetheart."

Jennifer shrank back shyly and immediately put her fingers in her mouth. They laughed.

"Amory was tied up at Court," he explained, "so we're the substitute welcoming party."

Brett looked into his eyes, seeming genuinely pleased to see him. She was heartbreakingly beautiful. "That's awfully nice of you," she said. "I figured I'd be taking a cab."

They exchanged a long look, and then, as if to underscore the latent affection, she leaned forward to give him a hug.

Elliot brushed his cheek against hers, catching her fragrance. She smelled of roses, making him remember that she had always smelled of flowers in India—lilacs or roses or jasmine. The memory had completely slipped his mind until he'd inhaled her perfume now. That evening they'd been together came flooding back.

Brett turned her attention to Jennifer, pinching her cheek. "You look just like your pictures, sugarplum. Such a pretty little thing."

Jennifer buried her face in Elliot's shoulder. He watched as Brett kissed the top of his daughter's head. "As you see," he said, "she gets her shyness from me."

Brett toyed with Jennifer's soft black curls. "She certainly favors you, Elliot."

He watched Brett, admiring her as she admired his child. India no longer seemed so long ago. The sight of her brought it all back. And yet, in truth, so much had changed, it might as well have been a lifetime ago.

"We brought your car," he said. "Amory said you wouldn't mind."

"Of course not."

He tried to take Brett's case, but she wouldn't let him. They began walking back along the concourse. No one spoke for a time. Then Brett said, "I hope Odie's been taking good care of you."

"She's been great. I think she's enjoyed Jennifer as much as Amory does. I'd have left Jen with Odie, but she's still a little skittish about being in new surroundings. She's been clinging more than usual."

"I'm glad you brought her. This is the first time I've seen the little dumplin', you know."

"It's only the second time *you* and *I've* seen each other," he said.

"It seems like it ought to be more than that by now."

"Does it?"

"I've been in the family long enough that I feel a part of it, but I guess that means nothing as between you and me. When you think about it, we are practically strangers, aren't we?"

"I'm only at the periphery of the Maitland clan," he said. "A part of it almost by default."

"Everybody's fond of you, Elliot."

"I must say it's a much more interesting group since you signed on."

Brett glanced over at him, giving him a little smile. "Are you trying to flatter me?"

"Sure, why not?"

Brett's garment bag arrived at the baggage carousel shortly after they did. Elliot insisted on carrying it to the car, even though he had Jennifer.

"I'll let you drive," Brett said to Elliot, "if we can convince Jennifer to let me hold her."

"I think we'd better consult her," he replied.

Brett brushed the little girl's cheek with her finger. "Are you going to sit on my lap while your daddy drives the car?"

Jennifer shook her head.

"I expect that is asking a lot," Brett said with a smile. "Looks like I'd better drive."

After they got the baggage into the trunk Brett opened the passenger door for them, then went around to the driver's side. Within minutes they were headed up the George Washington Memorial Parkway.

"I know it's no treat to come home from a trip to house-guests," he said, glancing over at her, "but we won't be intruding for long. I only agreed to stay because Amory insisted."

"It's his chance to play granddaddy," she said. "I wouldn't deny him that for the world."

"Still, I know it's a pain in the ass."

"I'm sure I'll enjoy your stay every bit as much as Amory will," she told him, sounding sincere.

Elliot wondered if it might actually be true. She'd been cordial toward him in India. Warm, even. And yet she'd also chided him that evening, accusing him of being cynical—with some justification, too. He wondered if it would be like that between them now—if in some strange, mysterious way they would connect again.

Already he'd felt a rapport with her. Did she feel it, too? It was difficult to tell what she really thought of him.

Only one thing was certain: She was still Amory's wife, still forbidden.

"I'm sorry about your uncle, by the way," he said. "Were you close?"

"No, just the opposite. We didn't have a good relationship at all."

"Then the trip wasn't as dismal as it might have been."

"I felt badly for my aunt, naturally. She and Earl had been married over thirty years."

"Any children?"

Brett shook her head. "My sister and I were as close as they came to having a family."

"You were an orphan for all intents and purposes, then. I didn't know that."

"Amory calls me the Horatio Alger of Supreme Court wives." She gave him a sly grin. "My detractors tend to think of Eliza Doolittle instead."

"You have detractors?"

"In Washington? Are you kidding, Elliot?"

"So the stories about you being a refugee from the backwoods are true. And an orphan to boot."

"Considering I haven't seen my father since I was four and have no idea where he is, I'm virtually an orphan, yes. It's the sort of thing people like talking about behind your back at cocktail parties."

"Does it bother you?" he asked.

"No, not really. I've adjusted. Once Amory explained that when people talk about you it means you are somebody, I stopped paying any mind."

"Amory is very wise."

She glanced over at him. "You lost your father when you were young, didn't you?"

"I was seven. The only living relatives left on my father's side are a couple of second cousins. Mother was an only child. So being without family is something you and I have in common."

Brett reached over and patted Jennifer's leg. "You have a daughter now."

"Yes. She's my family." He kissed the child's head.

"Who's that, Daddy?" she asked pointing at Brett.

"That's Grandpa's wife. She lives with him in his house."

Jennifer considered that. "How come?"

Elliot glanced at Brett. "Do you want to take a stab at that?"

Brett peered up the highway. "Do you have a teddy bear, Jennifer?" she asked.

The girl thrust her fingers in her mouth and nodded.

"Well, your teddy bear lives with you because you love him, and that's why I live with your grandpa."

Jennifer looked over her father's shoulder into the back seat. "Where's Teddy, Daddy?" she asked.

"He's at Grandpa's, angel." Elliot gave Brett a wink. "We're still very literal-minded, as you can see. The philosophical insights into the meaning of love come sometime after kindergarten, I think."

"Or after twenty-five," Brett said.

"Or after thirty-five, in my case," he rejoined. "Some lessons in life come harder than others."

She heard the pathos in his voice and knew he was referring to Monica. She assumed their separation had to be very painful, especially considering the baby. "I'm sorry about everything, Elliot. We were hoping you and Monica would be able to work things out."

"Some things never seem to change," he said. "In this case they only got more complicated."

"Has she abandoned the baby altogether?"

"It's hard to know what she's thinking. Her feelings for me are most definitely unambiguous. I can't say what she feels about our progeny here. It's something that will have to play out, I suppose."

Brett knew he was being cautious in his speech because of Jennifer, but he might not have been all that eager to discuss Monica, regardless. Maybe it was his diplomatic background, but she had trouble reading him, which was odd, really, because in India she had felt as if she understood him so well.

Elliot had aged some over the past three years, but he was as attractive as ever. Even though the first touches of silver were appearing at his temples, he didn't seem as careworn, as wounded, as he had in India. Maybe with his marriage finally over, he was more at peace with himself, despite the difficulties that naturally flowed from any breakup.

"Amory and I will do what we can to make things as easy for you as possible," she said. "We want you to feel at home with us."

"Thank you, Brett, but I really don't want you taking on any burdens."

"Nonsense. It'll be nice to have a little one in the house." She laughed. "Anyway, the work will fall on Odie's shoulders, not mine."

"So far she hasn't complained."

"Odie's a dear. Makes me feel superfluous sometimes, I have to admit." She chuckled. "I think Amory would just as soon let his law clerks go as his trusted housekeeper."

"Continuity becomes more important with age."

Brett wasn't sure if he was taking a jab at Amory, or if it was an impolitic slip. Or maybe she was just being defensive on her husband's behalf. Since Harrison's heart attack, she'd felt a lot more protective of Amory. He seemed older, more vulnerable somehow.

"I've come to rely on her a great deal myself," she said, choosing not to make a point of it. "I'm not much of a housekeeper, so Odie and I together make the ideal wife."

Elliot seemed amused. "The lot of modern woman."

"Don't get me started on the subject," she said.

"Is it a sore point between you and Amory?"

"No, not really. He tries very hard to understand me. He's got a lot of past to overcome."

Brett glanced over at him. If he took her words as a knock on his mother, he gave no indication of it. She hadn't intended it that way—at least not consciously. But she did notice they both had a tendency to take subtle jabs at each other, to spar. It made her wonder.

She realized she liked Elliot a lot. That pleased her, but it also concerned her. He was vulnerable again, just as he had been in India. And she didn't want him liking her in the wrong way.

She was sure, though, that time would take care of things. Elliot would pull himself together and go on with his life. He was attractive, intelligent, and he could be very, very charming. Once his divorce was complete, it wouldn't take him long to find someone else. She suspected women would be lining up for a man like him.

She drove all the way to the Francis Scott Key Bridge before crossing the Potomac into the District. She decided to take the back way to avoid downtown Georgetown, then followed Wisconsin Avenue up toward Chevy Chase.

Their conversation had lapsed, but she felt Elliot's eyes on her. He was probably thinking some of the same things about her that she had thought about him. The chemistry between people could be strange.

When she glanced over at him, she saw that Jennifer had fallen asleep in his arms. "You like being a father, don't you?" she said.

"She's the joy of my life."

"I can see that."

They stopped at a traffic light. He was stroking Jennifer's arm. "Are you yearning to start your family?" he asked. "Or is that too personal a question?"

"You've been talking to Amory."

"No," he said, shaking his head, "not about that."

Brett was silent.

"I see it was something I shouldn't have brought up. I apologize."

"I'm not offended or anything, so don't apologize. It does happen to be a topic under discussion at the moment," she said. "Let me put it that way."

"I won't meddle, but as a parent with some experience, I caution against having children unless you're really dedicated to the idea—whichever of you is reluctant."

"It's me," she said. "There's no need to deny it. The issue is not if, it's when. Amory feels his age is a factor and is reluctant to wait too long. Otherwise there'd be no problem at all."

"I think the 'when' problem is better than the 'if' problem," he said. "We certainly didn't plan on having this one. Unfortunately Monica was in a difficult state when the key decision about whether to have the baby needed to be made."

"You mean whether to have an abortion or not?"

"Yes. Monica was in the middle of her breakdown. I didn't feel I could push the issue since it obviously impacted her a lot more than me, but by the same token I knew she wasn't in any condition to make a reasoned decision."

"That's rough, Elliot."

"It was a tough time for both of us. Fortunately, I like being a father, so Jennifer's not without a parent."

"Does Monica hate being a mother?"

"She loves the baby. To be fair I have to say that. But to answer your question, no, motherhood is not Monica's cup of tea."

"I'm sorry."

"It's not a subject to be dwelled on."

"Have you figured out what you're going to do?"

"I'm trying to get a post in Washington under the theory that it will be easier to cope here. I'll have to hire a nanny, which is going to be tricky. She'll effectively be a surrogate mother."

"This is a situation when your own mother or a sister would have come in very handy—even if you had to hire someone else to do most of the work."

"It's all part of the hazard of modern life, I suppose."

They turned off Wisconsin Avenue. The big shade trees lining the street had changed color. Theirs was a neighborhood of substantial homes—not quite stately, but more than respectable. How many young law-school graduates, just starting out, lived this sort of life?

Brett's thoughts returned to Elliot. "I must say, you're handling the situation well," she said. "My hat's off to you."

"If you want to know the truth, I'm whistling in the dark. The real challenge lies ahead, when I try to live a normal life—be a father and have a career at the same time."

"Not many men have to face that."

"It's eye-opening, I must admit."

"Call on me if I can be of help in any way," she said.

"Thanks. I appreciate the offer, but I think you've got a pretty full plate getting started in your new career."

"Actually, that's not true." Brett slowed the car as they approached the house, a large brick Georgian. "I'm taking some time to kick back a little while I wait for the bar-exam results."

She pulled into the drive, which ran past the house to the garage in back. She stopped the car and set the hand brake.

"I may refurbish Rosemont for Amory and Harrison," she said. "So there's no reason why I can't take on some surrogate-mother duties, as well—assuming you really can use the help."

Elliot stroked Jennifer's head. "Tell you what, we've planned an excursion to the zoo this afternoon. If you want to see if you're cut out for this sort of thing, you're welcome to come along. That way, you can get some hands-on experience and reconsider your offer, if necessary."

She gave him a look. "I consider that a dare, Elliot Brewster."

"No, it really was just an invitation. I made it for my benefit as much as for Jennifer's."

"How so?"

"To see if you're really the stepmother I've always dreamed about," he teased.

Brett gave him a whack on the arm. "Watch your mouth, Mr. Brewster. I don't take kindly to these swipes at my youth and inexperience."

"Is that what I was doing, taking a swipe at you?"

"Yes. Whether you realized it or not, that's exactly what you were doing. Come on, now, let's get that baby inside and feed her lunch."

* * *

Megan Tiernan drove down Connecticut, past the point where it touched Rock Creek Park at the zoo, and then went on to Dupont Circle. There were no parking spaces, so she pulled into a garage, barely waiting for her receipt before hurrying around the corner to St. Matthew's Cathedral. This had been John F. Kennedy's church and it was Harrison's now, unless he had abandoned God as he seemed to have abandoned her.

Inside the church it was cool, and she paused to adjust to the change in temperature. It was quiet and serene, in stark contrast to the chaos outside. She made her way to a pew in a dark corner of the sanctuary, knelt and locked her heart in prayer. A few days earlier in confession, she'd told the priest that she was considering an abortion. He'd admonished her sternly, just as she had expected.

But nothing he could say addressed her primary concern—Harrison. How could she win back his love? That was all that really mattered. Arthur Cadness had probably come closest to touching on the issue when they spoke, though Harrison's aide seemed more concerned with another worldly matter—the election.

The same day Harrison had been released from the hospital he'd sent Arthur to see her. She'd been home, ill with morning sickness and hopeful that Harrison would come to her. But Cadness, a slight, bookish man with horn-rimmed glasses too dark for his coloring, was the one who came to her door.

"Why are you here?" she'd demanded, even before he was in the apartment.

"Harrison couldn't come," the man had replied.

"Couldn't or wouldn't?"

"Couldn't," Arthur had said.

She'd let him inside, realizing that once again Washington was conspiring against her. It seemed so little to ask—to be with the man she loved, to have his child. But there was the matter of a wife. Undoubtedly Arthur had come to make that point.

The sanctity of the marriage vow was the one precept in the Church's teachings that Megan could least accept—and not only because it served her present circumstances. She had seen her mother's happiness destroyed because Megan's father was married to another woman.

She felt no malice toward her father's legitimate family, just as she felt no malice toward Evelyn. But she believed that a decision Harrison made in the 1950s should not preclude him from being with her now.

She had sunk into Harrison's chair the day of Cadness's visit and looked into his flat, unyielding eyes. "What do you want me to do?" she'd asked....

"Wait. Wait until after the election. Just five weeks is all we ask."

"*We?* What is this? Am I having an affair with a committee?"

"I'm sorry. I didn't mean it that way."

"I'm pregnant, Arthur. I'm carrying Harrison's child. Do you realize that?"

"Yes," he answered, bowing his head.

"No reason for you to feel bad," she said. "You weren't there."

"I know it's hard for you. I feel badly."

"*You* feel badly? Don't you see? I don't give a goddamn what you think! It's Harrison I care about. Why isn't he here? Is it because you and all the other geniuses running his life wouldn't let him come?"

"Things are very delicate with the election so close. Five weeks, Megan. That's all."

She began to cry then. She couldn't help herself. Cadness shifted uncomfortably. After a while she wiped her eyes. "Okay, Mr. Genius, what am I supposed to do about this baby while I'm waiting for the election to be over?"

"I can't tell you what to do about that. My job is to evaluate the political consequences of everything we face."

"Arthur...Jesus Christ...this is not a vote on an abortion bill, it's my goddamned life!"

"Are you considering an abortion? I thought you were a Catholic."

"I am. And I'm a human being, too. Right now I want to know just one thing—how Harrison feels."

Cadness looked uncomfortable. He pushed his glasses up off his nose. "I think you know that he loves you."

"Great!" Megan said, with undisguised sarcasm.

"Five weeks," he repeated. "If you want an abortion, get one."

Megan's heart slowed to a half tick. "Is that you talking, or Harrison?"

"It's me," Cadness said.

"And what does Harrison say?"

"He'll come to see you in five weeks."

Frustration had welled in her like steam in a pressure cooker. "For God's sake, who does he think he is—Richard Nixon? Why is he stonewalling me?"

"He's not, Megan. He's a United States senator who has to go before the voters in just over a month. He's married to a decent woman who knows nothing about any of this. He recognizes his responsibility to you and he's prepared to meet it. But he cannot do anything until November 8th, including divorce his wife and marry you."

"Is that what he said? Is that what Harrison said, Arthur?"

He half nodded. "In effect, yes."

"In effect." She shook her head. "God help this country."

"What shall I tell the senator?"

She looked at Cadness with sad eyes. "Tell *the senator* I won't soon forgive him for deserting me like this. But also tell him I love him. Like the rest of the voters, I'm willing to blame his faults on the sonovabitches who run his life."

Cadness got up, took a business card from his pocket and handed it to her. "You'll call me if you need anything," he said.

"You mean if I consider doing something rash—something that wouldn't look good in the papers."

He went to the door. She stayed in Harrison's chair. Cadness said, "He did tell me to say this. This past week, all that's happened to you, has been the most trying experience of his life. And he did say he loves you. That's a direct quote."

"Thank you," she said, tears overwhelming an attempted smile. It was the best she could do....

Megan spent another fifteen minutes in the cathedral, praying. But then she realized her prayers had brought her no insight. God, it seemed, had abandoned her just as everybody else had.

She returned to the garage for her car, her eyes on the sidewalk, her heart beating like a weary metronome. There were three weeks left before the election, but she could wait no longer. It had come down to either killing the child or herself. But she would do neither before she talked to Harrison.

Twice she had tried to reach him. Each time, Arthur Cadness had returned the call. Megan had insisted that she had to speak to Harrison. She'd begged. But Arthur was unrelenting.

She held her stomach as she climbed in behind the wheel of her car. She didn't show yet. Whenever she looked at her naked body in the mirror, the changes she saw were only marginal, the pregnancy mainly evident in a softening of her flesh. But she was pregnant, all right, with a child Harrison didn't want.

Her head dropped forward onto the steering wheel and she began to cry, sobbing mournfully. When the attendant came over to see what was the matter, Megan put the car in gear and drove home.

When she got back to her apartment she got out Harrison's Glenfiddich and poured herself half a glass. Standing at the kitchen counter she quaffed the Scotch, hating herself for what she was doing. Then she went to the telephone and called Harrison's office.

"Tell him," she told the receptionist, "that if he doesn't return my call, he may never again see me alive."

* * *

By the time Brett had unpacked, Odie Johnson was standing at the bottom of the stairs, announcing that lunch was ready. A heavyset black woman, Odie believed that because of her size and advanced years, it was within her province to use her voice when it effectively saved steps.

As Brett went downstairs, she could smell the soup simmering. It brought on a sudden appetite. She'd settled for coffee on the plane, so she hadn't eaten yet that day. When she entered the kitchen, Odie was at the stove, ladling the soup into bowls.

"That sure smells good, Odie," she said.

"I hope so, Miz Maitland. Ain't nothin' special, though. Mostly out of cans with a little of this and a little of that added to the pot."

"It's the this and the that that make the difference."

"You go on 'bout my cookin' that way, Miz Maitland, I don't never dare have no failure."

"My greatest success in the kitchen wouldn't compare to your worst failure, Odie. I'd hate to have to be the one responsible for feeding Amory."

The housekeeper dismissed the comment with a wave of her hand. "You want to do somethin' helpful, ma'am, you can find that man and his chile. They gone off somewhere. I think out back."

Brett went to the back porch. There was a small gazebo at the foot of the garden and Jennifer was chasing Elliot around it, whooping and laughing with joy. She watched them playing in the autumn sun. It had been cold and rainy in Georgia, but Washington was enjoying Indian summer, a time of year she especially liked.

"Is anybody hungry?" she called to them. "Soup's on."

Elliot turned and waved in acknowledgement. It was a deep lot and so it took awhile for them to make their way to the house. Brett waited for them. Jennifer was clinging to her daddy's hand as they wound through the flower beds that were well beyond their summer brilliance.

Over the years Brett had pictured what it would be like to be with her father. Her fantasy had been that he would come for her and Kady and take them home with him to his big house in the city where there were bicycles and sidewalks to ride them on. And he would love them, and tell them that he'd never leave them again.

"*Soup's* the magic word," Elliot said, breaking her reverie. He had come to the bottom of the steps.

She acknowledged the comment with a smile. "Odie makes the best in the world."

He carried Jennifer up the steps, holding the door for Brett. The table in the breakfast nook was set and the piping-hot bowls of soup were waiting. Elliot put Jennifer on the makeshift high chair they'd constructed of old phone books.

"So, did you get unpacked?" he asked as he took a half of a sandwich from the tray and put it on Jennifer's plate.

"Yes, I'm all ready for the zoo." She had changed into fawn pants and a lightweight white cotton sweater.

"We don't mean to coerce you into going if you're tired."

"I stayed at an airport hotel in Atlanta last night so I wouldn't have to leave Mount Ivy at three in the morning. I feel fine."

Elliot gave her a crooked grin, like he knew she was going along because she wanted to be with them, and wasn't just being sociable. He passed her the sandwich plate.

Odie came to the door. "'Scuse me, Miz Maitland, but I gotta know what you be wantin' to do about supper. Justice Maitland, he tell me I should ask you."

"Well, let's see," Brett said, considering the question. "We could go out tonight. What do you think, Elliot? Is Jennifer up to dining out?"

"She's a champ. Considering her mother's distaste for the kitchen, we went out all the time in Geneva. Small children in restaurants aren't much appreciated by the Swiss, incidentally, but it was a matter of survival. We're flexible, though. Whatever's easiest."

"Amory and I like Chinese food and they're pretty good for family dining, if you think that might work."

"Fine. Jennifer isn't a fussy eater."

"Don't worry about dinner, then, Odie," she said. "We'll be going out."

"Suits me just fine, ma'am," the housekeeper said. "Won't hear me complainin' none." She waddled back to the kitchen.

Brett watched Elliot handing Jennifer her cup of milk. "Where is Monica, by the way?" she asked. "Did she stay in Switzerland?"

"No. She's in New York, visiting her family. I expect she'll be coming down here before long to see Jen. If she follows form, she won't be going back to Geneva. Her boyfriend there was a prominent doctor. He wasn't willing to leave his wife for Monica, so she doesn't have a lot of choice but to move on. I'm sure she's recovered from the disappointment by now, and will be on the lookout for another adventure."

There was no indication of pain or sorrow in Elliot's account. He was surprisingly matter-of-fact. Brett glanced at Jennifer, who was busy trying to spoon soup into her mouth. She was too young to follow the conversation. "I take it you left Monica, not the other way around."

"The baby made it tougher than it otherwise would have been, but yes, it finally got to be too much. I pulled the plug."

"Certainly no one can blame you. I don't know Monica, but from what little I've seen and heard, you've had to put up with a great deal. Amory and I both thought it might be over when we saw you in India."

"It was over, Brett. The pregnancy held things in abeyance."

"Bad timing."

"The first thing everybody wondered was if she was mine," he said with surprising candor. "These dark curls and green eyes ought to tell the story, but being the suspicious type, I also spoke to the doctor about blood types and so forth." He shook his head. "So, by default, it turns out my daughter is mine. A sad commentary on the state of my marriage, isn't it?"

"I can't blame you for wanting a divorce."

"Monica told me Robert Farrens was unable to have children." He smiled self-deprecatingly. "She said it more with regret than relief, I might add. That right there pretty well sums up her attitude toward me."

Brett was embarrassed for him. She dabbed her lips with her napkin. "I didn't mean to pry, Elliot."

"No, I've found it's better to be candid. People imagine things to be as bad or worse than they are, anyway."

Jennifer dropped her sandwich on the floor and Elliot picked it up. She did not look pleased to have it back. "Dirty, Daddy. I want a new one."

Elliot got her another half sandwich and cut it in two pieces. "Try to be careful with this one, angel."

"Has Monica agreed to let you have custody?" Brett asked.

"She's ambivalent. That would probably be the best way to put it. I really don't know what's in her mind. I don't think she knows at this point herself."

"It's a shame—for everybody's sake."

"It's been a long time in coming, Brett." He sipped some soup. "But no point dwelling on the morose. What's new at the zoo? It must be a hundred years since I've been."

"It's quite nice. I went with a community children's group when I was in law school a couple of years ago."

"That's right, you're an activist and a politician these days. Destined to be the first female president of the United States."

Brett shook an admonishing finger at him. "As I recall, Mr. Brewster, that was to be our little secret."

"I've never mentioned it to a soul," he said, "though I'm sure the Republican National Committee would pay a small fortune to get their hands on that particular piece of intelligence."

He winked and Brett tossed her napkin across the table at him, which elicited a whoop of delight from Jennifer.

"Just pretend you didn't see that, honey," he said to his daughter. "Ladies are permitted to do that only when they're extremely embarrassed and wish to express their adamant disapproval to a gentleman."

"You've certainly got that right," Brett rejoined.

When she laughed, Jennifer and Elliot did, too. The little girl clapped.

"Let's finish eating and get to the zoo," Brett said. "They've got a new Smokey the Bear, you know."

"Hey, how about that, Jennifer?" Elliot said. "A new Smokey the Bear."

Jennifer responded dutifully with an excited grin, though she clearly didn't know what her father was talking about. He glanced up at Brett.

"You don't realize how much there is in this world to learn until you have a child with no life experience to draw on."

"Jennifer's lucky to have a father who's both sensitive to the issue and who cares. I would have given my soul for that when I was a child."

Elliot's gaze slid down her admiringly. "I'd say you turned out pretty well in spite of the deprivation. Now Amory's the beneficiary."

She blushed like a teenager, taking a sip of iced tea to cover her embarrassment. Jennifer had eaten her quarter sandwich, so Elliot gave her the other piece.

"Smokey the Bear, angel," he said, tousling her curls. "That's somebody you'll be happy to meet."

"Is he like my bear, Daddy?"

"He's bigger, honey. And like all politicians, he has a constituency. But that's politics, not exactly my area of expertise. If you have political questions, you'll have to ask Brett."

Brett gave him a reproving look. "You may not be a politician, Mr. Brewster, but you're definitely a slippery diplomat."

Elliot tilted his bowl to get the last of his soup. "Oh, how you politicians love to flatter."

"Jennifer," Brett said, politely, "may I borrow your napkin?"

It was a perfect day for the zoo. School had started, and since it was a weekday there were few visitors. They tried to make the tour systematically, but Jennifer had gotten obsessed with Smokey the Bear. She expected to see him in each cage or exhibit they came to, and the postcard Elliot bought her only seemed to whet her appetite. So they gave up their planned tour and went directly to Smokey's habitat. They found him asleep. If Jennifer was disappointed, it wasn't evident. She pointed out that her teddy bear slept a lot, too.

The Chinese panda exhibit was comparatively crowded, but they endured the wait because none of them had seen a panda before. Jennifer was not overly impressed.

"How quickly they become jaded," Elliot observed.

"Children or women?" Brett asked, laughing.

He chuckled. "You're definitely a lawyer, Brett. I can see I've got to be careful what I say around you."

They saw the big cats and a few more exhibits before thirst set in. Elliot bought them juice and they sat down at a table in the shade. As they drank, Brett observed him.

Amory's stepson was a very interesting man—elusive, wry. The rapport between them was difficult to define. It wasn't the usual man-woman thing, and yet it wasn't just another friendship, either. Their backgrounds and life experiences had been so different, and yet they seemed to share something.

Elliot watched her watching him. He'd almost asked what she was thinking, but he already knew. Brett was thinking about him, just as he'd been thinking about her. He liked that a lot. And he liked the way she looked, too. Brett had an elegance, even a sophistication about her, yet she was very real. Under the confident facade, he sensed her vulnerability.

In Delhi, he'd felt that she and Amory were mismatched. He understood why she'd married him, he'd even believed her love for Amory. But as he got to know her, he realized that her feelings for Amory were mostly cerebral and that the basis for the attraction went back to her deprivations during childhood. She'd been looking for a father, a relationship that was a refuge. She'd found all that in Amory.

Brett was playing pattycake with Jennifer, relating to her as Monica had never been able to. He watched them, wondering if Brett's reluctance to start a family might not be because she knew subconsciously that Amory wasn't the man she'd spend the rest of her life with. She was a woman of uncommon passion and depth. Amory had intellectual depth, all right, but Elliot would have bet his soul that his stepfather didn't have the slightest inkling of the passions that burned in his wife.

"What are you thinking, Elliot?" Brett asked him. "You have the strangest look on your face."

He chuckled. "If you must know, I was thinking about you...us...the way we seem to relate to each other."

"I don't think that's so surprising," she said. "Friends do relate, don't they?"

"I'm not so sure it's just friendship, Brett."

She was taken aback by the comment and looked at him strangely. His comment had clearly flustered her.

Elliot decided to press ahead, figuring the truth was the truth. "When we met, I was rather taken by you. I was jealous of Amory, to be frank."

"You were having difficulties with your marriage," she said, trying to dismiss it. "It isn't surprising to be envious of someone just starting out and happy."

"What I saw in you had nothing to do with my problems with Monica."

Brett studied his eyes. She swallowed hard. "What are you trying to say, Elliot?"

"Just that I admire you as a person, as a woman." He gave her an unabashed grin. "Knowing you, seeing you

again like this, has brought home just how unfortunate i
love I've been.''

Brett folded her hands in her lap. ''I assume you mear
that as a compliment, and for that I thank you. But I'm no
so sure it's a good idea to take it any further than that.''

''Why? Does it frighten you to be admired?''

''Of course not.''

''Then why are you upset?''

''I'm not so sure we're just talking about admiration, El
liot.''

''My feelings for you are a problem, then.''

She looked him square in the eye. ''Maybe I'm con
cerned because I'm not sure where all this is leading.''

''Where do you want it to lead?''

''I'd prefer that you regard me more like a stepmothe
than . . . whatever it is you regard me as.''

''I regard you as a friend, first and foremost.''

''That isn't what I was hearing just now.''

''Perhaps I was a little too candid about my feelings,'' h
said. ''Shall I withdraw my comments?''

''That might be a good idea.''

''Okay. I withdraw them.''

She smiled politely. ''Well, I trust you've got that out o
your system. I wouldn't want there to be any problems.''

''No, Brett,'' he said. ''Nor would I.''

Despite her nonchalance, she knew her cheeks wer
burning. The intimacy and suggestiveness of his words ha
knocked her off-balance.

Worse, she wasn't sure what his intentions had been. Ha
he been testing to see how receptive she was? Or did he hav
an agenda? Even though he was appealing and clearly ha
a way about him, Brett was fairly certain he wasn't a wom
anizer by nature. This wasn't a routine bid for sexual con
quest, a game. So why had he been so blatant, as though h
half expected a favorable response?

A sudden thought struck her. Could he have taken he
openness and attempt at kindness to be flirtation, a signa
of some kind? Or maybe he'd read her own feelings o

awareness, the attraction she felt, and had drawn unwarranted conclusions.

She quailed at the thought that she could have incited him. Dear God, she hoped that wasn't what had happened.

Elliot seemed not to be upset in the least. Actually, he was smiling.

"You have the most tragic expression on your face," he said. "Are you upset?"

"I guess I am," she said.

Jennifer had started getting antsy and Elliot took her, putting her on his lap. "There's no reason to get upset," he said. "In my work I obfuscate. In my personal life I tend to be direct, say what I think."

"So I see."

"If you understand that, there shouldn't be a problem, then."

Brett wasn't so sure.

They'd finished their drinks, and Jennifer was ready to see more animals. The walk-in Great Flight Cage was next, and it turned out to be the biggest hit of all. Brett watched as Elliot lifted Jennifer high into the air so she could pretend she was soaring with the birds. Jennifer giggled with glee.

An elderly woman standing nearby told Brett that she had an adorable little girl. "I do enjoy seeing happy young families together," she said. "It's not so common anymore." Brett didn't destroy the illusion on either score.

As they headed for the elephants Jennifer wanted to run, so she and Elliot went on ahead. Strolling alone, Brett thought again of the suggestive comments he'd made.

The best way to regard it, she decided, was as a simple difference of opinion as to what their rapport and attraction implied. By letting her know his feelings, he had, in effect, forewarned her. Accordingly she could make sure that nothing would happen.

There was no need to panic. Elliot hadn't actually done anything. Nor, for that matter, had he suggested anything untoward. Harrison, after a few Scotches, had been much

worse. The second time she laid eyes on him, he'd proposi
tioned her, not realizing that she was already falling in lov
with his brother.

No. The best policy was to overlook it. Considering wha
Elliot was going through, she'd allow him his small trans
gressions. It would be up to her, though, to keep things i
perspective.

Elliot and Jennifer were waiting for her at a drinkin
fountain. Once she got there, they started off together. El
liot put his arm around her shoulders in a friendly, casua
way.

"I'm concerned that I offended you, that you're upset.'

"No, don't worry about it. I'm not easily offended," sh
said with good humor. "I consider it very important to b
on good terms with my husband's family."

"I'm glad. I'd like for us to be able to get along."

"We will if we both try hard." She glanced at him from
the corner of her eye. "Speaking of Amory..." she said.

"Were we speaking of Amory?"

"I was. Well, I was thinking of him, anyway."

"And?"

"He'll be getting home soon. Maybe we'd better ge
back."

"Whatever you want," he said.

"I want things to be normal and happy. For everybody'
sake."

"Jen and I will be getting a place of our own soon." H
gave her a wry smile. "That should make it easier for you.'

"I'm fine about things, if you are," she said.

"Amory offered to let us stay at Rosemont for a while
but I'm wondering if it wouldn't be better to get Jennife
settled in someplace here in town."

"In this weather the East Shore would be delightful," sh
said evenly. "I'd take Amory up on his offer, if I were you.'

He contemplated her. "Will you be coming over to th
East Shore?"

"Amory and I might on a weekend. I know he'd like t
see Jennifer as much as possible."

He slowly nodded. "Well, there's lots to consider, isn't there?" Jennifer began complaining, so Elliot swung her into his arms. "Next we see the elephants," he said to her. "Then we have to head for home."

"No, Daddy, let's see Smokey again."

He laughed. "How about if we go see Grandpa instead?"

Megan Tiernan had been lying on her bed for hours. Arthur Cadness had called every thirty minutes or so, but she refused to speak to him, hanging up after a stern rebuke, her voice growing more slurred with each glass of Scotch.

By seven, she'd barely been able to stagger to the bathroom. Apart from aspirin, the most pernicious drug she could find was an over-the-counter sleeping tablet. She dumped the contents onto the counter, raking the tablets into a pile. Several times she tried counting them, but she couldn't focus. There were enough, she decided, however many there were.

She wove back to her bedroom. She'd try one more time before she ended it all. She dialed Harrison's home number, mumbling a prayer. It took three tries before she dialed right. The room was spinning as she collapsed onto her pillow and waited for someone to answer. "Dear God," she sobbed, "please help me."

Evelyn stood at the stove, sautéing the veal, when the phone rang. She took the pan off the burner, wiped her hands on a bar towel, and went to the telephone in the front hall. It was probably one of Harrison's staffers. They never left him alone. This was the first time he'd been home for dinner in two weeks, but that wouldn't stop them.

When she took the receiver and said hello, no one replied. "Hello?" she said again. Then came a faint response, the voice slurred.

"Could I speak with Harrison, please?"

The woman didn't sound familiar. Occasionally cranks or petitioners of one sort or another had managed to get their unlisted number. And so Evelyn was cautious. "May I tell him who's calling?"

"Megan."

"Megan," Evelyn repeated, reflecting on the name. "Does Harrison know what this is regarding?"

"Yes. Please put him on. It's an emergency. Please."

There was a desperation in the woman's voice that Evelyn found alarming. To make matters worse, she sounded as though she might be drunk. "Hold on," she said, and went upstairs to see if Harrison was out of the shower.

He was in the dressing room, toweling his salt-and-pepper hair.

"Darling," she said, "there's someone on the telephone for you. Megan. She says it's an emergency."

He showed only the slightest reaction, but it was enough. His current love interest now had a name—Megan.

"Oh, her," the senator said smoothly. "Staffer. Armed Services Committee. I'll take it here, darling. Thank you."

Evelyn left the room. As she reached the top of the stairs, she heard Harrison's voice.

"Yes, Megan," he said affably, "what seems to be the problem?"

By the time she reached the table in the entry and picked up the receiver, Evelyn could only hear weeping. She listened, but the critical information—whatever it was—had already been imparted. Harrison was making reassuring sounds, and the woman, Megan, was sobbing.

"All right. I'll come over," she heard her husband say. "But I don't appreciate this. I'd planned a quiet evening at home with my wife."

In a moment or two he hung up. Evelyn replaced the receiver, deciding that the guilt she felt about listening in was misplaced. She went to the kitchen and put the pan back on the burner, though she expected Harrison to appear momentarily with a story. It was another four or five minutes before he came downstairs.

"I'm afraid the silly girl has gotten embroiled in a personal problem I'm expected to solve," he announced.

"You?" Evelyn said blandly. "Why you?"

"She adopted me as her father confessor sometime back. The worst part is she's somewhat unstable. And has a drinking problem."

"But is it something *you* have to deal with?"

"Only because she seems to be in pretty bad shape. I'll only be gone a short while, dear, just long enough to make sure she's okay. I'd like to ask a favor, if I could."

"What sort of favor?"

"Would you call Arthur Cadness and ask him to go to Megan's right away? He's been dealing with her and should really handle the matter. I just want to make sure they've got her under control."

"Certainly, Harrison."

He kissed her on the cheek. "You're a dear."

"What seems to be Megan's problem?" Evelyn asked, before he could make his exit.

"She a bit starstruck. New to Capitol Hill. You know."

"You're saying she's in love with you?"

"A crush, perhaps. I may have misled her with the teasing. I'm lighthearted with everybody, as you know. She misunderstood."

"That *is* a problem, isn't it?" Evelyn said, unable to conceal the sarcasm entirely. "I must admit I admire your candor."

He kissed her cheek again. "You *are* my wife, dear. I couldn't fool you for long, even if I wanted to."

"No," she said. "I think not."

There was a touch of uncertainty on Harrison's face, but he didn't dally. "I'll be back in an hour. Perhaps less. Her problem is drink more than anything." Harrison turned for the door. "This can't go on," he said. "Arthur has been advising strong measures and I've resisted—out of misplaced compassion, I suppose." He glanced back, giving a jaunty wave. "Don't wait dinner if you get hungry."

He went to the front hall, grabbed his jacket and went out the door. He'd been smooth, but he realized Evelyn had been smoother, giving him the rope with which to hang himself. To her credit, she hadn't hit him with a broadside. His dear wife was shrewd, levelheaded, but not without her limits. He would hear more on the subject later, he had no doubt.

Megan was another matter. Even drunk, she had to know she'd taken a fateful step. It was virtually an ultimatum, a ploy that could only end in disaster. If this thing blew up now, he would never forgive her.

Harrison backed his Chrysler Imperial sedan from the garage, cursing Megan aloud. It was so typically female, what she had done. Why couldn't she have waited?

He followed P Street east to Dupont Circle, then up Connecticut Avenue to Megan's building. Arthur Cadness hadn't arrived, so he decided to wait in the lobby. If things got messy, he wanted someone he could hand the mop to.

When his aide showed up ten minutes later, Harrison met him at the circular drive out in front. Cadness was a pro, completely trustworthy, totally reliable. He did look strange, though, with his bookish glasses and pasty white legs and running clothes. But Harrison didn't give a hang about the appearance of the people who worked for him—unless it was a woman—in which case his interest might not be primarily professional, anyway.

"I'll go up first," Harrison said, "and deal with her if I can. She was hinting about killing herself. I thought you should be here just in case she'd done something foolish."

"Right," Cadness said.

Now that the situation could be managed, Harrison permitted himself to worry a little. "I hope she's all right."

Cadness nodded. "She's had a rough time."

"Shit, it'll kill me if I've mishandled this."

"What else could you have done, Senator?"

Harrison braced his shoulders and turned to go inside. The ride up in the elevator seemed to take an eternity, yet he dreaded what he would find.

Harrison knocked on Megan's door first, then used his key. The apartment was dark and smelled of Scotch. He heard no sound, even after he called her name. A sense of dread rose in him. He began to fear that she was dead.

He tiptoed to her bedroom where soft light spilled through the doorway. His heart started an upward skip, jolting him into a recollection of his heart attack. How ironic that if it were to happen again, it should be with Megan. God might pay closer attention to these things than Harrison had allowed.

He saw her on the bed, her auburn hair arrayed on the pillow, her hand still resting on the telephone. She was wearing his robe. Her face was deathlike. The possibility that he might be too late made his gorge rise. He stared at her chest. When it moved minutely, he nearly cried out with relief.

He sat beside her, letting his heart find a more normal rhythm. When he'd calmed some, he reached out and touched her face. His anger had been subsumed already by his fear. Now a sudden joy displaced them both. "Meggie," he whispered.

An eye fluttered open. She looked at him for a long moment before she recognized him. "Harrison," she said. And then she began to cry.

He pulled her into his arms, cradling her like a child. "Meggie, Meggie," he said again and again.

"I was afraid you had forsaken me," she sobbed.

"No, my darling. Never."

"They wouldn't let me see you, Harrison. I've been dying, but they wouldn't let me."

"I know. I know. I wish I didn't need them."

She looked up at him, bleary-eyed, her skin blotchy. "I've ruined our baby," she said. "I'm not supposed to drink like this."

"Why did you?"

"I couldn't take it anymore!" she cried, growing hysterical almost instantly. "Oh, Harrison, you don't know how I've suffered. I must know that you love me."

"I do, Megan. I love you."

"And you won't abandon me? Promise you won't?"

"I won't."

She pressed her face against his chest and clung to him, her body trembling. "Oh God, oh God..."

"Megan, you can't do this to yourself. Or to me. It was a mistake to call me at home. You aren't supposed to do that. You knew."

"I'm so sorry. I didn't want to, but I couldn't help myself. I had to see you. I *had* to. I was going to die, Harrison. I was going to kill myself."

"Don't talk that way. Don't think it."

"I can only live if I have you," she said, her fingers digging into his arm. "If you leave me, I'd rather be dead."

"Meggie..."

"Do you hate me?"

"No, of course not."

"What about our baby?"

Harrison hesitated a second. "I love it, too."

"But you'd be happier if I wasn't pregnant, right?"

"It hasn't come at a good time. I should have been more careful. I've blamed you, and that isn't fair. But I've got this election to get through—a few weeks, several days. That's all."

"Everything would be all right if I wasn't pregnant. It would be like before, when we were happy. You'd come here and we'd make love. You wouldn't let those goddamn advisers get between us. And after the election you'd marry me."

Megan sank back on her pillow. Harrison pushed the damp locks of hair off her brow.

"Meggie, all I know is I have to get through these next few weeks. I can't think about anything else. I love you. You know I do. Beyond that, you must trust me."

She stared up at him, and he could feel her probing his soul. She was fighting through her intoxication to reach out to him. Harrison could see he'd made a dreadful mistake by putting her through this. He was probably more to blame for her call to his home than she.

"All I ask," she said, "is another chance."

"I promise you, after the election it will be just as it was before." Harrison leaned down and kissed her tenderly. She kissed him back, probing his mouth for the familiar taste of him. He held her face between his hands, then slid his palm down over her swollen breast. Megan reached for his crotch, and found him firm, distended.

But he took her hand away, kissing the back of it. "I can't now," he whispered. "I have to get home. Evelyn's suspicious." He kissed her again, but he didn't let it deepen as he had before. He stood, but kept hold of her hand. "Will you be all right?"

"Yes."

He smiled as he had smiled at her a thousand times before. He blew her a kiss and went quietly to the door. Megan lay perfectly still until she heard the front door close. Then she bit her lip.

Harrison hadn't told her what to do about the baby. He hadn't even discussed it. But he'd made clear what he wanted. Megan knew. She might burn for an eternity, but now she knew what she had to do.

Talbot County, Maryland

Brett stood at the window of the study, gazing out at the Tred Avon, glistening in the morning sun. Amory sat behind her at his desk, studying the briefs he'd brought along for the weekend. As she looked at the water, she thought about Elliot and Jennifer. They'd gone sailing in Amory's dinghy, enjoying the crisp autumn day. They were out of sight at the moment, having moved beyond the point of land to the south.

Ever since Elliot had left Chevy Chase, Brett had found herself in a peculiar mood. She'd thought about him a great deal, and plainly that wasn't good. Back in India she'd welcomed the connection between them, thinking it might be a basis for friendship. But at the zoo, when he'd said he had special feelings for her, everything had changed.

True, Elliot had made no further overtures. He'd behaved perfectly. But the damage was done. He'd made her question whether there was something more far-reaching buried in their feelings for each other. And not knowing how to handle that left her confused and uncertain.

The problem was she liked Elliot...a lot. Everything about him seemed to fit—his mind, his sense of humor, his irreverent outlook and strong passions. But she knew she had to keep her distance from him. And that would be difficult.

If their conversation at the zoo had put her on edge, dinner that evening had given her cause to worry—not because of anything else he'd said or done, but rather because of her own feelings and her growing awareness. Jennifer had been cranky, so they'd left her at home and the three of them had gone out for Chinese at the Golden Dragon, a Hunan restaurant on Wisconsin Avenue.

After a tentative start, the evening turned festive. She and Elliot consumed copious amounts of TsingTao beer—a mistake in itself—though Amory was a stabilizing influence. He'd stopped after one beer, saying one of them had to be able to drive.

She'd been in a funny mood, wanting to drink more than was usual for her. Perhaps Amory's presence gave her the courage to let loose a little. She sat close to him, sometimes holding his hand or leaning against him, yet she was terribly aware of Elliot. And he was no less aware of her.

The whole situation was arousing, in a curious sort of way, and Brett found herself drawn into it, craving the titillation, despite everything she'd said earlier. It was such an uncommon feeling for her to have that she wasn't sure what to make of it.

Elliot had seemed completely in control of himself. At times he was serious, at other times amusing and wry. She tried not to think about how much he appealed to her, but everything seemed to lead her right back to her awareness. It made her wonder if he hadn't understood right off what she'd been denying—that something very serious was going on between them. It was a distressing thought. And it made him dangerous.

After a few days of separation her obsession hadn't gone away. If anything, it had worsened. She found herself on edge, eager to see him, yet afraid of what was happening to her. She'd done her best to rationalize her feelings, to dismiss them as meaningless. But still, she had an overwhelming compulsion to tempt herself, and to test Elliot.

Staring at the river, Brett noticed the sail appear from behind the trees out on the point. For an instant she wasn't sure it was them. When she saw that it was, a shameful sense of joy fluttered through her.

"There they are again," she said.

"The kids?"

Brett turned to Amory, noting the irony of the comment that he, in his distraction, had missed. Maybe, she thought, he'd been equating her with Catherine. "Yes," she replied, "they're going by now."

Amory slowly got up, setting his brief aside. He stretched and ambled over, slipping an arm around her shoulder to watch the dinghy running before a southerly wind. "Look at that!" he said with a sailor's glee. "Jennifer must be in seventh heaven."

"Why don't you and I go sailing?" she asked rather abruptly. "I enjoyed it that time last summer when we went out."

"That's right. I'd promised you more lessons and we haven't done it, have we?"

"It's not too late," Brett said.

"Yes, and we'll be getting into nasty weather season pretty soon, too." He glanced back at his desk, betraying the train of his thought. "I wish I wasn't so loaded down this weekend." He shook his head. "You know, I haven't even thought about tennis. Used to be I couldn't come to the East Shore without playing a few sets. Suppose I'm getting old?"

Brett gave him a look.

"No point in depriving you, though," he said. "No reason why you shouldn't get out on the water."

"It's not important," she replied.

"To the contrary, I think you should try to get in some sailing. This may be the last good opportunity until spring. Why don't you have Elliot give you a lesson? God knows he's a better sailor than I."

"No," she said. "I'd rather you teach me."

He chuckled. "Why?"

She shrugged indifferently. "You're a patient teacher. Besides, in the future we'll be sailing together. I'd rather learn from you."

He accepted that, though she could tell he considered her rather silly. In truth, she probably was.

Elliot brought the dinghy about and began tacking up-wind. They watched for a minute or two.

She wondered if Amory sensed the rapport between her-self and Elliot. At a superficial level it had to be apparent. But had he intuited more? She couldn't bear the thought of hurting him. Even sparking the smallest disappointment would be unfair.

She took Amory's hand and pressed it to her cheek, wanting to draw all the warmth and reassurance she could. It was the only way she knew to keep everything in perspec-tive.

When the dinghy disappeared from sight again, Amory gave a wistful sigh. "I envy Elliot. What I wouldn't have given once upon a time to have taken my own daughter sailing."

"You haven't given up on the dream, have you?" Brett asked.

He turned to her, taking her by the shoulders. "I didn't mean that as an editorial comment."

"You sounded so forlorn. It made me sad. I want you to take our children sailing."

"It wasn't my intention to bring that up, darling. I don't want you to feel pressured."

Brett kissed his chin. "I didn't take it that way. I've been feeling selfish ever since our talk. I don't want you to think it's not what I want. I've been giving it a lot of thought."

"And?"

"I'm still torn, to be honest. But I'm not closed to your point of view. I understand how you feel."

Amory folded her into his arms. "I don't want you wor-rying about it, darling."

She felt happy just then. As happy as she ever had.

Mrs. Mallory rapped lightly on the open door, causing them to part. "Excuse me, Mr. Justice," she said. "Would you and Mrs. Maitland like your tea now?"

Mrs. Mallory, a bone-thin widow in her early sixties, had been a housekeeper for the family since Anne Maitland's day. She came to cook and clean whenever the family was in residence.

"Wonderful idea," Amory said. "How about if we take it out on the terrace?"

He liked his morning tea, whether he was in chambers or at home. His secretary, Bernice, had always been solicitous of that, as had Odie Johnson in Chevy Chase, and Mrs. Mallory when he was on the East Shore. The housekeeper thoughtfully offered to bring Brett a shawl because of the light chill in the air.

They went out onto the terrace and sat in the large garden chairs, facing the river. A couple of minutes later Mrs. Mallory wheeled out the tea service. She handed Brett the shawl. When the telephone rang, the housekeeper left to answer it.

The small sailboat was not in sight. Brett and Amory sat, silently enjoying the pungent breeze, ripe with autumn smells and salt air. The shawl felt good and Brett cradled the teacup in her hands to keep them warm. The hot liquid was wonderfully soothing.

Despite Elliot's troubling presence, she felt a degree of contentment, sharing Amory's ritual tea. Seeming to share the sentiment, he reached out and took her fingers.

Mrs. Mallory came back out, looking stricken. "That was my niece in Florida calling," she said. "My brother-in-law has been in an accident at work. He was run down by some heavy equipment and is in serious condition."

"Oh, how terrible," Amory said.

"If you don't mind, Mr. Justice, I may have to go down there to be with my sister. I'll be calling her tonight to see if she needs me."

"Of course, Mrs. Mallory," Amory told her. "Whatever you need to do."

"I'll stay here till tomorrow for sure, but after that, I don't know. If I have to go I won't be able to look after Mr. Brewster and the little girl."

"Don't you worry," Brett said. "We'll see that everyone is taken care of."

"Oh, thank you, Mrs. Maitland," she replied. Shaking her head, she went off.

"Poor thing," Brett said when she was gone.

Amory's expression reflected his concern. "Life is certainly unpredictable." He squeezed Brett's hand. "That's why we must savor every moment."

His words made her feel guilty. If she'd felt joy the last few days, it was because of Elliot, not because of her love for her husband. Brett knew that was wrong and shameful, but the more she fought it, the more powerful her growing obsession seemed to become. Still, Amory afforded her a safe harbor and she took comfort in the companionable silence they shared.

It didn't keep her mind from wandering, though. Elliot seemed to drift into every silence, just as each train of thought eventually led back to him. The only way she knew to fight it was to occupy her mind with other things. She tried to find a topic of conversation.

"What are you working on now, darlin'?" she asked.

He named the case, but she'd forgotten what it was about and had to ask him to remind her. During the drive over the previous evening, he'd told her about the key cases that would be argued before the Court during the November session. Several in the area of criminal rights had sounded interesting.

Not having read the briefs, as she often did, Brett couldn't comment, though his work was something they frequently discussed. They both enjoyed the interaction. She regarded it as one of the pillars of their relationship.

Still, Amory was careful never to betray a trust. She'd learned early on not to ask how he would vote—nominally because he often didn't know, but also because of the principle involved. She respected his feelings and let that set the tone of their relationship. But there was a matter coming before the Court this term that haunted her—the abortion issue. They hadn't discussed it in detail because it was so emotionally charged. And yet, Brett couldn't just let it lie.

She pulled his hand over to her lap, squeezing his fingers tightly. "Is this a bad time to bring up a sore subject?" she asked.

"What would that be?"

"I was wondering when you will be hearing arguments on *Russo v. Clayson,* the abortion case."

He nodded, as if to indicate her appreciation for the delicacy of the subject. "I expect we'll be going 'round and 'round on that one, won't we?"

"Not if you don't want to. I know it's hard enough for you without having a petitioner's advocate in your own bed."

He leaned over and kissed her on the cheek. "I'm always interested in what you have to say, darling." He smiled at her in his kind, benevolent way. "The chief scheduled arguments for the January session. The pleadings are apparently voluminous. With amicus briefs still pouring in, we expect to be inundated."

The choice of January was not surprising because a full month separated the end of the December session with the beginning of the January session, allowing more time for the preparation of upcoming cases and writing opinions on ones that had already been decided.

Proceedings of the Supreme Court were highly structured. The Court sat in session two weeks out of every month to hear oral arguments and vote. During the two weeks between most sessions, the justices read briefs and wrote opinions.

Since only the nine justices attended the conferences where votes were taken, the deliberations were secret. The world never became aware of the outcome until weeks or months later, when the written opinions were released.

"I trust I'll have a memo from you to read with all the others," he said.

"Would you mind terribly?"

"No, of course not," he said.

Brett let the conversation rest and Amory was content to do the same. He poured more tea for each of them. Then the dinghy reappeared. Brett stared at Elliot, flickers of torment starting to play again at the edge of her brain.

"Ah," Amory said. "There they are!"

This time the boat moved toward shore, the sail full with the steady breeze. It was making a graceful arc through the gray-green water when it seemed to falter. Brett saw a sudden movement and something small tumble overboard—the baby. "Oh, my God!" she said.

Amory got to his feet.

The boat veered back, the sail going slack. It appeared for a moment that Elliot was going to maneuver back to where Jennifer had fallen in, but he apparently abandoned the notion. They saw him dive into the water.

They went to the edge of the terrace. A hundred and fifty yards away, Elliot grabbed hold of Jennifer and began swimming with her toward the dinghy.

"He had a life vest on her," Amory said. "But they'll both be chilled. Would you mind getting some blankets from Mrs. Mallory while I go down to help them off the dock?"

"Of course."

When she came back out with the blankets, Amory was at the dock. Elliot and Jennifer were nearly ashore. Brett ran down to the water as fast as she could. She got there just before the boat glided in.

Jennifer was crying. Elliot, his dark hair hanging over his forehead, seemed terribly upset. Amory got down on his knees to grab for the bow of the dinghy as it nosed up to the dock.

"She was in the crook of my arm," Elliot said. "I reached for a line to trim the sail at the same time she lunged for a gull. In just one second she was in the drink." He stepped out of the boat, handing Jennifer to Brett, who had an open blanket waiting.

Brett clutched her protectively as she handed Elliot the other blanket. He wiped his face with it. By then Jennifer made it clear she wanted her daddy, and he took her back, kissing her wet little face.

"That cry sounds healthy enough," Amory said, as he lashed the line to the dock.

"She might have gotten a few mouthfuls of water, but I don't believe the damage was severe. With the vest on, she was bobbing like a cork."

Brett took a corner of the blanket and wiped the child's face. "Poor darlin'. She's scared, that's all."

"She's not the only one," Elliot said.

Amory put the second blanket around Elliot's shoulders. "Come on up to the house. We've got to get the two of you in a hot bath."

They walked quickly up the sloping lawn, Amory on one side of them, Brett on the other. Mrs. Mallory had already run a tub in the guest bath. Elliot quickly stripped off Jennifer's wet clothes and put her in the water.

"I'll help her," Brett said. "Why don't you go jump into our shower?"

Amory, who was standing at the door said, "Yes, by all means."

The men went off and Brett bathed Jennifer, despite the fact she wanted her father there. They discussed the troublesome sea gull that had caused the accident, and the scary plunge into the water.

Brett was drying her with a big fluffy bath towel when Elliot came back. He'd slipped on a pair of jeans, but his chest and feet were bare. His hair was still wet, though he'd toweled it partly dry.

Jennifer practically leaped into his arms. For a moment Brett watched father and child cooing. It gave her a profound sense that all was right in the world. Amory had gone downstairs to see Mrs. Mallory about some hot soup for Jennifer, so the three of them were alone.

Elliot looked at her, obviously relieved. "I guess we gave you and Amory a scare."

"Yes," she said. "I guess you did."

He looked at her then, as though for the first time since they'd come inside. He was fully aware of her. And she was conscious of the physical man, half naked, his child in his arms.

Elliot was one of those men with a muscular, but elegantly lean body. His chest was a mat of dark hair. Brett looked him over as subtly as she could.

"Well," she said, sensing her awareness was noticed, "shall I get a change of clothes for Jennifer?"

"No, don't worry about it. I'll dress her."

She gave him a tentative smile and looked away self-consciously. "Perhaps I'll go downstairs then and see how they're coming with lunch." She brushed past him, not waiting for a response.

Elliot watched her disappear down the hall. He'd felt it again—her embarrassment in his presence, an unwillingness to look him straight in the eye. The effect he had on her gave him a certain satisfaction, though it wasn't triumph.

He couldn't help the attraction he felt. There was a rapport between them—a rapport that displeased her as much as it pleased him. That had been evident at the Golden Dragon. Had the two of them been alone, the evening would have gone quite differently.

Brett's marriage struck him as more unfortunate than ever. Despite the fact that she was totally committed to Amory, he wasn't deterred in the least. The attraction he felt for her was as strong as any he'd experienced, and it wasn't just sexual. It was different; intensely emotional; the most remarkable emotion he'd ever felt.

What was worse, he seemed powerless to deal with it, as though it was completely beyond his control. What could he do? Walk away? Deny the reality of it? Hope that it would pass?

The most troubling thing was that his own feelings weren't the only ones to be considered. There was Brett—not to mention Amory. And yet every time he looked at her he felt weak. Helpless, even.

Brett lay on their bed, a stack of briefs beside her. One was open on her lap, but she had been reading the same page for five minutes, unable to concentrate. She kept hearing Jennifer's light cough.

The poor thing seemed to be coming down with something. She'd been cranky at lunch and Elliot had put her down for a nap right afterward. She'd slept for three hours and woken in an even worse mood. Elliot had tried to comfort her, and Brett had read to her for an hour.

Jennifer seemed to appreciate the attention, but then had grown lethargic. At times it seemed she was hot, though there was no obvious fever. Elliot said if she didn't improve by morning, he'd take her to the doctor.

Brett was hardly an expert on children, but she tried to reassure him, as did Amory. Finally, they left him seated by Jennifer's bed and retired to their room. For a while they'd read together, then Amory went off for a long soak in the tub. At the moment he was taking a shower, which he often did after a hot bath.

Brett finally gave up on her reading. She kept picturing Elliot seated beside Jennifer's bed, the light of the small bedside lamp casting shadows on his face. He'd added a fisherman's sweater and loafers to the jeans he'd first put on. His black hair had long since dried and he'd combed it, but he still had the casual look of a sailor just off his boat.

Elliot Brewster was a man of many dimensions, many layers. But it was the hidden side of him that Brett was most aware of. She was sure she saw parts of him that no one else did. And that wasn't because he'd allowed her glimpses of himself others were denied. Most of it wasn't even conscious or overt. She could understand him simply by looking at him, observing him for a moment or two. They shared things—an awareness that wasn't easily defined. And oddly, the more she was around him, the easier it became.

Until he'd shown up at Washington National to meet her flight, she'd thought of Elliot Brewster as the man at the ambassador's dinner party in New Delhi, darkly handsome in his tuxedo, dashing, clever, with a droll sense of humor and a distinctive charm. He was different now. The distance between them, the comfort zone, was gone. Elliot had gotten inside her.

That was troubling, even terrifying. Elliot had shaken her confidence. She was no longer in command of her emotions. In the past, even when she was most vulnerable, she'd always been in control of her feelings. When Drew Croft had hurt her, when Amory had signaled his feelings for her, she'd always been able to rule her heart.

Her marriage had not been a compromise. She'd chosen Amory deliberately. She loved him—the person he was, everything he stood for. She'd been absolutely certain there wasn't another man in the world for her besides her husband.

So what did her feelings for Elliot mean? That she was weak? That she had a vulnerability she wasn't even aware of? The solution was simple, of course. She had to stay away from him.

Eventually the novelty would wear off. After all, she'd gotten accustomed to Harrison. Now he was just Amory's brother. She had him in perspective. It would be the same with Elliot.

The shower was off now and Amory was undoubtedly drying himself. Brett had an urge to sneak in and embrace him while he was naked, but she couldn't always predict how he'd react to that sort of overture. So she decided she would wait until he came out.

She'd thought about sex off and on all evening. When she'd undressed earlier, she'd slipped in her diaphragm, so as not to have to interrupt any lovemaking later. Though Amory didn't feel strongly about birth control, she was always mindful of his Catholicism and didn't want to create a problem unnecessarily.

She heard the whir of the hair dryer and knew it wouldn't be long before he left the bathroom. Stacking the briefs, she took them to the dresser. She looked at herself in the mirror and wondered if Amory would be in a mood to make love. She hoped so, because her need for him just then was especially strong.

She'd thought about having sex with him the past few nights, though she couldn't exactly say her desire had been overwhelming. But now she felt a wave of insecurity and wanted the assurance of her husband's love.

By the time Amory came out she was lounging on the bed, waiting for him in her sheer gown. She was more blatant than usual, but her desires were more blatant, too. He had on nothing but a robe. Noticing her, and smiling with approval, he went to the dresser for his pajamas.

Brett couldn't say that their sex life was completely satisfying. Amory sometimes lacked the energy for anything more arduous than affection, which he never spared her. In the three weeks since the court term had begun they hadn't made love, so she was almost certain he would have the energy and desire for her tonight.

Amory was not the sort of man who measured his sex life by his own need for release. He didn't reserve the last ten or fifteen minutes before sleep for sex, though on occasion Brett would have welcomed even that. Rather, he wanted sex to be the manifestation and culmination of an act of love. He was selfless in that respect, always concerned about her comfort and her satisfaction.

His goodness was one of the reasons she loved him. But his selfless attitude also made her feel unworthy at times. Why that was, she didn't know.

The desire she felt for him now was intense. She stared at Amory's terry-clad back as he went through his drawer, feeling a craving that was as strong as when they first became lovers.

"Before you put on your pajamas, would you come lie here with me for a while?" she asked.

Amory turned at the question, a pair of light blue, neatly pressed pajamas in his hand. He looked at her, immediately understanding the meaning of her words. He casually tossed the pajamas onto a chair and walked to the side of the bed nearest her.

He smiled down at her, his pale eyes a trifle weary. Then ne leaned over and kissed her lightly, his skin fragrant with the scent of soap and shampoo.

Brett scooted over so that he could stretch out beside her. She slid her hand into the opening of his robe and caressed his chest.

Amory had once had an athletic physique and was still reasonably fit from tennis and careful eating habits, though his skin showed the sponginess of age. She opened her mouth slightly, and he pressed his lips firmly against hers. Brett forced her hand down the opening of his robe, so that the tie pulled open and she could touch the soft flesh of his abdomen.

They got up then and together pulled back the covers. Brett removed her gown. Amory turned off the lamp and slid into bed beside her.

As their bodies touched, Brett heard the baby's muffled cry, and she immediately thought of Elliot. The image of him, bare-chested in the bath, came to mind. She remembered how she had wanted to touch him. Fighting off the notion, she focused on Amory, who was running his hand lovingly down her side.

"It's been too long," he murmured.

Brett had an insatiable craving for penetration. She bit at Amory's lip and said, "You don't have to wait, darlin'. Take me now, if you want."

"I can wait," he replied, running his fingers lightly over her breasts.

She didn't object. Better they do it his way. But she kissed him forcefully all the same. When Amory had become sufficiently aroused, he slid over her, careful to keep his weight from pressing down too heavily. He guided himself into her and Brett gasped pleasurably at the sensation. He rocked on her gently and, though he lasted a long time, she was not quite ready when he came.

Then, down the hall, Jennifer cried out. As before, Brett's thoughts went to Elliot. She pictured his face, his expression softly mocking. At that moment she hated him—hated him for intruding on her lovemaking with Amory, for making her think of him, for making her imagine what it would be like to be in his arms, in his bed. Lord, what was the man doing to her?

The next evening Brett sat on the bed, her half-packed suitcase open beside her. Amory's bag was already by the door, ready to be taken to the car. He was downstairs, discussing arrangements with Elliot.

The day had been a traumatic one. Jennifer had had a terrible night, having developed a fever. Elliot had been up with her, and had gotten hardly any sleep. Then, right after breakfast, Mrs. Mallory had received another call from Florida. Her brother-in-law was dying and she was needed at her sister's side. Brett had told her to go immediately; the house would survive until she was able to return.

Then, while Brett had been helping Elliot give Jennifer a sponge bath, the child had become sluggish, almost delirious. It had scared them and Elliot had decided to take her to the emergency room at the hospital in Easton.

They had admitted the child for tests, fearing she might have meningitis or something else as virulent. So Brett and Amory had spent the better part of the day at the hospital with Elliot. It wasn't until dinnertime, after Jennifer had fallen asleep, that the three of them had come home. Elliot planned to return to the hospital for a few hours that night after she and Amory had left for Washington.

While they were packing, Amory had hinted that if she wanted to stay on to help Elliot, he'd understand. With Mrs. Mallory gone, her assistance would undoubtedly be welcome. But she didn't want to be alone with Elliot. She was afraid of her own feelings.

Sitting on the bed now, she agonized. Amory couldn't know how Elliot affected her. Still, she knew darn well that she shouldn't have to rely on Amory to protect her from herself. She had to take responsibility for her own life. But would she really be doing Elliot any favors by staying?

She heard Amory coming up the stairs, and felt torn. When the door opened and he stepped into the room, she looked at him dolefully. His expression was solemn.

"Brett, darling, I hate to pressure you," he said, "but would you mind staying to help Elliot? He asked me if I thought it would be too great an imposition on you."

"He asked that I stay?" she said, flushing.

Amory nodded. "It's up to you, of course. I'm just passing along the request."

She knew Elliot's motive wasn't innocent, and it made her angry that he would use Amory that way. She didn't like the cynicism implicit in that. "I'm sure he's just trying to be polite. He'll be spending all his time at the hospital, so what could I do to be of help?"

"I expect he'd like the moral support as much as anything. But he knew it would be an imposition. He said not to pressure you." Amory rubbed his chin thoughtfully. "If anyone should stay, it's me. It's my family, not yours."

"You can't be absent from the court, darlin'. If leaving Elliot alone truly concerns you, I'll stay. I don't want it weighing on your mind. I just..."

Amory waited. "What, Brett?"

"Oh, nothing. It's too bad it isn't summer and the court wasn't in session. I'd rather you be here, too."

He put his arms around her. "I hate abandoning you both," he said.

"Well, if Jennifer needs a lot of care I suppose we can hire a nurse to help Elliot. She'd be able to do a lot more than I."

"I don't think it's nursing that Elliot cares about. He's very fond of you, Brett."

She was surprised. "Why do you say that?"

"He told me. Anyway, I could tell. I'm pleased."

Not wanting him to see her color, she turned away. "I want everybody in your family, all your friends, to like me," she said.

Amory took her into his arms. "The whole world adores you, Brett. But nobody so much as I."

She kissed him on the cheek and returned to the bed and started unpacking. "There's really no good reason not to stay," she said, trying to make Amory feel better. "I'm not doing anything but sitting around waiting for the bar results."

Amory didn't reply but she knew he was pleased. She would endure whatever she had to for him. And if she suffered, she'd suffer in silence.

Amory waited until she'd finished unpacking, then he took his bag and they went downstairs together. His bulging briefcase was sitting in the entry hall. Elliot sat on an upholstered bench by the door, leaning on his knees, his head bowed. Despite her resentment, Brett felt sorry for him. Jennifer's illness was real enough. Maybe she'd been too quick to be critical. Any feeling Elliot had for her might be the last thing on his mind at the moment.

"I'm going to stay for a day or two," she told him. "Until you and Jennifer are back on your feet."

He didn't quite smile, but he looked pleased. "I would appreciate it, Brett," he said.

She and Amory exchanged glances. "I'll be going now," he told them. "Please let me know how the baby is doing." Amory clasped Elliot on the shoulder.

A sad, sardonic smile tugged at the corners of Elliot's mouth. "Life can throw a lot of curves, but a sick kid is one of the worst."

"I'm sure she'll be fine," Amory said reassuringly.

"I just called the hospital and the nurse said Jennifer's still asleep, but she's got a high temperature. They've put her on an ice bed to break the fever. The doctor will do the spinal tap tonight and I want to be there."

"I'll go with you," Brett volunteered, knowing it was what both of them wanted to hear.

"Thanks," Elliot said. He looked at his watch. "I thought I probably ought to give Monica a call. She's entitled to know what's happening." There was a trace of bitterness in his voice. "I'll try to reach her now."

Neither Amory nor Brett said anything as they watched him head for the study. Then Brett told Amory she'd walk him to the car. As they went out into the dark night, she slipped her arm through his.

"I wish you were staying, too," she said, shivering in the brisk air.

Amory sighed. He was oblivious to what she truly meant. But then, Brett herself was unsure. Had she taken secret pleasure in what had happened? Was she glad that she'd been forced to stay, that the decision hadn't come by her own initiative?

If only she could come right out and discuss it with Amory. But she couldn't, even in the most careful, diplomatic terms. Anyway, nothing had happened. If she'd been unfaithful, it had been only in her imagination.

"I love you, Amory," she said, pressing her head to his shoulder.

"I know you do," he replied, stopping at the side of his car. "And I love you." He kissed her lightly. "Take care of them."

She nodded, staring at his dear face, faintly lit by the light coming from the porch. She felt her throat thicken with emotion. Amory kissed her and got into the car. She had a powerful urge to run around to the other side and get in with him, but he had to go, and she had to stay.

Amory backed the car around, the brake lights flashing in the darkness as he stopped and changed gears. He went out the drive, the tires crunching the gravel like it was a pit of bones. She waited until the two red taillights were out of sight. Then she went back to the house, feeling lost and apprehensive.

They left for the hospital within minutes after Amory had gone. They hardly said more than a few words during the drive. Elliot's mind was obviously on Jennifer, and hers was on Amory. But the fact that they were alone now was inescapable.

At the outskirts of town she looked over at him.

"Were you able to reach Monica?" she asked.

"Yes. She's coming down as soon as she can get a flight."

"That will be nice for Jennifer."

"Yes, I suppose it will."

In a few minutes they arrived at the hospital. Though it was late, the doctor, a young, heavyset man named Dormann, was there to greet them. He took them to a small reception room where he told them he suspected that Jennifer had meningitis.

Elliot listened intently. "How serious is it?"

"It can be very serious, Mr. Brewster. But we got her early, we're keeping the temperature down. Jennifer's not a happy camper at the moment. If it's meningitis, as we suspect, the crankiness is consistent. The infection causes a swelling of the membranes covering the brain, creating inner cranial pressure that can be very uncomfortable. Adults have been known to become violent. I'd like to get her on a course of antibiotics as soon as possible."

The necessary paperwork was brought in. Elliot signed, then they went to see Jennifer. She was awake and in a foul temper. Her crib was covered with a net to keep her from climbing out. Elliot had to reach through the bars to touch her face.

Jennifer wore only a pair of underpants and she was shivering. She cried at the sight of her father. Brett saw tears fill Elliot's eyes and a lump formed in her throat. She pulled up two chairs so that they could sit beside the bed. Jennifer whimpered as Elliot stroked her head.

A short time later the technicians took the child away. They went to a waiting room, and sat down across from each other. The coffee table between them was piled high with old magazines.

"I'm really sorry this had to happen now," she said. "You don't deserve it."

"It was my fault for taking her out in the boat."

"You don't know that's when she got the bug."

"Well, the shock couldn't have helped."

"You're a wonderful father, Elliot."

Her words appeared to cheer him, but he was clearly distressed. He said nothing for a while, then told her he hoped she wasn't upset that he'd arranged things so that she would stay. "It was for me as much as for Jen," he said.

She searched his eyes, wanting to know what he meant, and at the same time not wanting to know. "I hope it isn't a mistake," she said warily.

"Being alone with me?"

She nodded.

"It can't be a mistake unless you make it one."

"I know how *I* feel, Elliot. My concern is with you. I don't want you to misunderstand. If we're here together, it's for Jennifer's sake. It's important that you know that."

"I've been duly warned," he replied.

Brett looked away, biting her lip. "I hate having to say something like that, Elliot. It makes me feel . . ."

"Feel what?"

"Hard-hearted," she said, looking directly into his eyes. "I don't like this . . . what's happening between us."

The faintest smile touched his lips. "At least it's mutual—the feeling, I mean. I'd hate to think I have to go through it alone."

"Don't make too much of it," she said, letting her pique show.

Elliot studied her. Brett got up and walked across the room. "God, why am I talking this way? You'd think we'd had an affair or something." She laughed bitterly. "This is crazy, Elliot. What's the matter with us?"

He didn't answer. The same question may have been troubling him. She paced back and forth for several moments, feeling more and more anxious.

"You can take the car and go back to the house, if you'd prefer," he finally said.

"I know that. I'm here to help. So I will. Just forget what I said. I don't even know why I opened my mouth."

"Dealing with my feelings toward you isn't a picnic for me, either," he said. "It's like being on a double date with the wrong girl."

"Please," she said. "Don't talk that way."

"I'm being honest."

"Right now, honesty is not what's called for."

"What is called for, Brett?"

"Decency. Honor. Integrity. Loyalty. All the qualities we need to be showing, but aren't."

Again Elliot did not respond. He didn't have to. Finally her courage failed and she looked away.

"Maybe I'll go out and walk for a while." She went to the door, feeling his eyes on her. "I saw a water fountain up the hall," she said. "I'm going to get a drink." She left the waiting room.

Elliot sat staring at the wall, thinking about what she'd said. She'd conceded that she was obsessed, and yet, he could hardly take heart from that admission. Each step only led toward trouble. He'd known that when he'd spoken to Amory about Brett staying, but that hadn't kept him from making his request. He'd plunged ahead, knowing exactly what it could lead to.

If there was any good in it, it was that things were finally coming out into the open. Brett, to her credit, hadn't tried to pretend. He supposed she saw a tussle as inevitable and wanted to deal with it head-on.

She returned and a moment later Dr. Dormann came in. The spinal tap had gone well, he told them, and once everything was analyzed they could proceed with heavy doses of medication, probably within the hour, assuming the tests turned out as he expected.

He and Brett returned to Jennifer's room, and they waited for her to be brought in. Lying listlessly in the nurse's arms, his daughter barely recognized him. But when he'd held her for a few minutes, stroking her head, she cuddled against him and fell asleep. The nurse took her then and put her in the bed. After fastening the netting, she left.

They sat in silence, side by side. A pale green light faintly illuminated the room, creating a sense of unreality. Elliot gradually relaxed, with his hand resting on the arm of

Brett's chair. For several moments the only sound was the soft whir of the ventilation system.

Then he took Brett's hand. She didn't recoil as she might have. Her demeanor was passive. "Thanks for being here," he said. "I don't know if you realize how much I appreciate it."

"I do, Elliot."

He caressed her limp fingers. Her flesh felt cool. When he glanced at her, he saw she was watching his hand touching hers. She almost seemed removed from what was happening, and for once, he couldn't be sure what was in her mind.

"What are you thinking, Brett?" he asked. "Please tell me."

"Nothing."

"No, I want to know," he said.

"I was thinking about my father, if you want to know the truth. Seeing you with Jennifer tonight brought back memories from my childhood." Tears filled her eyes without warning and began running down her cheeks. She pulled her hand free and wiped them. "But never mind, I'm just emotional. You're the one in need, not me."

As if to emphasize the point, she got up and went to the window, pulling the blackout curtain aside to be able to look out at the night. She could hear the wind and shivered, though the temperature in the room was quite comfortable.

The lights of Easton were sprinkled in the darkness. Overhead she could even see a few stars. A sense of loneliness filled her. She recalled a thousand autumn nights like this in Mount Ivy when she was a kid, growing up. Lonely nights when she pressed her face close to the windowpane and peered out.

She only half heard the sound of Elliot's chair as he got up. She became aware of him standing behind her. Then she noticed his face reflected in the glass.

She flinched when he put his hand on her shoulder, though she'd expected that he might touch her. He slid his hand down her arm, and then, tightening his grip, he turned her toward him. She looked into his eyes, feeling a curious weakness, a helplessness in the face of what was coming.

Without a word he folded her into his arms and held her.

At first she felt wooden. But the seeming sincerity of the gesture neutralized her resistance. She closed her arms around his waist. He stroked her head, as he had Jennifer's earlier.

She pressed her face against his neck, half laying her head on his shoulder, trying not to think or draw implications from what was going on. It simply had happened; that was all.

She was aware of his good, masculine smell and the comfort she felt. In some form this had been coming, and now that she was in his arms, a burden had lifted. They were simply acknowledging the closeness they felt. The high emotion of the evening had given them the excuse.

Her feelings were ambivalent, though. She was equally disposed to cry or laugh. What they were doing was both wrong and right.

When he kissed her hair, her eyes began to well with tears. But then they moved apart, their hands the last thing to touch, lingering before falling away.

It was all her conscience could endure and Elliot seemed to understand. They'd shared simple affection, a little human contact. There couldn't be more than that. There just couldn't be.

Even before Elliot's eyes opened, he realized where he was because of the stiffness of his neck and the distinctive scent of the plastic covering on the couch. He held his wrist up to read his watch. It was nearly eight in the morning. He'd been asleep for over two hours—ever since Brett had come in to relieve him.

They'd arranged it so that one of them would always be with Jennifer. It had worked out well; the sleep they'd managed to snatch with each respite had enabled them to go on.

Dr. Dormann, who was going into the child's room as Elliot made his way along the hall, seemed to have made it home the night before. He had on a fresh shirt and tie. He greeted Elliot pleasantly.

"The nurses say our young lady had a comparatively comfortable night," he said.

"Compared to what?"

The doctor chuckled. "Some meningitis patients."

They went into the room and Brett, who was resting, her head propped in her hand, got up. They stared at each other. It was the look of people who knew something the rest of the world didn't.

While he'd been alone with Jennifer, he'd thought about Brett a great deal. In a way, she'd already given in to her feelings for him much as he'd given in to his feelings for her. And yet he wasn't quite sure how to interpret it. But now that morning had come, they would be facing the new reality in a different light.

The blinds had been drawn to protect Jennifer's eyes, but daylight was slipping through the cracks. He glanced into the crib. Jen was still dozing, though judging by the way she'd begun fidgeting, she was about ready to wake up.

The nurse removed the netting and the physician rubbed the child's tummy to waken her. "I know you'd like to snooze, Jenny," he said, "but we've got to have a look at you."

Jennifer awoke and, as Elliot and Brett watched, the doctor examined her.

"I would say the medicine is beating the bug," he announced. Then, with a smile at Elliot, he said, "She looks pretty good, Mr. Brewster, all things considered. If we continue to progress, she could be out of here in a couple of days."

"That soon?"

"Kids have a way of bouncing back quickly. The fever's under control. Now she just needs to get her strength back." The doctor looked at Brett, pausing before making his next statement. He knew she wasn't the mother, and to an outsider the relationships had to be confusing. "Getting lots of juice down her will be up to you two."

Elliot was heartened by the news. He glanced at Brett, who was smiling, too.

"We'll need to do some tests now, so it might be a good time for you to have breakfast."

They decided it was a good idea and went off together to the cafeteria. They each got a cup of coffee and a pastry, then sat across from each other at a Formica table in the corner of the room. Whatever self-consciousness had existed before was gone. They had, it seemed to Elliot, passed their Rubicon.

"We must look like a couple of vagabonds," Brett said, running her fingers back through her hair.

Elliot rubbed his stubbled chin. "I do, anyway."

"I feel like I was born in these clothes."

"Maybe we can run upstairs after we finish and see how Jennifer is doing, then I'll drive you home," he said. "I'm sure you could use some sleep."

"Not as much as a hot bath."

Their eyes locked and a flicker of distress crossed her face. He felt that a delicate equilibrium had formed and he didn't want to upset it. He sensed keeping the conversation going was called for.

"When we get home, I think I'll go for a long run. Or take my scull out on the river. I've got to burn off some energy."

They finished their breakfast and went back up to Pediatrics. Monica was there waiting for them. She was standing in the middle of the room, holding Jennifer, while the nurse looked on.

Monica only gave Elliot a cursory glance before her eyes fixed on Brett. "Well, I had a hunch the surrogate mother I've heard about would turn out to be Stepgrandmama, but I wasn't sure."

Elliot and Brett exchanged looks.

"Hello, Monica," Brett said.

The other acknowledged her with a nod. Then she shot Elliot another glance, this one more accusatory. "This is as fast as I could get here. It's too bad Jennifer wasn't with me instead of you, Elliot."

"That could easily be said on a number of other occasions when she needed a mother, and you weren't available," he replied caustically.

Monica pointed her finger at his heart. "Don't you start on me, you sonovabitch!"

He glanced at the nurse, then gave his wife a dark look. There was no point in getting into a shouting match, so he chose to ignore the profanity. "I take it you want some time with Jennifer," he said evenly.

"I didn't fly down here to shoot the breeze with you."

Jennifer wriggled uncomfortably. The nurse took a few steps toward her, but Monica refused to give her daughter up.

"How long do you plan to stay?" Elliot asked.

"Seeing as the baby is past her crisis, I guess I won't have them put up a cot. But I want to talk with the doctor and spend a few hours with her anyway." She arched a brow. "Does that meet with your approval?"

He ignored the sarcasm. "I merely wanted an idea. We're going home. I see no point in hurrying back if you're going to be here. I'll let you have your time with her."

"You'll *let* me! How very kind, considering I'm her mother."

"Well, now's your chance to show it, Monica. I'm sure the nurse will brief you on Jennifer's need for liquids." He took Brett's arm and they moved toward the door.

"It would suit me just fine if you never came back," Monica said.

Elliot glanced over his shoulder, catching the dark look on his wife's face as the nurse took Jennifer from her arms. "Oh, I'll be back," he said. "If there's one thing you can count on, it's that."

* * *

It was midafternoon before Brett awoke. Amory's pillow smelled of him and she clutched it to her face, comforted by his scent, just as she had been when she'd fallen asleep.

Her internal clock was thoroughly confused, she could tell. She'd had a good rest, though, so she got out of bed, dressed and went downstairs. There was a note from Elliot on the bench at the foot of the stairs. It said he'd returned to the hospital and would stay with Jennifer until she'd gone to sleep for the night. He wrote that she shouldn't wait dinner, that he'd fix himself something when he got back.

At first she was miffed that he'd gone off without her, but when she thought about it she decided she was glad. She'd needed the sleep and some time to be alone and think. She wandered into the sitting room where Anne Maitland stared down at her from the portrait over the fireplace.

Perhaps it was Anne's dour, admonishing expression, but Brett suddenly realized that she hadn't phoned Amory with an update on Jennifer's condition. It had been thoughtless of her. So she went to the study and telephoned him at the Court building in Washington. He came right on the line.

"Oh, the poor little child," he said, once Brett had filled him in.

"The doctor feels it wasn't nearly as bad as it could have been."

"That's a blessing. How's Elliot doing?"

She told Amory about Monica's visit.

"Well, I suppose that's to be expected."

"She seemed very possessive of Jennifer," Brett observed. "I hadn't expected that, somehow."

"Well, despite whatever else Monica is, she's still the child's mother."

"Do you think she may have changed her mind about custody?" Brett asked.

"It's hard to predict what's in that woman's mind. Her history indicates she likes to be difficult. Anything to jab Elliot. I suspect, however, that having the full burdens of parenting are not what she's after."

"I hope not," Brett said. "From what I've seen so far, I don't much care for Monica." She sighed. "So what's new with you, dear?"

"Busy as always. I did have a strange call from Harrison just before lunch."

"What about?"

"Apparently his people are getting very optimistic about his reelection. . . ."

"That ought to please him."

"Well, you know Harrison—enough is never enough. Anyway, he wanted to know what I was going to do in the *Russo* case."

Brett was shocked. Justices didn't discuss such things with senators, even with one who happened to be a brother. "You mean, how you were going to vote on abortion?"

"I guess so. Apparently he had some sort of inkling Donlevy might spring the abortion issue on him in the last weeks of the campaign, and Harrison wanted to make sure I didn't do something that would end up making him look bad."

"What did you say?"

"I told him I hadn't even seen the briefs and that the opinion wouldn't be handed down for at least six months. He got the message, but wasn't very gracious about it, I must say. I don't know what he was thinking. Harrison hasn't been himself since his heart attack."

"At least he called you before making a foolish statement of some kind in public," Brett said.

"I suppose we have that to be thankful for."

Amory's voice, so familiar, made her long for him—his love, his reassurance. She wondered how Elliot could have distracted her so.

"Well, I've got the chief dropping by in a moment to discuss a draft opinion. I've got to go, darling," he said.

"Okay. I'll call tomorrow and let you know how the baby's doing."

"I'll be in chambers all day and at home all evening. You can reach me anytime."

"I love you, Amory."

"And I love you, darling."

She hung up, feeling a stab of sadness. And also guilt. Why did her words of love feel so hypocritical?

At least their conversation had brought a breath of reason to her thinking. It helped her to remember who she was and what she was about. Elliot, and this strange identification she felt with him, were something she'd have to learn to live with. That's all there was to it.

Still, there was no denying that something notable had happened. The titillation she'd been feeling had given her the first tremor of doubt she'd ever had about her marriage. She hated that; hated the fact that in Elliot she'd found something she hadn't experienced with Amory—a deep longing, a nearly overwhelming desire to be with him. It was a physical thing, and it was very powerful.

Brett paced restlessly, alone in the big house that was her husband's and Harrison's, not hers, trying to decide what to do. Finally she settled into the wing chair facing the fireplace and stared up at the portrait of the woman who would have been her mother-in-law, had she lived. The eyes were accusing, making her feel guilty.

The next few hours passed slowly. Brett watched the evening news in the den. George Bush's now commanding lead in the polls was the principal story. The election was all but over, according to the report. Any chance there'd been to reverse the self-indulgent excesses of the Reagan years was lost.

She turned off the television and tried to decide what else she could do. She didn't want to read. And she didn't want to be alone with her thoughts anymore. Whenever Elliot entered her mind she got anxious.

She went to the kitchen to brew a pot of tea. While it was steeping, she sat at the table, watching the second hand moving around the old yellowing plastic clock on the wall. After she'd drunk two cups of tea, she rinsed the cup and saucer and set them aside.

Glancing out the window over the sink, she saw that the dark clouds that had come in at dusk had signaled stormy weather. The wind had picked up, whistling around the eaves of the old house. Being alone didn't frighten her, but she was eager for company all the same.

It wasn't certain that Elliot would be back for dinner, but she decided to cook enough for him, just in case. They could always warm it up. She went through the pantry, searching for something imaginative to prepare. There was a case of Bordeaux that she and Amory had delved into several times in the past. Brett selected a bottle, wondering if it might seem inappropriate. In the end she decided their relationship was too open for games. She would do as she wished.

Mrs. Mallory had left some fresh chicken stock, so Brett made vegetable soup and put a couple of small sirloins out to thaw. When Elliot still hadn't returned by eight-thirty, she began to wonder whether he'd already have eaten at the hospital. Or maybe Jennifer had taken a turn for the worse. The thought of that made her start to worry about the child. Once again she'd been so preoccupied with herself that she'd lost perspective.

She went to the front hall to peer out at the dark road leading to the house. There was no sign of Elliot.

Brett paced about the empty house, listening to the wind. It had grown stronger over the past hour. Gusts occasionally rattled the windows, making her shiver. She went up to her room and got a sweater. She was back in the salon, again contemplating the portrait of Anne Maitland, when she heard a car. She practically jumped to her feet.

By the time she got to the entry, Elliot appeared on the porch. She opened the door to a gust of wind and he came in. He looked tired.

"How's Jennifer?" she asked.

"Much better." A smile replaced the lines of weariness on his face. "When I left she was sleeping like an angel."

"I'm so glad. I was beginning to worry when you didn't come back."

"I left a note."

"I know. I just expected you before now."

They looked at each other as he removed his coat and tossed it on the bench. They stood facing one another.

"Are you tired?" she asked.

"Yeah."

"Well, I've got a nice dinner planned. I hope you didn't eat at the hospital."

Elliot shook his head. He was staring at her, that now familiar somber expression on his face. He looked as though he might want to take her into his arms. Just to be close. She moved toward him and he did embrace her.

Her body trembled a little—she was more aware of the physical man than she'd been when they'd embraced at the hospital.

When he kissed her temple, she realized it had become more than she intended. She stepped back then, slipping from his arms. "You must be so relieved that Jennifer's better," she said.

"I am."

"Well, come on," she added self-consciously. "Let's eat." She led the way back through the house to the kitchen.

"So, I guess Monica was happy, too," Brett said.

"She'd left by the time I returned."

"Oh?"

"She'd put in an appearance, done her duty as she saw it, and took off."

"Did she go back to Boston?"

"I don't think so. She told the nurse she'd be in Washington for a few days and left a number for them to contact her. I didn't inquire further."

Brett pointed to the table. "Hope you don't mind the informality. Sit down. I'll put on the steaks while you have some soup. There's wine there. You pour."

They talked about Jennifer while they ate, but their awareness of each other dominated the conversation. Brett tried not to do or say anything suggestive, but it was hard not to feel the intensity of his presence.

Elliot, exhausted, drank his wine freely. Brett pushed her glass away after consuming half of what he'd poured. Her fingers trembled, so she hid them in her lap.

"For someone who can't cook, you did pretty well," he said. "You went to extra trouble. I appreciate it, Brett."

"It was the reason you asked me to stay, wasn't it?"

Elliot smiled faintly, but didn't respond.

When they'd finished eating, she cleared the table and put the dishes in the dishwasher. Elliot sat at the table, sipping the last of his wine.

"Shall we go into the salon and have a cognac?" he asked when she'd finished.

"I'll join you, but I really don't care for more to drink."

"Why?"

She looked for a clue to his meaning, but found none. "No particular reason. I just don't feel like it."

They went into the salon and, while Elliot poured himself some brandy, she stepped over to the windows and looked out at the night. When she turned around, Elliot was standing across the room, staring at her. He slowly walked toward her and then she knew. The whole evening—the dinner, the wine—it was all coming down to this—whether she'd consciously intended it or not.

Standing beside her at the window, Elliot looked out at the night, too. The only light was at the Daughton place on the far bank of the Tred Avon.

"What are you afraid of?" he asked.

"You, of course," she said. "Isn't it obvious?"

She needed a little distance from him and walked over to the fireplace to stand under the portrait of Anne Maitland, half hoping the family matriarch might somehow protect her.

Elliot waited at the window. It was easier with him at a distance.

"I called Amory," she said, "and told him about Jennifer. He was happy. He just adores her, you know."

Elliot didn't respond.

Brett saw the brooding look in his eyes and felt a rush of apprehension. She was sorry, now, that she'd stayed on the East Shore.

"Aren't you tired?" she asked. "I slept until the middle of the afternoon. I was exhausted. You must crave sleep."

Still he said nothing. He seemed to be looking at the painting on the wall above her as much as he was looking at her. Brett glanced up at it.

"Did you know Amory's mother?" she asked.

"Sure. But we were never close. She didn't care much for my mother, and she regarded me as an outsider. I avoided her whenever I could, and never saw her again after my mother passed away. She died a few years later."

Brett looked up at Anne Maitland.

"Is that what you aspire to?" he asked.

"What?"

"Being like Amory's mother."

"I'm not sure what you mean. I'm my own person, Elliot."

"Are you?"

She frowned.

"What is it you want?" he asked. "Who are you trying to be?"

"I don't know what you're asking. What are you getting at?"

"I'm asking what you expect to accomplish being married to Amory?"

A wave of anger went through her. "I think you've had too much to drink, Elliot. Please don't try to provoke me."

He went over and sat down in one of the chairs near her. "I'm not trying to provoke you. I'm trying to understand you, and I don't."

"Well, I don't understand you, either."

A half smile crossed his face. "We have a problem, don't we?"

Brett rested her hand on the mantel, near Anne Maitland's antique rose vase, the one Amory told her had been passed down for generations. Elliot observed her frankly, as though he had every right. She knew he was thinking of her sexually, and for the first time she felt truly threatened. "I believe I'll retire now," she said. "You may not have the sense to get some rest, but I certainly do."

"If you want to go to bed, I can't stop you," he said.

She turned toward the front hall. "Good night, then," she said.

"Good night," Elliot replied. He watched her go, letting his eyes sweep down her, taking pleasure in the sight of her.

How could he pretend that he didn't want her? Whenever he looked at her, it was all he could think about. Brett knew it, too. She wasn't happy about it, but she'd decided to tolerate it, so long as he didn't cross the line. But that was the problem. He *did* want to cross the line. His desire was so strong, he could hardly think of anything else.

He quaffed his brandy, letting the alcohol sear his insides. He put down the glass, staring vacantly at Anne Maitland, and thought about her son.

Amory stood for all those heroic and noble things in life that he had rejected for something more obscure and less well defined. Sometimes Elliot thought he'd lost track completely of what he'd wanted. With his marriage a disaster, he'd focused on his career; he'd set goals and made achievement his reason for living, all the while cynically doubting his course.

Perhaps he'd lost faith. Nothing anymore was real and immediate enough for him but his desires. It was often said that a good marriage and happy home life were essential to a man in his work as well as his life. He'd never understood that so well as now.

Amory had a loving wife and a happy home. Elliot coveted both. It was not a happy thought. He didn't want to take anything from Amory, but what choice did he have? Brett was already married when he met her.

She was the most exceptional woman he'd ever known. Accepted mores, not to mention simple decency, dictated that the right thing for him to do was turn away. But that would be impossible. He had sensed, virtually from the beginning, that he and Brett had a common destiny. And no force on earth could stop him from discovering it.

Monica sat alone in the dining room at the Waterman's Inn. She'd had time to kill so, after leaving the hospital, she went to the inn for a couple of drinks, then dinner. She was nervous about meeting Robert Farrens. The last time she'd seen him had been in Delhi. She was curious about him and, having heard he was in Washington, decided to give him a call. And Robert, bless his soul, had sounded as eager to see her as she was to see him. It had been a long time, but something in his voice had told her he hadn't forgotten.

Good old Robert had been different from the others, though she hadn't fully appreciated that at the time. She'd been so damned unhappy with Elliot, and Robert had been a welcome change. At first that had been enough—the illicitness, the discovery of someone new. In retrospect, maybe she'd wanted something more.

Gérard, her lover in Geneva, had only been a way to pass the time. She hadn't really loved him—not the way she loved Robert.

The Scotches she'd had in the lounge hadn't done much to allay her anxieties, though. She hadn't been all that hungry, but she decided she'd better have something to eat before they met. Judging by the state of her nerves, Robert meant even more to her than she'd realized.

The last time she'd seen him had been one of the saddest days of her life. He had sneaked into the clinic at the embassy compound to say goodbye. It had been an emotional parting. His eyes had teared up, and so had hers. "What's important is that you get through this thing," he'd said. "I don't need to tell you that."

"Once I do, once I'm better, I'm coming back, Robert," she'd said to him. "I promise."

"I'll be here, kiddo."

That was Robert. Stoic. He hadn't said a lot more. He'd kissed her goodbye, and then he'd gone. *Have a good life,* she'd remembered thinking. Oh, Robert.

And she'd have gone back to him, too, if she hadn't been pregnant. But once she discovered she was carrying a child, her world had been turned upside down. Elliot, it seemed, had gotten the ultimate revenge.

During the few days she'd been at her brother's home in New York, she'd thought about Robert a lot. She'd tried to picture his face but, strangely, she could only conjure up indistinct impressions. Mostly she remembered his cynical sense of humor, and his to-hell-with-them attitude. Above all, he was a symbol of the salvation she so badly needed.

Robert hurt inside, like she did. Underneath the jokes, the cynicism, the self-deprecation, he hurt badly. They had that—and booze—in common. Something told her she had to get together with him. It had been more than three years, but she had to try.

When she'd called, she'd said right off, "Fuck it, Robert, I'll have another gin and tonic."

"Jesus Christ," he'd said, stunned. "Monica Brewster."

"Guess you survived India, huh?"

"I guess I did."

"You married?" she'd asked, seeing no point in beating around the bush.

"No. How about you?"

"For the moment. But it's over. We're separated. For good."

He was silent for a second or two. "Where are you?"

"Long Island."

"What in Christ's name are you doing there?"

"Calling you. Sometimes a woman has to go back to go forward."

"You aren't exactly around the corner."

"I'm staying with my brother, but I'll be in Maryland tomorrow. The East Shore. Family business."

Robert was silent.

"I suppose you heard I had a baby," she'd said.

"Yes, I did."

"She's the reason I didn't come back, Robert. When we left Delhi, I didn't know I was pregnant."

"That's what I assumed."

"I started to write to you a hundred times," she'd said. "I thought of you a lot, but it seemed so pointless as long as I was with Elliot."

"You finally left him, then."

"It was inevitable. I knew it the day I first met you, Robert. You didn't believe me when I told you that in Delhi, but it was true. Things had to run their course, though."

Robert hesitated, his mind obviously turning. "So, what did you have in mind, Monica? Why the call?"

"How about a few gin and tonics and dinner?"

"Like old times?" Robert Farrens had said.

"Yeah. Like old times."

He'd paused to assess his options. "I've got a dinner engagement tomorrow evening, but I could probably get away early. Would you settle for an after-dinner drink?"

"Sure, as long as it's with you."

They'd agreed to meet at an out-of-the-way place just across the Chesapeake Bay Bridge. Monica had decided that the prospect of seeing him would make dealing with Elliot less onerous. But more than that, she had to know if she still loved him, if the fire was still there.

After she paid for her meal, she had some time to kill, so she returned to the cocktail lounge. She didn't enjoy going to bars alone, but the Waterman's Inn in Easton was about as harmless a place as you could find.

She ordered another drink, switching to gin and tonic in honor of Robert. God, how they'd loved their gin and tonics. The first time they'd gotten drunk together at Robert's club in Delhi, he'd asked her why she'd married Elliot. She'd told him she didn't know. "It seemed like the right thing to do" was the best she could come up with.

But over the past couple of years she had come to realize that in Elliot she'd married an idea more than a man. When they'd met she was living in Boston, dating her cousin's friends, lawyers mostly. Elliot seemed both suitable and different—a combination that had impressed her.

She'd always been the adventurous type when it came to men. At Radcliffe she'd go slumming to Southy every once in a while with Julie Moss, who also liked her sex down and dirty. They'd find a couple of Italian or Portuguese studs and ball them till the guys couldn't take it anymore. When Julie had wanted to move on to Roxbury, Monica had called a halt. Kinky was all right. Dead wasn't so good.

Elliot had happened along just as she was getting involved with a young associate professor at Tufts. David had taken her to an alumni reception at the Fletcher School of Law and Diplomacy, where Elliot was a student at the time. While she'd listened to David's academic prattle, she and Elliot had made eye contact—he sipping his champagne on one side of the room, she sipping hers on the other side.

When she'd slid over to the bar to get another drink, Elliot had come up behind her. In the crush, the front of him had bumped up against her ass. She'd turned around and said, "Is that thing of yours hard for any particular reason?"

With a straight face he'd said, "I've got a room at the Mayflower. My car's the black Porsche at the near end of the parking lot. I'll wait five minutes." Then he'd walked away.

They'd spent two days in a suite, interrupting their love-making only for hot baths and room service. Elliot had made love to her, whispering in French, which she took to be an omen. She'd lost her virginity to an Algerian student in Paris when she was sixteen. She'd never cared much for France, but Kudir could fuck and so could Elliot.

Somehow she'd managed to overlook the fact that Elliot wanted to spend his life abroad—she'd never liked to travel a whole lot. But there was money in his family, which would please her father, and the thought of playing the role of a lawyer's wife and screwing the gardener for variety was sounding less and less appealing, the older she got. So she'd married Elliot Brewster in the garden of her father's home on Long Island three months after they'd met.

Even if she'd been a little shortsighted, Monica knew why she'd married. But she'd never quite understood what Elliot's motivation had been. He'd imagined her to be someone other than who she was; that much was certain. During a bitter fight he'd once told her he'd proposed because of some dark impulse that had possessed him. Monica had believed it. But even after things had started to go wrong, there'd been passion in his feelings for her, and she'd actually thought for a while that he loved her.

After a year or two of marriage they'd begun resenting each other deeply—she hating him for making her feel inadequate, Elliot hating her for not loving him as he wished. And so their marriage had been a long siege of mutual punishment.

When the bartender asked if she was ready for another, she decided it was time to go meet Robert. Leaving a five, she went out into the blustery night, climbing into her rental car for the drive across the bay. God, how she hated the East Shore.

Once she'd crossed the Chesapeake Bay Bridge, she felt a tremendous sense of relief. There was something about the Talbot County and the Maitlands that she found stifling, suffocating. More so even than Elliot.

Monica liked cities and people, crowds and anonymity. She liked strange men and men who were strange. But she especially liked a man who understood her, someone in tune with her—someone like Robert Farrens.

It was after ten by the time she exited Highway 50, just north of Annapolis. Thinking about Robert had made her hornier than she'd been in a long time. The town of Waterview, situated on an inlet off Chesapeake Bay, wasn't far. Robert had given her directions, telling her it was sufficiently funky that they could sink as deeply into the muck as they wished, unnoticed by the world. Only Robert could understand how appealing that was to her.

Monica liked that about him—that they could play together, and she never felt ashamed or inadequate. She felt like she was all right when she was with Robert.

It was remarkable, considering that they'd only known each other a few months before she had her breakdown. For the first time in her life, sex hadn't been the catalyst of the affair. In fact, it had been secondary. That, more than anything, convinced her that she might love him.

It seemed an incredibly fortunate development that Robert was in Washington, just when she needed him most. Perhaps fate was trying to tell her something. Still, she was unsure what Robert's attitude would be. For all she knew, he was involved with someone, or when they saw each other the old spark would be gone.

Entering Waterview, she turned before the small bridge and drove along a street that ran by the shore. Facing the water was a string of white frame buildings—ramshackle bait shops, a hardware store, a grocery identified by a Coca-Cola sign, two nondescript bars and, at the end of the road, the restaurant, sitting opposite a marina. It was marked by a large sign on the roof that simply said Seafood in large black letters. There were a dozen vehicles out front, inauspicious except for a dark blue Buick Riviera, which Monica decided must be Robert's. She parked next to it and got out.

The wind had died down, the worst of the front having passed through. She noticed the pungent smell of the bay, fishy in a pleasant sort of way. The dark sky was moonless. Stars twinkled through the broken clouds as she walked toward the entrance. A veranda covered with tables spanned the building. A month or so earlier, people might have been sitting there, enjoying the evening air. It was too far into autumn now for outdoor dining.

For some reason she thought of the cafés along the waterfront in Rhodes where she and Elliot had gone for their honeymoon. Another omen, perhaps. Another new beginning.

Inside, the sweet aroma of whiskey greeted her. She saw Robert sitting alone on a barstool toward the back, smoke curling over his head. In his hand was both his drink and his cigarette. Seeing her, he put them both down and stood, a wide smile on his face.

"Gawd, you look terrific!" he said, extending his hands He took her into his arms, holding her against him.

Monica suddenly felt very emotional. He leaned back then, and she looked into his eyes.

He looked older, a trifle paunchy, the edges of his face worn by years of hard living. His smile was still warm, but the predominant impression was one of sadness. The bags under his eyes were dark and larger than they'd been in India. His brown hair had thinned, but the charm and energetic affection hadn't abandoned him. He was a welcome sight.

Robert gave her a kiss. "What a damn nice treat, Monica."

"It's good to see you," she said. "Damned good."

"You're thinner," he said, looking her up and down.

"I'm not pregnant."

He stared at her for a moment. "Was it Elliot's? I always assumed so."

She nodded.

"Come on," he said, leading her to the bar. "Let me buy you a drink."

The bartender placed a gin and tonic in front of her. Robert drained his glass and signaled for another. She fingered her cocktail nervously, waiting for Robert's drink to come. When it did, they toasted each other.

"It ain't India," he said wryly, "but it's gin."

She took a long swallow, liking the burn of the alcohol on the way down. "I can almost smell the tropical air."

"No, sweetheart," Robert said. "I think that's the crab pot."

She leaned over and kissed his cheek. "How come I'm so fond of you, after all this time?"

"I don't know," he said, taking a drag on his cigarette. "It was a whirlwind romance we had, wasn't it? Memorable, but much too brief."

"I assumed you were just lonely after Nora died."

"No, her death freed me, God bless her soul. Our marriage was purgatory. Now I can go to hell, unencumbered." He smiled sadly. "So, things aren't copacetic with Elliot."

"We're coming to the finale."

"Too bad. I sort of liked him. He was decent enough, considering."

"Robert, please."

He reached up with his cigarette hand and pushed back a strand of her dark hair, letting his fingertips linger on her cheek. She shivered.

"I've thought about you," he said.

His words sent a wave of hope through her. She was glad she wasn't the only one who'd anguished. Even when she was with Gérard, screwing on the couch in his office, frequently she thought of Robert. "I often wondered if what we shared in Delhi was love," she said.

"You were as lonely as I."

"I guess." She took another drink, practically draining the glass. "Do you think that's all it was between us—loneliness?"

He leaned away from her, as if to see her better. "It's an easy way to dismiss it, but seeing you, it's all coming back."

"Maybe you're still lonely," she said.

"Maybe."

"Well, I'll be honest, Robert. I'm not interested in clandestine meetings to fuck. Elliot and I are going to the mat on this divorce if I don't give him what he wants. It's not going to be a cakewalk. I need a friend."

He drew on his cigarette and exhaled toward the ceiling. "You're refreshingly direct, my dear."

"I'm thirty-four, about to be divorced. I've got a daughter I've got to figure out what to do with. Why be coy?"

"Is that the problem—the child?"

"It will be, if I don't just walk away and let him have her."

Robert signaled for another round. "What is it you want out of the deal?"

"I don't know. I don't know," she lamented. "I love Jennifer, but when Elliot told me he was leaving and taking her with him, I actually felt a sense of relief. In the days since, I've developed second thoughts. I guess I'm confused."

He contemplated her. "So you're looking for a friend."

"I don't want to be misleading."

"Why is it I feel this conversation ought to be taking place in bed, afterward?"

Monica smiled. "In a way it is. The intermission was just a little longer than we figured. That's all."

He covered her hand, looking at her through the smoke drifting between them. "You know, I think I did love you, Monica. And maybe I will again."

She moved close to him and he put his arm around her shoulder. The affection made her feel all misty. He kissed the top of her head.

"I think you want your daughter," he said. "And I think what you're looking for is assurance and somebody to help you."

"Maybe you're right, Robert. I know Elliot will think it's just to be difficult. He's convinced I'm a shitty mother, and maybe he's right. But if he wasn't so goddamn self-righteous, he'd realize I'm not so bad as he thinks. In fact, if I wasn't married to him, I might not be so bad at all."

The barman brought their cocktails. Monica picked up hers at once. It made her feel better to drink. It always did. She turned to Robert. "But don't worry, I don't intend to shove my burdens on you. I've got to tell you, though, it's damn nice, knowing you care."

"It's been a long time since I've done anything important," he said, fiddling with the ash of his cigarette. Then he looked into her eyes. "Maybe it's time I did."

Brett awoke to the smell of bacon and coffee. For the briefest instant she thought she was in Mount Ivy and that Aunt Leona was downstairs cooking breakfast. Then she realized where she was.

When she entered the kitchen, Elliot was at the stove. He had on a charcoal-gray cashmere sweater and pale gray slacks. One of Mrs. Mallory's aprons was tied around his middle. He was in a cheerful mood.

"There's a lady who looks to be in dire need of a cup of coffee," he said.

He seemed to be pretending that nothing had happened the night before, when the truth was that he'd all but propositioned her. Maybe, though, he'd had second thoughts and wanted to forget about it, to put it off to having had too much to drink. "Good morning," she said coolly.

"Amazing what a little sleep will do for the disposition, isn't it? I feel like a new man."

"Does that mean you'll be on good behavior today?"

She'd dressed conservatively in a wool skirt, blouse and cardigan, but Elliot looked her over anyway. He was showing that he was always aware of her—always—regardless of the circumstances.

"I'll try not to offend you, Brett."

It wasn't a direct answer, but it was a start. As long as he recognized that what he'd said—and particularly what he'd implied—was inappropriate, things would be all right.

She'd worried about him before falling asleep, trying to convince herself that her marriage was strong enough to endure any temptation Elliot might represent. There was no question that being alone with him in the house was playing with fire. And yet, she couldn't bring herself to flee. Danger had never held any particular appeal before. Why now?

"Sit down, Brett," he said. "I'll fix you breakfast."

She went to the table.

"I called the hospital," he said. "Jennifer's doing great. She's started taking more liquids. The doctor's really pleased."

"That's wonderful. Will you be going to see her soon?"

"Right after breakfast."

"Mind if I come along?"

"Not at all. I was hoping you would." He took the strips of bacon out of the pan and laid them on a plate covered with a section of paper towel. "How do you like your eggs?"

"How many ways do you do them?"

"How about fried?"

"Just what I'd have asked for."

Elliot laughed and stared at her for a moment, admiringly.

After they'd eaten, they cleaned up the breakfast dishes and left for Easton. By the time they got to the hospital, Jennifer had had her bath. A nurse was trying to get some orange juice into her as they walked into her room.

The little girl was pleased to see her father. Elliot took her into his arms. After getting some more juice down her, he began to read her a story, asking Brett if she wanted to join in. She declined, saying he seemed to be doing just fine on his own.

As she watched Elliot in the role of father, Brett's imagination started running wild. She imagined herself and Elliot as Jennifer's parents. Was it her maternal instinct that had taken hold, or was it Elliot who was doing this to her?

She'd never had these little fantasies of motherhood with Amory. So why with Elliot? No sooner had that question entered her mind than she chastised herself for her disloyalty to her husband. She had to stop constantly drawing comparisons between them. It was a dangerous game she was playing.

"Do you think it's important that I stay at Rosemont much longer?" she asked when he'd finished the story. "Or would it be all right if I got back to Washington?"

Elliot looked up at her. "Why? Do you want to go?"

"If you don't need me, yes."

He brushed Jennifer's cheeks with the back of his fingers. "*Need's* a funny word, isn't it?"

"Does that mean you do or you don't want me to stay?"

"I'd like for you to stay."

He didn't explain and Brett didn't know if she should demand that he justify the request, or simply accept it. If she did question him further, he might say something she didn't want to hear. "I'll think about it," she said.

"Good." He put the empty juice cup on the table. "Maybe the problem is I haven't kept you busy enough. How would you like to read to Jennifer while I talk to the doctor? I'd like to get an idea as to when we might take her home."

Elliot handed Jennifer over to her, along with a couple of books. In the process his hand brushed her arm. Then, as if to accentuate the point, he touched her deliberately, signaling a possessory intent. Smiling, he left the room.

Brett opened one of the storybooks, but in the back of her mind she was worrying about Elliot—wondering what he meant by his gestures and looks. She felt like she was in quicksand. Escape was already impossible.

They left the hospital late in the afternoon after Jennifer had been put down for her nap. The weather had turned cloudy again. They drove home under a threatening sky.

Elliot had gotten progressively more quiet as time passed. His mood seemed to hang heavily, like the changing weather. Brett couldn't imagine how to account for the transformation.

When he pulled into the drive and turned off the engine, he said, "I could use some exercise. Care to go for a walk?"

Brett interpreted the invitation as an offer to have a talk, perhaps to confront their feelings head-on. The hospital had hardly been a suitable place for serious conversation. Maybe a walk and an attempt to get to the heart of things was just what was needed.

"All right," she said. "But I'd like to change my shoes."

Elliot waited for her outside. When she came back out of the house, they went around to the river side where there was a path that ran through the woods. She'd grabbed a jacket, but decided it probably would have been smarter to take a raincoat.

He looked up at the sky. "Maybe we'll be lucky."

"And maybe we won't."

Elliot didn't say a lot as they walked, though from time to time he touched her, taking her hand to help her over a log or through some bushes.

They heard thunder in the distance.

"Sounds like there might be some squalls out over the bay," he said.

"Maybe we should head back."

"You don't like to tempt fate, do you, Brett?"

"I've already taken chances I shouldn't have."

"What's the worst that can happen? We get wet?"

"Maybe you have a death wish, Elliot," she said. "Or do you just like pushing things to the edge?"

His only response was a smile.

They proceeded, even though the sky got darker and darker. When the wind started gusting and the first raindrops fell, she stopped. "Even if we turn back now, we'll get soaked."

"We'll have to find shelter," he said.

"In the woods?"

"If my recollections are correct, there's a shed out here somewhere. I thought we'd have come to it already."

She looked at him warily, not sure what game he was playing. There'd been no need to go to such lengths to get her alone. They had the whole house to themselves.

The rain started coming down more heavily, but Elliot soon spotted the shed. It was off the path in a thicket of trees. The shelter was open on one side, and fairly dilapidated, but the roof was in halfway-decent repair.

He dusted off a wooden box they could use as a bench. Brett sat, leaving room for him beside her on the narrow box. He sat down, too, pressing his leg against hers. She clasped her knees and looked out at the falling rain.

"It was stupid of me not to have gotten a raincoat," she said.

"You took a chance, after all," he said.

"I wasn't thinking. So many things are done in life without thought. That's how we get in trouble."

"Do you feel like you're in trouble, Brett?" His voice had deepened and was taut with emotion.

She looked into his eyes. "You want me to say yes, don't you?"

"I'm wondering how you feel, what you're thinking."

"I . . . think you brought me out here on purpose, hoping to provoke something."

"Like what?"

Emotion built inside her. It wasn't all annoyance, but part of it was. "Why do you keep pressuring me?"

"Because I don't think you're being entirely honest with either me or yourself."

"Why don't you just say what you mean?"

He looked into her eyes. "Is our relationship ready for that degree of candor?"

A rush of apprehension went through her. She got up and went to the edge of the overhang, the falling rain only inches from her. She leaned against a post and hugged herself against the cold damp air. Then, after a minute, she turned around. "Don't do this, Elliot. Please."

"I'm sorry," he said, "but some things can't be helped."

"I'm leaving as soon as we get back," she said, trying not to sound as desperate as she felt. "I'm returning to Washington."

He got to his feet. "Is that what you really want?"

"Of course."

He moved near her, stooping slightly so that his head wouldn't brush the roof of the shed. She was as far from him as she could get without backing into the rain.

"I don't believe you," he said. "I don't believe you want to go." His voice was soft, unthreatening, but it made her heart race just the same.

When he stepped closer, his eyes moving back and forth between hers, she knew he was going to kiss her. She shook her head, trying to ward him off, but he wasn't deterred. He took hold of her, his fingers sinking into the flesh of her arms. Then he kissed her.

At first she resisted, but Elliot knew her mind. She faltered then and, with a groan of surrender, slipped her arms around his neck, letting him kiss her deeply.

She was immediately overwhelmed by a rush of excitement. There was no hesitation, no apprehension. She'd wanted him for days, craving this even as she'd fought it. And now she couldn't hold back. She couldn't get enough of him.

Elliot held her against him, his lean, angular body pressing into hers, taking the breath right out of her. They kissed more and more desperately. She moaned. Her body quivered and she felt herself moisten.

"I want you, Brett," he murmured into her lips. "I want you now."

His words had a sobering effect. She realized he wanted to make love with her, right there in a shack in the woods.

"No—" she stammered, breaking free. "We can't do this—we can't."

He kissed her again, and she only resisted for a moment, kissing him back, even as she told herself to stop. She hated herself for wanting him, yet she couldn't help it. When he touched her breast she pulled away, hating him, wanting him, loathing herself and him both. "No!" she said as emphatically as she could.

Reluctantly, he allowed her to move away from him. He was annoyed, even angry, the vapors from his breath dissipating in the chilly air. "Brett, you want me as much as I want you. Why fight it?"

Without a word, she turned and dashed from the shelter, running as fast as she could up the path. Elliot called after her, but she didn't stop. She had to get away from him at all costs.

Every once in a while he'd catch a glimpse of her ahead of him. She'd stop running for a while. Then, when he got closer, she'd start again. She might not want to be with him now, but at least he knew what was in her heart. Still, what good did it do him if she ran back to Washington without giving him a chance?

He'd taken a calculated risk, done what was necessary. He couldn't spend the rest of his life regretting, wondering. He had to reach out to her, to try. She was the most compelling, fascinating and desirable woman he'd ever known. And rational or not, he could deal with the consequences later.

When the house came into sight, he saw Brett waiting on the porch. As he crossed the gravel drive, she glared at him. She was as soaked as he, her blond hair plastered to her face, her clothes dripping. She was on the verge of tears.

"Why, Elliot?" she demanded as he mounted the steps.

He saw the pain in her golden eyes; he saw the hurt.

"What about Amory?" she cried. "Did you think about him? Even for a second?"

Her agony was worse than he expected. He couldn't answer her. He couldn't speak. She began sobbing. He wanted to weep along with her; weep for her, for himself.

"Don't you think it's been hard for me being attracted to you?" she cried through her tears. "You know I've been fighting it. Why couldn't you respect that?"

It was all he could do not to grab her. But he stood still, listening as she went on with her lament.

"If I give in to this," she sobbed, "my life will be over. Don't you see that? Don't you care?"

"Of course, I care. I love you." He took her face in his hands. Her lashes were wet, making her eyes larger, more beautiful than ever. Using his thumb, he wiped away a smudge of mascara on her cheek.

She took his wrists and pulled his hands from her face, but she didn't let go of him. "Don't, Elliot," she begged. "Please, don't touch me."

He could think of only one thing: having her; regardless of the consequences. "I have no choice, Brett. The strength to resist died a long time ago. I've only been waiting to know how you feel. And now I do," he said.

She stared into his eyes for a long time. He caught her chin between his fingers, but he didn't kiss her. He let the longing in his eyes speak for him.

Brett slowly turned then and went into the house. He followed her, closing the door. She dragged herself up the stairs, her shoulders slumped. He trailed along behind.

She went to her room, but didn't close the door. He watched from the hall as she entered her bath. She peered at him through the crack before closing the door between them. A minute later he heard the water running. He went to his room where he stripped and got into his shower.

When he'd finished he put on his terry robe and returned to Brett's room. The door was still open. She was in bed, covered by a sheet, her damp, amber hair fanned out across the pillow.

He sat beside her on the bed. She looked at the ceiling, tears running from the corners of her eyes into her hair. Elliot touched her cheek.

"Will God forgive us?" she asked, her voice childlike.

Elliot didn't answer. He leaned over and lightly kissed her lips. "I love you, Brett," he whispered. "I love you."

Thunder rumbled, shaking the windows, making her tremble. He rested his hand on her shoulder and she whimpered like a frightened animal.

He saw her as he never had before—the tiny lines around her eyes, the perfect ovals of her nostrils, the smooth slope from the ridge of her nose to her cheekbones. Each contour of her face invited his touch. Her eyes glistened, making him feel cruel, as if he were her tormentor rather than her lover. And yet he couldn't help himself. He needed to taste her lips, already swollen from his kisses. He had to have her.

She was different now than she'd been before. Her surrender had changed her. He saw it in her eyes.

Exhilaration swept over him. It wasn't lust he felt; it was love. The physical craving was almost secondary. What he wanted wasn't to conquer, but rather to possess, to have and to hold, as in the marriage vow. He touched her face with awe. It was a moment to cherish—the acceptance of all that was to follow.

He pulled back the sheet. Her nipples rose from her breasts like fingertips. He touched them—first with his thumb, then with the tip of his tongue. She closed her eyes and moaned, her lips slightly parted.

He ran his hand down her side, molding the curve of her hips. The silk of her skin aroused him, and his penis lifted.

"Please hold me," she said, shivering. "I feel like I'm going to die."

He took off his robe and climbed into the bed. His thigh and hip pressed against hers. Her flesh felt cool. He ran his hand over her body, then pulled her closer, so that her breasts bumped against his chest and their bellies pressed together.

She stared at him with wide eyes, her chin lifted, her lips slightly open. She made a mournful sound. He slipped his tongue inside her mouth and his penis pressed against her.

When he touched the soft curls between her legs they were already moist. He moved over her then, sliding down her body, kissing her breasts and stomach and the fringes of her mound, before he spread her legs and began pleasuring her with his tongue.

Brett shivered and cried out, almost as if she were in agony, but she didn't shrink away. Instead she scooted forward just a bit, and pressed his face into her.

He stroked her steadily with his tongue. Brett writhed and moaned and whimpered. But it wasn't until he pulled back enough to slip his finger into her, all the while caressing her with his tongue, that her climax hit and she called out his name.

Then her body grew slack, her hips gradually sinking into the bed. He kissed her belly, awed by the intensity of her pleasure. He wondered if anyone else had done that to her, wanting to believe there had been no one but him.

He rose to his knees then and waited. A minute passed before she opened her eyes. She saw that he intended to take her; she offered no resistance.

When his phallus pressed against her opening, then entered her, she dug her fingers into his rump, forcing him deeper. She tightened her legs around him with surprising strength, but he held back. He wanted to be in her as long as possible.

They stopped to kiss, breathing as one. He was overcome by the joy of possessing her. Her body was his. Her arms and legs, her flesh, her blood, her breath—all his.

She arched against him and he couldn't hold back any longer. His orgasm came violently, his body shuddering before he collapsed on her, exhausted. He held her for several minutes before he rolled onto his side.

She hadn't spoken. That bothered him. Brett had been involved in the pleasure, yet somehow detached from him.

He looked into her eyes. They glistened as she stared at the ceiling, her arms at her sides. She seemed wounded. He knew then he'd hurt her—not her body, but her soul.

Tears were running down her cheeks. There was no pretending, now. He understood, as he hadn't before. There would be a price to pay. Brett, he realized, had known that all along.

It took an hour for the storm to blow away, leaving the Chesapeake in a state of relative calm. The rain had stopped shortly before dusk. Brett lay on sheets still damp from perspiration and their lovemaking.

Beside her Elliot dozed, his heavy arm across her stomach, his warm flank against her side. She had come out of her fever slowly—more slowly than at any other time in her life. Perhaps she was reluctant to face the realities ahead.

She hadn't been able to think about Amory yet, or about the magnitude of her sin. For a while she lay replete, devoid of thought.

Then she began questioning what had happened, and the answer came back: pleasure, just pleasure. She'd given herself to Elliot as though nothing else mattered, but she knew, as sure as she breathed, that the heaviest of consequences would fall upon her.

She wasn't ready to deal with that yet—to square her conscience. How could she now live on as though it had never happened? But those weren't thoughts for the moment. They were for tomorrow.

In the dim light she could barely see his profile, his ruinous appeal.

Then when the telephone on the table across the room rang, she jumped. Elliot lifted his head and looked around. The phone rang again.

"God, who could that be?" he mumbled.

Brett took a breath, her heart racing. "Maybe it's the hospital."

"I'd better get it."

Elliot made his way to the phone. She could see the pale skin of his rump, the lean muscular lines of his legs and torso. He picked up the receiver.

"Hello? Oh ... hi, Amory."

Brett flinched.

"Jennifer's much better," he said. "The doctor thinks we might be able to bring her home tomorrow. Day after at the latest.... Yes, we're pleased...."

She could see Elliot turn toward her in the dark. Her shame was crushing.

"No, Amory," Elliot said, "she's upstairs sleeping. It's been an ordeal for her, as well as Jennifer and me. We've sat up nights with the baby."

She heard the practiced voice of a liar and felt deep contempt. Perhaps it was Elliot's diplomatic training, or simply his character; she didn't know. Yet, at the same time, she was grateful to him for having spared her. Had he put her on the line, she would have dissolved in tears. How could she ever face Amory again?

Across the room Elliot said, "I'll wake her if you want.... Okay, sure. I'll tell her. Any other message? Right. Good night, then."

He put the receiver back quietly, as though she might somehow still be asleep and he didn't want to wake her. He returned to the bed and crawled over beside her. Brett stared at the ceiling, her heart aching. From the corner of her eye she could see him. He was leaning on his elbow.

When a tear welled up and overflowed, Elliot wiped it away.

"What have we done?" she whispered.

He took her chin and turned her face toward him. "We made love. We did it because we both wanted to very badly. I'll never regret it, Brett. Under any circumstances. Ever."

"That doesn't make it right."

"I love you," he said.

"That doesn't matter."

"It does matter. It makes all the difference in the world."

She felt quivery inside and her voice shook. "I wanted to make love with you. But even while I was doing it, I knew it was wrong."

"It won't do any good to torture yourself."

"What am I supposed to do?" she sobbed. "Pretend it didn't happen?"

"It did happen. And I'm not sorry. We'll just have to deal with things as they come along."

"I think I should go home."

"You belong here with me." His voice took on a forceful tone.

A feeling of helplessness had come over her. She felt wretched and despicable. She tried to stay calm. "What did Amory say?"

"Nothing. He sends his regards. He'll talk to you tomorrow."

Elliot's words sounded heartless, cold. She began sobbing into her hands. After a minute she wiped her eyes. "How will I ever face him?"

"Don't think about that, Brett."

"What am I *supposed* to think about?"

"Us. Think about us."

"I can't."

He turned her face to him again. "Listen to me. What we did, didn't happen by accident. It was what we both wanted. And there was a reason for it. It wasn't just sex. You wanted to be with me as much as I wanted to be with you. And we've got to find out what it means."

"What *could* it mean?"

He stared at her, his face hidden in the darkness. She could barely see his features. "That we belong together."

Could he possibly be right?

"This happened for a reason, Brett," he said.

What reason? What did he mean? That she should divorce Amory so that she could be with him?

She turned away. If only Amory hadn't called. She'd been all right until then. Was her marriage over? Is that what had happened? "This is his bed, Elliot," she said. "We're in Amory's bed."

"We can take care of that easily enough. Come on," he said, getting up. He went around the bed and took her by the hand. "Come on. Get up."

She got to her feet, her shoulders slumped, her head bowed.

"Think of us," he said. He lifted her chin and kissed her tenderly.

His lips tasted of her, their lovemaking. When he gathered her into his arms, pressing her breasts against him, his chest felt familiar, his whole body did. She couldn't remember if Amory had ever held her that way, standing naked in a dark room. She couldn't remember what her husband felt like. It was as though he were dead.

"We're moving into my room," he announced.

Elliot led her to the door. "First thing, we have a shower. I don't know about you, but I need one."

They went to his room. Elliot turned on the light. She winced at the brightness.

"Come along," he said. They went into the bathroom.

He started the shower, and steam began billowing.

"Too bad we didn't meet ten years ago," he said.

"I was sixteen then."

He shrugged. "You'd have had ten happy years by now."

But she hadn't been unhappy—not since she'd married Amory. The only negative feelings she'd had toward her husband were because of Elliot and the doubt he'd created.

Without waiting for her to comment, he tested the shower and pulled her into the stall with him. The warm flow cascaded over them and Elliot hugged her tightly. She relaxed in his arms and the soothing comfort of the water. Gradually Amory slipped from her mind.

Brett stood at the French doors in the salon, watching the wind toss the branches of the trees. It had turned colder. She could feel the chill through the glass. The sherry Elliot had given her had warmed her insides. She took another sip.

He was in the kitchen, whistling and humming as he cooked. He'd insisted on making dinner, just as he'd insisted on washing and drying her hair. In the shower he'd lathered and washed her from head to toe, caressing her as he did. And he'd have made love to her again, right in the shower stall, if she'd let him. But she'd stopped him—only because she was sore.

Elliot came into the room. He smiled at her, reflecting his high spirits. Brett wasn't feeling nearly as jovial, but his upbeat mood had helped keep her anxiety at bay. For the most part she had managed to think about him instead of Amory, but it took a mammoth effort.

Since she'd come into the sitting room, she hadn't looked at Anne Maitland's stern visage. But now that Elliot was there, she felt a little braver and sneaked a peek at the portrait.

Elliot noticed and put his arm around her. They faced Anne together.

"My stepgrandmama would not approve of this," he said, "in case you're wondering."

"I hardly think she would," Brett replied, her voice thick with irony.

"Don't mind Anne, though. She had her secrets and her crosses to bear, as do we all."

Brett stared at the woman, feeling more courageous now that Elliot had addressed the issue. "If Amory found out about this, it would kill him," she said.

"He's more of a realist than you might think."

Brett looked at him with disbelief. "You think he wouldn't care? Is that what you're saying?"

"No, that's not what I'm referring to."

"What *are* you referring to?"

"This is not a profitable line of conversation."

"We can't run from it forever."

"Not everything that happens is meant to be broadcast," he said.

"What do you mean?"

He gestured toward the painting with his glass. "Look at Anne there, with her rose. And her rose vase sitting on the mantel. You know about the rose, don't you? To the Romans it was a sacred flower, with special significance to Harpocrates, the god of silence. They decorated meeting rooms with carved roses to ensure that anything said there, under the rose, would be kept confidential forever—*sub rosa*. What happened today, like other things that have happened in this house over the years, happened as intended—under the rose."

"How will you be able to look Amory in the eye?" she asked.

"How would I have been able to look myself in the eye, if I hadn't made love with you?"

She shook her head. Elliot rested a hand on each of her shoulders.

"Do you love me, Brett?"

"I feel tremendous attraction—irresistible attraction. For days I haven't been able to think about anything but you...."

A half smile touched his lips. "Could you learn to love me?"

She lowered her eyes. "Perhaps I already do, in a way. But it's all been so fast. A week ago, Amory was the only man in the world."

"I think I've loved you ever since India. I didn't know it then. Not clearly. But this time, when you came back into my life, there was no denying it."

"It's easier for you, Elliot. You're getting a divorce."

He lowered his head and kissed her. "Give me this week," he whispered. "Just this week."

That night Brett slept in Elliot's bed. She awoke just before dawn after a somber dream. For a while she lay awake, fighting off morose thoughts. When Elliot got up to go to the bathroom, she waited for him to return, then took him into her arms, seeking his reassurance and affection. They'd gone to bed naked—something she and Amory never did. After hugging him for only a minute, she became aroused.

The mat of his chest hair rubbing against her breasts made her nipples hard. When he pinched them, they tingled. She begged him to lick them again, as he had that afternoon.

After he did, he had her sit astride him so he could hold her breasts in his palms. Then, when she leaned forward, he was able to suck her nipples, sending a wave of heat through her. In minutes she was ready for him. When she lifted her haunches to receive him, he entered her.

Brett moaned as he sucked and licked her breasts. She gyrated, grinding him deep inside her. They came a few minutes later, both at the same time. Brett cried out, digging her fingers into his shoulders.

Her orgasm was different this time—more sudden and jarring, stabbing deep into her core, taking her breath away. Afterward, as she lay panting beside him, he kissed her face and her swollen lips.

"Dear God," she murmured.

They lay in the cool air of the room, holding hands until he finally sat up and pulled the covers over them. It was beginning to get light outside and neither of them had slept much.

"How would you like to go sailing?" he asked, after lying quiet for a long time.

"Now?"

"Sure. There's no more invigorating way to start a day, unless it's skiing nude."

"Elliot, you're crazy."

"It'll make the hot shower and coffee afterward all the better."

So they went out in the dinghy, gliding over the flat water as the rose-colored sun appeared in the eastern sky. They sat hip to hip, their feet pressing against the opposite gunwale. Brett looked up at the pink and crimson clouds. Elliot had one hand on the rudder, the other held the sheet. He nudged his knee against hers and gave her a kiss.

She snuggled against him, listening to the hiss of the hull as it cut through the water. The air was brisk, but they were bundled against the cold. She rested her hand on his knee and inhaled the salt air.

"Out here, it's like nothing else exists," he said, nuzzling her cheek.

A part of her would have liked to sail off with him, to run from responsibility. And she knew he hadn't made the comment to provoke thoughts of Amory; it was his carefree soul speaking. Elliot, she'd learned, was a romantic. It wouldn't have surprised her if he envisioned that at week's end she would be running away with him to Hong Kong or Rio de Janeiro or wherever he decided to go.

During one of their midnight talks at the hospital, he'd confided that he'd gone into the foreign service because he was not the sort of man for life in the suburbs, with its commutes and country clubs. American civilization never had fulfilled him completely.

The wind wasn't heavy that morning, but running with it, they managed a brisk pace. When Elliot brought the dinghy about at the dock, he asked if she wanted to accompany him to the hospital to see Jennifer. Brett said she did.

After they'd had breakfast and cleaned up, they drove to Easton. Jennifer was up and ready for action. The doctor told them that he wanted her to get some exercise that day, to start rebuilding her strength. Tentatively he planned to release her the next morning, though he wanted her back in a couple of days for a checkup.

While not yet her normal self, Jennifer had become a handful again. Between stories and strolls down the hallway, she managed to keep them busy. From time to time Brett's eyes would meet Elliot's. She could tell by his look that he was thinking of her astride him that morning.

When she permitted it, a thousand snapshots of the past twenty-four hours went through her mind—Elliot as he shampooed her hair, their easy camaraderie as they sailed, the sensation of him thrusting, hard and firm, inside her.

Jennifer's lunch tray arrived, and for the first time she seemed enthusiastic about eating. This pleased Elliot immensely and, as he and Jennifer each took a spoon so they could alternate bites, Brett slipped out of the room, saying she would be back in a moment.

In fact she'd decided to try and reach Amory. She didn't want to tell Elliot, but the truth was she couldn't hide from her husband forever. She'd dreaded hearing his voice, but she thought that by calling him at the Court, she might catch him when he was distracted and less likely to notice anything unusual.

As she listened to the phone ringing, her stomach was in knots. But Amory wasn't in chambers. Bernice told her he had gone to lunch with Harrison. Brett left the message that Jennifer was doing much better. Once the child was released, she would stay on the East Shore a day or two longer, then come home.

Amory's absence from chambers had given her a reprieve, but only a brief one. She still had to face him. Fighting her growing anxiety, she returned to Jennifer's room. Elliot looked at her uncertainly. She felt as though she'd betrayed him. The scope of her deception, and her sin, was finally sinking in.

Somehow she managed to get through the day. That evening, once Jennifer was asleep, they left the hospital and drove to Oxford for dinner. Seated at a window table overlooking the waterfront, Elliot told her about his fantasy of spending a year or two on an island in the South Pacific. He'd take a hundred books, he said, and the woman he loved.

It was an invitation of sorts. At one level the notion appealed to her. What woman wouldn't want a blissful year of what she'd had for the past two days? Sex alone wouldn't be enough, of course, but with Elliot there was so much more. She could talk to him more easily and honestly than to any person she'd ever known, including Amory. And she genuinely liked him. That was probably more important in the long run.

When Brett stopped and realized what was going through her mind, she was flabbergasted. She was actually contemplating leaving her husband!

As Elliot talked about his island as the candle flickered between them, she wondered if she could actually go with him. She would have to give up so much. And she loved Amory. That was something she couldn't say yet about Elliot—not with the same certainty. She told herself that her relationship with her husband had dimensions this love affair couldn't possibly have. She and Amory had built their marriage on mutual respect—respect she had now betrayed.

But, even as she thought about her husband, Elliot was beginning to steal her attention. He rubbed his fingers over the back of her hand and looked into her eyes. He made wry comments—sexual allusions that got her to thinking about him and the things he could do to her body.

By the time they were headed for home, she was obsessed with the prospect of making love. Elliot seemed to know that. He stroked the inside of her knee, making her wet with a deep, hungry craving for him.

They entered the dark house and didn't even bother with the lights. They were at each other almost instantly. At the bottom of the stairs he undressed her and she undressed him, clothes flying in every direction. They nearly made love there, but she managed to pull free and run upstairs to his bed. He found her there, waiting, ready for him.

They made love for hours, exploring each other's bodies, trying every position they could imagine. By the end, the sheets were a jumble, the covers askew, their bodies soaked with perspiration. He was behind her, slowly surging into her derriere. He'd come twice already and she'd come so many times she could no longer tell where one orgasm ended and the next began.

She was alive with sensation, yet exhausted. Even her wildest weekends with Drew Croft hadn't approached this. Perhaps it was her maturity or her need, but she was obsessed with having this man.

His pace increased and she knew he was close to coming again. The suggestion alone was enough to get her started once more. In seconds her orgasm came rolling over her, making her shove her rump back against him. When it was over, he collapsed onto her. Neither of them could move.

"We might as well die," she moaned. "There's nothing left to do."

He sank his teeth gingerly into her shoulder. "There's tomorrow."

Brett groaned. "Elliot, you're insatiable."

"Only with you."

She held his hand against her cheek. "Wasn't it ever good with Monica?"

"Why do you want to know?"

"I just do."

"Sometimes it was," he replied, accommodating her. "Especially at the beginning. Sex was usually empty, though. Loveless. And sometimes cruel."

"I'm sorry."

"You're a wonderful lover," he said. "But that's not what attracts me to you."

"What does attract you?"

"The fact that I always want to be with you. When I'm inside you, I want to stay forever. You give me something I didn't know existed and take a part of me I didn't know I had. And that's okay with me. I love you for it. We're good for each other, Brett. We belong together."

A heavy silence fell over them. The only sound was their breathing.

"Don't think about Amory," he finally said.

Brett didn't reply. It was the one subject they couldn't discuss. The one subject on which they were at odds. "What are you going to do once Jennifer's well?" she asked.

"Take another week of leave. I think I've finagled a job at Foggy Bottom for a year or two. But if it proves advantageous to get out of the country, I can probably pull an assignment somewhere else—maybe not the best job, but somewhere."

Brett took that to mean he could take her away, if she wanted to leave Washington. The suggestion had a heart-stopping authenticity that gave her pause.

Her mouth went dry, and she asked him to come out of her. She rolled onto her back and lay there, her hands over her heart, trying to calm herself. "What do we do when we wake up one morning and this is all over?" she asked.

"I don't expect that to happen."

"But what if it does?"

"Then it does."

"What about our lives, Elliot?"

"They'll go on. If necessary, under the rose, like everybody else's. I don't expect any disasters."

"What *do* you expect?" As soon as she asked the question, she regretted it. She wasn't ready to form conclusions, make plans. She was still in a perfectly sound marriage with a man she loved—or at least, that had been true until a week ago.

"I expect for us to be in love for a long, long time," he said.

He had answered obliquely. She was grateful for that.

Their body heat had dissipated some. Brett shivered. Elliot got up and pulled the covers onto the bed. Then he held her, kissing her hair, her ears, telling her again that he loved her.

His warmth, her exhaustion, the comfort of his body, made her drowsy, and she began to drift off. She and Amory slept together well enough, but never like this. No man had ever been like Elliot Brewster.

Late the next morning Elliot brought Jennifer home. Brett had the house fixed up and a lunch ready. Shortly before they had arrived another front had moved through, bringing thundershowers and heavy rain.

But they were cozy inside the big house. After lunch Elliot sat in an overstuffed chair in the salon with Jennifer on his lap, looking at picture books with her. She was practically her old self. It cheered Brett to see it. She watched the pair as she sipped a cup of tea and listened to the thunder rolling in off the bay.

The three of them had dinner together while the storm raged. Lightning flashes lit the evening sky, making Jennifer jumpy. She began whimpering, and Elliot would hug her. Before they'd finished eating, the power went off, and Brett dug some candles out of the drawer.

Soon after dinner it was evident that Jennifer was ready for bed, but the continuing storm and the darkness frightened her. They took her upstairs, Brett lighting the way with a couple of candles. Remembering how storms in the night had sometimes frightened her as a child, she held Jennifer in her arms and sang to her, just as Leona had done for her.

Elliot sat in a chair listening. Then, when Jennifer was nearly asleep, he went to the bed and kissed them both, telling Brett he would build a fire and she should come downstairs as soon as Jennifer was asleep. As he went off, she couldn't help speculating whether one day she might not end up stepmother to the child in her arms.

When Brett got downstairs, Elliot had a fire blazing. He opened a bottle of champagne and they sat together sipping it and watching the fire.

It was dreamy and warm before the hearth. Each night she was with him seemed to offer a different pleasure. Yet she knew it couldn't go on much longer.

When he unbuttoned her blouse and kissed her breasts, the same old yearning pulsed within her. There had been something else on her mind these past days. She had her diaphragm with her and yet she hadn't used it. But she simply had to, now. That was all there was to it.

With Amory she hadn't hesitated to use birth control, but with Elliot she'd been totally irresponsible. The reason was completely beyond her.

When he unsnapped her bra, she excused herself so she could go upstairs and make herself comfortable. As she undressed, the storm grew violent, and thunder crashed over the roof of the house. She shivered, slipped on her robe and went to look in on Jennifer, who was managing to sleep through the tumult.

On her way downstairs Brett stopped in Elliot's room to grab his terry robe, in case he would want it later. She descended the stairs, holding the flickering candle before her.

Later, reflecting back on those critical moments, she couldn't recall whether she might have heard the sound of a vehicle, or the flash of headlights had been mistaken for lightning. Her mind had been on Elliot.

When she got to the salon, she found him on a blanket that he'd gotten from the hall closet and spread out before the hearth. He'd stripped off his clothes and he was lying on his side, propped up on his elbow. The sight of him aroused her again.

She tossed his robe on a chair and set down her candle. Elliot extended his hand, inviting her to join him. Brett unfastened the tie and let the robe fall to the floor.

He ran his hand up the inside of her thigh as thunder shook the house. Her eyes were focused on his, and when he touched her between the legs, her head fell back and she moaned.

Then, for a reason she couldn't explain, Brett suddenly sensed that someone was watching them. She opened her eyes and looked at the French windows. There, through the water-streaked pane, she saw a woman standing in the pounding rain—dark-headed, grim-faced, motionless. It was Monica Brewster.

PART IV

Chevy Chase, Maryland

November 8, 1988

Brett exited the polling booth and walked past the voters waiting for their ballots. Amory hadn't finished, so she stepped outside the building for air. Her cheeks felt hot, and she was glad for the brace of the autumn breeze. She took a deep breath and leaned against the wall.

A couple of small boys ran by an elderly woman making her way up the walk. Three little girls bundled against the cold skipped past, chattering excitedly. It was impossible for her to look at children without thinking of Elliot. She closed her eyes and fought back the all-too-familiar emotion.

The elderly woman arrived at the door and said good-morning. Brett returned the greeting, then began strolling along the walk strewn with crimson and gold leaves. She hoped Amory would finish soon. She wanted to go home.

At breakfast he'd been chipper, perhaps deciding that her mood of the past several days was best countered by cheerfulness. But it was only making things worse. When he talked about the first time he'd voted in a presidential election—the Dewey-Truman race of 1948—she'd grown depressed for no particular reason. That morning she had almost told him she didn't feel well enough to go to the polls, but she didn't, sensing that it was important to him that they go together.

More of their neighbors arrived at the school to vote. She said hello to a couple she recognized, then watched them greet Amory as he came out of the building. He chatted with them for several moments before joining her.

"Well," he said with good humor, "was it a relief not having to see Ronald Reagan's name on the ballot?"

"No," she replied. "I've gotten used to being on the losing end of elections, no matter who the nominees are."

"Don't despair," he said as they walked to his car. "These trends have a way of reversing themselves. With the exception of Ike, we Republicans had a pretty long dry spell until Dick Nixon resuscitated himself and the party."

Normally eager to discuss politics, Brett couldn't bring herself to utter a word. Her mind was on one thing: Elliot. When Amory climbed into the car beside her, she had a sudden urge to break down and confess her affair. All those terrible, haunting recollections that wouldn't go away.

Again she pictured Monica at the window, watching them make love. She remembered running to her room naked, horrified at what was happening. While Elliot dealt with his wife, Brett had paced in near hysteria, not knowing what to do, what would happen.

As they raged at each other downstairs, she listened like a child locked in her room. It was apparent what Monica wanted—Jennifer. When Elliot finally gave in and carried the sleeping child down to her mother, Brett was horrified. She realized that his life was also in a shambles. It was too much for her to bear, and she began throwing her things in a suitcase, desperate to get away.

She was packed, her coat on and tears running down her face, when Elliot finally came to her.

"I'm sorry," he said. "Monica's gone now."

"Sorry? My God, Elliot, do you realize what's happened?"

"It can be handled."

"That was your wife who caught us making love!"

He tried to take her into his arms, but Brett pushed him away, horrified that he would try to touch her. "Don't you see? Everyone will know what we've done!"

"It's under control."

"Is it? What about Jennifer? You gave her to Monica!"

"It was the easiest way to calm her down and buy some time. When she's gotten off her high horse and thought about this, she'll be more reasonable."

Brett stared at him in disbelief. There was nothing she could say. Absolutely nothing. "I'm going home," she announced, struggling to control her emotions. "I'm going home to Amory."

He looked incredulous. "Why? This incident isn't the end of the world. Monica means nothing to me and I mean nothing to her."

"That's not the point."

"It is! You're blowing this all out of proportion," he said. "I know it was a shock. But we can deal with it."

She shook her head. "No, Elliot, this just proves how wrong we've been. What fools we are."

"No, Brett!"

"Look what I've done to Amory! This will destroy him. You're his stepson, for godsakes!" She moaned at the horror of it all. "And look what's happening to Jennifer!"

"Brett, I love you!" he said, his voice rising. "That's what matters."

"It doesn't!"

He paced back and forth in front of her. "You're talking nonsense. You're upset. You aren't thinking."

She went to the telephone.

"What are you doing?" he demanded.

"Calling a taxi."

"That's ridiculous." He tried to take the telephone from her, but she pushed him away. "Brett, for Chrissake! I'll drive you back to Washington, if you insist on going."

"No, I don't want to be with you."

"Then take my car!" He was so angry he was shaking.

She felt anger, desperation, even hatred. All that mattered was that she get away. In the end she took his car and drove to Chevy Chase, arriving just before midnight. Amory was in bed, and when she came into their room, he awakened.

"Darling?" he said, sitting up.

She collapsed onto a chair and stared at him in the darkness. He was looking at her, disoriented and confused.

"Brett, what's the matter?"

"Oh, Amory..." she moaned.

"Darling, what is it? What's happened?"

She sat there for a long time, feeling thoroughly incapacitated. Amory turned on the lamp, got out of bed and came over to her. She grasped his hand and pressed it to her face. He knelt before her.

"Brett, tell me what's happened."

"Monica came back," she said with a sob. They were the only words she could bring herself to utter.

"And what happened?"

"She and Elliot fought." Brett could feel herself slipping into half-truths, half-truths leading to outright lies. It had been like that when she'd tried to explain to Leona about Drew. How could she possibly tell her husband she'd been unfaithful with his stepson?

"Fought? Over what?" Amory asked.

She'd broken down then, weeping in his arms. All she could say was that it had been a terrible, emotional scene. Monica had taken Jennifer. It must have seemed like a gross overreaction, but Amory hadn't questioned her. He was so fond of Jennifer himself that he could only assume she'd gotten emotionally involved with the child.

The next morning Amory had left for work before she awoke. For half an hour she lay in bed, unable to believe the nightmare was real. She got hold of herself finally, realizing that she had to find a way to get control of things. She needed to find out what Monica was thinking.

Brett decided to call Elliot. But before she'd dressed and settled on the tack she wanted to take, the telephone rang. Odie Johnson, who'd come in early because it was her day to clean house, answered downstairs.

"Miz Maitland," she called to Brett. "You home, ma'am?"

Brett appeared at the landing.

"Well, you is home, I see. I tol' Mr. Brewster you was suppos' to be over on the East Shore, but he insist you was here. I see now he was tellin' the truth, all right."

"Is that Elliot on the phone?"

"Yes, ma'am, it sure is."

Brett's courage almost failed her, but she recovered herself and said she'd take the call. She went to her room.

"Brett, what's happened?" He was clearly upset.

The sound of his voice made her weak. It was a struggle to speak. "Nothing. Nothing's happened."

"You haven't told Amory...."

"No, not yet."

"Don't. Not until I've seen you."

"I can't be with you again, Elliot. Not ever."

"Dammit, Brett. Don't do this. Monica's showing up had nothing to do with us. Nothing."

She drew a shaky breath. "Maybe you're right. But it woke me up. I pray to God it's not too late."

There was a long, angry silence. Then Elliot said, "I'm coming over there."

"No!"

"You can't stop me from seeing you."

"I'll refuse. I'll call Amory at his chambers. I'll tell him everything."

"What in the hell is the matter with you? We'd have faced this eventually, whether Monica happened along or not."

"I know that. I'm facing it now."

"Like hell! You're completely ignoring the facts. I don't believe for a minute this past week was meaningless, and you don't, either! I'm coming to see you."

"No, Elliot, please! Give me a few days to work things out in my mind," she said. "If you care, you'll do that much."

He didn't say anything.

"Is that asking too much?"

"If I agree," he said, "I want a definite time I can see you."

"In a week. Not until the election. I'll call you then."

"That's too long," he said.

"You have problems of your own to take care of in the interim."

"If you mean Monica, it's being worked out. I've already talked to her this morning. I'm meeting her at her hotel later."

There was a long silence before she spoke. "If she wants to do anything terrible, will you tell me?"

"Terrible for you ... or for me?"

"For either of us," she replied.

Elliot kept his word. She didn't hear from him all week. Nor did she find the courage to confess to Amory. Around home she was catatonic. Alone she agonized, alternately craving Elliot, and hating him and fearing the sight of him. She cursed her weakness. But she resolved never to be with him again. Even if Amory pitched her out, she wouldn't go to Elliot. It was over....

When Amory turned onto their street, Brett tried, without much success, to put Elliot from her mind. She looked out at the houses along the tree-lined way. They were stolid, respectable ... and unforgiving. Everything around her, everyone in her life, seemed accusing. It was all in her imagination, of course; no one knew a thing, but her confidence was in shambles, her pride destroyed. And she had only herself to blame.

Amory pulled up in front of their house. Brett was relieved. She wanted nothing more than to climb into her bed and hide from the world. Amory reached over and took her hand.

"How would you like to go out to dinner this evening?"

"It isn't necessary," she replied. "I'd just as soon eat at home. Unless you really want to, of course."

He brushed her cheek with his fingers. "Darling, what's the matter? You just haven't been yourself lately."

She stared out the windshield at the near-barren trees of autumn. She bit her lip, her eyes growing liquid. "I've let you down," she murmured. "I just feel terrible."

"Because of Elliot and the baby? Don't be silly. He understands your concern. Besides, Jennifer's back with him now. He's sorry you were stuck in the middle of it. He told me so."

Her head whipped toward him. "You spoke to Elliot?"

"I called to see how things were going."

Her heart leapt. "What did he say?"

"Just what I told you. He knows you took it hard. And with your life up in the air now, it's not easy."

"Oh, Amory...I don't deserve..."

"Deserve what?"

She shook her head. "I'm keeping you from work." She wiped her eyes and tried to smile, but it was almost impossible to look at him.

"Would you like to get away this weekend?" he asked.

"If you would."

"We could go over to the East Shore and see Jennifer. The two of us. And maybe, if the weather holds, we can do a little sailing."

"No," she said abruptly.

Amory blinked.

"I mean, I'd really rather not."

He looked at her strangely and she wondered if at last he hadn't felt a spark of suspicion.

"I honestly think I was in the way over there. Elliot is completely self-sufficient." She felt the crimson rising in her cheeks.

"I think you're much too critical of yourself," he said with a touch of impatience. "They both adore you."

Brett felt so miserable she thought she might be sick. "Let's have a quiet evening at home together. And, if you don't mind, let's not go away this weekend."

Amory leaned over and kissed her forehead. "Whatever you wish." He glanced at his watch and gave her a sad look. "I'd like to stay with you."

Brett pressed his fingers to her cheek. "No, I've distracted you from your work enough. Don't worry about me, Amory. I'll be fine. See you tonight." She climbed out of the car and stood at the curb as he disappeared up the street. She went to the house then and, as she reached the front door, it swung open, startling her. Odie Johnson's corpulent body filled the doorway.

"Odie," she breathed. "I didn't expect . . ."

"I left you a note, Miz Maitland. Yesterday. Remember? I said I comin' early this mornin' so I can go see the dentist this afternoon. Didn't you see it? I left it right on the entry table here."

"I guess I forgot."

"Mr. Brewster is here. He's waiting in the living room."

Brett's heart began to race. "Oh, Lord . . ."

Odie gave her a suspicious look. Not a lot escaped Odie's notice.

"Well," Brett said, "he must want to talk about Jennifer." She pushed the door open and entered the house.

Brett took off her coat, handed it and her purse to Odie and walked to the front room. Elliot was sitting in an overstuffed armchair in the far corner. He glanced up at the sound of her step. Brett stopped and they gazed at each other. His expression was sober and unsmiling, and she became afraid. "So, how's Jennifer?"

He slipped his hand into the pocket of his tweed sport jacket. The intense expression on his face remained. "She's fine. At the moment I'm more concerned with you."

Brett nervously fiddled with her fingers. After a while she said, "This is not a very good time to talk."

"It's the only time."

"Then it's not a very good place."

"Let's go somewhere else."

She thought for a moment. "I'll get a sweater and we can sit out in the garden."

She got Amory's heavy cardigan from the hall closet and slipped it over her shoulders. When she returned to the front room Elliot noticed what she had on, but didn't comment.

They went to the dining room and out the French doors into the backyard, heading toward the gazebo. Brett led the way. Entering the gazebo, she pulled one of the yard chairs around so that it faced the other and sat down.

Elliot sat across from her. Brett held the bulky sweater closed at her neck. When she inhaled the crisp air she noticed Amory's scent on the cardigan. It gave her courage.

"So," she said. "You wanted to talk."

He felt the cavernous distance between them. It was remarkable that she could be so vulnerable one day, then dig in her heels and be so heartless the next. Where was the passion she'd felt for him? "What's made you change?" he asked. "Guilt?"

"I feel guilty, yes. So guilty I could die. But that's not it."

"What then?"

She looked down at her hands. "With time," she said, trying to modulate her voice, "I've managed to put things into perspective. . . ."

"Brett, my God! It wasn't just sex. Or lust. Or weakness. And it wasn't a goddamn mistake! I love you and you love me! Jesus! What's the matter with you?"

"Listen to you, Elliot! How can you talk about love? You sound as if you'd like to kill me."

"You're right. To be honest I could strangle you for falling into this stupid, pious, moralistic game that Amory lives by." He shook his head. "It's not you, Brett!"

"Who are you to tell me who I am? You don't even know me. Not at all!"

"And Amory does?"

She shook her head in disbelief. "How can you sit there and talk about him like that? Have you no shame? Have you lost all sensitivity? Does he mean so little to you?"

"No, Brett, you mean that much."

She sat trembling. His stony expression told her how very differently they saw what had happened. And yet, staring into his green-flecked eyes, she could recall how they had gotten to where they were. She'd been led astray before and could be again. She clutched at the sweater, fighting the urge to flee. She knew that she had to make him understand.

When he continued to glare at her, she got up and went to the back of the gazebo. In the tree behind the fence a squirrel hopped along a naked branch. She watched it absently, realizing how confused her existence had become. She knew she couldn't give in to her passion. She turned to face him.

"I don't want to hurt you, Elliot, but I don't love you and I never have. Not really." She took a deep breath to fortify herself. "I know it's impossible to love two people at the same time, and I do love Amory. I love him with all my heart."

"I don't believe you."

"It doesn't matter what you believe."

"So the time we've spent together was nothing more than a mistake. Or sex... or something else equally frivolous."

"Don't make fun of me. I thought you were what I wanted. Maybe I'm just weak, I don't know. I can't justify what I did. But now that I'm back home, I know this is where I want to be. With my husband."

"So that's it, huh? End of the story? Thanks for the memories?"

"I have to be honest with you."

He stared, his eyes piercing her. "I don't believe you, Brett. I never will."

"That's your pride talking."

"It's my heart. And my mind. I know you belong with me. And someday you'll realize it."

"You're wrong." A terrible sadness came over her, washing away her anger and her fear. Tears ran down her face and dripped onto Amory's sweater.

"No matter what you say, no matter what happens, I love you," he said. "I always will."

She stood looking at him.

"I'll go," he said, "if you insist this is the way it's got to be. But I have some advice for you. Don't tell Amory. For his sake. There's no penance for something like this, and no point in trying. I'm not saying that for myself. I could be on an airplane tomorrow and never come back. I don't need him, and he doesn't need me."

She nodded. "I know."

He got up and moved behind his chair, resting his hands on the back of it. "If you made a mistake, it was today, not over on the East Shore. I hope you realize it soon. In any case, I'm going to wait until you do."

He pivoted then, and walked back up the path to the house. As Brett turned to stare at barren branches of a neighbor's tree, the brisk autumn wind rose, sending a few more swirling leaves to the ground.

Washington, D.C.

November 9, 1988

Megan Tiernan was waiting for Harrison; waiting for the sound of his key turning in the lock of her apartment door. She went and sat on the arm of the wing chair she had bought especially for Harrison. The past weeks had been hell, but she'd been calm ever since he'd called that morning.

"Meggie," he'd said right off, "how's the supply of Glenfiddich?" That was it. No, "How've you been? Mind if I come over? I think we need to talk." Just, "How's the supply of Glenfiddich?"

"Ample," she'd replied.

"Good. I've got a press conference in Baltimore midafternoon. That should put me back in Washington by five. How does six sound?"

"Perfect."

"I'll see you then."

It had been the first time they'd spoken in three weeks, though Arthur Cadness had called four or five times. Harrison had known that she was alive and well. Once the vile deed was done, her weeping had ceased—at least in front of others.

Megan had managed to find the peace that comes when events have passed beyond one's control. The doubt, the uncertainty, were over now. It was only Harrison's state of mind she'd been worrying about. At last, now, he was coming home.

That afternoon she'd bought a new dress. It had been a pleasant change to slip into something sleek. In the dressing room she'd admired her figure, which was rapidly growing trim again. But then, as she stared at herself, it had hit her why. Her face had crumpled, and she'd cried for perhaps a minute. When it was over, she'd wiped her nose and resumed her search for the perfect dress.

What she'd done to their child had gotten to her—one minute she was blissful, the next sobbing. The emotion never lasted long, though. She refused to let it.

She was still seated on the arm of the chair a few minutes later when she heard Harrison's key in the lock. The door opened slightly. Then she saw him—the man she loved.

He closed the door, removed his trench coat and tossed it on the straight chair by the door. The light from the lamp was dim, but she could see the irreverent grin on his face.

"How was your day?" she asked.

"Hell. But that's nothing new, is it?"

Megan stood. Harrison looked at her dress.

"Goddamn," he said. "You look beautiful."

"Shall I get your Scotch?"

"Not until I have my kiss," he replied.

He walked over to her. Her excitement rose. She looked into his eyes, noticing the deep lines at the corners, indicative of the grueling pace of his life.

For a moment he just stood there, taking her in, noticing her hair, which she'd lightened some, inhaling her essence with a certain bestial pleasure. She could hear him breathing through his nose, the sound a bit labored. The mildest tremor touched his lip, foretelling a smile. He touched the sleeve of her dress without touching her, muttering, "Jesus. You look great, Meggie."

"I've missed you, Harrison."

He hugged her then, squeezing her tightly as he twisted back and forth. "I can't tell you how good you feel. I've missed you, honey."

She drew back so she could see his face. Then she clasped her hands behind his neck, resting her forearms on his shoulders. He took her waist in his hands, squeezing her flesh. As he felt her, a suspicious questioning look played on his face.

"I understand congratulations are in order," she said, ignoring the hands that continued to explore her middle.

"If you're referring to my two-percent landslide victory last night, it was a piece of cake."

Megan laughed, letting her lip drop open invitingly, and tossing her head back. Harrison kissed her, taking her mouth hungrily.

When he let her go free, she laughed again, running her fingers through his hair like an exuberant child. Harrison clamped his pelvis against hers. She could feel his erection through their clothing.

"Haven't you been eating?" he mumbled.

Megan slithered from his arms. "Less." She patted his cheek. "How about that Scotch?"

When she returned with a tumbler half full of Glenfiddich, she saw that Harrison had removed his suit coat and tie and was seated in his chair. She handed him the Scotch and took a seat on the arm of the chair opposite him, instead of beside him as she usually did.

Harrison seemed to be studying her, trying to decide if what he suspected was true. Arthur Cadness hadn't asked. And she hadn't volunteered the information.

Megan crossed her legs at the ankles and lifted her chest. She knew how much Harrison adored her tits. He'd once told her if he could only have one part of her, he would choose her breasts. She hadn't been offended. She couldn't think of any better choice. What good were her mind and heart without her body?

Harrison's drink rested in his hand, untouched. He scanned her a couple of times, still thinking. Then he looked into her glistening eyes. "You aren't pregnant anymore, are you?"

"No." The response was barely a whisper.

Harrison put down his drink and got to his feet. When he reached for her hand, she let him pull her up. Then he held her. He didn't say anything; he barely breathed, though the strength in his arms didn't flag.

Suddenly Megan felt the bittersweet joy of triumph and loss, of victory and damnation.

"Meggie," he finally said. "I love you."

She stroked him fervently. "I know, Harrison. And I love you."

Their cheeks were pressed together. When he pulled his head back she could see that his eyes were glistening. "I know how hard it must have been," he said. "I want you to know that someday, soon, you'll be my wife."

Megan almost broke down, but she wouldn't let herself. He was saying the words she most wanted to hear, but even at this triumphant moment her dignity was important. Not knowing what else to do, she kissed him long and hard. Then, murmuring her love, she lay her hand on his chest and thanked God for giving her another chance.

Washington, D.C.

November 18, 1988

Brett and Amory arrived at Le Lion d'Or on Connecticut Avenue at seven-thirty. A large jovial group had entered the restaurant just ahead of them.

"You certainly have a festive atmosphere tonight," Amory said to the maître d' as they checked in.

"That's a group from the White House, Justice Maitland," the man replied. "They're celebrating Governor Sununu's selection by President-elect Bush to be the new White House chief of staff."

Amory turned to Brett. "I hope having to share the place with a bunch of happy Republicans won't spoil your celebration, darling."

"Of course not," she said, embarrassed.

"A special occasion, Mr. Justice?" the maître d' asked.

"Mrs. Maitland found out today that she successfully passed the bar exam," Amory said proudly.

"Oh, Amory." Brett squeezed his arm.

"I think the whole world ought to know," he whispered to her. "It's quite an accomplishment."

The maître d' came around his lectern, with two menus in hand. "This way, please." He led them to their table, helping Brett with her chair. After handing them the menus, he said, "Congratulations, Mrs. Maitland, on your happy news." Then to Amory, "I'm sure we can find a very special bottle of champagne to honor the occasion, if you like, sir."

"That's an excellent idea."

"I'll send over the wine steward." The maître d' went off.

"If I'd known you were going to make a big deal of it, I wouldn't have agreed to come," she said.

"I couldn't be prouder of you. Allow me that, Brett."

She smiled at him appreciatively, her eyes shining, fighting hard to keep from breaking into tears. The nicer her husband was to her, the harder it became to endure her shame. For over three weeks now, her sin had been weighing on her. She'd been wrestling with it, one day convinced that she had no alternative but to confess all; the next, certain that doing so would devastate Amory and accomplish nothing but to unburden her soul. Elliot had advised her to say nothing and thus far she'd taken the advice.

"So tell me," Amory said, "having had a few hours for the reality of it to sink in, are you eager to get out into the fray?"

"I'm not exactly ready to go to court, but I suppose I will have to start thinking more seriously about the future," she said. "I don't have an excuse for putting things off anymore, do I?"

"With a new administration coming in, there'll be a lot of jobs changing hands and there are bound to be some openings," Amory told her. "It's not a bad time to be looking in government, assuming you don't want to join a firm."

"I did get a call from John Horgan this afternoon," she said. "He congratulated me and asked if I was interested at all in talking to the managing partner of his firm."

"That's a nice compliment. What did you say?"

"I'm having lunch with John and Graham Staynor next week."

"That's wonderful, darling."

The wine steward came. Amory discussed the champagnes with him. Brett watched her husband, feeling sick inside. He was so good and decent and oblivious. The poor thing wouldn't have guessed in a million years that she'd been unfaithful. He deserved better. She'd let him down as well as betrayed him. How could she survive years of marriage with her treachery constantly weighing on her soul? She wondered if the pain would ever go away.

A few minutes later the wine steward opened a bottle of Cristal champagne and poured some into their glasses. Amory toasted her achievement, saying it was one of his proudest moments. Brett couldn't stop her eyes from flooding. She tried to smile through the tears, thankful that her husband had no idea what was really behind them.

They each sipped the wine. Brett immediately put her glass down. For some reason the taste didn't agree with her. It was probably nerves. For several days now her stomach had been upset. She wasn't eating right, either. Amory had noticed she was not herself, but he'd passed it off to Elliot's troubles with Monica and anxiety over the coming announcement of the bar results.

They opened their menus, but Brett had trouble making herself think of food. A cup of tea and a piece of toast would have been much more welcome than rich French cuisine. But she was determined to get through the evening in good spirits for Amory's sake. She owed it to him to do her best, not only tonight, but for as long as they were together.

Brett decided on a consommé with chanterelle mushrooms and a poached fish. As she put her menu down she glanced up, noticing a couple entering the dining room. The man, in his forties, with brown, thinning hair, she didn't recognize, but the brunette with him was all too familiar. It was Monica Brewster.

Brett was horrified. She felt her cheeks start to burn. At first Monica didn't notice her, but as the maître d' was helping her with her chair, she looked up, her gaze falling on Brett. There was surprise on her face for a brief moment, then, upon seeing Amory, a smile.

They were two tables away, with Monica facing her. Brett felt such utter humiliation that she considered telling Amory she wasn't feeling well and that she wanted to go home. It was all she could do to raise her eyes and meet Monica's gaze.

Amory, who'd been intently studying his menu, finally set it aside and began discussing John Horgan and the merits of a possible offer of employment with his firm. Brett did her best to engage in a dialogue with him, but all she could think of was the fact that Monica was sitting not twenty feet from her, probably gloating. When she did venture a look in Monica's direction she was greeted with a sarcastic smile.

Mercifully the waiter arrived, standing squarely in Monica's line of vision. After they had ordered, the waiter withdrew. Then, to her horror, she saw Monica rise and come toward their table. Her stomach clenched and she knew something dreadful was going to happen.

"Seeing my in-laws, I couldn't resist coming over and saying hi," Monica said, beaming.

Amory was caught by surprise. "Well, Monica," he said, rising to his feet.

"Sit down, please, Amory," she said. "You know I'm not one to stand on ceremony."

"Brett and I are celebrating the fact that she passed the bar exam," he said.

"Congratulations," Monica said to her. "You've had a big month, haven't you? All kinds of firsts."

Brett shot a glance at Amory, who didn't seem to find significance in the comment. "I appreciate your thoughtfulness, Monica," she said, her voice tighter than she would have liked.

"Will you join us for a glass of champagne, Monica?" Amory said.

"No, thank you. I'm with a friend. Just wanted to say hello." She gave Brett a stiff smile. "Funny, the places you run into people, isn't it?"

Brett colored again, wondering if Monica was cruel enough to humiliate her publicly. She would die if she did—not for her own sake, but for Amory's.

"Lately I've gotten a reputation for being a real party pooper," Monica went on. "I used to be considered kind of wild, but the world seems to be catching up with me. Maybe it's motherhood. What do you think, Brett?"

"I'm sure having your daughter with you has brightened your life," Brett said.

"Folks find their thrills where they will, I suppose."

Brett lowered her head, unable to look at the woman.

"Well, I don't want to interfere in your celebration. Married couples do cherish their privacy, I know." Monica patted Amory on the shoulder, said, "Toodle-oo!" then went off.

"That was certainly strange," Amory said after she'd gone.

"I think Monica was showing her bitterness," Brett said. She hated herself even as she uttered the words. Monica's transgression was nothing compared to her own. If anything, she owed her a debt of gratitude for showing at least a measure of discretion.

"She made very little sense," Amory said.

"I suppose she doesn't like us," Brett said weakly. The truth probably was that Monica was so overjoyed at catching her in a compromising position that she couldn't help gloating. She must have enjoyed seeing her turning slowly in the wind.

When Brett glanced over, she saw that Monica was talking to her companion, a triumphant look on her face. She was laughing. Brett could hardly hate her, considering what she herself had done. But she did continue to feel sick to her stomach.

The first course arrived. Amory had dismissed Monica from his mind and picked up their conversation where they'd left off. Brett wondered if this was the way their marriage would be in the future—her living in constant fear of being exposed, of seeing her husband discover what sort of woman he had actually married.

Brett tried to eat, but after a few spoonfuls of the consommé a wave of nausea come over her. She knew she had to get to the rest room. "Will you excuse me, Amory?" she said, rising. "I think that champagne didn't agree with me." Before he could say a thing she was on her way.

When she got to the rest room, a woman was combing her hair but the place was otherwise empty. She went directly to a stall, locked the door, bent over the bowl, and started retching. She had the dry heaves for a minute or two before her stomach finally calmed down. Then she stood, feeling so weak she had to lean against the partition.

When she'd finally regained her strength, she opened the door to find Monica leaning against the counter, her arms folded, waiting for her.

"Not feeling well, sugar?"

Brett stood, utterly frozen.

"What is it?" Monica asked. "Morning sickness or guilt?"

For a moment Brett thought she might pass out. She wasn't sure she was up to a battle, but she managed to meet Monica's gaze. "What do you want?"

"Just to see you squirm, honey child," she said, mocking Brett with a faux Southern accent. "You can't imagine what a pleasure this is after all the stones that have been hurled my way over the years. *Elliot's mistress.* I can't tell you how much good this does my soul to say those words."

"That night was a terrible mistake, Monica," Brett said, her voice shaking.

Monica laughed. "Actually, it looked like fun."

Tears began rolling down Brett's cheeks. "I'm ashamed of what happened. I want you to know that. I'm not sure how you feel or if you even care about what we did, but I want you to know it's over between Elliot and me."

"Save it for church," Monica said, waving her off. "I couldn't care less about Elliot, and you know it. I find the hypocrisy amusing, though, I must say."

Even at the lowest moments in her life, Brett had never felt such humiliation. "What do you plan to do?"

"I'm not going to scratch your eyes out, if that's what you're afraid of. Maybe I'll just bide my time and see what happens. It's not often a woman catches her husband red-handed." Monica smiled. "And with a relative, no less."

"I won't defend what happened," Brett said, "but nothing that was done was intended to hurt you. My husband was the one who was wronged. I'm to blame for that."

"Your contrition is really very sweet, but I don't give a rat's ass about you. All that matters to me is my daughter."

Brett studied her, trying to understand the implications.

Monica laughed. "It's Elliot's tit that's in a ringer, sugar, not yours. I hate his guts, but you aren't important enough for me to care about." She observed her, smiling. "What do you think of your stepson, by the way? The man can fuck. I'll give him that."

Brett sagged against the stall. "It's all over, Monica. I'm sorry for what I've done. Since you weren't hurt, can't you just forget it?"

"Hold the tears. If I wanted to tell Amory, I would have. But I've got a bit of advice for you. If you're going to fuck around, do it with your chin up. When you crawl, people kick you. That's especially true if you're a woman. If fucking Elliot leads to a scandal, you'll get more of the blame than him."

Brett had never felt so despicable, so low. After savoring her moment of triumph a bit longer, Monica started for the door, her heels clicking on the tile. Then she stopped and turned. "That retching you were doing. It's not morning sickness, is it?" She smiled. "That's how I found out I was expecting Jennifer."

A look of horror filled Brett's face. "No, of course not."

Monica shrugged. "These things can happen when you get laid." She laughed and left the room.

Brett drew a ragged breath. She'd answered Monica's question quickly, without thought. Why, just because she was ill, did Monica assume she was pregnant? It was true she felt wretched—both emotionally and physically—but that hardly meant . . .

Clearing her head, Brett tried to evaluate the situation rationally. She'd been so preoccupied—so obsessed with the torment in her life—that her body had hardly entered her thoughts the past few weeks. Her period was late, but surely she wasn't pregnant. Dear God, she couldn't be!

Washington, D.C.

At dusk the dome of the Capitol building looked muted against the gray Washington sky. Amory knew it was cold out. The wind was brisk, blowing an occasional flake of snow past his window. The last of the autumn leaves tumbled up the street. It was just after four, but the cars and buses had on their headlights.

Three months ago at this time of day, tourists in shorts and T-shirts were climbing the marble steps to have their pictures taken between the white Corinthian columns. Now the winter solstice was approaching, the days were short, the nights cold and, to him, an ominous feeling was in the air. It was the abortion case that was on people's minds, *Russo v. Clayson.*

He had been thinking about it a great deal. He'd already decided to devote a major portion of the December-January recess to studying the briefs and preparing for oral arguments. Nothing could be known about the outcome with any certainty until the conference, but the briefs appeared to focus on the core issue. All the abortion decisions since *Roe v. Wade* had touched on tangential issues, but in *Russo* the litigants were pressing the justices to face and define the fundamental right of privacy.

Amory had faced some difficult issues during his time on the bench. A few had touched the depths of his soul. But none had been so troublesome to him as abortion. It represented the clash of two fundamental values—liberty and life. Additionally it touched on the core beliefs of his religion, the foundation of his judicial philosophy, and even his relationship with his wife.

Brett had engaged him in discussions on the subject on his own terms. She had made his impending decision a personal as well as professional one. And yet, ultimately, the decision as to how to cast his vote was his and his alone.

Amory turned from the window to look at the telephone. He hadn't called Brett that afternoon to see how things had gone at the doctor's, to see how she was feeling, because she'd insisted that she didn't want to distract him from his work. "I'll be fine," she'd told him that morning when he'd left the house for the Court. "We can discuss it when you get home. There's nothing to worry about."

But he had worried. Something was wrong. Brett hadn't been herself for weeks. At first he'd been convinced it was emotional, but she'd finally admitted she hadn't been well. The Monday after he'd taken her to Le Lion d'Or she'd gone to see the doctor. All she'd said was they weren't sure what was wrong, that she'd have to go back in a week for more tests.

Whatever it was, it had shaken her. Brett simply wasn't the same. She seemed listless and pallid, her spirits were definitely down. Then, Wednesday night, Evelyn had abruptly canceled Thanksgiving dinner, saying she was ill. Odie had already had plans to be with family, so he and Brett had been left high and dry. He'd always enjoyed the traditional Thanksgiving meal and had no particular desire to go to a restaurant, so at Brett's insistence he'd picked up a small turkey at the supermarket and she'd improvised a Thanksgiving meal.

But she'd hardly touched her food. Brett had made an effort to be festive, setting the table with candles and making a centerpiece for the table with holly branches and leaves from the yard. She'd done her best, but the dark circles under her eyes told him she wasn't well—in body or spirit.

Knowing she was likely home from the doctor's by now, he was very tempted to call, despite her insistence that he not trouble himself. And if his worries over Brett weren't enough, Harrison's office had called an hour earlier to ask if Amory had a few minutes to see the senator.

It was an unusual request, first because his brother had never been shy about picking up the phone, and secondly because he almost never came to see him at the Supreme Court building. Their offices were only a block apart, but if they did see each other during the day, it was invariably in Harrison's office or at a restaurant.

He had asked Bernice if Harrison's office had indicated what the senator wished to discuss and she'd said they hadn't—only that it was very important. Amory couldn't imagine what it was, unless it was Evelyn. Lord, he hoped her illness wasn't serious. She'd been vague when she'd called about Thanksgiving dinner and seemed to be repressing emotion. He'd been so preoccupied with Brett, he'd hardly given it much thought.

After a final look at the swirling snowflakes, Amory returned to his desk. Bernice had gathered the *Russo* materials and briefs, and had stacked them on the corner of his credenza. On top of the pile was a memo from William Brown, the clerk he had designated to take the lead on the case.

Brown was a bright young black attorney from Yale, and the most ideological of his four clerks. Amory had always enjoyed give-and-take with bright young intellectuals, though the function of a law clerk was theoretically to assist the jurist with research, not advise him or her what to do. William Brown had a reputation for speaking his mind whether he was asked or not. Two other justices had rejected him for appointment on that basis, but Amory had decided the stimulation would be refreshing, and so had hired him.

Two weeks earlier, when they'd had their first discussion about the case, Amory had lamented the difficulty in choosing between two such important principles as the right to life and the right to privacy. "I'm convinced, William," he'd told his clerk, "that the issue must be settled on constitutional principles and constitutional principles alone. There is nothing to be gained by framing the issue as life versus freedom.''

William had pushed his gold-rimmed glasses up off his nose. "I agree, sir. What the Court has to do in *Russo* is decide who makes the choice—the woman or the state. And if a woman's right to control her body isn't protected by the Constitution, then the door is open for the government to do anything—even make abortion or sterilization mandatory, if it wanted. The Founding Fathers recognized that freedom of speech couldn't be selective, otherwise whoever was in power would decide what could be said and what couldn't be said. The same is true of the right to privacy.''

"A thoughtful analysis," Amory told him, "but I am here to interpret the Constitution, not rewrite it.''

They had resolved nothing, of course. The difficult issues were never clear-cut. But he had told Brown to write his ideas down so that he could study them along with the briefs.

He'd intended to take a copy of the memo home to Brett, thinking that a little intellectual stimulation would help raise her spirits. On reflection, he wasn't sure it wouldn't be counterproductive. His wife's health was definitely a concern. He could only hope her visit to the doctor would help.

Brett was sensitive about her independence and was adamant about being equal in every way. She'd even talked about separate finances once she was working. But she didn't hesitate to look after him when he was ill, as he'd been on their honeymoon. No, he decided, there was nothing wrong with being concerned. He picked up the phone and dialed home. Odie answered.

"She ain't come home yet, Mr. Justice. No, suh. She said she was goin' to see the doctor, but she not back. I gettin' worried, to tell you the truth. She say she wouldn't be but a few hours.''

"What time did she leave the house, Odie?''

"Must been 'bout one-thirty this afternoon, suh.''

"I imagine she'll be home soon. Have her call me, will you, Odie?"

"Yes, suh."

Amory hung up, his concern growing. He buzzed Bernice and asked her to call Dr. Sullivan, their family physician. When she got the doctor's office on the line, he was informed that Brett hadn't had an appointment that day. He hung up, perplexed.

For several minutes he sat at his desk, rubbing the bridge of his nose, his eyes closed, trying to figure out what could have happened. He considered the implications, telling himself there was no reason to panic. Brett was, after all, an adult with the freedom to do what she wanted, including misleading her housekeeper about her whereabouts, if she so chose.

Amory sighed wearily. It being Monday, the justices had been on the bench all day, and he was exhausted. Problems seemed to be crowding him from every quarter. He was looking forward to the December recess.

The intercom buzzed just then and he picked up the phone, expecting Bernice to tell him Brett was on the line. Instead, she told him that Harrison had arrived. Amory went to the door to greet him.

Harrison, who usually managed to look upbeat, regardless of the circumstances, looked grim. He went to one of the high-back leather visitor's chairs and dropped into it heavily. Amory did not return to his desk, but took the other visitor's chair instead.

"How's Evelyn feeling?" he asked warily.

Harrison looked away, distracted, rubbing his chin. "She wasn't sick," he mumbled. "That was a diplomatic illness."

Amory was thoroughly confused. His brother wouldn't meet his gaze.

"We're calling it quits," Harrison finally blurted out. "Evelyn and I are getting a divorce."

"What?" Amory was incredulous.

"We're getting a divorce."

"Why? What's happened?"

"It's over, that's all. There's no point in going on when the love's gone."

"Harrison, you're talking nonsense. You don't divorce a wife of thirty years because 'the love's gone,' as you put it."

The senator slapped his knee distractedly. He was still avoiding his eyes. Finally he said, "All right, you might as well know. There's somebody else."

"Another woman? Who?"

"Megan Tiernan," Harrison said, showing annoyance for the first time. "She's a staffer, somebody I've known and worked with for some time."

"This is insane, Harrison. You can't divorce your wife just because you've had a relationship with some woman."

"She's not just some woman," he snapped. "I love her. This is not an overnight thing. I've been fighting the situation for months. I know now that I want to marry her."

Amory tried to absorb the shocking news. He could see that his brother was adamant. And he understood the timing. Harrison had just been elected to a new six-year term—long enough for his constituents to get used to a new wife. But he wasn't going to point that out.

"The reason I've come here is because I thought you should know before it becomes public. I moved out over the weekend. I'd also like your help, Amory."

"My help?"

"I'd like for you to talk to Evelyn."

"What for? To make your case for you?" Amory regretted his words as soon as he'd said them.

"Evelyn respects you," Harrison said. "I'd like you to convince her that it's in her interests to handle this privately and quietly. Raising a stink will not do either of us any good."

"What *is* her attitude?"

Harrison sighed, rubbing his jaw. "Basically, she doesn't accept it. She refuses to believe it's really what I want. She thinks I'm going off half-cocked. But how do you tell a woman you don't care for her anymore, that the love is dead?"

"Is it, Harrison? Is it really?"

"Look," he said, annoyed again, "I didn't come here to make a case for my feelings for Megan. The only issue is how Evelyn and I are going to end this thing. You can make a difference, Amory."

"You want me to tell her to let you go, quietly, to forget the teachings of the Church that she embraced out of love for you."

"Please!" Harrison insisted, getting to his feet. "Don't preach to me." He walked to the window to watch the snow flurries that were getting heavier as the daylight faded to darkness. "I know I questioned the wisdom of you marrying Brett, but having expressed an opinion, I didn't harangue. And I certainly didn't moralize and throw religion in your face. Let's leave our personal philosophies out of this."

"Do you really think Evelyn will let you go quietly just because I ask her to?"

Harrison turned around. "Just convince her not to get into a public pissing match. That's all I ask. I'm sure once she's had a chance to reflect, she'll see that's the best course."

"Is she threatening to raise hell in public?"

"Not exactly. She wants me to delay my decision until after the holidays, not to make any public announcements. I'm not sure why. I suppose she thinks I'll come to my senses."

"She may be right."

"This is not a precipitous act on my part, Amory. To the contrary, I even tried to end it. I couldn't. This woman means too much to me. So much that I'm willing to risk everything for her."

Amory was tempted to ask why Harrison waited until after the election to make his decision, but saw there was nothing to be gained by being snide. The important thing was to work things out in the best way possible for all concerned—particularly Evelyn.

"All right," he said. "I'll talk to Ev. But offhand, I think her request is not unreasonable. If you'll agree to delay making an announcement until after the holidays, I'll do what I can to make the divorce as private and quiet as possible."

"I'm not moving back to the house. I'm living with Megan and intend to continue living with her until we marry."

Amory got to his feet and looked at his brother sadly.

"I'm curious. How do you separate love and lust, Harrison?"

"I don't know. I can only go by how I feel."

Amory looked at him uncertainly.

"You want to know what finally convinced me this was what I wanted?"

"What?"

"I want to have a child."

"A child?"

"You want one, don't you, big brother?"

"Yes, but I wouldn't have thrown Catherine out just to find a woman who'd give me a child."

"That's not the reason I'm divorcing Evelyn. And it's only part of the reason I want to marry Megan."

Amory had never seen Harrison's amorality and selfishness so clearly as he did at that moment.

"I can see you don't approve," Harrison said, going to the door. "All I'm asking is help with Evelyn." Another faint smile touched his lips. "I know you'll talk to her—for her sake, if not mine." With that he said good-night and left the office.

Amory went to his desk and sat thinking for a long time. Then he got up, put on his coat, and told Bernice he was going home to look after his sick wife.

The house was dark when Amory arrived home. His worry over Brett had grown stronger during the long drive from Capitol Hill. Where could she have gone?

He left the car in the drive and climbed the steps to the front door. The house was silent. He put his topcoat in the closet and started for the staircase. Then he heard it—a faint weeping sound. He stopped and listened. It was coming from upstairs.

Hurrying, he reached the upper hallway. The sound was more pronounced there. He went to their bedroom door. In the dim light coming from the bathroom he could see her lying on the bed.

"Brett?"

She stopped crying, raised her head and looked back at him, startled by the intrusion. But realizing it was he, she began sobbing again, more violently than before. He went to the bed, turning on the lamp on the bedstand.

Brett was on her side, curled into a fetal position. She was in a blue knit dress, her eyes were red, her face blotchy. She looked miserable.

"Darling, what is it?" he asked. "What's the matter?"

She turned into the spread, clutching it with her fists.

"Brett, tell me. What's happened?" He sat beside her, stroking her head.

She struggled to get control, finally rolling onto her back. She searched his eyes for reassurance, trying to speak, to find her courage.

"Amory..." she said. "I'm... pregnant."

He was stunned.

She watched him through eyes bleared with tears, waiting for a reaction.

"Why... darling... that's wonderful news! Why are you so upset?"

Her face started to crumple, but she managed to hold herself together.

Then he realized the problem. She had just passed the bar exam, was on the verge of starting a new career, and now everything was suddenly up in the air. "Darling," he said, his voice thick with emotion, "I know how important your career is, but a baby can be wonderful, too."

She shook her head. "You don't understand."

"I do understand. Listen, you don't know how worried I've been the past few hours, Brett. All sorts of terrible visions were going through my mind. I called Dr. Sullivan's office and they said you didn't have an appointment today."

"I went to the gynecologist."

"I understand that now. But I was afraid it was something else, a serious disease or something of the sort. The past few weeks I've been very, very concerned about you, Brett." He stopped to take a breath, peering happily into her eyes. "So you weren't sick, after all."

"I had a pregnancy test last week. It was positive, but I wanted to have another to be sure. The doctor said it was a virtual certainty, but I didn't want you to know until I was sure."

He couldn't help smiling. Then he leaned over and kissed her lightly on the lips. "I hope you don't hate me for being pleased. I would like so much for you to be happy, too."

She sat up and put her arms around him, burying her face in his shoulder. "Amory," she said, "I don't deserve you." She clutched his coat sleeve.

"Don't be silly. I could say the same."

She shook her head. He pulled back and took her face in his hands. Her eyes filled and tears rolled down her cheeks. He brushed them away. She lowered her eyes.

Amory lifted her chin, making her look at him. "Darling, I love you so much."

Her damp lashes dropped again.

"How far along are you?" he asked.

"About six weeks."

"Then . . . it would have been . . . let's see . . . that time on the East Shore."

She slowly nodded.

"We were talking about a baby about then. Remember?"

She nodded again.

He sighed deeply. "I know how momentous it seems," he said, holding her against him. "And I can't blame you for feeling the way you do. But I want you to know that I'll do my best to make it all right."

Brett started sobbing then, and he could only assume it was because of the high emotion. He'd heard that women got emotional during pregnancy. That had been the reason for the change he'd seen in her. It all made sense now.

He stroked her head as she continued to cry. The poor thing, her heart seemed to be breaking. His only worry was that she would resent her baby; but she was a good person, she wasn't selfish. She'd adjust. She'd love her child. It was in her soul. He knew it. He had no doubt.

"I'm sorry to be like this," she mumbled through her tears. "I'm so sorry."

"Don't be silly, darling. I understand."

It was then that he thought of Harrison's awful news. Brett was very close to Evelyn and she'd want to know. She would probably call her. But he decided that this wasn't the best time. Later, after she'd calmed down, he'd tell her.

He held his wife tightly in his arms. She was really shaken. And so was he, when he stopped to think about it. What irony. Only that afternoon his brother had talked of having a child. Amory didn't want to think about the effect the news was likely to have on him. This would be just one more thing that his brother would resent.

It was after ten when they pulled up in front of Elliot's building in Cleveland Park. Monica glanced at the entrance, then at the child sleeping in her arms. Robert turned off the engine.

"I'll carry the bag for you," he said.

"No, I can manage." She got out, and Jennifer, a dead weight in her arms, moaned. Monica pulled the fur-trimmed hood snugly around her daughter's head, then hoisted her onto her shoulder. Farrens handed her the bag.

"You sure?" he said.

"Yes, I'm fine."

There were snow flurries, and the ground was lightly dusted with frost. Monica made her way to the building.

Once inside, they went up in the elevator to Elliot's floor, then along the musty hallway to his apartment. This was her third trip to his building. They'd been trading Jennifer back and forth every few days for the better part of a month. Elliot had let her set the schedule, mainly because they both knew she had him by the balls.

Elliot answered the door wearing cords and a sweater. He appeared rumpled, tired. He hadn't been the same since she'd caught him with his hand in Brett's pants. Illicit sex, it seemed, was the great equalizer.

He invited her in, taking Jennifer from her arms. "Do you have a minute, Monica?" he asked. "I'd like to talk to you."

"A minute, maybe," she replied. "Robert's waiting out front."

"Let me just put Jen to bed."

He took the case and went off with the child. Monica glanced around. The room was bland, a touch shabby, though more because of age than neglect. It was the kind of apartment that widows of career military men occupied when they were without family. Elliot had filled it with rental furniture. She took off her coat and sat in the only armchair in the room.

Their things were in storage in Virginia. Neither of them had yet settled in a place that would accommodate all their furniture. They'd scarcely discussed their possessions. The process of dividing up was yet to come. There were very few pieces that she cared about and she suspected Elliot felt much the same way. Jennifer would be the bone of contention. Monica imagined that was what he wanted to talk about.

After a few minutes Elliot returned to the front room. He sat on the sofa. Newspapers were scattered about. He folded a couple of the sections and tossed them aside.

"I'd like to know what you want," he said. "We both have to make plans. We can't go bouncing Jennifer back and forth like a Ping-Pong ball forever."

She gave him her impatient, annoyed look. "I haven't decided what I want to do."

"When I left Geneva, you seemed to have no particular interest in raising Jen. I gather that's changed."

"You gather correctly."

"But you don't know what you want."

"No, goddamn it!" she snapped. "My life is a little up in the air right now. I just don't know yet. But whatever I decide is the way it's going to be. You'll just have to wait until I'm ready."

That familiar dark look crossed his face. "Is Farrens a factor in this?"

"Yes. Robert is very special. He's the only decent man I've ever been involved with, if you want to know—present company included."

"So Gérard was just a ship passing in the night?"

"Look, asshole," she said, shaking her finger at him, "don't get holier-than-thou with me. At least I didn't fuck around in the family. Of course, if you want to boff the princess, be my guest. It's your business."

"Is it really my business, Monica?" he asked. "Or have you made it *your* business?"

She crossed her legs and smiled. "It's nice to see you trying to be diplomatic with me, Elliot. Is it for your mistress's sake or Amory's?"

"Brett and Amory really have nothing to do with this," he said curtly.

"Oh, but they do, my love. Only they don't know it yet."

He gave her an uncertain look. "What's that supposed to mean?"

"It means you'd better not be going off half-cocked, because I'm holding all the trump cards. I'll do as I please and you'll have to accommodate me."

Elliot studied her. "Listen, Monica, I've got no problem with you seeing Jennifer on a regular basis, but her welfare has to come first. If you and Farrens are going to be together and you expect Jennifer to spend time with you, then we've got to talk about your drinking."

"What in the hell do you mean by that?"

"A couple of alcoholics have no business trying to raise a child."

"You sonovabitch!"

"I'm not going to jeopardize her welfare."

"And you can go to hell, you pompous bastard!"

"I know you wouldn't be negligent intentionally," he said, ignoring her anger, "but people who drink heavily are not always in control of themselves."

She scooted to the edge of her seat, her jaw taut. "Listen, mister. I would never do anything to endanger my daughter, and I resent the suggestion that I would."

"Have you given up booze?"

"I don't have to account to you."

"No, but you'll have to account to the court."

"Oh, so that's the way it's going to be," she said, lifting her brow. "Well, I've got some advice for you. Before you go making threats, consider how the court is going to look on Mr. Goody Two-Shoes fucking Stepgrandmama. Or do you consider that a wonderful example for a child?"

"Don't try to make something out of nothing, Monica. Brett has no bearing on my suitability as a parent—and that's all the court cares about."

"Oh, you mean to say they'd be pleased to know you're fucking a Supreme Court justice's wife? Judges get off on that sort of thing, is that it?"

"It's not relevant, Monica."

She laughed. "Relevant to who?"

His eyes narrowed. "The issue is Jennifer."

"Goddamn right, it's Jennifer! And it's you, and it's me. And you might as well know if you sling mud, I'll sling it right back. You might not care, but I can assure you that your little sweet-assed mistress does."

"What are you talking about?"

"Didn't Brett tell you about our conversation?"

"You've talked to her?"

Monica smiled. "Well, you mean you two really are quits? I thought she was just saying that."

"Monica, what the hell have you been doing?"

She pursed her lips. "My, my. What's that I hear in your voice—love or fear?"

"Monica, don't play games with me! Jennifer is not a football!"

"Well, goddamn it, she's not a football as far as I'm concerned, either."

"What do you want, then? Money?"

"Fuck you."

"War? You want to fight because you've got nothing better to do? Why don't you and Farrens do something constructive—like sobering up, for example?"

Monica got to her feet, taking her coat. "You can go to hell, Brewster." She shook her finger at him. "I guarantee you that I'll be deciding what happens to her, not you. When I've made my decision, you'll be hearing from me. In the meantime you just plan on doing what you're told."

He did not reply. He sat on the sofa without moving as she slipped her coat on and went to the door. Before going out, she turned to him.

"I hope you don't sneak that bitch in here for orgies when my daughter's around. I assure you, Elliot, I won't put up with it. And I won't forget what I've seen. Count on it!" With that, she went out the door.

Chevy Chase, Maryland

December 24, 1988

Brett ran a brush through her pale hair, then turned to look at her profile in the mirror. She'd worn the same red knit dress at Christmas the year before, and she could honestly say it wasn't much snugger. Her stomach looked practically as flat as it ever had.

More than once she'd wondered if the doctor could have made a mistake. But her morning sickness was very real and there had been subtle changes in her body. Her breasts seemed different, and there was a distinct glow to her skin. Her flesh had gotten softer, too. No, there was nothing to be gained from pretending it wasn't true.

Brett put down her brush and took a bottle of perfume from the tray on the vanity. Applying a little behind each ear and on the insides of her wrists, she went back to the bedroom. The door was open and she could hear Amory's Christmas music coming from downstairs. He had an impressive record collection, some recordings dating back to the Thirties and Forties. Leona had been in ecstasy, having listened to records most of the day.

Her aunt had arrived two days earlier. The trip had been Amory's idea. He'd known it would be Leona's first Christmas alone, and had thought it might be nice if she were to join them.

Brett had told her aunt about her pregnancy first thing. She had to share the news with someone. Leona was delighted, nearly as joyful as Amory. "Honey, that's just wonderful!" she exclaimed. "The judge must be a happy man."

Amory had been virtually euphoric the past month, though he'd been very concerned about her frame of mind. He'd been solicitous, constantly asking after her, doing what he could to cheer her. Brett had made an effort not to mope or complain. She didn't want to spoil Amory's joy, even though she was dying inside.

He'd wanted to make an announcement that night, saying that Christmas Eve was a perfect time since everyone in the family was coming over. She'd wanted to curl up and die when he suggested that. The mere thought of Elliot being there while her husband told everyone she was pregnant was more than she could bear. God knew, she had enough to live with, considering the guilt. But trying to pretend in front of Elliot would be beyond her. It was too soon. If she had to face him, better it be later, after some time had passed.

Of course, Amory hadn't understood her reluctance. She'd explained that she wasn't ready to be fussed over quite yet, and he hadn't questioned her, but she'd seen the uncertain look in his eyes. As it was, she couldn't avoid seeing Elliot. When the invitation to dinner went out, she'd prayed he would decline, but he'd accepted, though his note did indicate he wouldn't be able to stay long. Monica had a flight booked to New York late that night and would be taking Jennifer with her.

Brett hadn't seen Elliot since election day, though at Amory's invitation he'd brought Jennifer by for a visit one Sunday afternoon. She'd arranged to have lunch that day with a friend from college, and thereby managed to avoid him. Elliot had made no other attempts to see her.

Still, she couldn't forget how insistent he'd been that they belonged together, that he was sure she would realize it eventually and would come to him. He couldn't know how wrong he'd been.

Brett went downstairs to join her aunt in the front room. Leona, cheeks rosy with rouge, had on the new green silk dress Brett had bought her the day before. Though her hair was getting grayer, and she was a little gaunt, she looked much better than she had at Earl's funeral.

She held up a half-eaten Christmas cookie as Brett sat beside her. "I don't know if it's the climate or what, but these just don't seem the same as when we make 'em down home."

The evening before, the two of them had baked, just as they had when Brett was a girl. It was a nostalgic experience, making her think of the things she would be doing with her own child one day. And then she'd gotten upset, wondering if she'd ever be able to look into her child's eyes, knowing who its father was.

"The house looks so nice," Leona said, making conversation.

Brett looked around the room, trying to put herself into the frame of mind of a hostess. This year, she had decorated more formally. Having nothing to do, it had kept her occupied.

She'd longed to be working, but it seemed pointless to start a career and a pregnancy at the same time. So she decided to put off practicing law. It was a penance of sorts, and besides, it would be better for the baby.

"Well, well," Amory said from the entrance to the dining room. "Has the mother-to-be come down?" He had on blue suit pants, a white shirt and bright red tie.

"Amory, I wish you wouldn't say that. Our guests will be arriving soon. If you get in the habit, you might slip."

"No, I've promised you discretion, and discreet I'll be. Can I bring you an eggnog, darling?"

"A plain one. No bourbon."

Brett folded her hands on her knees and stared at the tree. Bing Crosby and a choir were singing "O Come, All Ye Faithful."

"Why, Brett honey," Leona said, "you're tremblin' like a leaf. You don't have a chill, do you?"

"No," she replied, looking down at her hands. "I'm just a little excited. I always am at Christmastime. You remember that."

But that wasn't it at all. In not too very long, Elliot Brewster would be arriving. That's what was making her nervous.

Amory brought in Brett's eggnog and one with bourbon for himself. The three of them sat chatting, though Leona was still noticeably intimidated by the justice. About twenty minutes later, when the doorbell sounded, Brett jumped. Amory went to the entry hall and she followed. It was Evelyn.

They'd invited Harrison, but he'd remained steadfast in his devotion to Megan Tiernan. When Brett had talked to Evelyn the week before, her sister-in-law had virtually given up hope. She was beginning to accept the fact that he wasn't coming back.

Brett went to the entry to greet her. They embraced. Evelyn looked her over, pinching Brett's cheek playfully.

"Don't you look radiant," she said.

Brett looked into her eyes, suspecting that Evelyn knew— or at least had her suspicions. She would tell her soon, but not now. Not yet.

Evelyn put down her shopping bag of presents and Amory helped her off with her full-length mink, which she'd told Brett she only wore on private occasions. She'd had the coat and matching hat long before fur had become politically incorrect, but Washington was obsessed with symbolism.

Amory bussed Evelyn on the cheek. "I'm sorry Harrison won't be here," he said, wisely getting the subject out in the open.

"I'm realizing that's the way it's going to be."

"This will probably be the first of several Christmases without him," Amory said. "But life will go on. We'll always be here for you, Ev."

Evelyn's eyes turned glossy, but she managed to smile. Brett touched Evelyn's arm. Amory picked up the shopping bag. "Come in and meet Brett's aunt."

They all returned to the front room. Evelyn was very sweet to Leona, though their worlds and backgrounds were light-years apart. Amory put Evelyn's presents under the tree, and got them all more eggnog. "It's wonderful," Evelyn said at one point, "how the holidays bring people together."

Brett admired Evelyn's courage and her spirit, wondering if there wasn't a lesson somewhere there for her. But their situations were not at all comparable. Evelyn was an aggrieved party, she a wrongdoer.

After half an hour, Brett began looking at her watch. It wouldn't be long before Odie was ready to serve and Elliot still hadn't arrived. Amory seemed aware as well. "I wonder where Elliot and the baby are?" he said.

"I hope he doesn't poop out," Evelyn said. "I was counting on seeing that little girl. How long has it been since any of us have had a Christmas with children around?"

Brett went off to the kitchen to check on dinner. She was talking to Odie when she heard the doorbell. Her heart tripped.

"Don't you worry about a thing here, Miz Maitland," Odie told her. "Your guests is a-comin'. I's got everything under control. Go on, now. Have yourself a good time."

Brett knew she couldn't hide in the kitchen forever, but she stalled for a minute or two longer. By the time she returned to the front room, Elliot was on the sofa next to Evelyn. Jennifer was standing at his knee. The little girl recognized Brett and ran over to her. Brett embraced her. She glanced at Elliot.

"Merry Christmas," she said. "I'm glad you finally made it."

"Sorry to be late." He leaned over and gave her a perfunctory kiss on the cheek. "Merry Christmas."

Brett tried hard to take him in stride, to pretend nothing had ever happened between them, but it was impossible. The only solution was not to look at him. She turned her attention to Jennifer. "You've gotten so big, sugarplum!" she said. "And it's been only a few weeks since I've seen you! What's your daddy been feeding you, anyway?"

Jennifer was clearly pleased by all the attention. She proceeded to tell Brett a story about a new teddy bear, which her daddy had given her for Christmas. Brett listened to her, trying to ignore Elliot completely, but when she did glance at him and catch his eye, she felt her cheeks color.

In another fifteen minutes they all drifted into the dining room. She'd arranged the seating so she wouldn't have to sit next to Elliot. Even so, she couldn't help noticing that he was watching her. Whenever she glanced in his direction, he was looking her way, studying her. But he didn't address her directly, which came as a relief. But then she worried that her frosty attitude toward him might arouse suspicion, so she made herself speak to him.

"How's your new job, Elliot?" she asked when there was a lull in the conversation. "I'm not even sure what it is you're doing."

"Policy planning," he replied. "It's a staff position. I'm keeping busy. It gives me a chance to make some good contacts in the department."

"Are you looking forward to going abroad again?"

"It's not likely in the near future, but I'm sure I'll be ready when the time comes. How about you? Having trouble sorting through all the job offers?"

Brett glanced at Amory. "I'm weighing my options."

Odie wheeled in a serving cart with their dinner, which got Brett off the hook. When conversation resumed, Evelyn asked Elliot how long Jennifer would be in New York.

"Just until the New Year. It's longer than I would have liked, but Monica insisted."

"Is Monica living in New York now, or is she still down here?"

"She's spent the last few weeks in an alcohol-abuse program somewhere in Virginia. Claims to have turned her life around. She and Farrens, both."

"Well, that's good news," Evelyn said. "Isn't it?"

"Good for Monica. Not so good for me. Our attorneys have been talking. She's starting to make sounds like she might want Jen. But for the moment it's still up in the air."

"Oh, dear," Evelyn said.

Brett listened to the conversation, chancing an occasional glance at Elliot. She wondered if Monica had given him a bad time about catching them making love. He'd assured her that everything was under control—that he could handle Monica—but she had seen the woman in action and doubted she had a reasonable bone in her body.

"Farrens is the chap from India, isn't he?" Amory asked Elliot. "The one she had the affair with?"

Elliot nodded. "Yes."

Brett felt her stomach begin to knot.

"Is she serious about him?" Amory asked. "Are they going to marry?"

"I don't know," Elliot replied. "It wouldn't surprise me. She's been in this program with him and claims he's a stabilizing influence. If he's done her some good, so much the better. I only hope we can resolve our differences amicably."

Brett exchanged glances with him. She knew they were suffering the wages of their sin. What if he knew she was pregnant with his child?

"I'm always suspicious of these eleventh-hour conversions," Amory said. "I can imagine Monica giving up drink, but not changing her stripes. People are what they are."

Amory's words cut deeply into Brett's soul. She was no better than Monica. The only difference was she'd been sneaky and deceptive. Dishonest. Monica at least made no attempt to hide the person she was.

Brett felt sick with guilt. She longed to get up from the table and go to her room. Was this what she had to face for the rest of her life? How could she live with this burden? She had to, though. For Amory's sake, she had to endure.

After Odie cleared the table Amory suggested they check under the Christmas tree to see if there were any presents for Jennifer. They would have their dessert later.

Brett situated herself as far from Elliot as she could. She wasn't as tense and fearful as she was when he first arrived, but his presence was definitely having its effect. For weeks she'd been trying to distance herself from him emotionally. But seeing him again, she began remembering the man she'd succumbed to, the man who'd broken down her defenses, the man who'd expressed his undying love.

She tried not to think of him that way. She tried to concentrate on Amory and the others. But Elliot was there, just across the room, forcing himself into her consciousness, whether she looked at him or not.

She did her best not to let her anxiety show, praying she'd survive the evening.

Noticing Odie looking in from the hallway, Brett found a way to escape. She slipped from the room and went with Odie to the kitchen.

"Whenever you want your dessert, Miz Maitland, just holler," the housekeeper said.

"We'll have it in a while, Odie. But you don't have to wait. I can clean up the dessert dishes. You go on home."

"You sure, ma'am? I can stay if you wants. Nobody home waitin'. My nephew, he don't come till tomorrow."

"You've had a long day. Go on home."

After the housekeeper got her coat and purse, Brett handed her an envelope with a check from Amory as her Christmas bonus.

"You's awfully kind, Miz Maitland. And I sure do appreciate it."

They hugged and Odie went off to say goodbye to the others and catch the bus home. Brett remained in the kitchen to start the coffee. While she was cutting the pie, she heard someone come in the swinging door. She glanced over her shoulder. It was Elliot.

His sudden appearance gave her a start. She took a breath to say something, but the words weren't there.

"The others are having fun with Jennifer," he said. "I wanted to talk to you."

"We have nothing private to say to each other, Elliot."

"There's plenty to say. But there's no time now. Have lunch with me this week."

The request was worse than she could have imagined. The looks he'd given her all evening were bad enough, but she hadn't expected him to make an overture. "No," she said, shaking her head. "No!"

"I have to talk to you."

"If it's about us," she said, lowering her voice, "there's nothing to say! I swear to God, I don't want to speak to you or even see you again. For Amory's sake I'll do what I did tonight, but no more. Please!"

He stared at her broodingly.

"Please," she begged. "Let me be!"

He stood motionless for a long time, saying nothing. Finally he retreated to the door, where he stopped, his hand resting against the doorjamb. "I don't want to hurt you, Brett," he said, "but I still don't believe this is what you want." He left the room.

Brett sagged against the counter, weak with anxiety. Her heart was pounding, she was on the brink of tears. The pressure had built to the point where she couldn't help herself. She began to cry.

Chevy Chase, Maryland

January 10, 1989

A cold wind was blowing out of the north, whistling through the eaves outside their bedroom window. It was nearly midnight. Brett had lain awake for an hour, her mind moving over the same familiar terrain. Whenever she thought of the child in her womb, her mind naturally moved on to Elliot.

Ever since Christmas she'd worried about Elliot's stubborn determination to change her mind, though he hadn't attempted to contact her, as she half expected he would. In a way, that was worse. He'd become an invisible danger, capable of alighting on her doorstep at any moment.

Amory remained oblivious. He had his own problems. He'd talked with Harrison, hoping to persuade him to reconcile with Evelyn, but Harrison stood firm. He'd had discussions with his attorney and was going to file for divorce at the end of the week, at which time he was going to make a public announcement. Evelyn was resigned. She'd finally given up hope.

On top of everything, Amory was going through the most difficult crisis of his career. On Monday the Court had heard oral arguments on *Russo v. Clayson,* the abortion case under appeal. Brett had been in the gallery. Amory, now second most-junior member of the Court, had listened glumly, saying little, giving no indication what was in his mind. Even Brett couldn't be sure how he would vote.

Amory had hardly said a word when he'd gotten home that night, and she thought it best not to ask how he felt about the day's events. Today had been much the same. She'd watched for signs that he'd finally made up his mind, but she'd seen none. She was beginning to think that even now, the night before the justices would meet to cast their vote, he was undecided.

When she heard him sigh, she turned her head and saw him staring at the ceiling, his eyes glistening in the faint moonlight coming in the window.

"Are you awake?" she whispered.

"Yes," he muttered.

"Thinking about tomorrow?"

"Yes. This has never happened to me before," he said. "I've never been torn like this."

She put her hand on his shoulder, trying to lend what comfort she could.

"The funny thing is, it's not the moral issue. I know how I feel about abortion. I simply don't know how I feel about *Roe v. Wade*. If I were a legislator, I'd support a bill to prohibit abortion, as long as it made exceptions for medical necessity."

Brett said nothing.

"I know you don't like to hear that, but it's the truth."

Brett agonized. Amory's feelings about abortion had not been a secret, but it always bothered her when he stated them.

"I'm sensitive to your arguments about a woman and her body," he said, reading her thoughts. "But in my heart I'm convinced it's not a sexist view. I could vote to put the same restriction on men."

"If that's the way you feel, why are you having so much trouble making a decision?"

"Because I'm not a legislator. I'm an arbiter and defender of rights. Some of my brethren don't see that as the role, but I'm coming to realize it's our true function. And to compound the problem, I know now the ultimate ruling will come down to my vote. Five are all but announced already. I'm fairly certain how the other three will go. When the count is made tomorrow, there will be four votes against and four in favor of the right to abortion. And then there's my vote."

Brett could hear the anguish in his voice. Her husband was a man of principle, but also one with compassion. She felt for him, knowing how hard he was struggling to find the right course. The issue had always been so clear to her, and yet she couldn't fault him for not seeing it.

"Until Monday I was leaning toward overturning," he said, rambling on. "It struck me as the cleanest solution. The notion of putting the decision in the hands of the legislators seemed to me eminently democratic."

She felt a well of hope. "But you were persuaded otherwise by something you heard in orals?"

"No, frankly it was something William said."

"William Brown?"

"Yes, he's been waging a one-man crusade to win my vote for the pro-choice cause. His argument is that ours is a society in which individual rights are more important than collective goals."

"I've never thought of it in those terms," Brett said.

"Nor have I. Not that way, precisely. There are people, including some on the Court, who couldn't agree with the notion. But it may be the hook on which I ultimately hang my hat."

"It sounds like you have made up your mind, after all."

"I'm still at war with myself, darling. It's not easy to vote against values and beliefs and goals that you treasure. I wish abortion didn't exist. But I can't will it so. That baby inside you tells me one thing, but I'm afraid it's more in the nature of the collective good than individual liberty. The more I think about it, the more I see that I may have to become the instrument of something I personally abhor."

Brett understood what he was saying. He was probably going to vote to sustain *Roe*. Ironically, she felt no triumph. She felt empty, lost, adrift in a terrible sea of personal failure. Still, her husband's nobility shone through it all.

She found his hand under the covers. "Whatever happens, Amory, whatever you decide, I want you to know I love you."

He reached over and touched her face. "Darling, that's as important to me as anything on earth."

She began to cry then. Silently. For Amory's sake, more than for her own.

Brett knew Amory would be depressed when he got home from the Supreme Court that night, regardless of what action he took. She decided the best way to cheer him up would be to suggest they make plans to announce they were expecting. In not too many weeks she would begin to show anyway, so they couldn't put it off much longer.

Amory might want to do something at the Court to celebrate, she thought—a luncheon or something. The justices weren't given to socializing with each other a great deal, though. They might also host a family dinner and invite a few friends. But who was left in the family besides Evelyn?

She was more restless this morning than usual. Brett agonized, knowing that at that very moment Amory and the other justices were making their monumental decision—one that would affect millions of lives for years to come. All she could do was stand around wringing her hands. It wasn't the life she'd envisioned, staying at home while others made the important decisions, but it was the one she'd condemned herself to, at least for the next few years.

She was feeling sorry for herself again. Brett knew she had to guard against that. What could she do for Amory?

Sunday, after he had returned home from mass, they'd gone for a walk around the neighborhood. It had been a brisk but sunny day. Amory had talked about the baby. At one point he'd asked why she hadn't bought any baby things yet. Brett had told him she would in due time, but that she wanted to wait until she was further along.

She hadn't been entirely truthful. Actually, she wanted to avoid any reminder of her sin. She realized that was selfish. Amory would be pleased if she had a few baby things waiting when he got home that night. She had to face up to the reality of her pregnancy eventually. Perhaps today was the day to start—for his sake, if for no other reason.

Brett decided to drive to Georgetown. She'd noticed a cute children's boutique on Wisconsin Avenue. She could pick up a few things, have lunch and maybe afterward give Evelyn a call. Her sister-in-law had a rough couple of months. If Brett didn't have a job to devote her energies to, she could at least lend support to someone in need.

She hastily scratched out a note to Odie, who wasn't scheduled to come until afternoon, saying she was going shopping and would be home late. Getting her coat, she left the house and drove down Connecticut Avenue to Georgetown.

The boutique was filled with all sorts of adorable things. Just seeing them made her feel pregnant and maternal. But her feelings were mixed. Whenever she thought about Elliot being the true father of her child, a shimmer would go through her. What if it looked just like him? What if her baby grew up to be a clone of its father?

She'd picked out a tiny sleeper and an adorable little knit sweater when a tall dark-headed man and a little girl entered the shop. Brett had a start until she saw that it wasn't Elliot and Jennifer. Whenever she saw a toddler, she immediately thought of the hospital in Easton, the ordeal they'd gone through, and their lovemaking—"under the rose," as Elliot had called it. When those memories filtered into her mind, the woman she'd been seemed like someone else—someone from a different world, a person she didn't know.

Her heart slowly regained its normal beat and Brett carried her selections to the counter, asking herself how long this anguish would go on, how long the torture would last. She made her purchases and walked down the street to a gourmet deli that she and Evelyn had visited a couple of times for lunch.

Georgetown was not far from Foggy Bottom, so employees from the State Department sometimes would come up for a gourmet sandwich. Brett didn't know if Elliot had ever frequented the place, but the possibility of running into him gave her pause. Still, what were the chances?

As she entered the deli she noticed that the place was already fairly crowded. A television was on behind the counter, which seemed to have most of the customers' attention. They appeared to be listening to a news bulletin.

"What happened?" she heard somebody ask.

"Maitland's dead," came the response.

Brett's heart stopped.

"Who?" someone asked.

"Senator Maitland, from Maryland. Heart attack."

Arlington, Virginia

January 14, 1989

It was a bitterly cold day for a funeral. As the procession crossed over the Potomac, Elliot looked out the window of the limousine at the bleak countryside, the mist-shrouded hills up the valley fading from gray to white. The ranks of Harrison Maitland's mourners had thinned some since the mass of the Christian burial at St. Matthew's Cathedral.

The president and First Lady had returned to the White House; the secretary of state went back to Foggy Bottom; and much of the congressional delegation had returned to the Hill or gone on home. Among the top-ranking members of the administration, only Frank Carlucci from Defense had hung in there, loyal to the end. George Schultz had been considerate, insisting that Elliot take his limo to the internment. Jerry Falwell and a few of Harrison's closest friends in the Senate were the only other major public figures to accompany the family to the cemetery.

With the Bush inauguration only days away, Washington seemed anxious to get past the dismal business of the funeral. There were parties to prepare for, tickets and dresses and tuxedos to arrange. Guest lists, publicity and gossip were the preferred commodities of the season. The feeling was that Harrison Maitland had picked an unfortunate time to pass from the political scene.

Of course, to a few people in Washington the senator's death meant more than a jog in the seniority system and a change in committee assignments. Leaving St. Matthew's,

Elliot had noticed a young woman in the company of a couple of Harrison's aides. Judging by her tear-streaked face, she had to be Megan Tiernan. The three of them had fallen in at the end of the procession headed for Arlington. The woman was apparently determined to see her lover laid to rest.

To Elliot it was understandable. There were times when appearances seemed not to matter. This was probably one.

As far as the world was concerned, Harrison had died leaving a grieving widow to whom he'd been happily married for thirty years. But within hours of his death, all the Washington insiders knew the true circumstances of his passing.

Elliot had heard the story the day Harrison died. The senator's aides had rushed to Meg Tiernan's apartment where they'd found the paramedics wheeling Harrison out on a stretcher. He was already dead, having suffered a massive heart attack while locked in the embrace of his mistress.

When the emergency crew arrived at the apartment, Megan was still astride the senator, naked and frantically administering CPR. By the time the first staffer arrived, she had put on a jogging suit. She'd ridden in the ambulance with the body, her feet in slippers, her face smudged with tears and mascara.

Megan was still standing beside the gurney with Harrison's body when Evelyn arrived at the hospital. The senator's aides had taken Megan away then. The story was the two women didn't encounter each other directly, though they may have passed in the hallway. The press and media reports were, of course, quite different.

On television that night Evelyn was shown arriving at the hospital. Megan was nowhere to be seen. The statement issued by the senator's office had him collapsing in the middle of an early-morning meeting with a group of staffers at one of their homes on Connecticut Avenue.

In the cathedral that morning, Elliot had sat in the pew behind Evelyn, Amory and Brett. Whenever he'd had a glimpse of Brett's face, he'd wanted to lean forward and touch her. He'd wanted to look into her eyes. In his heart he knew they belonged together, yet, as the weeks wore by, his ability to fight for her had begun to wane. The more time passed, the more he was beginning to see that her true feelings weren't nearly as important to her as what she *wanted* to believe she felt.

At first he'd felt guilty about what had happened. God knows, that was easier than trying to conjure up resentment or jealousy of Amory. Elliot knew he was the interloper, the troublemaker. But he also knew Brett belonged with him, that they were destined for each other. About that he was absolutely certain. God or fate or the collective conscious—whoever or whatever controlled destiny—was not permitting the inevitable to come easily to him. He was beginning to realize that he would have to pay dearly for whatever fate he was finally accorded.

At work he'd gone through the motions numbly. He put in the hours they expected of him, but he thought of little else besides Brett.

Jennifer was the sole exception. She was the only other human being he could honestly say he loved. She'd kept him functioning, if only because she was dependent on him. Of course, he hated it that a woman had to be hired to watch her during the day, especially since Monica was now claiming she was sober and ought to have Jennifer in her care.

Having reformed herself, Monica was getting bolder in her demands. Till now he had dismissed her as being contentious for the sake of her own pride and self-esteem, but he was beginning to realize her motives ran deeper, and that she was dead serious. Only the day before, his lawyer had called to say Monica was now demanding sole custody. Elliot had laughed when he heard the news, but the lawyer insisted that it wasn't posturing.

"What does she want?" he'd asked. "A mudslinging contest?"

"For starters, she wants a meeting," the lawyer had told him. "Just the two of you. No hearing. No counsel on either side."

"Why?"

"Her attorney would only say she has her reasons."

The proposal had given Elliot pause. Experience told him Monica was capable of anything. "Have her call me," he'd said.

He'd wondered several times during the past months whether Monica might make good her threat to use his affair with Brett against him. He'd assumed she was mainly interested in gloating at his expense, but as time went on, the implications were becoming more worrisome.

His lawyer told him that the days in which a parent's morality was scrutinized by the courts were pretty much over—unless there was danger to the physical or emotional well-being of the child. The question was how much credence would the court accord Monica's few months on the wagon. And what would Elliot have to do to turn back the threat? Catch Monica dead drunk and flat on her ass?

The funeral procession entered the gates of Arlington National, and Elliot's thoughts returned to Brett. She was in the car ahead of him, with Evelyn and Amory. Outside the cathedral, as the mourners had made their way to their vehicles, Brett's eyes had found him. She'd held her vacant gaze for only a moment before turning away and taking Amory's arm, but it was enough to send him into a blue funk.

Now, whenever he saw her touch Amory, it set off a quiet rage within him. He tried not to think of them together. He had had no desire for another woman, and he couldn't imagine how she could want another man—not after what they'd shared.

The cavalcade came to a stop on the hillside near the center of the cemetery. He'd hardly noticed, but it had begun snowing. There was more than half an inch of dry, crystalline snow on the ground.

For a moment Elliot remained in the limousine, staring at the darkened rear window of the vehicle ahead. He could see the hearse and the attendants beginning to unload Harrison's casket. After a minute the door of the limo opened and Amory emerged, bareheaded but in a black topcoat with a white silk scarf at his throat. Evelyn exited next, taking Amory's gloved hand as she climbed out. Then he closed the passenger door. Brett, it seemed, would not be getting out. Elliot wondered why.

He got out of the car, buttoning his topcoat as he made his way to Amory and Evelyn. Some officials approached them as he reached Evelyn's side. Amory said something to one of the men, and Evelyn looked at Elliot with red-rimmed eyes. She smiled faintly before taking his arm.

"Thank you for coming, dear," she whispered.

Amory greeted him with a nod, then the three of them followed the men bearing the casket. They walked along the sanded path, their feet crunching the brittle snow.

Elliot wanted to ask why Brett had stayed in the limousine, but there was no way it could be done diplomatically. Evelyn was clearly in need and, along with Amory, he lent her his support.

It had been years since Elliot had been to a funeral—not counting ceremonial attendance at the services of some foreign official. The funeral that always stood out in his mind was his mother's. He and Amory had been together that time, too. He morbidly wondered who would be next.

But as the other mourners gathered at the grave site, he kept thinking about Brett back in the limousine. Even when the snowflakes stung his face, he thought of her. Elliot bowed his head mechanically as a prayer was said. Then he watched Evelyn go forward with Amory to place a flower on Harrison's casket. He was still off in thought, thinking about being with Brett on the East Shore, when Amory leaned over and whispered, "Could I ask a favor?"

"Certainly."

"Brett wasn't doing very well during the drive and I'm worried. Would you mind checking on her for me, Elliot?"

The request came as a surprise. "Is she ill?"

"Not exactly." Amory glanced at Evelyn. "She's pregnant."

Elliot was stunned, disbelieving. He started to ask for an explanation, but caught himself. Pregnant? The word came back through his mind a second time. He managed to collect himself. "Yes, certainly. Of course."

He turned and slipped through the crowd, noticing Megan Tiernan standing in back with two of Harrison's staffers, nearly prostrate with grief. Passing by her, he quickly made his way along the path.

The vehicles were still at some distance, but he made out Brett's limo. The driver was standing at the open passenger door, looking in. Just as Elliot got there the man closed the door.

"Is Mrs. Maitland all right?"

"She's pretty sick, sir. She asked me to get her some water."

"Yes, please do. I'll look after her."

The man went off and Elliot opened the door. He leaned over to peer in at Brett. Her face was white as a sheet. She was startled at the sight of him. He climbed in beside her, closing the door before she could say anything.

"Elliot . . ."

"Amory said you weren't feeling well. He asked me to check on you."

She swallowed hard, wiping her mouth with a handkerchief. "I'm all right—just a bit upset. There's nothing to worry about. Tell Amory I'm fine."

"Brett, he said you're pregnant."

She froze for a second, then took a long breath. Finally she leveled her gaze on him. "That's right, Elliot. I am."

"When did you get pregnant?" There was a ring in his voice. Accusation.

"The baby is Amory's."

He felt as though she'd kicked him in the stomach. He shook his head. He didn't believe her. Something was wrong.

"I'm sorry that you had to find out this way," she said, her voice firm now. "I know it isn't very pleasant for you...."

"Not pleasant! Jesus Christ, Brett."

"Well..." She was at a loss for words.

"How far along are you? Were you already pregnant when we were together?"

She looked away, her mouth tightening into a thin line. "No," she whispered, her head slightly bowed. "Amory and I have wanted a child. I decided now was a good time. And so I got pregnant."

"I don't believe you." There was accusation in his voice again.

"Well, it'll be obvious soon enough."

Elliot sat, shaking his head. "How could you?"

"How could *I*? What about what *we* did, Elliot? That's what we should be asking ourselves. How could *we*? I want this baby very badly. I shall always feel terrible about what I did to Amory. I can only pray God will forgive me."

"Brett, this is insane."

"I know you're upset. I was hoping that when you found out, you'd understand, that you'd see that now there can never be anyone in my life but Amory."

Elliot was still incredulous. "Does he know about...us?"

"No. I took your advice. And I won't tell him unless I have to. It would hurt him terribly, and for no good reason. But this child is my bond with him, and if he should find out about us, then I pray he will forgive me—for the baby's sake."

"The only reason you got pregnant was because you were afraid of your feelings for me. You love me, Brett. I know you do."

The expression on her chalky face grew solemn. "I *don't* love you," she said. "It's over. Accept that. Please."

Elliot was beginning to see that he had lost her. His hope had been fading for weeks, but now the reality of it had hit him in the face. He did his best to draw himself up. "I guess there's nothing left but to wish you well, then," he said.

She lowered her head.

Her hand was resting on the seat. He reached over and covered it with his. "I'll never truly accept this," he told her. "Not in my heart."

Brett sniffled. "I'd like to think that...someday...we could be...friends."

Until the last, she'd maintained control. But at the end her voice had broken and her eyes glossed. She turned away.

The door opened. It was the chauffeur with a plastic cup of water. Elliot took it from him and handed it to Brett. Then he slipped out of the limo and into the bitterly cold Potomac air. Just before the man closed the car door, Elliot heard Brett sob. It was faint and muffled, but it was undeniably an anguished cry of pain.

Washington, D.C.

January 28, 1989

Elliot watched Jennifer kneeling on a chair at the window in the living room, peering at the tranquil gray hues of Cleveland Park at twilight. A month or so earlier she had spent a lot of time there looking at the Christmas lights, carrying on a hazy conversation with herself about Santa Claus. Now the lights were gone and so was Santa.

Elliot felt a bit isolated from the uncertain world. And not only because they were living in a furnished apartment that was neither home nor alien territory. His life was on hold. He was waiting for Brett.

The days after Arlington had been bleak. He was left without a clear sense of purpose. He spent the night of the inaugural ball at home, just like the Dukakis camp. But Brett's life, like the Reagan-Bush revolution, went on. Word of her pregnancy had been in the gossip columns. Among the pictures in the paper from the inaugural ball was one captioned, "Supreme Court Justice Amory Maitland Dances With His Wife, Brett, Who Is Expecting Their First Child in July."

Elliot had stared at the picture for ten or fifteen minutes, numbed by public confirmation of a circumstance he considered a profound injustice. His reaction had been to turn to Jennifer, spending every possible hour with her.

Jennifer spent her days with Mrs. Ingram, the woman he'd hired to care for her. Nights and weekends she passed with him, except when she was with her mother, which at

Monica's insistence had become more and more frequent. He'd offered no resistance to Monica's demands under the theory that, in time, mothering would become a tedium rather than a pleasure.

But his wife had showed no signs of tiring of the child. In fact, she'd grown more possessive with each visit. Elliot had been leery at first, but he could find no evidence that Jennifer was neglected or unhappy when she stayed with Monica and Farrens. She was always glad to see Elliot, but leaving him didn't seem a problem. As time went on, Jennifer seemed to accept the notion of two homes.

Watching his daughter at the window, Elliot had let his book drop into his lap. The baby-fine dark curls at the back of her neck made his heart ache with love. She turned around just then and, seeing him watching her, smiled.

"No more Santa, Daddy," she said, pointing with her little finger.

"No, angel, not for another year."

"How come?"

"Come over and sit on Daddy's lap and we'll talk for a while, okay?"

Jennifer climbed down from the chair and skipped over to him. He lifted her high into the air before she hugged him, pressing her round little cheek against his cashmere sweater. A lump formed in his throat. He had grown afraid of losing her.

"Is Mommy coming now?" she asked.

"Later, angel. After you're in bed."

He played with her for a few more minutes, then they went off to the kitchen to fix dinner. After they'd eaten she had her bath and Elliot told her a bedtime story. Before he turned out the light, he told her that he loved her.

"Love you too, Daddy."

The rite was a customary one. But this time there was more fervency in his words than usual. After kissing her forehead, he went to the front room to wait for Monica.

They'd agreed she'd come at nine. On the telephone Elliot had tried to learn what he could about her intentions, but Monica hadn't been forthcoming. "I want to resolve this thing, Elliot," she'd told him. "Once and for all."

Settling into his chair, he picked up the Sunday *Post*, which carried the latest story about the backroom maneuvering in the Maryland Republican Party over Harrison's senate seat. While Washington was busy celebrating Bush's inauguration, in Baltimore the two wings of the party had bared their claws, leaving the governor in the unenviable position of making enemies whichever way he went.

Evelyn's name had been floated as a compromise candidate, a kind of caretaker senator to hold office until Harrison's true successor could be chosen in a special election. She was a sympathetic figure, and the notion of her taking the office had great appeal to both sides, mainly because she was considered politically neutral. Elliot hadn't talked to her since the funeral, but he assumed she had some interest in the job, or the speculation would have been squelched.

He put his paper aside and looked at his watch. Feeling restless, he went to the window to watch the lights. The town lay under a cold, somber haze. There were many things about Washington that he liked, though it hadn't been particularly good to him. The associations with Monica were particularly untoward. Even their first trip to the capital together had been bizarre.

During the cab ride from Washington National, she'd tried to embarrass him in front of the driver. She'd stuck her hand under his coat and rubbed his crotch and talked about his wife being at home with the children. And later, at the hotel, she'd insisted on going to get ice wearing nothing but a sheer nightgown, delighting afterward in telling him about her encounter with a disbelieving guest.

At the time he'd half enjoyed her game, dismissing it as part of her irreverent personality. But he'd soon learned that he could be the object of her mischief. Time proved to him that Monica's problem wasn't the devil at large so much as the devil within.

Still, even when they'd been fighting incessantly, there had been a bond, if only of mutual suffering. Now their war had taken on a detached quality. They were distant adversaries, dueling at long range and with heavy artillery. Unfortunately one of them was destined to be seen the winner, the other as a loser.

Much as he hated her, Elliot had a begrudging admiration for Monica. Getting off booze couldn't have been easy. And forging a respectable relationship with Farrens had to be a challenge. His wife, it seemed, was finding herself in divorce as she never had in marriage.

When the buzzer finally sounded he went to the door to let her in. Surprisingly, Robert Farrens was at her side.

"Well, an entire delegation," Elliot said. "The first curve of the evening."

"Robert and I plan to marry as soon as the divorce is final," she announced coolly. "Since what happens tonight will affect him as much as me, I decided it would be all right if he came along."

"By all means," Elliot said, stepping back to admit them.

Monica strode in, looking around with her usual air of disapproval. Farrens, bemused, followed. He looked older, yet somehow healthier than before. They slipped off their coats. Monica was in a navy wool suit with navy pumps—the picture of respectability. Farrens wore one of his well-tailored business suits.

"I probably should have said something," she intoned, "just in case you wanted Brett here, too."

He glared at her. "If you want this to be a civilized discussion, Monica, I suggest you drop the sarcasm."

She tossed her head with amusement. "Oh, sorry, Elliot, dear. I thought you had more of a sense of humor than that."

He gestured for them to sit on the sofa, taking a chair opposite. "All right," he said. "You wanted this meeting. What's on you mind?"

She exchanged looks with Farrens, then said, "Your attorney has told you that I want Jennifer, I assume."

"Yes. I took it for what it was—posturing."

"Oh no, Elliot, darling. I'm perfectly serious. I want her. I will be generous about visitation, but I want her living with me on a full-time basis."

"That's out of the question. I'll share custody, but that's as far as I'll go."

Monica's look turned dark. "You don't seem to appreciate how shaky your bargaining position is, do you, Mr. Ambassador?"

"Monica, I'm prepared to litigate this, so don't bother trying to strong-arm me. Jennifer is more important to me than anything in the world."

"Oh?"

"Yes."

"Well, you sanctimonious sonovabitch, I guess I have to be blunt. If you don't comply with my demands, I'm going to have a conversation with Amory about you and Stepmama. He might consider it interesting that his sweet little pregnant wife has been fucking the foreign service behind his back."

"Monica, even you are not that low."

She laughed. "Isn't that one of the basic principles of diplomacy, Elliot? If you've got leverage, use it?"

"In other words, you're blackmailing me."

She gave a half laugh. "Yes, Elliot. In other words, I'm blackmailing you. The point is you have a choice. Give me my daughter or you and Brett can account to Amory for your sins."

Anger surged through him, but he tried to remain calm. "Don't you see you're playing with people's lives? Jennifer's well-being is all that matters. Don't you care about her?"

"Yes, Elliot, she matters to me so much that I'll do whatever it takes to have her with me. She's *my* child. *I'm* her mother, not some woman you hire to look after her. She'll live with me. And if you force me, I'll take down whoever I must to make sure that's the way it will be."

His jaw tightened. "I'll be damned before I let you get custody by blackmail. You can threaten to blow up the world, for all I care. I won't sacrifice her. As far as I'm concerned, you can go to hell!''

"Sacrifice!" Monica shrieked. "You talk like she's yours to give!"

"You lost your rights a long time ago."

Monica moved to the edge of her seat, looking as though she were ready to spring on him. "Listen, you bastard, I don't know what right you think you've got to dictate to me. Yes, we had a rotten marriage. You're goddamn right we did. Maybe I had a few problems, but they're behind me now. I know damned well you wouldn't hesitate to use my past against me, so I'm going to use yours against you!" Farrens put his hand on Monica's arm, but she ignored him. "How do you have the gall to talk about *my* rights to *my* child?"

"She's both of ours."

"I won't deny you access. I'll be as generous as you would have been to me."

"I didn't keep her from you, Monica, even before Brett. I wanted nothing more for my daughter than that she have a mother. But *you* abandoned her!"

"Well, I'm not abandoning her now. I'm prepared to be the mother to her you claim you want—not that I give a damn about what you think."

Elliot stared at her, knowing she was dead serious about going to Amory. The bitch was willing to destroy anybody who got in her way. Farrens leaned forward, looking directly at Elliot. He spoke with a calm, reasonable voice.

"I know I'm not one of your favorite people, Brewster, and because of that I was reluctant to come along. But I thought it might be good to be here in case things blew up as they have."

"Say what you have to say, Farrens. Save the diplomacy for the office."

He sighed, measuring his thoughts. "I know how close you are to Jennifer, and how convinced you are that Monica is a failure as a mother—"

"He's as much to blame as me," Monica interjected.

Farrens shushed her with his hand. "The point is she's changed. And the circumstances have changed."

"Oh, come on, Farrens. This newfound rectitude is window dressing. A few weeks on the straight and narrow doesn't make her a fit mother."

"Yeah," Monica said. "And a few weeks on Brett Maitland's ass makes you an ideal father, I suppose."

Elliot's eyes flashed. "Our sex lives aren't the issue."

"That being the case," Farrens said, "Monica stands on fairly solid ground. We've gone over this with our lawyers, as I'm sure you have with yours. Monica hasn't had a drink in a couple of months. Neither have I. We're engaged. I'm not rich, but I'm comfortable and I have a decent job, and Monica has considerable resources through her family. We offer a home, stability and a track record of clean living that lengthens by the day. On the other hand, you offer Jennifer evenings and weekends and the prospect of being raised by a governess."

"Nice, Robert, but I don't buy it. I won't sell my daughter on the basis of a wish and a promise."

Monica jeered. Again, Farrens quietened her. "The only way you can refute the case I've just made is to open up the past," he said. "What we're telling you is that if you do, we won't hesitate to use all the information at our disposal, however embarrassing that might be to you, Mrs. Maitland or the justice."

Elliot shook his head. "Christ, Farrens. You're a snake. You're as bad as she is."

Farrens smiled thinly. "I'll overlook the personal attack, Elliot. But you should think this through. Obviously Monica is determined to make a happy family life for Jennifer. A few months ago she didn't feel this way. Whether you believe it or not, we've changed."

"Congratulations. I wish you every happiness. But not with my daughter."

A flicker of annoyance passed over Farrens's face. "Look, we've all been blunt, but I don't believe you see how determined we are. You must be aware that Mrs. Maitland could be named corespondent, that suits for alienation of affection and the like are possible.''

"You've got to be joking.'' Elliot tried to maintain a brave front, but he was beginning to see he couldn't buffalo them. In the back of his mind he had wondered about the possibility of this happening, but he just couldn't believe Monica would take it this far. He was wrong.

"Such legal maneuvering probably wouldn't affect the outcome of a custody battle, but it would embarrass a lot of people,'' Farrens went on. "Considering that Mrs. Maitland is expecting, I would think a public battle over Jennifer would be doubly painful, especially to her and her husband.''

"You're a son of a bitch,'' Elliot said through gritted teeth.

"Poor Amory's the one I feel sorry for,'' Monica said. "Imagine, having this baby and wondering if it could be his stepson's.''

Elliot had the urge to haul off and deck her. Only the last vestiges of his willpower saved him from doing it. "You'll stop at nothing, will you?''

"I'm surprised you haven't wondered yourself, Elliot. Is the kid yours or Grandpa's?''

"And you expect me to turn my daughter over to this?'' Elliot said to Farrens disdainfully.

Monica sat shaking with anger.

"We've given you a lot to think about,'' Farrens continued coolly. "You can hardly be expected to make a decision now. Think about it, Elliot. Talk to Mrs. Maitland, if that would help.''

"I have nothing to do with Brett anymore,'' Elliot said. "I thought I'd made that clear.''

"Then keep your own counsel. But you should know we are determined. And we have absolutely nothing to lose by taking this to the mat.''

It was a telling point. They'd given him the worst possible dilemma he could imagine—spare Brett at the cost of his daughter.

"I'd like to make one last observation," Farrens said. "We're not asking you to give up Jennifer completely. Monica wants her to live with us but, as she said, there will be generous visitation rights. I would think you could see the advantages in that for you, as well as Jennifer. And if you're really worried about us, you surely know that if a court later found us unfit for any reason, the custody order could be amended. What I'm saying, in other words, is let us prove ourselves."

Elliot looked down at his hands, hearing the weight of reason. To a judge it would be a compelling argument.

"And I'll offer something else," Monica said. "Something you don't deserve. I propose to take Jennifer home tonight and keep her for the week. Anytime you wish to drop in on us and check the state of our sobriety, or see that Jennifer's bed is clean and that she's been fed, you're welcome. It galls me to offer that, but I will. For a week. Any time of the day or night."

"Your generosity is admirable," Elliot replied with thinly veiled sarcasm.

She smiled. "I didn't do this to you, honey bunch. You did it to yourself. Believe me, a person's really got to watch who they fuck."

On reflection, Elliot decided it was the wisest thing his wife had ever said. "Monica, you've become a paragon. I can't help wondering where all this virtue was during our marriage."

"Oh, it was there. It was just smothered, that's all."

"I don't recall being cruel."

"Maybe you weren't. But you didn't understand what I needed."

"What was that?"

"To find a life, Elliot. To find a life."

PART V

Washington, D.C.

April 8, 1989

Evelyn had removed the last of Harrison's things from their closet two months earlier, but at times she could still detect a whiff of his scent, which invariably brought back memories. The most recent were not such happy ones. He'd come back to the house only twice after moving out. Once, he'd come to pick something up. The last time she'd seen him alive—the week he'd died—he'd come by to discuss how to coordinate the public announcement of their divorce. Ironically, she'd buried him the day he was to issue the press release.

But the occasion that stood out most in her mind was not that winter day at Arlington, when she'd laid him to rest. It was the day he'd told her he was leaving. Harrison had packed his things while she sat downstairs. And after he'd gone off to be with Megan, Evelyn had cried for a while, then she'd gone upstairs to view firsthand the flotsam of her marriage.

He'd left behind a few old clothes he hadn't been able to throw away, but wouldn't wear—much like the wife he'd only then found the courage to abandon. His top dresser drawer he'd left nearly intact. At first she'd thought it was an oversight. It contained nothing essential to his daily living; only a few keepsakes—his Georgetown school ring, his ribbons and decorations from the Korean War, a gold coin and penknife his father had given him as a boy, the index cards on which his first Senate speech was typed, an envelope with a lock of his mother's hair.

Though she had disposed of his other personal effects, Evelyn hadn't touched the drawer. It was the one place in the house where her husband still resided. Eventually she would clean it out, but for the time being she guarded it as she guarded her private memories. Megan Tiernan had taken her husband, but she couldn't take the past.

Evelyn put on her pearl-and-diamond earrings and looked at herself in the mirror. She wondered if the black lace dress with the full taffeta skirt didn't signal too loudly that she was a widow. It was completely appropriate for a dinner party at the White House, yet it struck her as a touch too blatant. Well, she thought, it was too late now. In twenty minutes Amory and Brett were due to pick her up.

After smoothing back wisps of her graying hair, Evelyn opened Harrison's drawer to commune with him for a moment before going downstairs. She fingered the index cards containing his speech, glancing at the first words. She remembered the thrill she'd felt, listening from the gallery. How long ago it seemed. Now she had made a maiden speech of her own.

Harrison would have envied her the evening ahead. She was not only attending a private dinner with the Bushes, it was partly in her honor. Two freshmen Republican senators, Connie Mack of Florida and James Jeffords from Vermont, would be there as well as the majority leader, Bob Dole, and a few other key Senate Republicans. The evening was intended partly as a tribute to Harrison, but Evelyn wasn't so naive as to believe the past was more important than the present.

The key issue looming in the coming months was the budget. The president wanted to avoid a major defeat like the one he'd suffered in March, when the Senate rejected the Tower nomination for secretary of defense, and so he was marshaling Republican forces. The White House wanted to be sure Evelyn could be counted on in the same way Harrison had been.

The president's concern was not without basis. Evelyn had already proved to be a bit unpredictable with regard to domestic issues when she made it clear that she would not be a standard-bearer for the right-to-life forces, as Harrison had been. She intended to think for herself, and that made the right wing of the party nervous.

So she was off to the White House for an intimate dinner—a privilege never accorded her husband, though she and Harrison had attended a couple of important White House functions.

The doorbell chimed, and Evelyn looked at her watch. Amory and Brett were early. She went downstairs and opened the door. Megan Tiernan was standing on the porch. Evelyn was so surprised she was speechless.

"Oh...you're going out," Megan stammered.

"Yes, to dinner," Evelyn said, unable to keep the frost from her voice. "What is it you want?"

"I'm...Megan Tiernan, Mrs. Maitland," she said, clutching the collar of her little beige wool suit.

Evelyn tried to maintain a calm demeanor. "I know who you are."

"I was wondering if I could talk to you?"

"I'm afraid it's not a very good time."

"I'm leaving Washington tonight. I wanted to see you before I caught my plane. I'll only take a minute."

Evelyn looked out at the street, knowing that Amory and Brett would be arriving at any time. "I suppose I have a few minutes. Come in," she said, stepping back.

They went to the sitting room. Evelyn indicated the chair for her to take. Megan sat on the edge of the cushion.

"I know this is a shock to you, me coming here," she said, "but I thought about it a long time and finally decided I had to."

Evelyn said nothing.

"I'm sure you hate me," Megan nervously continued on. "And I'm sorry if my coming causes you any pain, but I had to tell you how much I regret what happened."

Evelyn took a deep breath. "Are you referring to Harrison's infidelity or his death?"

"Everything."

Evelyn stared at her, seeing a sister in mourning as much as an adversary. The sting of Megan Tiernan's unexpected appearance wasn't as painful as she would have thought. "If you've come for forgiveness, Miss Tiernan, you've got it. I don't hold grudges."

"I came because I wanted you to understand. I didn't intend for any of it to happen, Mrs. Maitland. Neither did Harrison. We just fell in love. We couldn't help it."

"I believe you."

"He loved you, too," Megan said. "I didn't like it that he did, but it's true. Even at the end."

Evelyn didn't know what to say.

"Harrison's feelings were a lot more complicated than you may have thought," Megan said.

Evelyn studied Megan closely. She had a wholesome beauty with a kind of voluptuousness that would have attracted her husband. This was a girl who could give sexual pleasure, yet Evelyn sensed there must have been much more. Sex alone wouldn't have been enough. Not for him to leave her.

"He did love you," Megan assured her.

"I was aware of my husband's feelings, Miss Tiernan. You don't have to tell me how he felt."

"He loved you a lot more than he let on," Megan said. "I was with him when he had that first heart attack. He wanted you with him, not me. At the time it hurt terribly, but I thought you should know that was how he felt."

"If this is designed to make me feel better, it isn't worth the trouble. There's no point now."

Megan lowered her eyes. "Whatever you might think, Mrs. Maitland, our relationship wasn't frivolous. I would have done anything for Harrison. And in a way, I did. I sold my soul for him. Even though I lost him after we were together only a few weeks, my only regret is what I did to you."

"What do you mean, you sold your soul?"

Megan hesitated, though her glossy eyes remained on Evelyn. "Last summer I got pregnant."

Evelyn gasped. "Dear God."

"I was happy until I discovered that I couldn't have Harrison and the baby both. So I got rid of my baby." She girded herself, obviously struggling to look brave.

"You had an abortion?"

Megan nodded, then looked away. "I damned my soul to hell for all eternity, just to be with him for a few months."

Evelyn closed her eyes. Megan's pain may as well have been her own. She never would have thought she could feel empathy for the woman who'd taken her husband, but she did.

"Harrison didn't ask me to do it," Megan said. "But I could tell he didn't want me to have the baby."

Evelyn felt a chill run up her back.

"I loved him, Mrs. Maitland. I loved him with all my heart." She took a ragged breath. "I don't expect you to feel sorry for me, or even forgive me, but I thought telling you this might help you to forgive Harrison."

Evelyn felt weak. "I know you mean well, but I must make my own peace, just as you must make yours."

Megan lowered her head; her hands were folded on her lap. Tears began running down her cheeks.

"You said you're leaving Washington. Where are you going?" Evelyn asked.

"Home. To Washington State. Ellensburg. It's what I need right now. To try to make a life without Harrison." She glanced up, smiling through her tears. Then she got to her feet.

Evelyn rose as well. She stared at the girl who'd rent her marriage and taken her husband. "Don't punish yourself," she said softly. "Just don't punish yourself."

"I've been punished already." Megan's voice cracked.

Evelyn stared at her, pity welling. "Goddamn this world," she said, and stepped over and put her arms around the girl. Megan cried against her for a minute. Then, for a brief moment, they held hands before Megan turned to go.

From the doorway Evelyn watched her descending the stairs. The April sky at dusk was clear except for pink clouds in the east. The air was brisk and smelled of vegetation and the perfume of some flowering plant.

As Megan went out the gate, a taxi pulled up out front, double-parking. Amory, in black tie, got out, pausing to watch Megan making her way up the street. He glanced up at Evelyn.

"Give me a couple of minutes, will you?" she called to him.

She went upstairs, checked her face and got her purse. She opened Harrison's drawer and stared at the contents, realizing that she would give it all to Amory except, perhaps, for the speech. Everything else belonged with him.

Downstairs she looked in the hall closet, fingering her mink before rejecting it in favor of her politically correct wool coat. Then she went out to join Amory and Brett for the ride to the White House.

"So how's the expectant mother?" Evelyn asked, as the taxi pulled away.

"As expectant as ever," Brett replied. "More, I guess, than when you saw me last."

Evelyn smiled. "You look wonderful. A picture of health."

Brett nodded appreciatively, resting her hand on the bulge under her beige silk dress. It was an Empire style with a beaded bodice. She had an antique silk shawl around her shoulders.

Amory leaned forward so he could see Evelyn. "Who was the young woman leaving as we came up?"

"Megan Tiernan. Harrison's . . . friend."

"She came to see you?"

"We kind of settled things, I suppose you could say."

"I can't imagine."

"I can," Brett said

Amory shook his head.

Evelyn said, "I think you'd have to be a woman to understand, Amory. Which reminds me of something else I wanted to tell you. There are a few of Harrison's mementos I'd like you to have. Some things your father gave him. A lock of your mother's hair, that sort of thing."

"I'd be delighted to have them, but are you sure you want to part with them?"

"I'll keep the ones that are meaningful to me." She turned to Brett. "So, what does the doctor say?"

"Things couldn't be better," she said with a hint of enthusiasm.

"Do you know yet whether it's a boy or a girl?"

"No, I told the doctor I don't want to know and Amory doesn't care whether they tell us or not. He says he already knows it's a boy."

"There hasn't been a girl in the Maitland line for five or six generations," Amory said.

"Listen to him." Brett chuckled. "He almost sounds like that's something to be proud of."

They all laughed.

"Well, thank God there are families around that do have girls," Evelyn said. "Otherwise you Maitlands could get kind of lonely."

"I'm the first to admit that, Ev," he replied. "Brett is the joy of my life." He reached over and patted his wife's hand.

"The way you've been working lately, I wonder if those clerks of yours aren't the real joy of your life," Brett teased. She turned to Evelyn. "He's been struggling with an opinion for over two weeks now, sometimes long into the night."

Evelyn wondered if Brett was referring to *Russo v. Clayson,* the abortion case. She had no idea how the Court had voted, but she wouldn't be surprised if Amory had been assigned to write the opinion. The job usually went to the justice with the swing vote.

Evelyn knew Amory well enough to know he'd never betray a confidence of the Court, so there was no point in asking questions. She glanced out the window. They were on M Street now, headed for Pennsylvania Avenue.

"Is this your first White House dinner, Brett?" she asked, finding a safer subject.

"Yes. I've been to a reception, but that's all."

"You were at the bicentennial dinner in honor of Queen Elizabeth, weren't you, Amory?" Evelyn asked.

"Yes," he replied. "Gerry gave me a seat on the Court and Betty gave me dinner."

They laughed again.

"You're certainly starting out right, Brett," Evelyn said. "A private party. Very few people can claim to have done that. My first White House dinner was a state affair for Nikita Khruschev when he came in 1959." She chuckled. "I guess that dates me a little, doesn't it?"

"How exciting that must have been, though—right at the height of the Cold War."

"Harrison and I were newly married and he was just crushed that he couldn't go. But my father, who'd spent time in Russia during the war and spoke the language, received an 'Honorable Ellis Daughton and Mrs. Daughton' invitation, even though Mother had been dead for years. The protocol people were so embarrassed, they let me come in her place. Believe me, it was a hot ticket and I was thrilled."

"You met Khruschev and everything?" Brett asked.

"Oh, yes. He about broke my hand in the receiving line. What a character. Standing there in his business suit with his ribbons pinned on his pocket, and Ike next to him in white tie and tails. Talk about a mismatched pair. Mrs. Khruschev wasn't quite as bad. She had on a short gown with a diamond brooch, as I recall. Mamie wore a long gold brocade gown with a diamond-and-pearl necklace. I remember the necklace real well."

Evelyn hadn't thought of that night for a long time, but it had been a sore subject between her and Harrison for years. He wasn't comfortable with her superior Washington connections until he'd eaten at the White House him-self—invited, he was wont to point out, in his own right.

But that September evening back in 1959 she'd gone to the White House with her father. A uniformed guard had taken their card of admission, then they'd been directed through the oval diplomatic reception room, where she had checked her mother's fur stole. A white-gloved military aide had di-rected them up the broad marble stairway to the foyer where they were greeted by a member of the White House social staff and given cards showing where they would sit in the State Dining Room. A second military aide had escorted them to the East Room.

When all the guests had arrived, the Marine Corps Band had struck up "Hail to the Chief." The Eisenhowers and Khruschevs had paused in the foyer for a brief photo ses-sion, then, following a color guard, they'd appeared at the doorway to the East Room.

The guests then had passed through the reception line, her father commenting to the chairman of the Council of Min-isters of the U.S.S.R. that they had met once in Moscow. Khruschev hadn't seemed very interested. He had been fas-cinated more, it had seemed, by the neckline of Evelyn's gown. She smiled at the recollection.

The evening had been a dazzling one, and was still vivid in her mind. Even though she'd been back to the White House several times—as recently as a year ago for a lun-cheon with Nancy Reagan and the Senate wives—the Khruschev state dinner had always stood out. But she de-cided the one tonight might change that. This time, she was going to be wooed for the vote *she* wielded in the United States Senate.

Still, Evelyn wasn't arrogant enough to think she was there by merit. But she did believe that Providence was re-warding her. Whether it was luck or compensation for years of wifely fidelity didn't really matter; it was what she did with the opportunity that counted.

They got out of the taxi at the southwest gate of the White House, just as she had in 1959. Though it was a private

party, the invitation instructed the guests to enter through
the state rooms, rather than the West Wing.

Evelyn glanced over at Brett, whose eyes were bright as
they strolled up to the mansion. Even with her pregnancy
obvious, she was radiant; her pale hair a bit shorter and
swept back, her shawl loose about her shoulders.

They entered the mansion and were escorted directly to
the Yellow Oval Room on the second floor, where the president and First Lady were receiving their guests. Spotting
Evelyn, George Bush stepped over to greet her, his familiar
grin spreading across his face as he pumped her hand.

Barbara, in a midnight-blue lace-and-taffeta Scaasi, and
a triple-strand necklace of huge pearls, was soon at his side,
adding her own gracious welcome. Behind her, Evelyn heard
the president asking Amory how things were going at the
Court. But the justice's response was drowned out by the
voices of the First Lady and Brett, who were discussing
when the baby was due. It was a nice moment, one she
shared with Brett vicariously.

Brett saw the little smile on Evelyn's face as Bob Dole
came up to say hello. The two senators went off and Brett,
her heart beating swiftly, took Amory's arm and they moved
on into the room.

"This is more exciting than I imagined it would be," she
whispered. "I've been pinching myself to make sure I'm really awake."

"Since when does a liberal belle from the hills of north
Georgia find a roomful of stuffy Republicans exciting?"
Amory teased.

"Oh, you know what I mean. The Bushes are very gracious. And he *is* the president of the United States. I can
overlook the fact that he's in the wrong party."

Amory laughed. "Well, don't get too accustomed to
dropping by for dinner. When the Court's opinions are released at the end of the term we won't be very welcome in
the hallowed halls of a Republican White House."

There was a sober quality in his voice that took her aback.

"Surely people won't hold your judicial decisions against you, Amory—not people in the top circles of government?"

"Darling, I will soon be one of the most hated men in America. Of course, those who don't despise me will revere me as a saint, but the flames of hatred will burn bright around me for months. I guarantee you that."

Brett had assumed that there would be a lot of public clamor when the *Russo* decision was announced, but she hadn't thought of it so much in personal terms—with Amory the object of public passions. Maybe she'd been naive, oblivious to how this would affect him personally, how it would impact their lives.

A waiter came for their drink orders. Amory asked for a light bourbon and branch. She asked for orange juice.

"Look at Evelyn," he said, signaling his desire to change the subject. "She seems to be in her element, doesn't she?"

Evelyn was across the room, chatting with her Senate colleagues, looking confident and very comfortable in the spotlight.

"My respect for her grows daily," Brett said. "She's going to be a wonderful senator. God knows, she's already a fabulous person."

In spite of the excitement of the evening, Brett couldn't help thinking about Megan Tiernan's visit. Evelyn's forgiveness was truly remarkable. Still, no matter how much she admired her sister-in-law, Brett doubted that she could be as generous. It seemed to her that she had more in common with Megan than Evelyn.

Sometimes she wondered if her terrible guilt would ever go away. A part of her had died when she'd betrayed Amory. Maybe it would be like any other death—it couldn't be undone, but the sting of it might diminish with time.

The waiter returned with their drinks. They each took a sip from their glasses and observed the crowd. Brett told herself that she ought to try to enjoy the moment.

Barbara Bush came over to them. "Justice Maitland," she said, "you may have the loveliest young lady at the party, but that doesn't give you the right to keep her to yourself. May I pry her away so the other guests will have a chance to enjoy her?"

Amory bowed solicitously. "Difficult as it is to give her up, I wouldn't want to deprive anyone of the pleasure."

She patted him on the arm. "I'll bring her back."

He beamed as the First Lady took Brett off for introductions. He'd been alone only for a moment when Evelyn appeared at his side.

"Don't tell me you've broken the Senate filibuster," he quipped. "I was sure you'd been buttonholed for the evening."

"The new kid on the block always gets a little extra attention, Amory. You know that. Once they know where I stand on their pet issues, they'll let me fade into the background. I have no illusions."

"You're too modest, Ev."

They turned to watch Brett being introduced across the room. The House minority leader was on one side of her, and the only Democratic senator in attendance was on the other. She was speaking to them with animation.

"Why is it I feel Brett belongs in politics?" Evelyn asked.

"Perhaps because she does," Amory replied. "If I live long enough, I may end up as the First Gentleman of the nation."

Evelyn smiled. "Does that upset you?"

"Heavens, no! I want her to be successful."

"It's important to encourage her, Amory. Brett needs to be somebody in her own right. Not all husbands could appreciate that, though I imagine if there ever was one, it would be you."

"You're much too generous, Ev."

They continued watching Brett.

"I'm so glad about the baby," she said. "I know it's hard on Brett to put aside her career for a while, but you really deserve a family. God knows, it was the disappointment of my life, not having children."

The ranking Republican senator on the Judiciary Committee came up and took Amory's arm. "When are we going to have that abortion decision, Mr. Justice Maitland?" he asked.

"In a few weeks, Senator," Amory replied. He winked at Evelyn, who nodded subtly and slipped away.

Circulating around the room, she listened to the political patter. She liked being a mover and shaker, not just an observer. But much as she'd taken to her new standing in Washington, Evelyn still had her moments of doubt, of nostalgia for the past and her life with Harrison. Having a sudden desire to be alone, she moved off toward the windows that overlooked the Truman Balcony and the South Lawn.

It was growing quite dark, but she could see the Ellipse, the Washington Monument and the Jefferson Memorial lit up in the distance. She reflected on what Megan had said about how Harrison had loved her—a strange thing to hear from the mistress of one's husband. And yet how very like him to have expressed his love that way. "Damn the torpedoes," she murmured to herself. "Damn the torpedoes."

"It's beautiful, isn't it?"

She turned to see Brett at her shoulder, flushed and glowing. "It is." Evelyn smiled. "Are you enjoying yourself, dear?"

Brett nodded. "Very much."

"Amory and I were speculating that you might be prowling these premises in your own right one day."

"Why, I thought my husband liked the Court," she rejoined playfully.

Evelyn gave her a wry smile. "You know exactly what I mean."

Brett's cheeks glowed. "Politics excites me, I must admit."

"As much as motherhood?"

"Eventually I'm going to have both," she said.

"I hope you don't have to wait as long as I did to step forward," Evelyn said. "You're fortunate, though, to have a husband who'll help rather than hinder."

"Yes, I know."

Brett rested her hand on the bulge under her dress. They both were silent for a time.

After a while, Evelyn said, "You knew Elliot went to France?"

Brett looked surprised. "Did he?"

"Yes. Very suddenly, a week ago. He called the day he was leaving."

Brett had heard that he'd agreed to give Monica custody—a development that had come as a shock—but leaving the country altogether was also completely unexpected.

"Why would he do that, Evelyn? Jennifer meant so much to him."

"Monica apparently made good on her vow to reform. Elliot told me he felt better about Jennifer being with her."

"Why Paris?"

"Monica's fiancé is being assigned to the embassy in London and Elliot felt he'd be able to see the child more if he were in Europe. The poor boy is reduced to following around his soon-to-be ex-wife. I've felt so sorry for Elliot. He's such a good father. He doesn't deserve what he's gotten."

Brett glanced out at the Ellipse and the Washington Monument, a well of sorrow rising in her heart. She'd been so focused on her own guilt that she'd given Elliot's situation little or no thought. But hearing about his suffering, his loss, made her heart ache. She'd guarded against feeling sorry for him because that's how she'd gotten into trouble in the first place—reaching out, only to fall victim to her own compassion.

Now, for the first time, she saw Elliot as the victim, too. Poor Elliot. She pictured him with Jennifer, loving her. And now he was alone. All alone.

"It's been a rough six months for the Maitland clan," Evelyn said somberly. "But there are bright spots." She glanced down at Brett's stomach. "Maybe this baby will be our salvation."

Tears formed in Brett's eyes, but Evelyn didn't notice because just then the president's voice boomed over the general din. "They tell me soup's on," he said, grinning. "Please join Barbara and me for dinner."

For a blessed, merciful moment, Evelyn's attention was directed elsewhere—long enough for Brett to recover. It was not a time to get obsessed with Elliot Brewster. She had to look to the future, not the past.

Georgetown University

July 8, 1989

Brett sat in a large leather chair in the office of Father President Andrew McNaughton, drinking the water they'd brought her. Amory had wanted to stay with her, but she'd insisted he go ahead and view the exhibit of Harrison's papers and memorabilia that had been put together in connection with the chair in law he and Evelyn were establishing in Harrison's name.

Now that she was in the final month of her pregnancy, her discomfort was at its worst. All she could think about was having her baby and getting it over with. And it didn't help matters that the temperature was in the upper nineties and the humidity almost as high.

Brett had spent a lot of time in bed the past few weeks and her doctor didn't want her to exert herself unnecessarily. Amory had suggested that she stay home, but she wanted to come to the ceremony. He was going to give a little speech, as was Evelyn. "Besides," she told him, "it would be nice to share something positive with you after all the unpleasantness this week."

"Unpleasantness" was a euphemism, to put it mildly. The past five days had been hell. On Monday the Court had issued its decision in the *Russo* case. And, as Amory had predicted, much of the rancor of the antiabortion forces was directed at him. Five justices had agreed on the decision, but the public had reserved its adulation, or blame—depending on which side of the fence a person was on—for Amory.

News accounts of the decision made it sound as if Amory had single-handedly decided the course of abortion in the country. Angry protests had been expected, but veteran observers were surprised by the depth of the outrage of the right-to-life forces. Brett shuddered as she watched the demonstrations on television, revolted by the angry, sometimes-shrill sound bites.

Protests outside the Supreme Court building had continued through the week, and some of the outrage had even found its way to Chevy Chase. The morning after the decision was handed down, blood was spattered on their front door despite the protection of the federal marshals.

There'd been an arrest following that incident, but it did little to calm Brett's nerves. She was not afraid for herself, but she was very afraid for Amory. He was stoic through it all, considering it part of the unpleasantness that came with a difficult job.

The hatred was hard for her to understand, though. "You'd think you were holding a knife to their throats, forcing them to get abortions," she said to Amory. "Nobody's trying to tell them what to do with their bodies. *They're* trying to tell me and every other woman what we can do with ours."

He'd said nothing in reply, and Brett had felt sorry she'd said anything. Amory did not feel her passion. Ironically, his personal morality was on the other side, which was why he suffered so. What strength it took to dispense justice, to protect liberty in the name of something that flew in the face of one's own conscience!

When they arrived at the campus that morning, a few hundred protestors had been there to greet them. Among them were some of the most hateful people Brett had yet seen. Two placards in particular caught her eye. One said, The Wrong Maitland is Dead! and the other, Kill The Judge Who Kills Babies! It sickened her to think it had come to that.

Despite the air-conditioning, Brett felt feverish. She ran the glass of water over her cheeks and forehead. Unfortu-

nately the dedication ceremony was to be held in the courtyard outside the administration building, which meant she'd
have to endure the heat. But both Amory's and Evelyn's remarks would be brief and the reception following would be
inside. Brett was confident she could get through it.

She was starting to feel better when the door to the father president's office opened and Amory appeared, looking concerned. He closed the door behind him and came
over to the chair where she sat resting.

"How are you feeling, darling?"

"Much better. I think it was the walk from the car in the
hot sun."

"It's shady where the ceremony will be held."

"Will there be a large crowd?" she asked, taking his
hand.

"It looked like two or three hundred people."

"That's quite a group."

"Harrison had his friends."

Brett looked into his eyes, seeing the burden he'd been
carrying. He seemed tired, as though the months since the
vote on the *Russo* case had finally gotten to him. She knew
he was glad the Court term was over.

"I'm happy you and Evelyn decided to do this," she said.
"Right now, the people we need to see are your friends."

"My friends are no longer friends in many cases," he replied. "In a way, I'm a bit adrift."

She pulled his hand to her mouth and kissed it. "You've
got me, Amory. And there are millions of pro-choice Republicans in the country. Harrison didn't speak for everybody in the party."

Amory smiled sadly. "Yes, I know. I suppose I'm just
feeling a little sorry for myself, darling. That's all."

"Evelyn's an ally, too. She's much closer to you in her
politics than she was to Harrison."

He laughed. "She's much closer to you, Brett!"

"Evelyn's a smart woman. What can I say?"

They looked at each other affectionately. Amory leaned
over and kissed her cheek, his expression growing wistful.

"You know, despite everything that's been happening, I've thought a lot about Harrison recently. In fact, when I was drafting my remarks for this ceremony today, I had an insight."

"Oh?"

"I realized I should be more forgiving of my brother."

"You mean for what he did to Evelyn?" Brett asked.

"Yes. For months I was bitter about the way he treated her. When he died in that girl's arms, I looked upon it as an act of divine retribution. Lately I've been thinking it was wrong of me to judge him."

"It's only natural, darlin'."

"I sit in judgment daily, meting out justice. But that's a job that was given me by the people, under the law. Neither I, nor anyone else as I see it, has the right to judge Harrison's immortal soul. I think I have a moral obligation to accept him for who he was, and leave the rest of it to God."

In light of her own transgressions, she couldn't help but be moved. How like Amory it was to be so compassionate. Looking into his eyes, she felt certain that he would have been equally forgiving of her.

It was as if in pardoning Harrison he had pardoned her. And yet she still believed she'd done the right thing by bearing her sin in silence. She would have to be satisfied knowing that there would have been forgiveness for her in his heart if she had asked for it.

She would always have to live with what she'd done. Her baby would be a constant reminder, but because of Amory's goodness, it would be all right in time. Her child would become his child in spirit, and that's what mattered.

There was a light rap on the door and Evelyn stuck her head in. "It's time," she said. "They'd like to start."

"Sure you don't want to stay here where it's cool?" he asked.

"No," Brett said, scooting to the edge of her chair. "I want to go with you."

Amory helped her to her feet. A slight dizziness came over her and she had to grab his arm. Evelyn stepped into the office.

"Are you sure you're feeling up to this, dear? It's hardly an occasion of monumental importance."

Brett drew a fortifying breath. She didn't want to be a wimp. She'd tried hard to be strong and self-sufficient during her pregnancy. She'd exercised and followed her doctor's orders to the letter. "I'll be all right," she said.

"Wait just a minute," Amory said. He went to the window. "Look at this. The father president's office overlooks the courtyard. You could stay right here at his window and see everything. No need to go out into the heat."

"But I want to be with you," she protested. It was a pro forma objection. The notion of staying in an air-conditioned office and still being able to observe the ceremony had great appeal.

"I think you should stay," Evelyn said.

"All right. Go ahead. I'll watch from here."

Amory pulled a straight chair over to the window so that she wouldn't have to stand. "Now you're all set, darling," he said.

Before leaving the office, Amory kissed her lightly on the lips. "The most important thing in the world is you, Brett," he whispered. "And that baby."

He touched her cheek, then left with Evelyn to join the others. Brett's eyes turned glossy and she bit her lip. Closing her eyes, she prayed to God to give her strength.

After a sigh, she sat in the chair Amory had carried to the window for her. The crowd was waiting. It was a sizable group. All the folding chairs were occupied and a number of people were standing at the rear and to the sides. Between the surrounding buildings and the trees, the area was mostly shaded. But Brett could tell it was hot because some people were fanning themselves vigorously.

She had a good view of the podium situated on a low stage that had been set up for the occasion. Her perspective was from the side, perhaps twenty or thirty yards from the lectern and high enough to see the stage well.

As she watched, Father President Andrew McNaughton, a burly man in his early sixties, exited the building with Amory, Evelyn and three or four others. The group made their way to the stage. Brett was able to hear the polite applause through the closed window.

The father president went to the lectern first. She could hear his muted voice over the public-address system. He spoke of Harrison and his career in public service. There was no mention of the abortion issue, and Brett was glad. It was not an occasion for debate or discourse.

After a gracious introduction, Evelyn spoke next. She talked about Harrison with respect and affection. She did not aggrandize her husband, but she referred to him warmly, in human terms.

Then the father president returned to the podium to introduce Amory. There was a polite round of applause, but before Amory could begin to speak a couple of people began heckling from the back of the courtyard.

Brett couldn't hear what they were saying, but there was no doubt in her mind what it was about. People were turning and looking. Craning her neck to see, she was able to make out one young man shaking his fist, red-faced as he shouted.

Several police officers started moving toward the heckler. As she turned her attention back to Amory, Brett saw a man moving abruptly toward the podium from the far side of the courtyard. He was in his thirties, and dressed casually. Amory didn't appear to notice him until the man was within a few feet of the stage.

The next thing she knew he was on the platform and raising his hand. It held a gun. There was a flash and a loud pop. Amory fell to the ground.

Gasping, Brett struggled to her feet. The man fired at her husband a second time, then turned and ran from the stage.

Brett screamed. Helpless, she stared at Amory's motionless body. It seemed to take forever for anybody to react.
Evelyn and the father president were the first to get to him.

"Oh, my God, no!" Brett screamed, over and over. "No,
no!"

She was able to see Amory's silver head through the
growing circle of arms and legs. He wasn't moving. Brett
had a glimpse of Evelyn, her hands clasped to her mouth in
horror as she looked toward the window where Brett stood
watching.

All she could think of then was that she had to get to him.
Brett turned and rushed toward the door, but she'd no
sooner touched the knob than a stabbing pain shot through
her. She winced, opened the door, took a couple of steps
into the outer office, and nearly collapsed after another
knifelike twinge. A terrible dizziness came over her. She
stopped to lean on the secretarial desk as her knees started
giving way.

Suddenly, the room was spinning and then everything
went black. Brett felt herself falling as she dropped to the
floor with a thud.

With pandemonium reigning all around her, Evelyn had
to fight her way onto the ambulance where they'd loaded
Brett's stretcher. She looked at her sister-in-law's face as she
settled beside her. Brett was moaning. She was only half
conscious, not having said a coherent word since Evelyn had
found her lying in a pool of water and blood in the father
president's outer office.

"What's her due date?" the paramedic asked calmly.

"The end of the month," Evelyn said.

"Well, this baby's coming now, ready or not," the paramedic replied.

The siren was screaming as the ambulance lurched
through the Saturday-morning traffic. Brett moaned, then
cried out in pain. She opened her eyes, and for the first time
appeared to understand what was happening. After staring

at the ceiling for several moments, she looked at Evelyn. A terrified expression crossed her face.

"Is Amory all right?" Brett asked desperately.

Evelyn took her hand. "They've taken him to the hospital."

"But is he all right?"

"He's very badly hurt, Brett. Very badly."

Brett stared at her. "He's dead, isn't he? Tell me, Evelyn. Is he dead?"

Evelyn tried to answer but her voice failed her. Finally she managed to speak. "I'm not sure. They were working on him as they took him away. I just don't know."

A wail issued from Brett's throat, and she began to cry. "I knew something like this would happen, I knew it. It's all my fault." Then she winced, crying out in pain.

"Excuse me, ma'am," the paramedic said, squeezing past Evelyn. "If you'll let me in here, I want to take her blood pressure."

Brett was sobbing uncontrollably, her body heaving. "My baby's going to die, too. I'm going to lose my baby."

"I don't think so," the paramedic said. "Not the way he's kicking."

But Brett didn't seem to hear her. She was lost in her pain, sobbing. Evelyn leaned back, completely drained, feeling as though she'd taken a bullet herself. Tears rolled down her cheeks. Her silk dress was covered with blood. Amory hadn't been breathing when they took him away, nor did he have a pulse. She was almost sure he was dead. The dear man had probably died even before she'd lifted his head onto her lap.

Talbot County, Maryland

August 23, 1989

They had left Washington that morning on the Anacostia Freeway, headed northeast against the flow of rush-hour traffic. Once on U.S. 50, they'd driven past Annapolis and across the Chesapeake Bay Bridge. Elliot and Evelyn were now making their way across the flat emerald landscape, the woods and watery vistas of Talbot County.

She had picked him up at the Mayflower Hotel on Connecticut Avenue. During most of the drive they'd chatted about politics and foreign affairs, especially events in Poland where Solidarity had wrested control from the Communists. "The Soviet Bloc is crumbling," Elliot had said. "A lot of people in Europe think the Cold War is all but over."

"Thank God. Now, if we can just get things straightened out in this country..."

Once they reached Easton, the conversation turned to Brett. "So, how is she, Evelyn?" he asked. He'd called from Paris a week earlier, telling Evelyn he'd be in Washington for a few days, and asked if she thought Brett might be receptive to a visit. He'd been back for the funeral in July, but hadn't seen her then. There'd been complications with the birth of her son and she'd claimed to be too ill to receive visitors.

The morning of the internment had been brilliantly sunny and warm. A perfect summer day. The decision had been made to bury Amory beside his parents in Easton. Not counting the media, only a few dozen people had been admitted into the cemetery. He and Evelyn were the only family members.

He had stood at Amory's grave, under a large shade tree, contemplatively listening to the priest read from the 23rd Psalm. His stepfather had been a great human being. He'd been good to him from the time Elliot was just a boy. And yet, his emotions were so ambivalent because Amory had also been the husband of both his mother and his lover.

Although the man had never done a single hateful thing to him, Amory's death had come as a relief. That alone made Elliot feel guilty. Just the same, he had never regretted his love for Brett. He'd refused to think it wrong, and he would die convinced they belonged together. But when would she be ready to face that fact?

He'd told himself a thousand times that she'd been through a lot, that she needed time to adjust to all that had happened. But a month and a half was as long as he'd been able to put off trying to see her again. He just couldn't wait any longer.

"Brett has really been suffering," Evelyn told him. "She's been torturing herself, as though Amory's death were her fault."

"How's her health?"

"The first few weeks were difficult. Her doctor felt the problem was emotional as much as physical. She's had a very slow recovery, Elliot. She's still weak. The doctor finally sent her over here to the East Shore, hoping she'd get some exercise and start eating right."

"Is she depressed?"

"I suppose so. The one thing that keeps her going is the baby. If it weren't for him, I don't know what she'd do. At times it seems that Tyler is all that she cares about."

"Thank God she didn't lose him."

"I don't know if she could have handled that," Evelyn replied.

Elliot glanced out at the sunny countryside. These were the same roads he'd traveled so often when Jennifer was in the hospital in Easton. That was less than a year ago, but it seemed more like a millennium to him now. Brett had turned her back on him. And if their week together had meant anything to her, she'd given no indication of it.

Still, her willingness to see him had given him some hope, though Evelyn had admitted that Brett hadn't been very enthusiastic about it. "Don't take it personally, though," she'd said when she called him back in Paris. "She's seen no one but me and her aunt. Brett seems determined to forget the past. As soon as Amory's affairs are settled, she wants to leave Washington."

"To go where?"

"Back to Georgia. She says she's going to start her life over."

Start her life over. What did that mean? Was she going to pretend that everybody she'd known these last years had died with Amory?

He understood now why he'd had only a pro forma note of appreciation in response to the letter he'd written her upon returning to Paris. He'd kept it low-key and respectful, but he'd made clear his desire to see her. Brett, it seemed, had kept her heart closed to him.

They were nearing Rosemont and Elliot began feeling the anticipation of their long-awaited meeting. Minutes later, as they passed through the gate to the estate, he took a deep breath, sensing that the rest of his life would turn on what happened over the course of the next hour.

They stopped in the gravel drive at the front and got out of the car. Odie let them in. According to Evelyn, Brett had wanted her with them because she'd been so good with the baby. Mrs. Mallory hadn't taken the intrusion well, but Brett's needs had to come first.

When they entered the sitting room they found Leona doing needlepoint next to the crib. She got up from her chair to greet them.

"Brett's out in the yard gettin' some air," she said. "I'll tell her y'all are here."

"Don't bother," Elliot said. "I'll go."

Leona didn't object. Before he went outside, Elliot went over to the crib. Evelyn was already standing there, looking down at the sleeping baby.

"Look at that black hair," Evelyn said. She ran the tip of her finger over his tiny clenched fist. "Isn't he adorable?"

"My brother, Jack, Brett's daddy, was dark," Leona said, "so his colorin' comes from our side as much as the judge's."

"When I first knew Amory he still had dark hair," Evelyn said. "He started going gray in his thirties."

"Hard to tell what color eyes the little critter's goin' to have," Leona said. "Baby's eyes change so much at first."

Elliot stared down at the baby, knowing, if things had been different, that Tyler might have been his son. He glanced toward the French doors, his mind back on Brett again. He saw the expanse of lawn sloping down toward the river, but there was no sign of anyone. "I'll go out and say hello to Brett."

It took a moment before he spotted her sitting on a lounge chair under a big shade tree, halfway between the house and the river. She was facing the water, her back to him.

He stepped down off the terrace and walked toward her. Rosemont on a balmy summer day was very different than it had been the previous October, and yet the mere fact of being there with her gave him a strange feeling. Waves of hope and anxiety washed over him. A lump formed in his throat as he neared her.

"They say you haven't been a very good patient, Brett," he said, coming up alongside her.

She rolled her head toward him. "Oh, Elliot, hi." She wore a pale yellow cotton dress and had on sunglasses. She hadn't fully regained her figure, but she was close. She glanced over her shoulder. "Didn't Evelyn come with you?"

"Yes, she's inside cooing at your son."

"Did you see him?"

He couldn't see her eyes because of the glasses, but the tone of her voice confirmed what Evelyn had said. "Yes," he said softly. "He's quite a handsome young man."

She bit at her lip and looked out at the water, sparkling in the midday sun. She was silent.

He squatted beside her chair, taking her hand. "So how are you, Brett?"

"Not a very good patient, as you said."

"I don't like to hear that," he said, rubbing her fingers.

Brett sighed. "I'll be all right. It takes time, that's all." She gestured toward another lawn chair nearby. "Pull that up. You might as well be comfortable."

He got the chair, setting it beside hers, but facing the house so that he could see her easily. She rested her head against the back of the lounge chair and stared off at the river. He was almost sure that she'd accepted his presence out of a sense of obligation, not because she wanted to see him.

Elliot thought about all the things he wanted to say, but now that he was actually with her, he was having trouble finding the words. He'd had a thousand imaginary conversations with her since the last time they'd spoken, but he was suddenly at a loss. The problem was he didn't know what was in Brett's heart.

"I appreciate you seeing me," he began. "I hope this isn't going to be too painful. For me, the worst part of the past ten months has been knowing that I've caused you so much anguish."

"That's over now, Elliot. It's behind us. The heartache I feel now is for another reason entirely."

"You're strong, Brett, you'll get over the pain of this, too. You've got your baby now, and your whole life ahead of you."

She gave him a faint smile. "I know you're right. I know I've got to pull myself up by the bootstraps, and I will."

"Evelyn said you're thinking of going back to Georgia."

"Yes," she said. "That's what I've decided. Washington—at least for now—has died right along with Amory."

He regarded her for a long time, wanting to ask how she felt about him, whether she could ever accept his love. But he knew that the first words had to come from her. "Brett, I'm trying to understand why you agreed to see me."

She turned her head toward him. "I want to tie up all the loose ends before I go. When you asked if you could come, I felt I owed it to you."

Owed. He didn't like the word. It gave him no hope. None.

"This might sound strange, Elliot," she went on, "but I do care about you. I care about you and Jennifer both. I've worried—especially about her."

"That's very thoughtful of you," he said. "It's been a rough few months, but Jen's all right. She's not suffering."

"It must have been terribly hard giving her up."

"Yes, it was. But I decided it was for the best."

"Jennifer's happy then?" Brett asked.

"Yes, I think so," he said, nodding. "I see her as often as possible. Since they got to England I've spent more weekends in London than in Paris. But believe me, it's hard saying goodbye on a Sunday night."

She nodded. "Monica's doing all right, apparently."

"She's staying off the sauce, as best I can tell. We talked about Jennifer coming to Paris for a few weeks before nursery school starts. I'm hoping it will work out."

He could see the compassion on Brett's face. A part of him wondered what she'd say if he told her what had really happened. Brett had suffered, and she'd lost someone she loved, but so had he. Whenever he went to Robert Farrens's place in London to pick Jennifer up, he'd get a lump in his throat at the sight of her. Invariably she'd come racing from her room and into his arms when he arrived. He always held her tightly, hoping she wouldn't see the tears in his eyes. He wasn't sure he'd ever get over having to give her up, though he thanked God it hadn't been worse. Monica could have cut him out of the picture altogether.

He saw that Brett had lowered her head. She was staring down at her folded hands.

"How about a walk in the garden?" he said. "It's a beautiful day. One that should be enjoyed."

"My doctor must have sent you over." Her smile was soft, wistful.

He studied her lovely face, hating the ache in his heart. "No, but I can see you need to get your blood moving."

"I'm weak," she said. "We can't go far." She swung her legs off the chair and sat up. Elliot helped her to her feet. "I'm not an invalid, though Aunt Leona and Odie have told me often enough I act like one."

He offered his arm and they slowly strolled down the gentle slope toward the Tred Avon. He glanced at her, thinking of his solitary walks in Paris, always imagining her at his side. They were together at last. Her hand rested lightly on his forearm, burning his flesh under the sleeve of his jacket, and yet there was a distance between them. She seemed so far away—her spirit detached, beyond his reach.

He wanted badly to find a way to touch her, to make her see him as she had before. The barrier was gone, but the separation remained. It frustrated him.

"I know why you're here, Elliot," she said when he'd anguished in silence for a time. "These past months you've sacrificed for me by staying away, and I'm grateful. I can't tell you how thankful I've been. But I want you to know that nothing's changed."

He stopped. "Brett, things *have* changed! You're a widow now. You're free."

She looked out at the water, her face filling with anxiety. "I can't think of you in those terms," she said, her voice trembling. "I'm sorry, but I can't."

"Why? I understood why you felt that way before. I didn't like it, but I understood. There's no reason now."

Her hand dropped from his arm. "Elliot, please don't give me a hard time. I know how I feel."

"You can't let guilt over the past rule your life. Don't you see? The only thing that was wrong between us was that I met you too late. We both suffered because of that, but that's behind us now. All I'm asking for is a chance. I just want you to keep an open mind."

She shook her head. "No, Elliot. Happiness can't be built on unhappiness, and we've gone through too many negative things together. I couldn't be in your arms without remembering. Every hour I was with you I'd be reliving the guilt, the pain."

He stared at her, noticing a tear appear from under the edge of her sunglasses and run down her cheek. He reached over and removed the glasses so that he could see her eyes. They were red and swollen. She began to cry, holding her hands to her face.

Elliot took her and held her against him. He stroked her head, but he wasn't able to touch her—not the way he wanted to. Her suffering, her misery, were beyond his reach.

"You know I love you," he said at last. "That hasn't changed. It never will."

She began sobbing heavily. It tore at his heart.

"You can't go on like this for the rest of your life, Brett," he insisted. "You've got to stop beating yourself."

"I know," she said, wiping her nose, getting control. "And I will, for Tyler's sake. I have a contribution to make. I'm going to fight through this."

Elliot held her by the shoulders. "It's only been six weeks since Amory died. I didn't come here thinking that things would have changed completely, but I wanted to believe you'd give me a reason to hope."

Brett wiped her cheeks with the backs of her hands. "I wish I could. Believe me, I don't feel the way I do to punish you. I owe it to you to be honest, and so I am."

"Maybe in time you'll feel differently," he said.

"I'd like to say I will, but I don't know what the future will bring."

His stomach churned. "Will you let me come to see you again?"

She bit her lip. "I don't want to hurt you, Elliot, but I don't think it would do either of us any good."

He looked into her bleary eyes, seeing that he was fighting a losing battle. "Don't say never. Please."

"All right. Maybe. But I can't promise you anything."

"How will I know when the time comes?"

"I suppose I'll contact you," she said.

"And in the meantime, all I can do is wait."

Brett nodded, fighting back her emotion. "I'm not a very good bet, Elliot. Some things are just not meant to be."

"I know you're saying that sincerely," he said. "But I want you to know I'm every bit as convinced of the opposite."

She tried to smile—without much success. "I guess time will tell."

"I won't give up hope," he said, his voice trembling.

Brett lowered her eyes, then turned away. He watched the soft warm breeze blow the hair at her temples. He wanted her so desperately, it was hard to hold back. Finally he took her by the shoulders and turned her to him so that he could see her face. "I'm going now," he said gently. "I've tortured you enough for one day."

"Elliot," she said tearfully, "I wish it weren't this way."

His eyes began to shimmer, but he managed to smile. Then he placed her sunglasses back on her face, leaned over, and kissed her lightly on the lips.

Brett reached out and took his hand, feeling each finger in turn, as a child would. She couldn't look up at him. "I'm so sorry," she whispered. "I wish none of this had happened."

"Whatever you say, we shared something very special. Nobody can take that away from us. Ever."

She nodded her assent, biting her lip. He took her arm and they started back up the slope, toward the lounge chair. When they got there, she sat down heavily. Their short walk had exhausted her. She stared up at him.

"Evelyn and I are dividing up the property here at Rosemont," she said. "We've talked some about selling the place. Is there anything here you'd like? This was your home, too, at least when you were growing up. How about the dinghy? Would you like to have it? I'm sure Amory would have wanted it to go to you."

He shook his head. "Maybe one day your son would enjoy having it." He looked at her sadly. "The only thing here I really want I'm told I can't have."

She continued staring up at him, anguished. Unable to resist touching her one more time, he reached out and brushed her face with his fingertips. Then he turned and began walking slowly toward the house.

PART VI

Washington, D.C.

A din of voices filled the large hall. Brett made her way through the crowd, having lost track of Evelyn. An assistant secretary, whose name she hadn't caught, had buttonholed the senator, doubtlessly to talk about business before the Foreign Relations Committee. During the ride over to the Department of State building, Evelyn had said the president was trying to build a consensus in the Congress for his most recent Bosnian initiative in the U.N., so she was destined to be wooed some.

The situation in the Balkans was on everybody's lips. The energy in the room seemed more intense than usual, though Brett was hardly in a position to judge. She'd been away from Washington for years now, having made only a couple of brief trips back before this visit. She'd witnessed the Persian Gulf crisis from her living room in Atlanta, so she hadn't been able to judge firsthand the mood in Washington during that time. But Washington still had an energy about it that appealed to her, whether the town was in the middle of a crisis or not.

Oddly enough, the events that had impacted her life the most over the past couple of years had taken place in Washington, not Georgia. Brett had been practicing family law in Atlanta in 1991 when the Clarence Thomas nomination to the Supreme Court reached the Senate. She'd watched what the Senate Judiciary Committee did to Anita

Hill during the hearings and decided it was time for her to stop sitting on the sidelines and get into politics.

Twelve months later, during "the year of the woman" in American politics, she ran for a seat in the Georgia legislature and won a narrow victory over a candidate who looked and talked a lot like Orrin Hatch and Arlen Specter. If she hadn't already been bitten by the political bug, that campaign had certainly done the trick.

Over the years, Brett and Evelyn had stayed in touch and when Brett had won her election to the legislature, nobody was more pleased than her sister-in-law. And so, when another political opportunity had come along this past January, Brett had phoned Evelyn to get her opinion.

"Randall Worthington has decided not to run for reelection come fall," Brett told her. "Everyone in north Georgia is eyeing the seat. I'm thinking of throwing my hat in the ring, as well. What do you think?"

"You'd be a fabulous congresswoman, Brett," Evelyn had told her. "If you want it, go for it!"

She'd decided it was exactly what she wanted, and she'd ended up as one of eight candidates in the March primary. She'd come in first, but the vote was so divided that she was thrown into a runoff later in the spring. Evelyn wasn't in a position to support her publicly because of the difference in their party affiliations, but she told her privately she'd do what she could to help.

Brett had come to Washington for a meeting with the Democratic Congressional Campaign Committee. A delightful staffer from California, named Stacey Krum, had spent all morning with her, discussing issues and providing briefing information. In the middle of the afternoon Brett had gone over to the Dirksen Senate Office Building to see Evelyn. They'd planned to have dinner together anyway, but Evelyn suggested Brett first go with her to a reception at the State Department.

"I won't promise it'll be fun, but it'll be a change from the state house in Atlanta."

Brett would have suspected that Elliot Brewster had somehow figured into Evelyn's insistence, except that she knew he was in France. Evelyn had said so earlier.

"He's always loved Paris, but they won't leave him there forever," she said. "I'm told he's one of the rising stars in the Clinton State Department. Rumor is he's in line for one of the undersecretary slots."

"When you're president, Evelyn, you'll have to appoint him secretary of state. You'll need at least one Democrat in the cabinet, won't you?"

Evelyn laughed. "My road to the presidency is about a hundred times longer than yours to the Congress, dear. But thanks for the compliment."

Nothing more was said about Elliot, but it seemed his name always came up whenever she and Evelyn spoke. Over the past five years she'd managed to keep up on his life that way—after a fashion.

Brett was circulating about the hall, nominally looking for Evelyn, but tall dark-headed men kept catching her eye, and once she actually thought she'd spotted Elliot. It would have been possible—a last-minute trip to Washington for an urgent meeting, then downstairs to the reception for a drink.

It was odd how he would pop into her mind from time to time. Over the past year or so, she'd thought of him as much or more than she had Amory. Maybe that wasn't so unusual. Nature intended that the dead fade from memory faster than the living.

She made her way over to one of the bars that had been set up in the lobby, and continued scanning the room for Evelyn. She was nowhere to be seen, which probably meant she was closeted with some of the secretary's people, discussing administration policy.

Working her way to the front of the line, Brett handed her empty glass to the white-jacketed bartender. "Vodka tonic, please," she told the man. "A light one."

He fixed her drink and handed it back. Brett withdrew from the crush, thinking she ought make use of her time and find someone interesting to talk to. Foreign policy came pretty low on the list of issues in a congressional race, but the subject had always interested her.

She sipped her drink and remembered the embassy party in New Delhi—her first close-up look at the diplomacy game. But what stood out in her memory wasn't the party so much as Elliot. She hadn't realized it at the time, but she had probably fallen for him that night. It had taken a while for the effects to be felt, but when she did succumb, she really did.

Over the years she'd often thought about that last time she'd seen him on the East Shore. It had been one of the sadder days of her life, not only because it had marked the end of an era, but because it had been so inevitable. She'd told him that some things were simply not meant to be, and she'd sincerely believed it.

Elliot had been so sure she was wrong; that time would be the healer. But he hadn't appreciated that when you travel a certain road long enough, it simply becomes impractical to turn back. That was what had happened in her case.

She hadn't regarded Amory's death as the end of her romantic life—she hadn't returned to Georgia with either the intent of finding someone or the conviction that she wouldn't. She often socialized, but it wasn't until the spring of 1990 that she'd had more than a casual date with a man.

That was when she'd begun seeing Marcus Jordan, a prominent Atlanta surgeon. He was eight years older than she and had lost his wife a year before Amory had died. Marcus was her usual escort and Brett was very fond of him. They had both come from poor rural backgrounds, had a lot in common, and very much enjoyed each other's company.

But Brett had not been in any hurry to get serious. She'd started her law career, and then had gotten into politics, which for a single mother did not allow much time for romance. From the beginning she'd devoted most of her energy to Tyler. She took motherhood very seriously and was determined that her son wouldn't be deprived, emotionally or otherwise.

"Why, Brett Maitland!" said a voice behind her in the crowd. She felt a cool hand on her arm and turned. The dark hair was different, the face a bit older, but still pretty. "You remember me, don't you, sugar?" she said. "Monica Farrens. I was Monica Brewster then."

"Hello, Monica," Brett said, extending her hand. "I remember you, of course."

Monica's tight little smile was insidious. "Lord, it's been years. When was the last time?" She made a show of it. "Let's see. It wasn't that fateful night on the East Shore, was it? No," she said, answering her own question, "it was after that. I know, it was in the ladies' room of some restaurant! You were retching your guts out, as I recall!"

"How sweet of you to remember," Brett said, returning the sarcasm.

Monica glanced around her as though checking out the crowd. Nobody seemed to pay any attention to them, much to Brett's relief.

"Aren't these receptions a pain in the ass?" Monica observed, opening her bag. "Personally, I hate them."

"I don't come to them as a rule," Brett replied, "so I'm not completely bored. Yet. But I'm making rapid progress in that direction."

"You have the sweetest little accent," Monica said, as she fumbled through her purse. "I always thought it was so cute." Finally she found what she was looking for—a pack of cigarettes. She offered one to Brett.

"No, thank you."

"That's right, you didn't have any vices, did you?"

"Look, Monica," Brett said, beginning to lose patience, "I'm not interested in trading insults with you. I don't see that you and I still have a problem. But if you feel we do…"

"Why sugar, I'm truly sorry if I offended you." Monica resumed her rummaging, now in search of matches. She stopped when a dark, Middle Eastern-looking gentleman extended his hand, holding a platinum lighter.

"Permit me, *madame*," he said, striking the flame.

Monica lit her cigarette and thanked him. When she didn't give him another glance, he withdrew.

"I don't recall you smoking," Brett remarked, watching her blow a puff of smoke toward the ceiling.

"I need at least one vice," Monica said. "And Robert would rather I smoke than fuck strangers. So what are you doing these days? The last I heard, you were back down in Alabama."

"Georgia. I practice law and I'm in politics."

"You can't play the grieving widow forever, I suppose."

"That's true. And what about you, Monica? Are you back in Washington permanently now?"

"Still in London, but it looks like Robert may be reassigned back here soon. He's here to talk to them about it, and I came along for the ride."

They stared at each other, adversaries by instinct, but now without a real bone of contention.

"How nice for you. It sounds like your life is well-ordered. You've got Jennifer. You've remarried. Are you happy?"

"Life's never quite as wonderful as it should be. But Robert's made a big difference. He understands me. I feel better about myself now."

"I'm happy for you."

Monica smiled. "That's what a good man and spending twenty thousand bucks on a shrink will do for you, I guess. But I'm sober. I keep busy collecting art and organizing exhibits. I guess I can't complain."

"You've opted for respectability."

Monica smiled with amusement. "I guess you could say that. But even in my darker days I was always pretty up-front. If I was fucking a woman's husband, she usually knew about it."

Brett could see the old fires hadn't gone out completely. "Look, if you've still got a problem over that, I don't intend to stand here taking a whipping. I'm not into blood sport."

"Oh, but don't you have a quick tongue, sugar. Elliot always liked that in a woman."

"Look, Monica, Elliot means nothing to me now, and I'm sure he means nothing to you. Personally, I'm not one to get pleasure from rekindling old grudges, so maybe it's best if we say goodbye."

"I'm sorry, Brett," she said, actually sounding sincere. "I don't mean to be such a bitch. I guess it's just a natural reflex."

"It's nice that you realize it."

"If you want to know the truth, I'm grateful to you for fucking Elliot. It saved my butt."

She blinked. "What are you talking about?"

Monica took a drag on her cigarette. "I'm referring to Jennifer, of course. Because of your affair with Elliot, I got custody. Weren't you aware of that?"

Brett blanched. "What do you mean by, 'because of' my affair?"

"I had Elliot by the balls, so I got custody. He had no choice." She laughed. "I figured he must have told you by now. Or don't you two speak?"

"I haven't seen Elliot since Amory died."

"Well, then, it doesn't matter, does it?"

"I would like to know exactly what you mean, Monica. Are you saying you used me against Elliot? That he gave up Jennifer because you threatened him in some way?"

"Honey, I blackmailed the sonovabitch." She let some smoke drift out of her mouth. "I told him I'd tell Amory everything if I didn't get full custody of Jennifer." She smiled again, clearly amused. "Jesus, I thought you could have figured that one out by yourself."

"Elliot didn't say anything," Brett said, coloring.

"I'm surprised. He always liked being a hero. God knows, you'd have owed him."

Brett was beginning to understand. Everything that had happened during those critical months suddenly took on a different light. Elliot had sacrificed himself for her—that's what it amounted to. She looked down at the drink glass in her hand, turning it nervously.

"So, he really didn't tell you, huh?" Monica said. "I wonder why?"

"He was too decent to, obviously!"

"Elliot's a fool. He should have gotten something for his big sacrifice. I'd have thought you'd have balled him till the cows came home for keeping his mouth shut. Jesus."

Brett glared.

"Oh, come off it," Monica said. "You can drop the vestal-virgin routine. You're no saint."

"No, I'm not. But what you did is no less disgusting because of what I did."

Monica took another drag as Brett continued to stare down at her glass. "Come on," Monica said, "let's lighten up. We're talking about ancient history. It's water under the bridge."

"You haven't kept Jennifer from visiting him, though, have you? He does get to see her?"

"Of course. He's seen Jennifer plenty. I've been generous. And she's happy with me and Robert."

Brett felt dreadful. Elliot had never once hinted at what he'd done. Obviously he hadn't wanted to add to her burdens.

Monica stopped a passing waiter and stubbed out her cigarette in an ashtray. Brett stared at her, still shocked, still amazed at all that had happened, all she'd been oblivious to. Perhaps she hadn't wanted to face the obvious. She didn't know. "I feel sorry for Elliot," she said. "He's the one who's lost all the way around."

"Elliot manages, sugar. He hasn't hung himself over any of this. He's doing fine. The rumor is he's in line for assistant secretary for European Affairs."

"I'm sure Jennifer means much more to him than any possible promotion," Brett said solemnly. "Poor Elliot."

Monica gave her a look of disbelief. "I probably shouldn't have said anything. It's too late to feel guilty. It's been five years."

That didn't make Brett feel any better. On the contrary, she really felt sick. She looked around, more eager to find Evelyn than ever. She wanted to get out of there.

Monica saw the anguish on her face. "Hey, the business with Elliot really upset you, didn't it?"

"Yes, as a matter of fact."

"Sounds to me like you're still carrying a torch, kiddo," Monica said, chiding her.

"Well, well," came a man's voice from behind her. "What an unlikely pair." It was Robert Farrens. He moved to Monica's side, slipping his arm around her waist.

"Just in time, Robert, to give Brett your hankie. We're talking about Elliot."

Farrens, still a touch dissipated, but well-dressed and looking content, nodded politely. "Hello, Mrs. Maitland, a pleasure to see you."

"Nice to see you, too, Mr. Farrens."

"So," he said, "the topic of conversation is Brewster?"

"It has been," Brett said, "but I don't really want to discuss the matter further. Frankly, I'm looking for Evelyn. You haven't seen her by any chance, have you?"

"As a matter of fact, I believe you'll find the senator back in that corner," he said, pointing. "Huddled with the top brass."

Brett offered her hand to Monica, but her smile was less than genuine. "It's been enlightening, if not a pleasure," she said.

"I hope not too much of a shock."

There was coyness in Monica's look. But Brett wasn't going to give her the satisfaction of noticing. "Things tend to happen for a reason," she said. "That's one lesson I've learned."

They parted, and Brett went off to find her sister-in-law.

It wasn't far from Foggy Bottom to Evelyn's town house in Georgetown. They planned to have a drink there and Evelyn was going to call her office before they went to dinner.

During the drive, Brett recounted how she'd run into Monica, but hadn't gone into any detail about the conversation.

"I haven't seen her in years," Evelyn said. "Is she still the same lovely person she always was?"

"Yes, though she seems to have found herself."

"No charity toward Elliot, I'll bet."

"No."

"I'm not surprised. Monica hated his guts while they were married. She certainly wouldn't treat him any better as an ex-husband."

Once at Evelyn's place, Brett settled onto the sofa while Evelyn went to get them each a vodka tonic. When she returned with the cocktails, she gave Brett a funny look.

"What's the matter, dear? You seem upset."

Brett had been thinking about Elliot almost constantly since her encounter with Monica. His sacrifice ate at her—it had been such a selfless act.

She felt dreadful knowing how she'd snubbed him after what he'd done for her. It also made her decision to withhold the truth about Tyler seem all the more heartless.

"Seeing Monica has gotten me to thinking about Elliot and Jennifer," she replied. "You have Elliot's address in Paris, don't you?"

Evelyn was surprised by the question. "Yes, of course."

Brett said nothing.

"Would you like it?"

"I was thinking of contacting him."

Evelyn waited, but Brett didn't comment further. "Did Monica say something that upset you?"

"Yes. But I'm not sure I want to discuss it. It's nothing against you, Evelyn. I'm in a strange mood."

"I could tell something was wrong."

The late-afternoon sunshine warmed the facades of the houses across the street as Brett stared out the front window. She had an odd feeling, as though she'd been a party to a tremendous injustice, and Elliot was the victim. She could clearly see his face in her mind's eye—the way it had been that day he'd come to see her at Rosemont. The poor man had been suffering a double tragedy and she hadn't even known it.

She took a long sip from her drink as Evelyn, sitting in the easy chair across from her, waited silently. The truth of Tyler's paternity—a secret that she had borne alone—suddenly felt overwhelming.

"Evelyn," she said, "can I tell you the darkest secret of my life without you judging me?"

Evelyn looked at her, curious. "Certainly, Brett."

"I wouldn't burden you with it, because I've thought all along I should shoulder it alone, but I really do need your advice."

Evelyn waited.

Brett lowered her head, knowing how a Catholic must feel in confession. She was overcome with a terrible anguish. It took a supreme effort, but she managed to say it. "Tyler's not Amory's child. He's Elliot's."

Evelyn sat very still. Her face registered no discernible surprise. Then she scooted to the edge of her seat, reached out and touched Brett's hand. Her expression made Brett want to cry, but she didn't.

"I knew, in a way," she said. "I sensed there had been something."

"I haven't told Elliot," Brett said. "In fact, I lied to him to protect myself."

Evelyn watched her with glistening eyes.

"Do you think—" Brett's voice cracked. "Do you think...I should tell him?"

"I can't answer that. Only you know what you want to do."

Brett slumped back onto the sofa, sighing. "Lord, I don't know what's right." She stared out the window at the rooftops. "Monica told me something at the reception that upset me. She blackmailed Elliot to get custody of Jennifer by threatening to expose our affair to Amory."

"Oh, my God. She didn't!"

"Yes, it's true. And Elliot never told me. He just gave his daughter to that bitch to spare Amory and me."

Evelyn looked horrified.

"I feel so dreadful I could die," Brett said, her eyes filling. "Just die." She ran her finger down the side of the glass, feeling such anguish. She glanced up at her sister-in-law. "I don't know if Elliot would feel better or worse, knowing the truth about Tyler."

"He might already know. Or suspect it at some level."

"That would probably be worse. He must hate me."

"To the contrary. I think he loves you, Brett. He's never said a word to me, but I've felt it for a long time."

"Recently? He's acted that way recently?"

"He always asks after you. He tries not to be blatant, but it's obvious he cares."

"And you tell him I'm doing just fine, that I'm happy as a clam?"

"I tell him the truth. You are happy, aren't you?"

"Evelyn, that's almost beside the point. Right now I feel as bad as I've ever felt in my life."

"I doubt that Elliot's interested in your pity. The real question is what you want, Brett."

"I thought I liked my life just fine."

"Then maybe that's your answer."

"But I'm not sure."

Evelyn sipped her drink and waited. Brett knew it had come down to a simple question. They looked into each other's eyes.

"It's not just Elliot's feelings or mine at stake," she said. "I've got Tyler to think about, his identity. He's only five, but he thinks that white-haired man in the picture on my dresser is his daddy."

"The truth is easily distorted. It can wear many coats."

Brett nodded. "I guess I've spent my life trying to find the coat I thought I wanted, lying to myself to get things to fit. Maybe it's time I stopped living that way, Evelyn. Maybe I owe both Elliot and Tyler the truth."

Paris, France

He stood at the open window of his town house and stared down into the avenue Émile-Deschanel, expecting her taxi to pull up at any moment. But none was in sight. The street was empty.

Damp cool air, smelling of rain, wafted in on him. It reminded him of that day they had walked in the woods near the Tred Avon, taking shelter in the old shed he'd played in as a boy. That autumn day had been the beginning. He'd finally broken down her defenses. He'd seduced her. Then one short week later, it was all over.

How brief their tragic love affair had been. Only moments in a lifetime. And yet those days he'd spent with Brett colored his very existence—to this day.

He had tried to go on. He did his work. He had a social life of sorts. But he was never able to forget her. She was always at the back of his mind, even after he'd given up waiting for a letter or a phone call.

He'd learned through Evelyn that Brett had gone on with her life. She was a politician, just as she'd told him she would be. She was raising her son. She was not looking back.

And so, when she'd called from Washington to say that she was coming to Europe and wanted to see him, Elliot had been dumbfounded. "If I could have an hour of your time," she'd said.

He'd offered to pick her up at the airport, but she'd declined, saying she didn't want to put him to any trouble. She was bringing her son; she thought Elliot might like to meet him. Tyler was nearly five.

And so they'd agreed that she would come by his place for a chat. The embassy wasn't conducive to private conversation. She didn't mind coming to his home, if he didn't mind. Of course he didn't. How could seeing her be a problem to him? They'd set the time for their meeting at three o'clock.

It was a few minutes after three now. He waited for her, feeling confused, curious, afraid to be hopeful, but hopeful nonetheless. What had happened? She wouldn't ask to see him for no good reason. Not lightly. Not on a whim.

Elliot glanced up at the gray sky before retreating to an armchair across the room. He sat and stared at the grouping of Chagall drawings on the moiré silk taffeta wall across from him. Having spent the morning at the Ministry of Foreign Affairs, he was in his dark gray double-breasted suit and Italian silk tie. He looked down at the toe of his highly polished shoe as he bounced his foot nervously.

Somehow he hadn't pictured that it would happen this way. In his imagination it was always in Georgia or Washington—him going to her. It was never in his milieu, on his turf.

He glanced around at the walls of the elegant town house. It was not his home. He didn't have one. He was a man without a home or a family. Shortly after becoming chargé d'affaires at the embassy, he had taken up residence in the elegant little town house in the seventh arrondissement, owned by a French investment banker. It was a few short blocks from the Champ de Mars, a good address, close in, the rent reasonable.

Growing impatient, Elliot got up and went back to the window. A woman was passing on the sidewalk, carrying an umbrella and pushing a large blue perambulator that was covered with plastic to shield the baby from the rain. There was no sign of a taxi. Dark clouds, heavy with rain, shrouded the city. He looked at his watch. Brett was late.

His heart was tripping. The wait had caused his anxiety to build. The world—or at least his world—was in suspension. Nothing mattered to him but their impending meeting, nothing had any significance but this. One little phone call, a two-minute conversation with her, had rekindled his obsession.

He heard a vehicle coming down the quiet street. The light mist had been replaced by large raindrops that plopped on the pavement. A taxi appeared, stopping in front of the house. His body tensed as the passenger door swung open. Her legs appeared first, then she climbed out. Elliot could see her blond hair, then had a glimpse of her pretty face when she glanced up at the house.

Just then the skies opened and the rain poured down. Brett dashed for the front door and he went to the foyer to greet her. He swung the heavy door wide and found her standing there, wet, her hair plastered by the rain.

They stared at each other for only an instant before he reached out to bring her inside, their hands touching for a moment. She was breathing hard from the dash up the steps, her smile the only sign of greeting.

All he could do was look at her. The usual words were not there. Unlike the last time he saw her, there was an eagerness in her eyes; but she was tentative, too. She gave a little laugh.

"Hello, Elliot."

He stood gazing at her. "You arrived with the rain."

She nodded, various conflicting emotions playing on her face. "Do you suppose it's a bad omen?"

"No," he said, shaking his head. "No, I don't." He helped her off with her coat and hung it on the rack behind the door. Then he faced her. She was in a beige silk dress, her hair cut stylishly short. She was beautiful, but it was a more mature beauty than before. Her figure was as trim as the first time he'd seen her. "I wasn't sure if you'd bring your son," he said.

Brett shook her head. "I thought it would be better if we talked alone first. Tyler's at the hotel with a baby-sitter, a nice old lady with a very thick accent. He seemed to accept the arrangement without too much complaint." She glanced around, then looked at him with the first hint of embarrassment. "I appreciate you letting me drop in on you like this."

"Brett, I couldn't be more delighted." He gestured toward the salon. "Come in and sit down."

"You have a lovely place," she said, checking out the room as she made her way to the love seat under the Chagalls.

"It's not really mine," he said, explaining the arrangement to her. "Home is wherever my briefcase and shaving kit happen to be." He was standing by the chair opposite her. "May I offer you a drink? Sherry? Wine?"

Brett had taken a handkerchief from her purse and was wiping her face. "Sherry would be nice, if you're having some."

He went off to the kitchen, returning in a moment with two amply-filled sherry glasses. After handing her one and putting the other on a side table, he pulled an armchair closer and sat down. He picked up his glass and toasted her. "Welcome to Paris."

They each took a sip. Elliot noticed that she was nervous, very much aware of him—unlike the way she'd been that last time he'd seen her at Rosemont.

"I understand you're well on your way to being president," he said. "You're running for Congress, I understand."

"I'm in a runoff for the Democratic nomination. The district is more conservative than I am, but the opposition's splintered. Traditionally, the primary winner is a walk-in, come November."

There was an energy in her voice. A confidence. Brett, he could see, was in her element. "You've strayed pretty far afield in search of votes, haven't you?" he chided.

She took a quick sip of sherry. "My supporters don't appreciate my absence from the campaign. That's why this is going to be such a brief trip."

They stared at each other for a long, poignant moment. Gone was her suffering, her anxiety, yet she was tense. It reminded him of the way it had been when they were first alone on the East Shore.

"Why have you come?" he asked softly.

She took a fortifying breath. "A couple of weeks ago I ran into Monica at a diplomatic reception in Washington." She hesitated. "Elliot, she said she'd blackmailed you to get custody of Jennifer. She told me how she'd threatened to tell Amory about our affair."

"Oh, God," he said with disgust. "What's Monica doing, stirring up trouble after all this time?"

"Why did you let her do that?"

He saw that Brett was quite upset. "I didn't have much choice."

She bit at her lip. "I can't tell you how badly I felt when I found out."

"Monica should have kept her mouth shut. That was our deal."

"Why didn't you come to me, Elliot? We might have been able to do something. Amory would have refused to be used that way. If I'd known, I would have—"

When he saw she wasn't going to finish the thought, he said, "Look, there's no point in hashing this over. It's ancient history. Everything's okay now. Really." He could see she was on the verge of tears. "I hope you didn't come all the way to Paris just for this."

She drew an uneven breath. "I couldn't let it pass without at least talking to you about it. You made a tremendous sacrifice for me. I want you to know how grateful I am for what you did."

"Gratitude acknowledged," he said with a smile.

She wiped the corner of her eye with her wadded-up handkerchief. "Considering how you feel about Jennifer, I don't know how you did it."

"I had very strong feelings for you," he said. "And I felt responsible for what happened."

Brett drank more sherry. "After talking to Monica I felt very badly about the way I've treated you. I've thought about you a lot the past few weeks."

"Brett, I don't want you feeling guilty. I appreciate the sentiment, I really do. But what happened with Monica was between her and me. You just happened to be in the line of fire."

"It's not only what you did to save me that's been on my mind. I've got other crosses to bear. There's something else I have to tell you, Elliot."

He didn't understand what she was getting at and looked at her questioningly. Brett frowned. He searched her eyes, waiting for an explanation.

She put down her sherry, got up and went over to the window. The rain was blowing against the glass, sounding a faint tattoo in concert with the ticking of the clock on the mantel. She stared out, partially in profile, a distressed expression on her face.

"What is it? What's wrong?"

She turned toward him. The silvery light from the window showed tear streaks on her cheeks. She wiped them away with her handkerchief.

"Elliot," she said, her voice trembling, "Tyler is not Amory's child." A half sob broke her voice. "He's... yours."

He couldn't believe what he was hearing. Her words stabbed at his soul. He was in shock. Tyler was his? He slowly rose to his feet. "What are you saying?"

"Tyler is *your* child," she cried. "He's not Amory's."

"You mean..."

"Yes, I lied to you, just as I lied to Amory. I lied to everyone, including myself. It was my penance, the burden I thought I had to carry to atone for my sin. It was the only way I could cope, to keep from hurting Amory more than I already had."

He started moving toward her. His heart picked up its beat.

"It wasn't until that conversation with Monica that I truly understood how you'd suffered, too," she continued. "I started seeing your relationship with Tyler in a different light. I'd been so intent on making him Amory's that I didn't appreciate the fact that I was denying him his father, and you your son. But Elliot, even if it's too late—even if you don't want to be a parent to him—you at least deserve to know the truth."

He was overwhelmed. It had come out so suddenly, and with such emotion, that he didn't know what to say. He peered into her shimmering eyes. "Brett..."

"Because of me," she said, "you lost your daughter *and* your son. I finally saw that you had no one, that I'd denied you your children. So I've come here to make my confession and ask your forgiveness." Her head dropped and a tear fell to the front of her dress.

Elliot moved closer to her. He took her face in his hands and made her look at him. "Brett," he whispered, "I can't tell you how much it means to me that you say that. But there's only one thing that matters to me now, and that's you." He leaned over and kissed her lips. "I love you," he murmured. "I always will."

She hugged him fiercely. "Oh, Elliot..."

He held her there by the window, rocking her back and forth as the rain streamed down the pane. Someone with a black umbrella moved by in the street below. A siren wailed faintly off in the distance.

"Life makes no sense," she whispered.

He pressed her body against him. "This makes sense," he replied.

She looked up at him. "I think I understand what happened to me. I couldn't come to you until I was ready. But I didn't even know that's what I was thinking." She sniffled. "I'm not afraid now, Elliot. That's what's different."

He held her again and she held him. The rain continued to fall. They stood there, the years that separated them melting away. He hardly knew where to begin, what had to come first.

"Deep in my heart," she said, "I've always known that I love you."

"And deep in my heart, I always knew we'd be together."

They kissed again. It was a long kiss, but a tender one.

Brett's tears kept flowing, but there was joy in them. And there was love. Elliot knew their time had come. Somehow, some way, they would make a new beginning.

New York Times Bestselling Author

Who can you trust when your life's on the line?
Find out this March in

Stevie Corbett is in jeopardy of losing everything—her career,
her future…her life. Her fate rests on keeping the truth a
secret, but there is one reporter who already knows too much.
She could lose everything…including her heart. All he has to
do is betray her trust.…

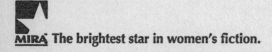

Over 10 million books in print!

Diana Palmer

An independent woman meets a determined
man this April in

Lady Love

Men had always wanted Merlyn Forrest for her
money, until she met handsome, serious and
dangerously seductive Cameron Thorpe. He
wasn't after her money, but he did want her
body—and her soul. She was too independent
to let any man control her life, but if he really
wanted her, he would have to play by her
rules...or not play at all.

Seduction most dangerous.

New York Times Bestselling Author

CHARLOTTE VALE ALLEN

Three women, three haunted pasts.

DREAMING IN COLOR

Bobby Salton is a woman on the run. With her young daughter, she finds refuge in a rambling house on the Connecticut shore. Alma Ogilvie is a retired head mistress, who, with Bobby's help, wants to regain the independence she lost following a stroke. Eva Rule, Alma's niece, is a successful writer who is trying desperately to put the past behind her—until Bobby shows up.

Now as they all begin to hope for the future, will past threats ruin everything?

Watch for *Dreaming in Color*, this April at your favorite retail outlet.

If you love the thrilling style of

JANICE KAISER

Then order now to receive another passionate story
by one of MIRA's rising stars:

| #66029 | LOTUS MOON | $4.99 U.S. | ☐ |
| | | $5.50 CAN. | ☐ |

(limited quantities available on certain titles)

TOTAL AMOUNT	$
POSTAGE & HANDLING	$
($1.00 for one book, 50¢ for each additional)	
APPLICABLE TAXES*	$_____
TOTAL PAYABLE	$_____
(check or money order—please do not send cash)	

To order, complete this form and send it, along with a check or money order
for the total above, payable to MIRA Books, to: **In the U.S.:** 3010 Walden
Avenue, P.O. Box 9077, Buffalo, NY 14269-9077; **In Canada:** P.O. Box 636,
Fort Erie, Ontario, L2A 5X3.

Name:_____

Address:_____ City:_____

State/Prov.:_____ Zip/Postal Code:_____

*New York residents remit applicable sales taxes.
  Canadian residents remit applicable GST and provincial taxes.

MJKBL1

MIRA